Damon Galgut was born in Pretoria. His novels *The Good Doctor* (2003) and *In a Strange Room* (Europa, 2010) were short-listed for the Booker Prize. His 2021 novel, *The Promise*, won the Booker Prize. He lives in Cape Town, South Africa.

ARCTIC SUMMER

Damon Galgut

ARCTIC SUMMER

Europa
editions

Europa Editions
1 Penn Plaza, Suite 6282
New York, N.Y. 10019
www.europaeditions.com
info@europaeditions.com

Library of Congress Cataloging in Publication Data is available
ISBN 978-1-60945-234-6

Galgut, Damon
Arctic Summer

Book design by Emanuele Ragnisco
www.mekkanografici.com

Cover photo © Steve McCurry/Magnum/Contrasto

Prepress by Grafica Punto Print – Rome

To Riyaz Ahmad Mirand
to the fourteen years of our friendship

"Orgies are so important, and they are things
one knows *nothing* about"
—E. M. FORSTER to P. N. Furbank, 1953

CONTENTS

ARCTIC SUMMER

CHAPTER ONE
SEARIGHT

In October of 1912, the SS *City of Birmingham* was travelling through the Red Sea, midway on her journey to India, when two men found themselves together on the forward deck. Each had come there separately, hoping to escape a concert that some of the other passengers were organising, but they were slightly acquainted by now and not unhappy to have company. It was the middle of the afternoon. They were sitting in a spot that offered sun and shade, as well as seclusion from the wind. Both carried books with them, which they politely set aside when they began to speak.

The first man, Morgan Forster, was thirty-three years of age and had come to think of himself as a writer. The recent publication of his fourth novel had been so successful that he felt financially able to make this journey. The six months that he planned to be away marked his first departure from Europe, and only his second extended absence from his mother. The other man was an army officer, returning to where he was stationed on the North-West Frontier. He was a few years younger than Morgan, a handsome fellow with backswept golden hair and numerous white teeth. His name was Kenneth Searight.

The two men had conversed a few times before and Morgan had found himself liking Searight, though he hadn't expected to. The ship was full of military types and their ghastly wives, but this man was different. For one thing, he was travelling alone. For another, Morgan had seen him behave with kindness towards the single Indian passenger on board, a kindness that was otherwise in short supply, and he had been touched by it. These small signs suggested they might have more in common than he had at first supposed.

Although he had only come aboard a week ago, Morgan was beginning to feel that he had been on the ship for too long. He was travelling with three friends, but even their company sometimes wore thin. His thoughts strayed constantly outwards, into the encircling sea. He would pace the deck for hours at a stretch, or sit at the rail, lost in aimless reverie over the flying fish that leaped at the bow, or the other creatures— jellyfish, sharks, dolphins—that sometimes showed themselves. He could sink very deep at moments like these. Once he had seen tracts of scarlet, billowing in the swell, which he was told were fish spawn, waiting to hatch. Life that wasn't human life, maturing and breaking out and expending itself, in a medium that wasn't human either.

He was stuck with the humans, however. The same set of faces awaited him each day. The ship was like a tiny piece of England, Tunbridge Wells in particular, that had broken off and been set in motion. For some reason, perhaps because they spoke more, the women were hardest to deal with. They assumed that he shared their feelings, when most of the time he did not. One of them, a young lady in search of a husband, had made a couple of sidling approaches, till his stony face repelled her.

But it was the casual vilenesses, flung out in airy asides at the dining table, that upset him most. He had set some of these down in his diary and brooded on them afterwards. On one occasion a matronly woman, who had been a nurse in the Bhopal Purdahs, had lectured him between courses on how deplorable Mohammedan home life was. And if English children stopped in India, they learned to speak like half-castes, which was *such* a stigma. "And this young Indian man who's on board," she added in a low voice. "Well, he's a Mohammedan, isn't he? He has been to public school in England, but has it improved him? He thinks he's one of us, but of course he never will be."

The Indian man in question, whose name he could never quite remember, had some acquaintances in common with Morgan, but he was a trying fellow whose company was unrewarding. Morgan had also begun to avoid him lately, but he knew that his table-companion meant something different by her aversion, and he disliked her for it. Though she was not in any way unusual: almost every other passenger treated the poor man with polite contempt. Only the day before, one of the army wives, a Mrs. Turton, had remarked, "They tell me that young Indian's lonely. Well, he ought to be. They won't let us know their wives, why should we know them? If we're pleasant to them, they only despise us." Morgan had wanted to reply, but held off, and felt bad about it afterwards.

So this chance encounter with the golden young officer held a tinge of promise in it. Something about Kenneth Searight—though it was hard to say what—did not belong in uniform, or with his air of impeccable politeness.

To begin with, they talked in a desultory way about the voyage. They had recently passed through the Suez Canal and the experience, for Morgan, had been curiously reminiscent of a picture gallery. And he had been disappointed by Port Said: it was, so everyone had told him, one's first vision of the East, yet it had none of the smell and vibrancy and colour he'd been expecting. There were no minarets and only a single dome, and the statue of de Lesseps, despite pointing commandingly towards the canal, appeared to be holding a string of sausages in his other hand. He had gone ashore, of course, and some of the Arabs were beautiful, but they had spoiled it by trying to sell him smutty postcards. ("Do you wa' to see something filthy? Noah? Well, perhaps after tea.") All in all, it hadn't been an uplifting experience.

"Except for the coaling barge," Searight said.

"Yes," Morgan answered. "Except for that." The memory of the barge came back strongly to him. More specifically, it was the figures on top that continued to trouble him: black with coal-dust, they had woken from a death-like torpor into a frenzy of activity, singing and squabbling as they carried their baskets on board. One of these figures, of indeterminate age and sex, had stood by the plankway after dark, holding a lamp, and the image, with its deep shadows and contrasting yellow glow, had seemed both hopeful and frightening to him.

Searight had also been there, Morgan remembered now; they had been standing close to one another at the rail, watching the scene. Although they had not yet met or spoken, the moment seemed in retrospect like a kind of complicity.

They began to speak now about their plans after landing at Bombay. They agreed they might travel as far as Agra together, after which Searight would head off towards Lahore and Morgan to Aligarh.

"You are staying with a friend there?"

"Yes," Morgan said, and then dared to admit, "He's a native."

"Ah," Searight said. "I thought that might be the case. I'm glad to hear it, very glad to hear it. You won't learn anything about India unless you mingle with the Indians, whatever anyone else might tell you. I myself have been close to many of them. Ah, yes. Very close."

"I can't imagine all your brother officers approve."

"There is more understanding than you might think, but of course you have to be careful. It's a matter of knowing your time and place." He laughed shortly. "Is your friend a Hindu?"

"He's a Mohammedan, in fact."

"Ah, yes. The Mohammedans. People think of the Hindus as sensual, because of all the decadent religious imagery. On the other hand, the Mohammedans are People of the Book, just like us. Well, I can tell you, the Pathans are a breed of young savages, and I intend to make friends with many of them. It's one of the delights of being transferred to Peshawar. I used to be in Bengal, you know, in Darjeeling, and I had a ripping time there. But I'm looking forward to the future."

Morgan had the uneasy feeling that the topic had slid away from him and that they were talking about different things. Nevertheless, he said, "So am I."

"You're looking forward to seeing your friend?"

"Very much."

"You've been missing him? How well I know this feeling, how well. And then I'm driven to seek consolation elsewhere. Fortunately one doesn't have to look far, not in India. More difficult in England, as you know."

"What is?"

"Consolation." He looked meaningfully at Morgan. "I did meet a horse guard in Hyde Park. Just a couple of weeks ago."

Alerted and alarmed by the turn the conversation had taken, Morgan decided to make a non-committal noise in his throat and to stare out at the water. Searight had turned towards him in his chair, his whole attitude confidential. After a pause, he began to speak about the heat. This seemed like a new topic, but it grew stealthily out of the preceding one. Over the last few days the temperature had risen dramatically; many of the passengers had taken to sleeping on deck. And had Morgan noticed how some of the men were wearing short pants? The older ones should not be allowed to do so, Searight said, their legs were not attractive. Very few Englishmen had attractive legs, it had something to do with their knees. But in India there were a great many attractive legs. Legs were everywhere on display, as Morgan would see. Flesh was generally more visible in India than at home; that was how they did things out there.

Morgan thought it best not to answer, but to wait and see what happened next.

Eventually Searight sighed and murmured, "I blame it on the heat."

"Yes," Morgan said carefully.

"One thing leads to another. It undoes people. I've seen it over and over. People go out there, to India, I mean, and they start behaving as they never would in England. I blame it on the heat."

"I shall wear my sola topi."

"It will not protect you."

"I assure you, it's of the finest quality—"

"No doubt. But it will not save you from yourself." Something in Searight's face had imperceptibly altered; his expression had become a little coarse and sensual.

"I'm not quite sure I follow you."

"Oh, I think you do."

At this moment there was a flurry of sound from deep inside the ship, a faint uproar of music and voices, eclipsed by the rush of water at the bow—a reminder of the normal world close by. Morgan looked around quickly, to be sure they were alone. "Perhaps we had better go and get ready for dinner," he said.

Before he could move, Searight leaned over and handed him the book he'd been holding on his lap. Morgan had barely glanced at it, assuming it to be a volume of poems like the one he himself was reading. But the fat bound notebook, green in colour, was something altogether more personal. It bore the mysterious word *Paidikion* on its front cover, and the many pages inside were filled with handwriting instead of print.

Though on the particular page that Searight's forefinger held open, there seemed to be, after all, a poem.

> *. . . I passed*
> *From sensuous Bengal to fierce Peshawar*

An Asiatic stronghold where each flower
Of boyhood planted in its restless soil
Is—ipso facto—ready to despoil
(or to be despoiled by) someone else . . .

"Oh, dear me," Morgan said. "What is this?"
"It is the story of my life, in verse."
"You wrote this?"

. . . the yarn
Indeed so has it that the young Pathan
Thinks it peculiar if he would pass
Him by without some reference to his arse.
Each boy of certain age will let on hire
His charms to indiscriminate desire,
To wholesome buggery and perverse letches . . .

"I blame it on the heat," Searight said, and laughed noisily.

* * *

He repeated the conversation breathlessly to Goldsworthy Lowes Dickinson in their cramped cabin that evening while they dressed for dinner. Even in recollection, a shock quivered through him and his fingers slipped on his buttons. It was amazing, he told Goldie; it was remarkable. To have spoken in that way to a near-stranger, to have exposed oneself so recklessly! It hadn't been a confession—there was no shame behind it. That was the truly astonishing thing: Searight appeared to be almost proud of who and what he was.

The two men glanced at each other in silence. Then Goldie enquired delicately, "And did he swear you to secrecy?"

"No. I think he took it for granted."

"Why did he believe that you wouldn't . . . ?"

"I don't know."

"And did you talk about yourself to him in the same open way?"

"Not at all. He didn't seem very interested in me. I told him a little about my home life and he changed the subject."

"Ah," Goldie said. His tone was commiserative, but his relief was obvious.

This was the way the two of them usually communicated, in little gusts of shared enthusiasm, followed by murmurous bouts of allusion. Much passed between them without being explicitly stated. They had known one another for some years now, since Morgan had been a student at King's, while Goldie was a don, though their friendship had been slow to flower and had only taken form more recently, once Morgan had left Cambridge behind. They were both fussy, worried men, elderly before their time, in whom a spinsterish quality was evident. Both of them had experienced love, but from afar and unrequitedly.

They understood one another well and therefore Morgan knew, though Goldie didn't say it aloud, that the older man mistrusted Searight. He thought that anyone so indiscreet could be dangerous. Goldie came from a generation where discretion was the first line of defence and any dropping of one's guard could lead to catastrophe. Oscar Wilde had gone to prison only seventeen years before.

Morgan, nearly two decades younger, was slightly less cautious, but only in theory. In practice, he was not nearly so afraid of the State as he was of his mother. He could not refer to his condition, even in his own mind, with too direct a term; he spoke of it obliquely, as being *in a minority*. He himself was a *solitary*. At Cambridge, among his own circle, the question was discussed, though from an angle, and safely abstracted. One could be forgiven for believing it was a matter of talking, not doing. As long as it remained in the realm of words, no crime had been committed. But even words could be dangerous.

* * *

Over the next few days, Morgan watched Searight carefully and observed that his life was broken into two. In his military existence he put on a public face, and in this area he was to all appearances vigorous and masculine. He was a member of the Queen's Own Royal West Kent Regiment, a fine, upstanding defender of the Realm; he could laugh and drink with his fellow officers in a hearty, backslapping way; he was popular and well respected, although he avoided the company of the women on board. That was one half of him—but of course there was another secret side, which Morgan had already seen.

This aspect of Searight's nature—which could be said to be his true character—he revealed only to those he trusted. But when the camouflage came off, it came off completely. That first conversation amazed Morgan, but it was followed by others soon afterwards. The very next day he took Goldie to the same part of the deck to meet his new friend, and almost immediately they were discussing things that Morgan had never voiced before, or only to his journal, and then cryptically.

A collection of von Gloeden photographs, for example, well worn despite careful handling. Morgan had seen these images before, but in a context that had required sober, aesthetic appreciation. That wasn't the case now. In Searight's hand, the sullen Sicilian youths, lolling among ruins and statuary, took on a carnal frankness. His voice became husky with awe on the subject of youthful male beauty. Flesh and feathery moustaches and defiant yet vulnerable eyes . . . "And look at his sultry cock, angled to the left at about forty-five degrees. It's a real beauty. To say nothing of the testicles, which are spectacular, especially the one on the right." In his telling, even the most tawdry encounter became luminous, operatic. He read a short story aloud to Morgan and Goldie, one he'd written himself, that made his own breathing become shallow and tortured. He let them peruse more of his epic autobiographical poem, which he called *The Furnace*. And he showed them several pages at the back of the green notebook that were filled with cryptic columns of numbers, before explaining in an undertone that they represented a tally of his sexual conquests thus far, all with statistical details of date, place, age, how many meetings and frequency of climax. These encounters were mostly with boys and young men, ranging in age from thirteen to twenty-eight, a great many of them Indian. Almost forty so far.

Almost forty! Morgan himself had never had a lover, not one. The world of Eros remained a flickering internal pageant, always with him, yet always out of reach. It had been only three years before that Morgan had fully understood how copulation between men and women actually worked, and his mind had flinched in amazement. His mother and father engaging in such physicality to produce him: it was almost unthinkable. (But must have happened, at least twice.) His father had died when Morgan was not yet two, and when he contemplated sex in any form it was the image of his mother, Lily—widowed, middle-aged, perpetually unhappy—that rose before him, to intervene. As she did now.

But he had left his mother behind in Italy, with her friend, Mrs. Mawe, for company. He was free of her, at least for a little time, and determined to make use of the freedom. Yet now he felt hopeless, looking at Searight across a great dividing distance. He had the sense that the other man's sexual practices involved tastes and behaviours that would shock him deeply, if he only knew the details, yet still he envied him the ability to translate yearning into deed. So much sex, so many bodies colliding! Morgan felt flushed and troubled by the images that came to mind. How had Searight done it? How had he set each seduction in motion, how had he known the right words to speak, the right gestures to make?

Perhaps there was a talent to it, a gift that Morgan simply did not have. Yet now he saw that there was another way to be in the world, a way to live more fully. Once he had realised this, nothing looked quite the same again. Anyone he knew could be leading an invisible, double life; every conversation could have a second meaning.

When, for example, on one of the nights following, he passed Searight in earnest colloquy with the little Indian passenger, he suddenly saw them differently. He had thought of it before as kindness, but he didn't think of it that way any more. They were standing close together, one of Searight's hands pressed gently to the other man's shoulder, speaking in low voices. They might have been discussing the weather, or the progress of the ship—but they might also have been talking about something else altogether.

* * *

As he pondered it now, Morgan wondered whether it wasn't his travelling companions who had given Searight his cue. Only he and Goldie were solitaries, but all four of them were unusual, and they had enjoyed playing up their differences from the other passengers on board. And perhaps their oddness had been a kind of signal to Searight.

Theirs was a happy group and it was something of a happy chance that they were journeying together now. Goldie had received a travelling fellowship and had decided to use it to visit India and China. He came in a spirit of social enquiry, wishing to catalogue jails and temples and hospitals, and thereby to understand moral progress in foreign places. Bob Trevelyan (known to most as Bob Trevy) had resolved at the same time that this might be a good moment to visit the East, without the hindrance of wife and children. Gordon Luce, a more distant acquaintance from King's, was passing through Bombay en route to a posting in Burma. And Morgan—well, Morgan was travelling in order to see his Indian friend again.

In the eyes of the other passengers, they were a peculiar lot. Certainly they were aware of their eccentricity and had not shrunk from it. At mealtimes they took pleasure in discussing important classical questions in loud voices, such as the relative merits of Tolstoy versus Dostoevsky, or whether Nero had shown any theatrical talent in the staging of his circuses. To the officers and civil servants and non-official Europeans who made up the bulk of the passengers, the antics of these giggling intellectuals were cause for suspicion. Once, when all four of them were lined up, drinking tea, a soldier sitting opposite them had collapsed in laughter. They appeared to belong, but did not, quite. They had no wives with them, and they did not participate in deck games or fancy dress balls. Their irony was construed as a lack of seriousness. So they had become known as the Professors, and sometimes as the Salon, in tones that mixed familiarity with malice.

Over the days that followed, Searight became an honorary member of the Salon, sitting with them at mealtimes and strolling with them on the deck. After an initial wariness, all of them decided that they liked him. Under the bluff military exterior, a poetic and romantic soul began to show itself. He was knowledgeable and charming and witty, easy to be near. His manner was generous, and he had led a highly interesting life, which he conveyed in a succession of amusing anecdotes, often told at his own expense, in a rich baritone voice that was somehow public and confiding at the same time. Soon he was insisting that they come up to visit him at the Frontier, and they were agreeing that it was an excellent idea. He would take them on a picnic to the Khyber Pass, he said; he would show them the edge of the Empire.

But for the moment there was still the remainder of the journey on the ship, the sea wide and bright around them. By now there was a general air of excitement and anticipation, which kept many of the passengers at the rail, glaring ahead at the horizon in the hope that it would yield up something solid. The first visitation came in the form of a pair of yellow butterflies, flittering around the deck. Morgan was thrilled, but the butterflies disappeared, and no land took their place.

The next morning Bob Trevy woke him with the news that India was visible. All four of them assembled in time to watch the dark line ahead of them break up into what it actually was: a bank of moody clouds in the distance. But later in the morning the horizon did thicken incontrovertibly into a graph of curious red hills, apparently devoid of life. For some reason, Morgan thought of Italy. He had already, at an earlier time, noticed an analogy between the shapes of southern Europe and Asia—three peninsulas, with a major range of mountains at the head of the middle one, and Sicily standing in for Ceylon—but this was an Italy he didn't quite recognise, as though it were a place seen in a dream, hinting at menace.

Then there was the arrival, with its predictable flurry and tedium, the last unpleasant meal among the same unpleasant people, before they were finally rowed ashore. As they toiled towards land, Morgan, who was sitting with Goldie at the rear of the little boat, saw Searight at the front, next to the Indian passenger, and suddenly an unsettling memory came back to him.

"I wonder why Searight wanted to kill him," he said.

"What?" Goldie said. "Whatever do you mean?"

He reminded Goldie of the incident, which had occurred nearly two weeks before, at Port Said. A strange story had gone around the ship: the Indian had reported his cabin-mate to the steward for wanting to throw him overboard, but then the two of them had made it up and became the best of friends again.

Morgan hadn't thought about it much at the time, but now it had returned to him, in the shape of this troubling question.

Goldie blinked in confusion. "Oh, but you're mistaken," he said. "That wasn't Searight."

"No?"

"No, certainly not. It was Searight who told the story to me."

"Of course," Morgan said, suddenly very embarrassed. "I don't know what I was thinking."

It was a leap of logic to assume that Searight was sharing a cabin with the Indian; such an arrangement was unlikely. Morgan didn't know how the idea had come to him. But afterwards, even when he knew it was untrue, he continued to be fascinated by what he'd imagined. Lust in close confines, under a hot, empty sky, breeding dreams of murder: he sensed the beginnings of a story.

CHAPTER TWO
MASOOD

The voyage to India had begun several years before, and on very dry land. In November of 1906, Morgan and his mother had been living in Weybridge, Surrey, for just over two years, when one of their neighbours, Mrs. Morison, who was friendly with the Forsters, made an unusual enquiry. Did Lily know of anybody who might be able to act as a Latin tutor to a young Indian man who was about to go up to Oxford?

"I wondered, dear," Lily enquired, "whether you might have any interest . . . ?"

"Certainly," Morgan said immediately. He had taught Latin at the Working Men's College in London for the past couple of years, but his curiosity ran deeper than his competence. Who was this young man from the other side of the world, what was he doing in suburban England?

"Well, it's a complicated story," his mother told him. "The young man is the Morisons' ward. You know that Theodore Morison was the Principal of the Mohammedan Anglo-Oriental College in, I forget where in India . . . "

"Aligarh, I believe."

"Yes. It seems that his grandfather was the founder of the college, so he is from a very good background."

"No doubt. But how did he come to be the Morisons' ward?"

"I am not exactly sure of that. You will have to ask him yourself. Mrs. Morison did explain it, but the story was unclear. They refer to him as their son."

"But the Morisons have a son."

"Well, it seems they have two." And Lily, who had been in a perfectly good humour till then, became unaccountably fretful and began calling peevishly for the maid, so that Morgan thought it best to retire to the piano room to practise his Beethoven.

The Indian man stayed with him, however, in the form of a mystery. A small mystery, to be sure, but with sufficient colour to stand out against the surrounding drabness. Since coming down from Cambridge five years before, he had felt himself gradually losing his way. The bright and interesting world remained, but for the most part he had to go out and visit it. Rarely did it come to visit him; much less with an appointment, and a desire to brush up on its Latin.

On the day arranged, Morgan hovered anxiously around the front door half an hour before the time. Nevertheless, his pupil was late. Syed Ross Masood was tall and broad and strikingly handsome, appearing far older than his seventeen years. His smiling face, with its luxuriant moustache and sad brown eyes, looked down on Morgan from what felt, on that first morning, like a remote height.

They had shaken hands in greeting, but Masood wouldn't release his grip. He announced solemnly, with a tone of accusation, "You are a writer. You have published a book."

Morgan acknowledged that the second statement was true. He had published a novel the year before, which had generally been well received, and he had two others upstairs in different stages of undress. Nevertheless, the idea of being a writer felt like an ill-fitting suit on him, which he kept trying to shrug into, or out of.

"That is a fine, a very fine thing. It is one of the noble arts, perhaps the most noble of all. Except for poetry. Have you read the poetry of Ghalib? You must do so immediately, or I will never speak to you again. Ah, that I could have lived in Moghul times! You have travelled to India? No? But that is a great crime on your part. You must come to visit me there one day."

The low, fast, sonorous voice, never really expecting an answer to its questions, continued without a pause while they went inside and settled themselves in the drawing room, and even while Agnes was serving tea, and only then fell suddenly silent. Now the two men took stock of one another more carefully. Masood was elegantly and expensively dressed, and gave off a hint of perfume. He looked, and sounded, and smelled like a prince. Morgan, on the other hand, had a crumpled, second-hand appearance, which made him seem like a tradesman of some kind.

"You need help with your Latin," he said to Masood.

"No, no. My Latin is beyond help. It is a lost cause." He was carrying a couple of textbooks under his arm, which he flung down in mock-despair. "Tell me rather about life at an English university."

"I know Cambridge, not Oxford."

"My father was a student at Christ's College, Cambridge. Did you know that? He was sent there by my grandfather, Sir Syed Ahmad Khan. My grandfather wished his Anglo-Oriental College to be like Cambridge, only for Mohammedan students. My grandfather was a great lover of the English, especially English education, oh yes! My father too, though he was not always well treated by his English friends. I, for my part, have yet to make up my mind."

"What did your father read at Cambridge?"

"Law, law. He was a barrister, you see, and then he became a High Court judge. But he resigned that position in unhappy circumstances."

Morgan asked carefully, "How is it that you came to live with the Morisons?"

"Ah. That is an interesting story. A very interesting story. But I think I do not know you well enough to tell it."

"Of course. I didn't mean to pry."

Masood reflected thoughtfully for a moment, then leaned forward in his chair, his dark eyes becoming darker. "Some years ago, when I was ten, my father lost his mind. He was very drunk, you see. Alcohol was the downfall of my father. It is the reason he resigned from the law as well."

"I am sorry to hear that."

"Yes. He took me out onto the lawns of the college one night. It was very dark and cold. He tried to show me how to use a wooden plough. He was talking a great deal of non-sense about the politics of agriculture. He wanted to teach me something, I believe, about what it means to be Indian. I was extremely afraid. My mother, too, was afraid, and she ran to call Mr. Morison, who came very quickly. He wrapped me up in his coat and took me home, and I have never left again."

"I see," Morgan said—though he didn't, really. There was a great deal about the story that he did not understand.

"Well, it is sad, terribly sad. The life of my father was a sad one. He has passed on now, a few years after this incident I mentioned." Having said this, Masood brightened consider-ably and asked Morgan, "Where is *your* father?"

"My father died a long time ago, when I was very young. I don't remember him."

"That is also terribly sad."

"I do not feel it to be so."

The two men looked at each other with renewed awareness. Morgan didn't know what to make of his visitor, who had been so utterly forthright in such an un-English way. Part of him was tempted to be shocked, but he decided instead that he liked this young man, precisely because he spoke without restraint.

And his liking only grew over the succeeding weeks, in which they met regularly. Very little Latin was learned, how-ever. Although Morgan prepared his lessons, when they sat down to the task Masood immediately began to writhe and squirm and to speak of other things.

On the third occasion, Morgan tried to insist. "You must attend to these declensions," he told his pupil. "It is the purpose of our being here."

"It is so terribly boring. Why don't we go for a walk?"

"When we are done with our lesson."

Masood looked mournfully at him. Then he sprang up and seized hold of Morgan, pushing him backward on the couch and tickling him furiously. It was shocking—for the first instant like assault and only then like play. Something in Morgan was thrown back in time to childhood, afternoon, the smell of straw in the heat. Ansell, his favourite of the garden boys, had frolicked with him like this.

That moment did it; Masood became his friend. The distance between them had closed.

* * *

India had encroached on the edge of Morgan's mind before now, not a place so much as an idea. It had become a tradition for Kingsmen to join the Indian Civil Service and many people he knew had gone out there to make their careers. It was spoken of at dinner parties, usually with extreme seriousness, as the vital cornerstone of the Empire. On the other side of the world, yet somehow part of England, it was not a place he had ever thought he might visit. Yet now, as he listened to Masood talk about his childhood, and sensed the homesickness in his voice, he began to imagine himself against the same background. Perhaps, yes, perhaps he would go there one day.

In the meantime, however, England was very much with him. The suburbs especially, with their hateful self-righteousness, and where his life seemed to consist of an endless round of tea parties and amiable, empty conversations, mostly—it felt to him—with elderly women.

One of these was his mother's great friend, Maimie Aylward. When Lily mentioned Morgan's new pupil to her, she put a hand up to her face.

"Oh, dear," she said. "I do hope he won't steal the spoons."

Morgan laughed politely, though he didn't feel like laughing. He had learned to feign enjoyment in conversations like these, and hated himself for the pretence. Although he was English all the way through, a great many English attitudes felt foreign to him.

For this reason, what Morgan found most interesting in his new friend was the strangeness of him, the exoticism imported into his drawing room. The most familiar topic, seen through Masood's eyes, became unpredictable, unusual. And what was ordinary to Masood seemed to Morgan remarkable.

Such as the casual mention one day that he could trace his ancestry back to the Prophet Mohammed at the thirty-seventh generation. "And to Adam at the hundred and twentieth," he added. The world, in that moment, felt very old and beautiful.

Though Morgan, of course, knew nothing about Mohammedanism, and this was irksome to Masood.

"Let me explain," he said patiently. "Not to drink wine. Not to eat the pig. There is one God and Mohammed is His prophet. To believe in the Last Judgement. Oh yes, and not to eat an animal that has died. Even a white man could follow these simple rules."

"In theory, yes. But I don't believe in religion."

"You mean you are a Christian."

"No, no. I lost my belief when I was at Cambridge."

"My dear Forster, all Englishmen are Christians. It is very sad. The English are a tragic race, I feel deeply sorry for them. I would like to help them, but they are too numerous, there is nothing to be done."

When Masood went up to Oxford soon afterwards, Weybridge felt immediately emptier. There was nobody left that Morgan cared for. But their communication went on in the form of frequent letters that stitched back and forth. In a continuation of the tone they had already established, Masood's letters were written in a faux-Eastern style, elaborate and overwrought, a mixture of sentiment and irony. He addressed Morgan in exalted terms: a great deal of *Thou* and *Thine*, and pledges of eternal devotion, against an imaginary background of minarets and muezzins. Very quickly, Morgan began responding in the same way.

Not long afterwards, he travelled to Oxford for a visit. Summer had almost taken hold; the few days passed in a dreamy haze of punts and walks and aimless conversation. Masood was by now in occupation of the whole town, as if it were one of his expensive capes that he could put on or drop at will. He was not so much interested in his studies, it seemed, as in playing an elaborate role, though the nature of the drama was not always clear. He liked to swagger around with a silver-topped cane, reciting Paul Verlaine in his mournfully melodious voice, or to prance about the tennis courts in his whites. He played a lot of tennis—and music on the gramophone, and practical jokes. In short, he liked to play, especially in his serious moments.

He was also the centre of a small coterie of admirers, most of them Indian, who lolled about in his rooms like the retinue of some indolent Emperor. Morgan went almost unnoticed in this company, sinking below the level of visibility, like a child or a spy. Often the talk around him was conducted in Urdu, only occasionally and laconically translated by Masood. But sometimes they all spoke in English, though the topics they discussed were almost a foreign language in themselves: customs in India, historical figures Morgan had never heard of, cities he had never seen.

To his great delight, these conversations also sometimes involved poetry, which was theatrically declaimed in Urdu or Persian, and sometimes in Arabic. The themes, as far as he could gather, were mostly about the shortness of love, or the decline of Islam. It was odd to hear lyricism in a social setting like this, but Masood explained to him that in the East poetry occupied a public place, not a private one, as it did in England.

"You so-called white people," he was told, "are too afraid of your emotions. Everything is arranged coldly on shelves. In India we show how we feel, without being ashamed."

"Why so-called?"

"Because your colour is far from white. More a pinko-grey, I'd say. Look."

When he and Masood put their arms together, to compare, he saw that it was true. He had never thought of his skin in this way before. His friend's colouring was infinitely more attractive.

Such ideas edged dangerously close to politics, which also came up as a topic among Masood's friends. But in these conversations the talk turned feverish and unintelligible, though it was easy to make out that Indian independence was a common and recurrent theme. It was only when they became aware of him that they would suddenly fall silent, and shift about.

When the time came for him to leave, Masood pressed a small parcel on him. "You'd better try them on," he said. "I have guessed at the size."

It was a pair of golden slippers.

"Oh, but I can't accept them. They're too beautiful."

"Certainly you will accept, or I shall never speak to you again."

The slippers fitted perfectly, holding his feet with a gentle, satiny grip. In his English trousers, which were a little too short, he seemed outlandish and a bit ridiculous to himself. But the only emotion he felt was gratitude—almost too much of it.

A month later he was back for a second visit, at the conclusion of which Masood cast around for another gift. Looking vaguely at the assortment of Indian articles that strewed the room—embroidered quilts, jewellery, carved wooden boxes of incense—he picked out something almost at random: a hookah, which one of his friends, a man named Raschid, had been smoking the day before.

"No. This I certainly cannot take."

"But you must."

"No. Thank you. But it is too generous. I am happy with my slippers."

An odd expression came over Masood's face, a wooden detachment that fitted over his kindliness like a mask. "I insist you have it. And you must not thank me again."

The pressure of his hands, as he pushed the hookah at Morgan, was almost impolite. But he had softened a little by the time they came to the railway station. "You must not thank me if I give you something," he said quietly. "And I will not thank you either."

"But why not?"

"It is only strangers who thank. Thanks are not given by friends. You are like family to me. Do you thank your mother for what she does for you? No, it is merely expected. No thanks are necessary."

"I do thank my mother. The English like to say thank you all the time."

"But I am not English. And when you are with me, you are not English either."

The absurdity of this notion didn't blunt its feeling, and a tiny point of gratitude stayed lodged in Morgan on the journey home. The hookah was much admired, on the train and in Weybridge, sending out glints of reflected light. But it was only when he was alone in his room that he allowed himself to feel again its true value, which was in what Masood had said to him. *You are like family to me.* The words stayed with him. He had always wanted a brother, a male figure close to him in age and sensibility, somebody he could confide in. Before his own birth, there had been another baby, which had died. He thought of that absent child as the brother he couldn't have.

He put the slippers on his feet and sat on the edge of his bed with the hookah to his lips. There was a faint and fragrant scent of old tobacco, almost imperceptible.

* * *

By this time his second novel had been published. It had been a pleasurable book to write, falling out of him with almost confessional ease, though at the same time, in a contradictory way, it had occasionally felt to him too symbolic and bloodless. The problem was that he was writing about men and women, about marriage, which were subjects he knew nothing about. It was an ongoing vexation to feel that his true subject was buried somewhere out of reach, and could perhaps never be spoken aloud.

He had dedicated the book to the Apostles, otherwise known as the Cambridge Conversazione Society, the exclusive group of intellectuals to which he had belonged from his fourth year at King's. Theirs had been a communion of minds, and his first and most lasting taste of friendship.

Many of the Apostles, and the sort of conversation they made, had featured in the story. Perhaps this was the reason they couldn't fully warm to it. He had tried to disguise them, or jumble them up, and in any case there was more of him in there than anyone else. One of the characters, however, was based to some extent on the Apostle he cared for more than any other. Hugh Owen Meredith—known as Hom to his friends—had occupied a central place in Morgan's affections until now.

He and Hom had become close in their second year at Cambridge. His dark, athletic good looks were immediately attractive, but his mind had a real power too. It was Hom, in fact, who had sponsored Morgan's election to the Apostles, though his influence had gone further than that. Almost as soon as they had become friends, he had started to work on Morgan's religious beliefs, questioning and undermining them with a rigorous and cynical vigour.

Morgan was ready to be challenged. The form of religion was one thing, but the content was something else entirely and, once he thought about it, the content started to feel very thin indeed. The idea of the Trinity was an absurdity. And Jesus was a humourless fellow, lacking in intellectual substance, who placed a perverse value on pain. If you knew he was in the next room, would you want to go and talk to him? No, Christianity was a distraction rather than a solution, and he came soon to a clear-sighted moment where he set it aside entirely. Afterwards, he felt almost physically lighter.

It was Hom who had given this lightness to him. But Hom himself had a heavy spirit, despite his outward cheeriness. Under all his conversation, a thread of defeat and futility ran deep. Morgan was drawn by this darkness, perhaps because he hoped to cure it. Certainly when the two of them were together they created a sense of hopeful excitement between them, in which a bright future seemed possible. What exactly that future contained was unclear as yet. But—in Morgan's mind at least—it might hold both him and Meredith in some blissful undefined companionship.

It had almost seemed possible for a while. His years at Cambridge felt like a high and radiant moment, where the world was on the point of opening for him. He had discovered the Greeks, and the ancient Hellenic universe, which was the first Empire, could justify so much. And it was under the cover of Plato that he had allowed himself to love Hom's body, rather than his mind.

He had left his student years at Cambridge behind by then; he was living with his mother in a hotel in Bloomsbury, and

Hom was nearby, studying at the London School of Economics. They spent a great deal of time together. One night, in the middle of a frantic discussion on the *Symposium*, they found themselves entangled on Hom's couch, fingers running through one another's hair. "I love you," Morgan told his friend, but the emotion had only risen in the wake of the words—fierce and freshly minted, true somehow for the very first time.

The words, and the feeling, had been rehearsed many times since. Yet the two men stayed in their clothes. Hands could range over the surface; fingertips could trace the outline of eyebrows, nose, mouth. On one especially heated occasion Morgan had dared to press his lips—fumblingly, inaccurately—against those of his friend. The brief touch, dry and tasteless, had fired a flare in his head. But he had felt Hom pulling back and away.

"We must take care . . . " he said, his voice trailing off, echoing nevertheless in Morgan's mind.

Care had to be taken. What felt so spontaneous, natural, was in fact dangerous. That danger could in itself be exciting, as Morgan was to learn on subsequent nights, when the embraces and fondlings continued. The possibility of discovery, the sound of other people on the far side of the wall: these gave an extra intensity, like a magnetic effect, to the movement of skin on skin. There were times when he thought his heart might stop. Nothing had ever felt so complete or so powerful as the encirclement of male arms. But he knew, even in the most ardent of clinches, that what was happening meant something different to each of them.

"Why are you doing this?" Morgan asked him once, when Hom's hand had fallen listlessly away from him.

"Why? Well, why not? If it was good enough for the Greeks . . . "

"Is that why, really? Simply to imitate the unspeakable vice of the Greeks?"

"We are speaking, aren't we, at this moment? Besides, we haven't indulged in any vice." In a sudden movement, Hom straightened up, pushing Morgan aside. "It hasn't been carnal," he announced, in a new, clipped voice. "We've merely expressed our feelings. Is that so unforgivable?"

"Not to me."

"Nor me. I am very fond of you, Morgan. Let's think of this as an experiment."

"An experiment? To find out what?"

"That we can only know by trying. I am sick of following rules that society has laid down. 'You may do this but not that, you may feel this but not that.' It's intolerable. I would like to go where my feelings lead me."

"I agree," Morgan said—but his feelings had ebbed for the moment.

He had taken to spending a lot of time among the Greek statuary at the British Museum and there were days when all passion seemed to be frozen in marble. The gods felt human to him, and the humans god-like. There was one statue in particular, a young man of ideal form—though an arm had broken off—which evoked a deep ache. It was the beauty of art, but also the beauty of the male body, that stirred him. And there was sadness in the stirring, because he did not think he would ever lie close to naked beauty like that.

To touch, to hold. To be touched. The yearning was so strong sometimes that it hurt. The more so because it could not be spoken. Not even—not really—to Hom.

Especially not after Hom told him casually, soon afterwards, that he had become engaged.

"To a woman?" Morgan asked stupidly.

"To Caroline Graveson." She was a friend of his from Cambridge. "We are thinking of starting a co-educational school together."

"What a good idea."

"Yes, it has given my life fresh power." Meredith was beaming. "She is so very lovely, Forster, and I know she is the right person for me."

"Of course." Morgan was trying to smile. This was an injury he had never felt before. He could see Hom's mouth working as he talked about his plans, but he couldn't hear the words.

At the end of the evening, when it was time to go, Hom pulled him close and held him. Morgan could feel the warmth of his body, and hear his breath. He experienced a great confusion of emotion, which continued when he walked back alone through the night-time streets to his mother.

Perhaps Meredith was right. Perhaps when all was said and done, one had to do the right thing. Marriage—a joining of lives—was the only possible way to be happy. But could it be his way? He had thought from time to time that, perhaps, if he only found the right person, it might be possible. But it was only with old ladies that he could be at ease. His dealings with young women were awkward, and the few occasions when he'd tried to show an interest had been mawkish and misjudged. During at least one episode, he had behaved in a way that reflected embarrassingly on him. In truth, most females felt like a different species to him; they made him afraid.

He had wrestled a great deal—invisibly, below the surface—with the whole question of marriage. In the end, it was a problem he could only solve in words. He worked it out of himself, knottily, in the bigger knot of his book. *The Longest Journey*, as it wound itself out of him, showed him strangenesses in his own nature that partly alarmed him, but partly pleased him too—because they confirmed what he hoped about himself: that he did not belong, not quite, in the deadly properness around him. No, there was a whole aspect of his character that was an unmentioned half-brother to his civilised side: drunk and disorderly and primitive, closer to the woods than the city. He even wrote a scene for this side of himself in which he capered, naked and goat-like, through a landscape that accepted him utterly. Then thought better of it later and struck out the pages.

He had had an encounter on the hills above Salisbury, where he had been visiting Maimie Aylward, that had showed him this secret face in a mirror. He had walked to the Figsbury Rings, the two Iron Age stone circles, with the twisted tree growing in the middle. He'd been there before, of course, but had never seen another human figure; something of the power of the setting derived from its loneliness. But on this particular day there was a shepherd boy, smoking at the centre of a crystalline silence. When Morgan had settled himself close by, the boy had offered him—unruffled, almost uncaring of his presence—a puff on his pipe. Morgan had held the pipe for a moment, feeling its faint heat, then returned it to the rough hand. He thought he ought to offer something in exchange, but when he held out sixpence the boy shook his head. In the soft exchange of conversation between them, none of which he could remember distinctly afterwards, the strongest impression he had taken away was that the boy had not called him 'sir', not once. He had not called him anything, in fact, but it felt as if he'd addressed him by name. It was only when the boy had stood up to go that Morgan had seen his club foot.

This conversation, and the place where it had happened, had stayed with Morgan afterwards; it had rippled through him, like the two concentric stone circles, moving outwards from some ancient point. Nothing had happened, but something had changed. The boy was real but he was also a sort of ghost. England had brewed him up.

Morgan had put him into the book, his rough truthfulness, even his pipe—as well as the landscape from which he could not be separated. But his club foot he had taken away from him and given to somebody else. The foot was not a foot; it was another kind of impediment, like a tongue that couldn't speak. Yes, he had put the foot onto himself, and himself into another life, one in which he did marry, although he ought not to. And the Apostles were there, and Hom too, and the suburbs that held him in their bloodless grip. It was all mixed up, all coded and undisclosed, too many opposites swirling in a muddle that he couldn't solve. But he liked it afterwards, this lack of a solution, because it was the truth.

* * *

Masood wrote: *Centuries may pass, years may turn into 2000 centuries and you never hear from me & you are not to think that the great affection, the real love & the sincerest admiration that I feel for you has in any way diminished . . .*

Affection. Love. Admiration. Morgan's head turned dizzily. But by degrees he detached himself and thought it through rationally. He remembered the other letters Masood had written him, their heightened, heated language. The little contact he'd had with other Indians, through Masood, had taught him that many of them spoke in this way. A few weeks before, in Oxford, a recent Indian acquaintance had told him earnestly that he was his very best friend in the world, and seemed utterly sincere when he said it. The words didn't mean what they did to the English. The language seemed bigger than it was.

And yet, despite himself, Morgan couldn't help responding. The tender declaration set something ticking. He understood, in that instant, what was happening to him. By a slow increeping, Masood was taking Hom's place in his heart.

By this time Hom was married—though not to Caroline Graveson. He had broken off that first engagement almost immediately, and had then suffered a breakdown of some kind, a long inward darkness, in which he'd seemed close to something extreme. Morgan had spent a great deal of time with him, speaking to him, and Hom had told a number of people that he only felt he came to life when he was in Morgan's company. And then he had got a little better, had taken a lecturing post in Manchester and met somebody else soon after moving up there. But although Morgan had felt it as a seclusion, a closing off, and his relationship with Hom's wife, Christabel, was coolish, the peculiar, lopsided bond between him and his friend was still in place.

For a time, then, Morgan had allowed himself to love both of them, Hom and Masood, silently and from afar, and in different ways. In the case of Hom, the happiness that Morgan might have felt was tempered by a sad certainty that Hom would never belong to him, not in any meaningful way. The most he would have were the chaste and clothed embraces that had marked the limit of their affections so far.

Masood, though, might be different.

* * *

Masood was in Paris for a few weeks, in the hope of improving his French. When he extended a casual invitation to come over for a visit, Morgan wavered only briefly. Aside from anything else, it would be an escape from his mother.

Masood came to meet him at the station. "It has been too frightful," he announced. "I will never learn to speak this language with any finesse at all. And the French are ruder than the English, which I hadn't thought possible. The white races are so damned ridiculous, it's an embarrassment to have been colonised by them. Give me your bags immediately."

He had taken rooms nearby, to which he led Morgan, talking incessantly. And their conversation barely ceased for the following week, in which they were always together. Morgan had never been to Paris before and everything had the power of freshness and discovery. Wearing identical hats they had bought together in the Latin Quarter, they walked aimlessly through the streets, wandering in and out of galleries and restaurants and theatres. The city became a vast set for their small, luminous drama. It was the first time that they'd lived together in such unbroken intimacy, without other visitors or family in attendance. Perhaps, Morgan reflected, marriage was like this: a kind of completeness between two people, like coloured shades closing off the rest of the world. He could live in this way, he thought, in a strange city with Masood, and never be bored or unhappy.

At some point in that week, they spoke about being in India together. Masood would be returning there when his studies were done, and it seemed natural—like an extension of this Paris sojourn—that Morgan should join him.

What was less natural, perhaps, was what Masood now offhandedly proposed.

"Of course," he said, "you will write a novel about it."

"What? India? That's not very likely, is it?"

"Why not? From the very first moment I met you, I knew that here was an Englishman who didn't see the world like the rest of his countrymen. You don't realise it, but you have an Oriental sensibility. That is why the book you'll write will be unique. It will be written in English, it will seem to be from English eyes, but its secret view will be from inside."

"If my mind is so like yours, why do I still find you so peculiar?"

But Masood was serious today. "You are offending me. If you can write about Italy, then why not about my country?"

Morgan considered it. An interesting notion, perhaps, but so far outside his own experience that it seemed impossible. He had read a few novels set in India, but they were all of a breathless female variety. Doomed love on the Frontier, that sort of thing. And there was Kipling, of course—but Kipling was always singing the virtues of the English and the inferiority of the natives, to say nothing of the gory glory of patriotic death.

They were walking in the street, a light rain falling, but the dampness and the slippery cobbles disappeared as his mind travelled elsewhere, either deep inside or far away. "My Italian novels," he said at last, "are really about the English. Italy was merely a backdrop."

"What of it? Write about the English in India, if it pleases you. Though I can tell you, they are a self-important, silly lot out there. Not the stuff of which heroes are made." But then, a moment later, his tone changed to one of affected outrage. "I demand to be a character in your novel! Or are the English the only worthy subjects? Oh, I wish I had lived at the time of the great Oriental despotisms—I would have ordered you to write me endless books, with no English characters in them." He went stalking ahead in pretended injury—or perhaps, for a moment, it was real.

This conversation stayed with Morgan. A novel about the English in India, one in which Masood also featured: it wasn't an unattractive idea. Though he would, of course, have to pay a visit to the East, and that seemed like a monumental endeavour, one to which his life wasn't equal.

On the morning of his departure from Paris, he woke early and lay for some time, looking across the room at the face of his sleeping friend. They had known one another for three years now, and yet it was only over the past few days that the final barrier had fallen. He had never felt closer to anybody. As he drifted back towards a doze, from some subterranean recess an understanding came to him.

Then he sat up, fully awake, in a flurry of panic. It was so obvious that he hadn't seen it, or had managed to call it by other names. But once the true name had been uttered, it couldn't be unsaid.

Yet even now he wondered. He had been aware for some time of where his true inclinations lay, and Masood didn't fit them. The previous year, through his friend Sydney Waterlow, he had been invited to dinner with Henry James in Rye, and an incident there had revealed his own appetites to him. The evening had been passably pleasant, though not for one moment had he felt truly at ease, truly in place. It had begun badly, with the Master emerging from his house, laying a plump hand on Morgan's shoulder and telling him, "Your name's Moore." That misunderstanding had been cleared up, but it had been followed by another confusion between Weybridge and Wakefield, and this awkwardness had stamped itself into all the social intercourse that followed.

It was only when he left Lamb House that something had become apparent. In the warm gloom, a labourer was leaning against the wall, smoking a cigarette, and the man's indistinct form, the red glow of the coal, had moved something in Morgan that all the high talk inside could not. He remembered the working-class men who had stirred him in his life, and remembered too a glimpse he'd had from a train window of two naked brown bodies sunning themselves in a warehouse. He had understood then what drew him; what his ticket was. Not just the lean outline propped against the wall, but the larger world he belonged to—the darkness, the evening under the sky, the smell of smoke and fields.

It was impossible, of course, because it was not his world. He belonged to what he'd just left behind: the polite, constricted ritual around the dining table, the buttoned-down conversation about books and travel and opera and architecture. Yet even there he could not keep his gaze from sliding sideways, to the figure of the servant who bent in to clear the plates. Although they brushed against each other, there was an immeasurable gulf between the two worlds, and something in him longed to close that gap. *Only connect*: he had set the yearning down in the book he was busy writing—yet it remained a yearning, an incurable ache.

And Masood, for all his difference, his exotic pedigree, belonged to Morgan's world. He had never for a moment been out of place in Oxford, or Paris, or at his mother's dining table in Weybridge. It was a matter of class; it nearly always was in England. It was not unusual in the least that Morgan should spend a week on holiday with Masood, but a week like this with Ansell, the garden boy, or that labourer outside Lamb House? Unthinkable!

All of this passed through Morgan's mind in an incoherent tumble, while Masood finally groaned and turned and yawned, coming to wakefulness. The realisation of love was important, but it also seemed improbable. They were too much alike, they fitted too closely together, for love to have taken hold. Love was what could never work; love was the longing across an insuperable barrier.

So it was something else, then, a misplaced fondness, a brotherly closeness. He put on his social face again. Yet something of his earlier disquiet lingered, making him unsettled and cold. At the station, when the time came to say goodbye, England was already upon him. He held out his hand to be shaken.

"Well," he said. "I had better run for the train. Thank you so much for everything—I have enjoyed myself enormously."

Masood stared at him, his handsome face becoming suffused with dismay. It took a moment for his voice to emerge. "What are you *saying* to me?"

Morgan was genuinely confused. "I am saying goodbye."

"This is how you say goodbye? To *me*? After the wonderful few days we have spent together, the sort of days I have never shared with anyone—" He broke off in a sort of strangled wail. "Oh, what is the use, what is the use?"

"If I miss my train, it will put my mother to great trouble. She and my grandmother—"

"I don't care about your grandmother!" Masood's eyes flashed, as if he might become violent.

So intense was this display that Morgan thought his friend was putting on an act. It took a few moments for him to understand that the performance was real. "I'm seeing you again in a few days," he said at last. "I didn't think sentiment was necessary."

"You are saying goodbye like an Englishman."

"I *am* an Englishman."

"Yes, I wish I could forget it for just a moment, I wish *you* could forget it! Are emotions a sack of potatoes, to be measured out, so much the pound? Are we both machines? Will you use up your feelings if you express them? Can you not speak from the heart, just one time? Oh, Morgan, you bloody fool," he cried fiercely, flinging his powerful arms around him and lifting him off the floor, "don't you understand, we're *friends*!" He made as if to throw Morgan onto the tracks, kissed him hard on the cheek, then set him down and strode off, a whole head higher than the crowds around him.

Morgan was astonished, and disquieted, and pleased. On the journey home, he thought confusedly back to that conversation on the platform, and to his half-wakeful thoughts that same morning. It had long been a problem, this question of his formality against Masood's natural extravagance. On his visits to Oxford he had been chastised for any gratitude, or for evaluating an experience in terms of how good or bad it was. These kinds of formality were cold, in Masood's opinion; he was above such petty distinctions. All manners should be washed away in a balm of friendly emotion.

For his part, Morgan had his doubts. Protocol and courtesy might be ritualised, but they had weight and significance too. And emotion could hide things as well as show them.

They would probably never agree on this point. It was a matter of nationality, of course—but there was also the larger matter of character. Perhaps Masood was right to mistrust the English tendency to properness, but he, Morgan, hid a very real feeling behind his apparent coolness. If Masood could only hear the words he would *like* to speak, perhaps he would be less keen on sentiment.

* * *

When a letter arrived a few days later, he carried it up to his room to open it, as if the words inside might be dangerous. Masood's handwriting, like his personality, spilled in every direction. The tone was at odds with the distress on the station platform, though Morgan was gently upbraided again for his avoidance of sentiment. But this time, dryly, Masood also explained himself.

There was a quality in the Eastern character, he said, called Taras, which made a man ever-alert, ever-sensitive, to what was happening around him. True sentiment implied the power of physically feeling the difficulties of another person. For an Indian like himself, walking into a room required immediately being perceptive to the surrounding emotions, and to his place in them. He knew that Morgan shared this quality, which was why he had always thought of him as Oriental under the skin. And that was why his reticence, his formality, were so difficult to accept.

He said all this, and then, at the bottom of the paper, he had scrawled a quote from some unnamed poem. *O love, each time thou goest out of my sight, I die a new death.* The emotion of these words, in complete contrast to what had gone before, was profoundly unsettling. The lines were written by some-body else, for somebody else, but they arrowed directly into Morgan, hurting him exquisitely. In a moment he knew, because he relived it again, that what he'd felt in the Paris hotel room was true.

It was his habit, on the last day of each year, to review the events, both inward and outward, that had shaped the preceding twelve months. On this occasion, just a few days after returning from Paris, he allowed himself to speak. He had very recently begun keeping his diary in a locked journal, and secrecy made him feel brave. *Let me keep clear from criticism & scheming,* he wrote. *Let me be him. You've stopped me. I can only think of you, and not write.*

He paused for a long moment before continuing. Once the word was set down, he felt, it would be irrevocable. It took courage to tell the truth, even if only to oneself. But he had gone too far to stop. Trembling slightly, he took up the pen again and went on.

I love you, Syed Ross Masood: love.

There. It was visible. *Love.* The word, separate from him at last, seemed to shiver and flutter on the page. But what use was it there? Action had to be taken. And though action was not his strength, in this case it felt easier to speak out than to keep silent, even though it was probably no use. The feeling was too strong to live on unconfessed. Whatever the shock, Masood's mind would surely right itself again. But even the thought of speaking undid him, so that his Chopin preludes, which he sat down to later, were wobbly and full of wrong notes.

They saw each other just a few days later. Morgan had recently turned thirty-one, and Masood insisted that he come down to London so that he could take possession of a birthday present. A painting, which they had looked at together in a gallery, and which he could certainly not afford. Morgan stifled the urge to admonish, for fear of being called formal again. But all his fears, which had multiplied like germs since he'd made his resolution, vanished in the presence of his friend. They spoke about many things: once again especially, memorably, of India, as a place in which both of them would be present together one day, just as they had been in Paris.

What they did not speak of was what Morgan truly wanted to say. The words rose up in him, reaching his mouth and swelling there. But they would not come out. This was the moment, surely: a perfect, possible opportunity. But as the minutes went by, his courage slipped away. He had a train to catch, after all, in order to get home, if he didn't want to upset his mother.

Another time; there would be another time, soon. In the meanwhile, things had changed—and only because he had insisted on going to Paris. The invitation had been tepid, and easily ignored; it might almost not have happened. But he had gone, and since then he had felt buttressed and buoyed up by a constant, consoling emotion.

In a letter a few days later, he addressed Masood as his *Dearest boy*. And signed it, after a slight hesitation, *from Forster, member of the Ruling Race, to Masood, a nigger.*

It was a measure of how far they'd come that he knew his friend would laugh.

* * *

India was creeping closer in other ways. After his third novel had been published, Morgan had received an effusive letter of appreciation from Malcolm Darling, whom he had known at King's. The book had been well received by the critics, but his friends had mostly not liked it, so this response was especially valued. Malcolm had joined the Indian Civil Service in 1904, and was writing from the tiny state of Dewas Senior, where he was tutor to the Prince. He had become very fond of his young charge. He had read one of Morgan's short stories to His Highness, he reported, and the Prince had been enchanted by it—which enchanted Morgan in turn.

Malcolm's life seemed fantastic to him, spiced by peculiar magic. In the letters that began to pass between them, carried across the intervening distance by ship, some of the strangeness and wonder of India carried too. Malcolm told him, with accumulating anecdotal evidence, the story of how Dewas State had split into two dynasties, Senior and Junior, in which every institution had had to be duplicated, with two competing bureaucracies. It was, so Malcolm said, the oddest corner of the world outside of *Alice in Wonderland*, and something in it did seem mad and ridiculous and bizarrely inspired, like an event that defied gravity.

Although they had not been close before, their friendship began to grow now in these letters. They had already generated great warmth before the next chance had come to see one another, when Malcolm had returned to England on leave, in order to get married. Morgan had visited him in London and some understanding, already agreed upon between them, had been cemented in that time.

But there had also been an incident, terrible and strange, which he could not forget.

He had been invited to eat at the Rendezvous, a restaurant in Soho, with Malcolm. "And I hope you won't mind, Forster, if I bring along Ernest Merz. He is my very best friend in the world, and he's to be a groomsman at my wedding."

"Of course not. How could I possibly mind?"

"He's a good sort. And a Kingsman too. Also, he's a bachelor like you. So there will be a lot to speak about."

Morgan wondered for a moment whether some coded message was implied by that word, "bachelor". But no, he didn't think so. Malcolm, for all his affable niceness, was a rigid fellow in his thinking. There were no secret codes in his social world, and bachelors were merely bachelors.

And Merz was indeed a good sort. He laughed almost more than he spoke, and the laughter increased as the evening wore on. They had, all of them, several friends in common, and it was as if some of the radiance of King's had descended on their little corner of London. It was in a genial good humour that they finally left the restaurant, strolling together through the summer evening.

Malcolm said goodbye to them soon afterwards, leaving Morgan and Merz to walk on. For the first time, a small silence embedded itself, uniting rather than separating the two men. Morgan was thinking of bachelorhood, his own, and what it meant.

Perhaps a similar thought was on Merz's mind, because he said, "Another one gone."

"What do you mean?"

"Oh, Malcolm getting married." He laughed shortly. "You've met Josie, of course. How did you like her?"

"We were only introduced recently. I haven't formed an opinion yet."

"I hardly know her myself," Merz said. "I didn't mean to suggest . . . "

"I quite understand. There's no need to explain."

As it happened, Morgan felt wary of Josie, as he was wary of all young women, especially those who laid claim to his friends. But she also seemed an overly impulsive sort to him, who spoke before she'd weighed up her words, and a couple of her political opinions had alarmed him. Nevertheless, he could see that Malcolm adored her and he hoped his friend would be happy.

He didn't want to discuss this with his new acquaintance, of course, even though he instinctively liked him. But he thought he'd detected, from Merz's side, a sadness underlying his jolly demeanour, and wondered what it meant.

"What about you?" he asked, trying to sound casual. "Is there a marriage on the horizon?"

"Me? No, no. That is, not at any time soon. There is somebody," he said, "somebody possible. But I'm not sure yet. Or not ready."

Their footsteps echoed off the brick walls close by.

"And you?" Merz added. "Any marriage for you?"

"No," Morgan said. "Not for me."

Both of them became aware of an awkwardness around this subject, and Merz hurried to cover it.

"You have written very sensitively about marriage, I think. How have you understood it so well without experiencing it yourself?"

"I'm glad you think I have understood it well. It doesn't seem that way to me. The little I know I have absorbed through my friends."

"Are you not lonely?"

"No," Morgan said quickly, though the question had pierced him. It was only later that he regretted not answering more truthfully, because by then he understood that Merz was talking about himself.

They moved on to other topics, with less edge, none of which Morgan could later remember. Merz had said that he was going to his club in St James's and, as they strolled down Piccadilly together, a young man emerged from the shadows and passed them. He was rough-looking but handsome, a working-class youth, hands in pockets, face half-shadowed by a cloth cap. But as he drew level with the two men, he smiled. It was an arch smile, loaded with knowing irony, and it silenced both of them in a moment.

They emerged from the silence, embarrassed. Morgan had to get to Charing Cross to make his train, and the time had come for them to part. "Well," he said. "I have enjoyed meeting you very much."

"I too. It has been an honour. You are a very fine writer."

"Oh, come." They shook hands, and Merz laughed, without apparent reason. Then the two men moved away from each other.

The news came the next day, in the form of a telegram from

Malcolm. The words, so sparse and incontrovertible, could not possibly be true. Yet they also could not be false.

Morgan rushed back down to London. He went to be a friend to Malcolm, but also for his own sake, to understand. But there was no understanding on offer. No note, no explanation, no *reason*. Merz had not, it seemed, visited his club after all. Instead he had gone back to his rooms in Albany, drunk a glass of whisky and hanged himself.

Malcolm was pale, shrunken with shock. "You were the last person to speak to him," he told Morgan. "Did he say anything that made you think . . . ?"

"Not at all. He seemed fine, he was normal."

Normal. The word, Morgan was beginning to think, had no meaning at all.

"But what did you talk about? He must have said something, he must have given you a clue."

"Really not. It was a perfectly ordinary conversation, like the one we had in the restaurant."

Was that true? Yes, in a certain sense—but in another way Morgan doubted himself. Perhaps there had been hints; clues, as Malcolm had put it. But they could not be understood unless you were part of the minority. A secret language, a secret way of speaking—which was also a way of not speaking. Morgan couldn't be sure that anything had actually been said.

Nor could any of this be spoken to Malcolm. Not directly. It would mean speaking about himself too, in a way that they had never spoken before. And Malcolm, with his closed, conventional thinking, might not understand. So even at one remove, when all either of them wanted was to find out the truth, they could only circle the subject obliquely, with hints and half-questions.

Not to anybody did he mention the young man who had passed them, with his knowing look. Had he been available, if one had the money and the courage? It was possible, Morgan thought, that Merz had retraced his steps and gone after him, and that something had taken place which had led to this calamity.

What had befallen Ernest Merz was a warning to him. There was an edge in daily life, invisible and almost underfoot, over which the unwary might easily step. And what made it especially dangerous was the seductive power of gravity. He felt it often, especially at this time of his life. Without warning, his body would throw up a pang of yearning so extreme that there seemed no reason to resist. On one occasion, passing a soldier in the street and meeting the flat indifference of his stare, he had conjured a mental image of the man's private parts that was shockingly vivid. He was nervously aware of every handsome face he saw and often changed his route, or his train carriage, to come closer to that sort of beauty. At night, before he slept, his brain would distil these various faces into a single, unattainable vision, passing across the ceiling.

It was lust, nothing more, and there were times when lust felt like a kind of idealism. But it was also a part of his nature he reviled. His own desire repulsed him. Though if he could not aspire to purity, then he was sufficiently aware of what his mother and certain others might think, not to give in to baseness. And that was a sort of goodness, he thought, which might substitute for the real thing.

Nevertheless, he was tormented. Lunching with a friend in the Bath Club one day, he suddenly fell through a weak spot in their conversation into an awareness of the pool attendant standing close by, wearing only a towel around his waist, folding up other towels and stacking them. The near-nakedness of the man and, beyond him, the shimmering blue-green oblong of the water, with more half-clothed male figures almost glimpsed beyond in the underlit smoky air: it was like a vision of some other country, a place of warmth and sensual appetites, that couldn't be England. It didn't seem possible that, just a few bricks away, London continued in its rainy tumult.

More worryingly, after lunch with the same friend at the Savile Club not long after, Morgan was talking in a loose, unguarded way about his teaching at the Working Men's College. He spoke without thinking about 'a charming boy' he had met there, and instantly one of the members sitting opposite him let down his newspaper and looked at him over it, with a glare that was stony but accusing, fired out of the double barrels of two sanctimonious, middle-class eyes. Morgan was quite unnerved, and he carried his consternation with him to the barbershop afterwards, where he realised after a few moments that the man had followed him. They looked at each other, looked away, looked back again. The man changed seats and came to sit next to Morgan. He started a seemingly innocent conversation which led, by a series of sharp turns, to a suggestion that he very much needed to borrow ten pounds to bet on a horse that afternoon. Morgan, flustered, had pretended not to understand and got up quickly to go, patting his pockets all the while. He had kept looking behind him and, though the man had disappeared, it felt to Morgan as if he'd been followed for the rest of the day.

* * *

He was reading, and thinking, about India more and more, all in preparation for a visit which he now knew was certain, though its timing was not. He did not have the money to go soon, nor could he take his mother with him, or conceive of leaving her behind. But he had faith that the moment would come. Perhaps his new novel, which was almost complete, might make it financially possible.

Although he had published three books, and his head was

jostling with short stories, still he did not think of himself as a writer. Not in the true, vocational sense. It was more like his piano playing: a frivolous but enjoyable distraction. Writing required courage, but a greater courage would be to give it up. And he might; he really might do it. He didn't need to work; he had received a legacy from his great-aunt Monie that kept him comfortably. Nevertheless, he thought that in time he would like to find a real job, as most of his friends were doing. He understood that they, his peers, were taking over from their fathers, grasping the levers of power, learning how to run the Empire, while he stayed at home with the women. And in just a few years, he knew, it would be too late. He would not even be able to write properly about them then. It was in work that people became most essentially themselves, but he only saw them when they were idle, like he was. He did not—he felt this anxiously—he did not truly know the world.

Never had he learned this more keenly than in the writing of his new book, despite the fact that at the heart of the story was an emotion very personal to him. This emotion had been with him since the age of thirteen, when he and Lily had had to move from Rooksnest, the house in Stevenage where his earliest and best years had been lived. That wrenching away had always felt to him like a fall from grace, a breaking from a time when life was somehow whole and complete, a perfect circle of loving and being loved. He could never recover that time, or find a place that moored him quite as deeply, and he poured all his loss and longing over it into the work. Where sincerity was concerned, at least, he did not doubt himself.

But in every other way, his writing felt to him light, insubstantial. He did not have the weight, he thought, to measure up to his themes. He was writing about money and power, among other things, and he bumped up every day against the thinness of his knowledge. Always he ran aground on the edges of what he knew, and found himself beached in ignorance. And here again was the old question of marriage, and the way that men and women behaved together. What could he say about these things?

Apparently too much. When the book was finished, and publication was imminent, he circulated the proofs among those close to him and almost immediately he became aware of a chilliness in the way some people responded to it. But worst of all was his mother. Lily appeared to be steeped in enjoyment at first, but there came a day when Morgan found her in the drawing room, stiff and pale, his pages scattered on the floor at her feet.

"What is it?" he asked her. "Has something happened?"

"Yes, something has happened."

"What is it?"

"It is," she told him, "it is . . . something. Oh, I cannot speak about it."

"You must speak about it. Please, tell me what has upset you."

"It is you, Morgan, who have upset me."

"What have I done?"

She had not looked directly at him until now, and when her gaze fell on him he felt the temperature drop. It had been a long time since he'd seen her so distressed, though in recent years disappointment had set permanently on her features, like a glaze. The thought had come to him recently that if he had any life's work to speak of it was not to rule the natives in some far-flung outpost, but to take care of his mother, and that the white man's burden was nothing beside his. When he was younger they had been good companions together, unromantically and chastely married, but lately his goodwill had been harder to maintain. She had become sourer and sadder as she grew older. Her rheumatism was bad, but she was also afflicted by spiritual abrasions that he struggled to understand. There were days when it seemed that she found nothing, absolutely *nothing*, worthwhile.

"Everybody we know," she said, "will read this book. Will talk about it. Did you not think of me at all?"

He understood, finally, that it was Leonard Bast's seduction of Helen Schlegel that had undone her so.

"It is human nature," he said. "People do these things."

"Whom do we know who does these things? I don't know anybody who behaves in this way. It is only the lower orders who lapse, and why should they be written about? I can't believe it of you, Morgan."

"Anybody can lapse," he said, with a quick flash of defiance. Then he immediately regretted it. "Let us not quarrel."

"Let us not talk of it at all."

He tried a different approach. "You know I would not want to upset you. Your Poppy would never do that." Poppy, Popsnake—words left over from childhood, part of a secret baby language between the two of them, in which his very voice changed, becoming wheedling and needy.

But the appeal didn't work today; her face was sealed against him. "I am feeling unwell, a headache, I am going to my room. Please send Agnes to me."

He sat on after her withdrawal, stewing in quiet misery. He too had misgivings about this part of his book, but on aesthetic, not moral grounds. Neither in books nor the real world did he know anything about the inner workings of women, their bodies or their minds. The seduction, the pregnancy: he had handled them badly, he hadn't pulled them off. The sequence was not sensual enough to be offensive; it had suffered more than any other part of the book from his deficiency of knowledge.

Lily tortured him for some time afterwards, not by talking about his crime, but by not talking about it. She was polite and cold in her dealings with him, reminding him at every opportunity, without ever saying it, that he had failed her, as he always seemed to do. Yet the topic was not mentioned again between them. He began to dread how others might respond. He had been raised in an encircling palisade of older women, all of whom had a particular idea of him, which he might be about to destroy. Those who had survived would judge him most harshly. There were still Maimie and Aunt Laura to deal with.

* * *

But Maimie liked his book.

And not only Maimie. The reviews were rapturous, and the word from those in his own circle was equally warm-hearted. Apparently he had written a masterpiece. He was talked about, and talked to, in a way that was new to him, and not entirely welcome. The word "greatness" was casually thrown about.

Fame was like a glow that soon became too hot, and he felt himself sweating in the glare. To his alarm, some people had begun to take him seriously. Through invitations and oblique approaches, he experienced the pull of literary society. He resisted; he would not feel at home there. He could only come to it as a supplicant. He developed a technique for dealing with praise, which involved staring down at the floor while being spoken to. One had to avoid listening, but to assume an attitude of modesty, while sending one's imagination down, down through the earth, to New Zealand on the far side. If you practised this assiduously, then fame did not matter so much.

The only possible benefit of all this attention was that his mother's outrage dwindled. She let it be known that she was bored by his literary success, but when the expected opprobrium failed to materialise, Lily withdrew into grudging resignation. Her son might not have learned to live in the way that real men did, but he had ventured into the world through his thoughts, and some of his acclaim reflected back on her.

Hom had written to say how much he'd liked the novel.

And then, in the same month that the book appeared, he came to Weybridge for a visit. Success made Morgan's skin glow; he could feel his own youthful confidence; he could sense that Hom found him attractive. On one particular afternoon, when his mother and Ruth and Agnes were all out of the house, the two men took tea together in the drawing room. Again, Hom spoke about how much he admired the book; it had made him feel close to Morgan, he said.

Just how close became apparent soon afterwards, when he set down his teacup and took hold of his host. They rolled around on the sofa for a while, and then somehow continued on the floor. For the first time Hom kissed him—not just once, but repeatedly—and put his tongue into Morgan's mouth. The sudden moist intimacy was startling, and all the more so because they had not touched each other in a year. Yet all that Morgan could think of was that Hom must have learned this from his wife.

The sound of Lily coming back from a social visit made them separate and return to their upright positions on the sofa. Morgan finished his cold tea, feeling dazed. He was thinking about his complicated history with his friend, everything that it had promised, how little it had delivered. Hom was very much married by now, and the father of twins. He had recently been appointed to a professorship in Belfast, and was moving over there. But his wife, Christabel, was refusing to go with him, and there had been a brouhaha among certain members of their social circle because, it was felt, she was not a good mother to the children.

For some reason, Morgan felt moved to address this issue now. "It's shocking," he told Hom, "that she will not accompany you. I intend to speak to her about it."

"She can't be forced. No, please do not bring it up. She will only turn against you."

"She already is against me."

"Morgan, that's untrue. She likes you very much. Speaking to her will ruin it. I implore you, in the name of everything that has happened between us . . . "

Pleased at this reference, Morgan softened. "Well, it is your concern, of course. But I think you should not allow a woman to undermine your life like this. If I were in her place," he added, "I would move to Belfast with you tomorrow."

"I hope you will come to visit me there often."

"I hope I shall."

The meeting had ended happily after all. Morgan could not know it yet, but this was to be the last time that he and Hom ever touched each other in this way. What he took away from the encounter was a warm, sad afterglow, like the fading radiance of a burnt-out fire, and it was still with him the next day, when he went to the opera with Masood.

Sitting next to his other friend, his Indian brother, their knees and elbows pressed together, he was nevertheless aware that he was not awake to his presence. His mind, his heart, were still rolling around on the carpet at home. It was possible to love two people at the same time, he reflected, but not on successive days. He was used to feeling desire. But what stirred him on this occasion, and stayed with him, was the knowledge that he had been desirable to somebody else. That was something he hadn't felt before.

* * *

He had spent a great deal of time with Masood in recent months, but on these occasions he had hardly ever been happy. Love had vexed his mind, making him irritable and irrational. There was something in human affection that was at odds with reason, he thought, like a kind of mild insanity. When he was with Masood, what he felt was that everyone around them was watching them with secret, pernicious judgement. The only time he was truly at ease was when they were alone together.

And yet his kinship with his friend had deepened. The tone of their conversation had changed now; it was more honest and more serious. Even in letters, Masood often dropped the baroque voice he had liked to use, in which he had played a fairy-tale king or slave. In one particular communication he had confessed, *I have got to love you as if you were a woman or rather part of my own body*. This was not the kind of declaration he would ever have made before, and it wasn't altogether welcome: it wasn't how Morgan wanted to be loved.

Just before Christmas, he and Masood went to the opera again, to *Salome*. Afterwards, as they wandered over to the Oxford and Cambridge Musical Club in Leicester Square, a regular haunt of theirs, they discussed what they had just seen.

"It's the mixture of lust and revenge," Morgan said. "Either one alone is a worthy subject, but together they are somehow squalid. And when the music is beautiful it only makes it worse."

"You see," Masood exclaimed, "it is what I have always said—lust and revenge are a very Eastern combination. You have an insight into these subjects."

This topic had been rehearsed many times between them and usually it was pleasing to Morgan, but tonight the rain was falling in cold, vertical lines and the heat of India seemed very far away. "You always tell me this," he said, "but it isn't true. There is nothing I know better than the English tea party."

"Nonsense, my dear chap. I have met many Englishmen and you are the only one with the power of true sentiment. You will see when we get to Turkey."

The two men had been making plans to go to Constantinople together; the idea was that they would travel in an Oriental city, a try-out for the real East. But at this moment even Turkey felt unreachable.

They had come to the club; there was a fussing with umbrel-

las and coats at the door, and a pause while they found an unoccupied corner to sit in. Masood was drinking whisky, and
Morgan wanted tea. They talked in a small, inconsequential
way while their order was brought, and then Morgan was hit by
a sudden plunge of mood. He said, "I am never going to write
another novel."

"Oh, you are, you are, not just one, many novels, or I shall
never speak to you again."

"You speak lightly, because you think I'm talking that way
too. I really mean what I say. You have too much faith in me. I
am not half the writer you seem to think I am."

"Oh, come." Masood's gaze flitted about, while he stroked
his big moustache with a well-shaped hand. He said confidently,
"You are the only living writer that matters. You are twice as
great as anybody else," and then suddenly broke off as he saw
Morgan's eyes fill with tears. "I'm sorry," he muttered, confused.
"I don't mean to joke. You know I am a foolish fellow."

The sudden switch from bluster to uncertainty was typical
and somehow touching. "It's all right," Morgan told him. "You
are my dear boy."

"I don't understand. What is the matter?"

Morgan himself didn't know what the matter might be.
Perhaps it was only the memory of John the Baptist's head, car-
ried bloodily on a platter. Surprising himself, he said quietly,
"You do realise that I love you?"

"Yes, yes. We have spoken of this many times. The feeling
is reciprocated."

"I am not sure you understand." Suddenly, he was filled
with a steady determination. "No, I'm not sure that you do."

For once Masood had no reply; he sat very still, looking at
the room around them. The place was very full tonight. There
were people close by, and a general roar of chatter and laughter, forcing Morgan to lean in closer to speak.

"I love you as a friend," he said, "but also as something

more than a friend. No, don't answer for a moment. I know what you are going to tell me—that in India friends can be like brothers, and you love me in this way. But I love you as more than a friend, and more than a brother too."

Now Masood's dark eyes focused on him with a puzzled, sorry look. He said, "I know," and touched Morgan's hand briefly on the table. A moment later he was calling for the waiter.

That was all. A year of waiting, while the pressure built up—then the truth spilled out in a handful of words. Perhaps the wrong words, words that did not fully speak their meaning. Yet the meaning had been there. Not long afterwards they were outside, in the wintry dark, saying their farewells and hurrying in different directions.

The feeling, at first, was euphoric. As he caught his train, Morgan was filled with a giddy sense of release. It had been so easy! And Masood had understood; there had been a quick pain in his eyes.

But even before he reached home, the happy mood was gone. The enormity of what he had said bore in on him. It felt as if he'd taken an irrevocable step, with consequences he hadn't properly considered. Masood had barely answered him. Although he'd been polite and friendly when they parted, might his manner not have concealed his true reaction? As he kept being reminded, his friend was an Indian and their social manners were different. Might Masood not have been horrified, or even disgusted, by him?

By the next day he was calmer. He trusted Masood's refinement of spirit and thought things would be all right. Nevertheless, he sent an anxious note, asking to be reassured. There was no response.

As the silence went on over the coming days, Morgan's equanimity was tested. There was no one on whom to vent his worry except his mother, and he found himself snapping at her, then feeling bad about his shortness of temper. His misery was small but deep, and it worsened when a birthday present from Masood arrived. It was an ugly gift, quite the most unappealing present his friend had given him—a tray with a candlestick, matchbox and sealing wax—and the note that accompanied it was bland. Reading and re-reading the empty words, Morgan concluded that the parcel must have been sent before his reckless announcement in the club. It felt like the forerunner of disaster.

He had to consider, then, the possibility that their friendship might be over. A life like his old life, in which he did not see or speak to Syed Ross Masood: it was a horrible thought. But in it there was a reckoning, and a choice. There was the simple temptation just to wall Masood off. It would be easy, so easy, to belittle him, and to think himself well rid of their friendship.

Upset and stirred by these thoughts, which were like voices calling up from some depth in himself, he went for a long walk alone. He felt he had to bring some order to his emotions, and so he dwelt on the association between himself and Masood, which had begun on the front doorstep of his home four years ago. Their friendship had come to seem like something separate from the rest of his English life—separate, even, to the two men who'd given rise to it. To turn away from the image of his friend would be a stain on what had joined them. The love that he had felt, however fruitless it might be, was like a kind of grace—that is to say, a gift bestowed from outside—and he had no right to refuse it. Even if the silence was permanent and they had to part, he would not give in to insult and regret.

Having achieved this resolution was a triumph, and one that lasted, if a trifle waveringly, past that evening. So that it came as something of a let-down when Masood did finally write, but without acknowledging the full weight of Morgan's confession. *There is nothing to be said, everything is under-*

stood. Well, that was true—but then he wandered on to other, everyday topics, infuriating in their smallness. It was obvious that he didn't want to say any more about it.

* * *

Constantinople came to nothing; six months later they went to the Italian lakes instead. They would spend some days on the Swiss side of the border and then, after Masood left, Morgan would join Goldie in Italy itself. It was a good substitute: Italy was the country where he had first felt his spirit stir in him. Travelling there with his mother, ten years before, he had been slowly wakened by the sensuality of heat and landscape and exotic ruins, till one day, out for a walk by himself near Ravello, a wild imagining had somehow become true.

He was in a forest, surrounded by tangled trees, and a wind had suddenly begun to blow out of the centre of a dry, still day. Morgan had stopped, staring around him into the moving leaves, and the fancy had come to him that this little breeze might herald the arrival of some old, pre-Christian god. Pan, perhaps. No sooner had this thought struck than the wind increased its power, till the branches had started to heave, and Morgan to run. He was genuinely afraid, but also thrilled: hot on his heels, on his neck, the ancient world pursued him. Only when he had emerged from the trees, and the modern roofs of the town had appeared below, did he stop and bend over to catch his breath. He felt frightened and ridiculous and amused by what had happened—or, more accurately, *not* happened—and only then became aware that a story had appeared in him, whole and entire. He could hardly get back to the *pensione* fast enough to put it down.

He had been back to Italy many times since, and had set two novels there. It had never failed to overturn the cold and ordered world of the English suburbs and to promise something pagan in return. He had similar hopes of this visit with Masood, but things had not worked out like that. There had been a joyous closeness between them, and one especially lovely moment on the train when they had knelt together in the corridor, looking out the window at the stars. But there was also sadness, because their time in England was drawing to a close; Masood was in London now, reading for the bar, and would be returning to India in a few months.

On one of the first days, Masood had begun to speak in a suggestive, nudging tone about a waitress at the hotel. It had been slow to dawn that what was being intimated was that he, Morgan, might like to approach her. An astonishing notion, after everything that had happened.

"Do you remember that conversation we had?" he asked. "I mean in the O and C Club, just before Christmas?"

A small frown appeared between Masood's eyes. He nodded slightly, it might have been in confusion.

"I'm not sure whether you understood me properly then. I don't think I made my meaning clear."

"I did understand you," Masood told him.

A silence opened up between them. They were in Tesserete, in the room they were sharing, and the waters of the lake were visible from the window. Morgan looked out on the grey, moving surface, rather than at the face of his friend. "Please allow me to speak," he said.

"Yes, please, speak, speak."

"When I say that I love you, I don't mean it in some passing way. I mean that I would like to spend my life with you. Not close to you, or parallel to you, but *with* you. I mean . . . " He trailed off, his meaning slipping away from him.

"You are always with me, Morgan."

"No, I'm not saying it correctly." He made a gesture with his hands, of helplessness and frustration. "What I want," he began bravely, "I mean to say . . . I want . . . "

What he wanted hung between them both, unsayable.

"I do understand," Masood said, a little crossly. "But it is not possible. Please believe me, if it were possible, I would give this to you. But I cannot."

Morgan looked down at his fingers. They seemed like something separate to him, pale and curious and segmented. He imagined them as he often saw them, holding a pen, setting words down in a line across the page, and the thought came to him that they would never hold another human body. Not in the way that he wanted.

"Yes," he said.

More softly, Masood went on. "I have known . . . I have *understood* . . . for some time, my dear. I was afraid at first, but then . . . " Now it was his turn to run dry. He shrugged his big shoulders, and blew through his moustache in a vexed way. "You are my very best friend, Morgan," he said at last. "I don't want that to disappear."

"No, of course not."

There was a strained silence, before Masood stretched and yawned ostentatiously, and said, "Now I think we should go for a walk. I need to build up an appetite before dinner."

So what mattered most was put away between them, and not mentioned again. The remaining days of their trip were spent in contented companionship, unbroken by any high emotion—unless it was Masood's seduction of the rather ugly waitress, which he only half-concealed from his friend.

* * *

He returned to England and the familiar morbidity. His maternal grandmother Louisa had died seven months before, and this event had shattered his mother. For his own part, he had loved his grandmother and thought she had lived fully and well. Her going brought sadness, but her life had been in every

sense complete; her final gift to him had been a sense of gratitude at being alive himself. But Lily was broken. She had wept
and cried aloud in Louisa's last hours, and something of that
dissolution had stayed with her afterwards. Her mourning
became a weight that she had to carry around physically, and
she did not cease from complaining.

He had hoped that something might change during his
month away. In the earlier part of the year, after the first time
he'd spoken out to Masood, his own health had taken a turn
for the worse. Perhaps disappointment had sapped him; certainly he had felt significantly older, as if time had shrunk.
Tuberculosis was mentioned. His opsonic index was low and
his doctor told him that he might have to go to a sanatorium.
But he had fought back, invisibly, under the skin, and both his
spirit and his body had recovered. He was determined that his
second disappointment would not return him to that state.

Yet here he was, battling not only his own sadnesses, but
those of his mother as well. Her grumbling and fault-finding
ate away at the solid ground beneath him. Worse, he seemed to
have arrived at a point where the way forward was no longer
apparent. He had published a collection of short stories
recently, but even this form, which he had always enjoyed, now
felt somehow out of reach. Instead, furtively, with a strong
sense of the forbidden, he had started to write another kind of
short story.

These were sexual in nature, a living-out of what he had
only dared imagine in his mind. He wrote them not to express,
but to excite himself. Although he liked some of them, he also
felt a certain repetition at work, a compulsion that centred on
the same figure: tall, dark, athletic and good-looking, when he
entered the scenario, the rest became inevitable. This man was
nowhere visible in real life—or he was everywhere visible, and
unattainable.

He could not show these stories to the world. Shame and

secret excitement: they had been the stuff of so much of his life, and they appeared now to have infected his words. He had started a new novel, too, which he called *Arctic Summer*, but he felt its emptiness, its diminishing momentum. The idea for it had seeded itself in him at Basel station, on his way back from Italy, when he had found himself in a horrible tangle of English tourists on the platform, and had almost been flung beneath a train. But part of the problem was that he had written about these people before. Hapless English travellers, finding or losing themselves in Italy—what more could he say about them? He knew them too well; he wanted to leave them behind.

Perhaps the answer lay further afield, in the Indian novel he'd been thinking about. In any case, India was becoming more certain in his mind. *Howards End* was selling strongly, and he had the money to make the trip. He had developed a daydream which he told to nobody else, which featured him travelling to India and vanishing. He would not die, exactly, but he would drift away, into a new life, a new identity, and he would never revisit his old one in England again. This daydream was most intense when his mother was at her worst.

On one particular evening she had worked on his nerves to such an extent, finding such fault with everything that he did and his manner of doing it, that he had almost lost control. She was supposed to be going out that night to call on a friend, but she wondered aloud how she could possibly go, when none of the household tasks had been attended to, the maid and the cook were away and Morgan could not be relied on to feed himself in her absence. And her back hurt, from bending over in the garden, or possibly it was the rheumatism.

"My body, my miserable body," she cried. "Why isn't it strong? Oh, why can't I simply walk away and be gone? Why can't I finish my duties and be gone? What is the point of all this talking? What is the point of *anything*?"

Eventually, she did depart. Alone in the house, Morgan

stood in the drawing room, feeling the silent furniture pressing in upon him with jagged, spiky lines. It was intolerable that he should have to share the house with this woman for the rest of her life, or his. And she was only fifty-six! Years and years of lustreless future stretched before him, drawing him in like a vacuum. He knew he couldn't endure it another moment.

Stepping up to the mantelpiece, he swept it clean of ornaments with a wild movement of his arm. The cacophony of brass and smashing china echoed a chaos in him. It was the end of his invisibility, the end of his hidden and smothered life. Who could have known, when he himself did not, that such violence had been cooking below his placidity? He bent and picked up one of the broken shards from the floor and without hesitation drew it across his throat. The pain, the bright line of blood, were a relief and escape. Then he rushed wildly out of the door, into the darkness and the cold.

Did he do any of this? No, he did not. He merely stood before the intact mantelpiece, watching his red and trembling face in the mirror, until normal breathing resumed and his natural colour returned. And when his mother came back from her outing later that evening, he was at the door, attentive and gentle, hating himself, her little Popsnake, to take her coat.

It was some time afterwards that he discovered that this night, with its reckless, non-existent events, was the anniversary of his father's death. Perhaps it explained his mother's unhappiness, or his own. Or perhaps it explained nothing; his father was so long-gone that his absence was almost a presence.

* * *

His father was to return only six months later, in the form of another biting conversation with Lily, on the subject of bad cheese. They were visiting West Hackhurst, the house in Abinger that his father had designed for his sister to live in. At lunch, which they took in the garden, Aunt Laura asked Morgan how he liked the cheese. He had just tasted it, as it happened, and it was nasty. But he couldn't bring himself to say this to her; he was in his armour of social politeness, and he said, "Oh, that one, I haven't tasted that yet."

Lily had seen him eat the cheese; she looked at him across the table. He gazed down, peculiarly humiliated.

"You have tasted it," she said, and when Laura turned to her she said, "The cheese is bad."

"Oh, how unfortunate. I'll have it taken away."

But in the end the cheese was only put to one side and remained, an offish whiff on the air, through the rest of the lunch. He knew that Lily was not yet done with him and later, on the journey home, she asked him in an amused tone why he hadn't spoken out honestly. He writhed and said, "It didn't seem important."

"Oh, what nonsense. You were afraid." She reminded him casually, "You are like your father. He always put his foot down at the wrong time, like you." She paused to rummage in her handbag for her lozenges, before murmuring a final judgement: "He wasn't a strong character."

He was disproportionately wounded by these little words. Although Lily had loved his father, something was always implied when she mentioned him: he had become a synonym for vacancy and ineptitude. The biggest legacy his father had bestowed on Morgan was the mistake of his own first name. Morgan was, in fact, supposed to be Henry, but on the way to the christening, when the verger had asked what the baby's name was to be, Edward had answered without thinking. So Henry had become Edward by accident, and everybody called Morgan by his second name instead.

Lily hadn't, it seemed to him, ever spoken against his father with such disparaging dismissal, but what really troubled him was her dismissal of himself. Through her eyes, with faint disgust, he saw "Morgan", and felt ashamed. Morgan was an ineffectual, useless entity; his life would always be a little bit ridiculous. He didn't have the strength of will, nor the substance of spirit, to shape his future in any way. That was how she saw him, and the knowledge hurt deeply.

Well, soon he would escape her—and perhaps it was that imminent prospect which had coloured Lily's mood. Because Morgan was going to India in just a few months. It had been decided that he would escort his mother and her good friend from Tonbridge days, Mrs. Cecelia Mawe, to Rome, where he would abandon them, at his own expense, to keep each other company, while he boarded the ship at Naples that would take him to Bombay, from where he would make his way northward to join Masood in Aligarh. Many other travels would braid themselves around it afterwards, but that moment of reunion was the centre and the heart of this whole journey.

Masood had left at the beginning of the year, and his going had been both more subtle and more difficult than Morgan had expected. It had left a deep hollowness behind it, in which every word or gesture seemed to echo slightly; a blankness had crept into things, and even the most heartwarming of English landscapes no longer quite consoled. Almost immediately afterwards, he had fled to Belfast to visit Hom. What had he wanted there? Some kind of comfort, some kind of manly embrace; but what he'd got instead was a watchful, hardened metropolis, and a great deal of political turbulence. Ulster was highly charged with rhetorical emotion, furious talk about secession, overhung by the visit of the First Lord of the Admiralty, Winston Churchill, bringing new proposals for home rule. A thin fault-line was opening into something much wider; civil war seemed possible.

Hom took him to tea at the house of a stalwart member of the Ulster Reform Club, resistant to home rule in any form. This man, pink and genial in every other way, informed them that, "Belfast will listen to anyone except a Judas or a turn-coat."

Morgan dropped a quick glance down at his own, and could not remember which side was originally turned outward. He repressed an urge to giggle.

"We are not," the man went loudly on, "we are not acting in accordance with any principle, and we don't pretend that we are."

His diminutive wife, nursing a baby in the background, suddenly interjected that, "It just shows the uselessness of principles," and then repeated it, more exultantly, in a high-pitched voice to the infant.

It was all most unsettling. He had promised his mother he wouldn't attend the mass meeting at the nearby football field, but everywhere you went the air was thick with the potential for violence. Four thousand extra troops had been brought in. He did go up to the Central Hotel, where Churchill was staying, and waited with the crowd in the foyer. He wasn't exactly sure why he was there, having a personal and political distaste for the man in question, but the moment felt historic. He'd heard the colossal booing from the street outside when Churchill showed himself at a window, and not long afterwards the short, great man had himself appeared, with the pale, unhealthy pallor of an underground root, and brushed against Morgan as he pushed through the mob to the door. Morgan, unsure of how else to respond, had raised his hat politely.

The sprouting seeds of religious conflict; the first loosenings of the Empire. It was with a sense of buried unease, a subterranean rumbling underfoot, that he had returned to England afterwards. And that unsettled, rootless feeling had remained with him, making it hard to stay quietly at home. His writing appeared to have petered out altogether, and without it his normal life seemed empty. He passed his days in eating too much and reading the newspaper, running the occasional errand for his mother or rowing her about on the river. He slept in his chair in the garden and played the piano with small enthusiasm. He seemed to himself like a man without an edge, lacking sufficient definition even to be disappointed.

So that when he heard that Goldie had received the first Albert Kahn Travelling Fellowship and was using it to visit the East, and that he had moreover persuaded Bob Trevy to accompany him, his mind was finally made up. He would go with them at the end of the year.

In the event, it had been surprisingly easy to get Lily to agree. A little mollification, a little pathos, and she'd succumbed. Of course, it couldn't have been a complete surprise.

"You had better do it before you're too old," she said. "And I'm relieved that you will have friends with you. You know you're hopeless when you travel. Always getting lost and forgetting the Baedeker behind."

"I don't plan to be with my friends all the time. But I have some Indian friends too."

"Masood, you mean." She mused on this for a while, then said, "Well, it's probably best for you to see him on that side."

"Why is that?"

She smiled sadly. "If he ever comes back to England, it won't be the same again."

A fter the much finer things he had seen on his journey, the caves were a little disappointing. The approach was almost more dramatic, for you were carried towards the Barabar Hills on the heaving back of the elephant across a parched plain, while the shapes of the giant rocks emerged from the haze. The first was the most astonishing: what appeared to be a huge, stony thumb pointing straight up at the sky. Only as you drew closer and saw it from the side did it slowly reshape itself as a mountain with an extended spine, and the single perched boulder on top became a fanlike arrangement of numerous similar boulders.

"That is Kawa Dol," Imdad Iman said, smiling.

"What does it mean?"

"It is the place where the crow . . . " He made a rocking motion with his hand.

"Swing, you mean? The crow's swing?"

"Ah, yes," the old man said. "Exactly." But the rock, however precariously balanced, did not look like a swing, and what seemed understood could possibly be understood differently. Whatever its meaning, the name stayed almost elementally with Morgan, along with his first image of the stone tower. Kawa Dol: the sound of it was ominous and old, evoking a darkness out of the earth.

It was not their destination, however. They toiled slowly past its base and on towards a second scattering of hills. Made of the same globular grey stones, piled atop each other in unlikely formations, they evoked other, living forms. While he appeared to listen to Imdad Iman, who wrote poetry in Urdu and felt warmly about many things English, from poetry to playing polo, Morgan's mind was elsewhere.

They were on an outing, which Masood had told him would be a wonderful experience. But he had said it without enthusiasm, and Morgan himself did not especially want to be here. This whole day had been planned, he knew, as a salve and consolation, because last night he had said goodbye to his friend for the final time on this journey. Although he was only halfway through his Indian sojourn, the rest of his wanderings would be completed without seeing Masood, and that knowledge pressed on him like a blue and suffocating weight.

When they drew abreast the second upthrusting of hills, the worn grey textures of their surface, unbroken except for greeny clumps of vegetation, distracted him from his melancholy. The place was so sudden, so violently improbable in the middle of the steaming flat plain, that it gave off an odd intensity. In a grove of trees at their foot were the tents of their advance party, with a line of smoke going up. But breakfast, which was supposed to be ready, wasn't; and they were advised that it might be best to see the caves first.

Nawab Imdad Iman was Masood's friend, and had been told to look after Morgan's every need. He was displeased at the tardy preparations and said that he would stay behind to oversee the food, so his two nephews—who were loutish and unlovely—accompanied Morgan up the nearest hill. They walked along a path under trees. Almost immediately they came upon a shrine, a hollowed-out alcove in the rock with a graven idol in the centre of it, garlanded with dying flowers, but if there was a holy man in attendance there was no sign of him. The path began to climb, lifting into light and heat. The trees thinned out, bird calls giving way to a buzzing of insects. None of them spoke, and the only sound between them was a panting of breath.

It wasn't a bad ascent. After only a few minutes they emerged onto a shoulder of the hill and the nephews steered him towards a long, rounded rock with a double-ridge on top, made of granite, looking something like a whale emerging from the deeps. The first cave was simply there, a rectangular doorway cut into the side. It was late in the morning already, and the night's coolness had long since departed the few remaining shadows. But the inside of the cave, at least, provided some relief.

A single domed chamber, perhaps thirty feet long. The walls were polished and smooth. There was nothing whatever inside it; nothing to see, nothing to admire. But immediately the nephews were wanting something from him, plucking at his sleeve insistently, saying a word over and over. He didn't understand; he said, "Yes, yes," impatiently, only to shut them up. He could tell already that these caves were going to let him down. Then the little party was outside again, in the brightness, and they were taking him up a flight of stairs in the side of the rock, to two more caves on the other side.

They led him to the second entrance first. This was the only cave with anything like an ornate doorway, a stupa-shaped arch with elephants carved in procession along it, and a sprinkling of what he took to be Pali. But compared with some of the statues and temples he remembered, what was on offer here seemed curiously unfinished. Through a square-cut passage you went into an inner chamber with a vaulted roof, which took you, by way of another short passage, into yet another dome-shaped room within. But the surface was only half-carved and its roughness was off-putting.

As he stumbled back towards the third cave entrance, the middle one of the three, he struggled to remember what it was that Imdad Iman had said about them, as they rolled atop the elephant. Buddhist caves, two hundred and fifty BC . . . ? It was the Emperor Ashoka who had ordered them to be made, he felt almost sure about that. But there was something else, something to do with the shape of the caves, that escaped him. Was it about meditation? He hadn't been paying close attention, his mind had been preoccupied, and now their purpose remained a mystery—as it seemed so much in this country was destined to, at least for him.

This cave was by far the most impressive. Again there was the vaulted first chamber, but in this one the rock had been worked to a planed and polished surface, so highly refined that it might have been done with a modern machine. And again there was a doorway leading to an inner room, high and conical, shaped like a beehive. The darkness here was total, till one of the boys lit a candle. Then another flame seemed to well up from inside the granite itself, and the rock revealed its grain in a swirling of red and grey. The walls had been polished to the consistency of glass and the hard smoothness, under his trailing fingertips, was pleasing and beautiful.

The two unpleasant nephews, who had very little English, were still repeating their word over and over, which he still couldn't make out. But the word—indeed, every word that was spoken in here—set off an overlapping mirror of itself, which hissed and rustled all around. Then at last he understood. The word was "echo", and that was why the cave walls had been so highly polished: to help the echo along. The dome-shaped room was meant for chanting, and the chanting was meant to reverberate. But the effect, like the caves themselves, was less than remarkable, returning every sound in the form of an indistinct surf-like roaring.

Then one of the nephews said, "Breakfast", and blew out his candle, and the expedition was apparently over.

They descended the hill again in silence, leaving the rocks and the darkness behind. But the caves were not what Morgan had supposed. They were not Buddhist, and the language inscribed around that third entrance wasn't Pali, though it was equally old and equally dead. The caves had been inhabited by a different sect, people who followed an ascetic path more extreme than most. Indeed, they had been avoided by those who followed gentler faiths, for their custom of abandoning their old and their sick, out in the open, to die. What exactly they believed, and their way of believing, was lost now. But some of their presence, perhaps, had remained behind, a kind of ghost, or another reflection in the stone, to brush against the visitor whose skin was receptive to it.

Breakfast was still not ready. The Nawab sighed and tugged at his beard in rumination and spoke fiercely to his nephews. Then, more kindly, he said to Morgan, "You go and see the other caves. After, we eat."

More caves! There had been nothing sufficiently inspiring in the ones he'd already seen to make him excited. But he plodded behind the nephews, who were sulking and hitting at weeds by the roadside with sticks, for a mile or two along the bottom of the hills. The sun was fierce by now, and the temperature seemed to match an emptiness he felt inside.

Nor did the other caves help. There were three of them, also carved out of boulders, and harder to find. They were similar to the ones he'd already seen, all variations on the same theme, with polished walls and geometric outlines, though none of them had the dark inner chamber where no light could reach. The last required a climb, up stairs cut into the stone. But when he got there, perspiring and weak in the knees, because he was really very hungry by now, he couldn't summon up the necessary enthusiasm. The inside of one rock was much the same as another and the echoes were all alike too.

By the time they made their way back to the encampment, breakfast was still not ready. The Nawab looked wretched. One of the nephews said angrily to Morgan, "You come." There was one last cave, apparently, part of the first group, which they had somehow overlooked. With his hunger very insistent now, and the start of a headache, he returned to where he'd begun.

The cave was off to the side, past a sullen pond of green water, over some slippery rocks. It really wasn't worth the effort; it was much rougher than the others, hardly more than a hole crudely hewn out of the hillside. But he lingered in it for a while, half-crouched under the low roof, to keep out of the sun. He became fascinated by a wasp that was clinging to the wall, trailing its yellow back legs behind it and, by the time he came to himself again, he realised that the nephew had departed, leaving him alone.

Wandering slowly back to the path, he decided to return to the middle cave in the first group, the one that had impressed him the most. It would be good to have a few minutes unaccompanied, sequestered in the rock. Looking out from the first arched room through the entranceway, he had the sense of the sunlit world beyond as a remote dream, which he was looking at through a window. Then he retreated deeper, into the second chamber. Instantly, he felt sunken profoundly into the world, or into himself. He spoke his own name aloud; the cave repeated it endlessly. He said Masood's name too, and then the word "love"—all of it rumbled back at him.

For the first time today, he allowed himself to experience his feelings. He had spent the last two and a half weeks with Masood in Bankipore, which was a small, ugly town on the outskirts of Patna. Masood had his legal practice there and Morgan felt a little like an intruder. But it was a benign intrusion, and they had managed to have a companionable, pleasant time together. The knowledge of his coming departure, however, had made him heavy for the past week already, and the previous day in particular had been long and slow and sad, culminating in their peculiar farewell in the middle of the night.

Morgan was making an early start in the morning, and had told Masood not to wake up. Although he'd said it firmly, he had wanted his friend to overrule him; he had wanted him to insist on waking and seeing him off on his journey. But Masood had yawned and agreed that he was very tired and that there was no point in getting up early. It was a sensible solution. So they had said goodbye just before going to sleep, in a stiff, incomplete way, both feeling shy, and then retreated. But almost immediately after, as he'd started to undress, Morgan had felt himself speared on the point of sharp emotion. He had gone back through to Masood's room and sat on the edge of his bed and taken hold, very tightly, of his hand. Cold anguish made certain details stand out, the white hanging shroud of the mosquito net, the shadows in its folds. Even if he'd been able to speak, he could not have said what he wanted. But the yearning had made him lean towards Masood, trying to kiss him. In the fizzing white burn of the lamp-light, his friend's face had been at first astonished, and then shocked. His hand had come up sharply, to push Morgan away, and that little movement had felt enormous, a force that could move a boulder. Morgan had accepted the refusal, because he'd known in advance it would come, and sat hunched miserably over his kernel of loneliness. By then Masood was merely irritated. He had rubbed Morgan's shoulder and patted him on the back, in a way that was both reassuring and dismissive. Neither of them spoke, but both of them understood. He did not feel as Morgan did; that was all. There was nothing else to say.

So in the end one had to make the journey back to one's own bed more alone even than before, the step down between the two rooms like the threshold between two worlds.

In the darkness afterwards, he experienced again what he'd just done with a fresh wave of shame. *Aie-aie-aie!* It was terrible, terrible—to have wanted so badly, to have been pushed so firmly away. The night and the land seemed to spread away around him, emphasising his smallness. He had cut himself open and showed the innermost part; it had been rash and unconsidered and regrettable. Now he had to close himself up again, to seal the carapace, and he began to do what was necessary. It was part of a willed cheerfulness he had learned, back in his childhood already, as protection against disappointment. The only defence against raw, naked feeling was reason. Understanding made sadness easier to bear.

So the thoughts that he followed, one by one, were like stairs ascending out of his misery, each of them valid and genuine, leading on from the one before. They went something like this: *Masood cares for me more than for any other man, I have known that for a long time. That is comforting. And much that has passed between us on this visit has made me very happy. That is good. To have a little, even a very little, can be enough to go on with; indeed, it's all I have. Better to hold to that than to yearn continually for what isn't possible.*

In the end, you had to return to your own life—which he did now with an effort, by swimming out, blinking and half-blind, into the vertical light, to let the normal day reclaim him. It was like emerging from the tomb. He hurried back down the hill faster than he needed to, as if he were being pursued, to the tents and the smouldering fire and the elephant, ponderously browsing.

Where by now breakfast was finally ready: after all the delay, a paltry smear of omelette with a cold chapatti and a mug of tea. But it was enough to restore his spirits and, as he sat in the shade chatting to Imdad Iman, he felt again the promise reviving in the vast landscape, with its blond, bleached colours, its scrubby bushes and old, tormented rocks. He knew already that this parting would eventually become a painful detail in a much larger event, one which was still unfolding before him.

Over the past three months, India had already violently rearranged his life, but it wasn't done with him yet; not by a long way.

* * *

His journey had begun in Aligarh. He had come all the way around the world for one reason only. And although his travels had barely begun, in another sense they felt already complete as he stood on a railway station platform at two-thirty in the morning, embracing Masood.

"At last, you are here," his friend told him.

"I believe I am."

"How do I look? Am I older?"

He had thickened in the middle, and some stray hairs had turned white, but Morgan said, "You look no different."

"Nor you. I have thought of nothing except this moment for the past ten years."

"You have only known me for six."

"Have I? Well, I speak metaphorically. My great love for you makes time seem much bigger." But Masood was already yawning as he swept out of the station and towards the waiting tonga.

When Morgan had woken up the next morning, it was into rather than out of a dream: the window showed an acre of garden, filled with loud, brilliant and exotic birds. Weird lizards scuttled across the walls and unusual insects hovered in the air. Masood had given up his bedroom to him and was sleeping in the sitting room close by; Morgan knew where he was, and yet he wasn't quite sure of anything. Here was an inversion of the world that had held them in England, where the view had always been known and tame, and it was only Masood who had been out of place. Now it was the Englishman's turn to be the stranger, the visitor. The idea of it pleased him greatly, and took him some way into another world—yet that world refused entirely to open for him.

When Masood woke an hour or two later and came lazily through to his room, almost his first question was what Morgan wanted to do that day.

"Honestly, the most important undertaking, as far as I can see, is to meet your mother. I would like to thank her for giving birth to you. Or else to punish her for it, I can't make up my mind."

He had been wanting to greet Mahmoud Begum for a long time already, and he had brought some small gifts for her from England. But the suggestion was answered with a solemn headshake.

"You can't do that, I'm afraid. My mother keeps strict purdah. She sends you her blessings, but she cannot show herself before you."

"But this is her house."

"Even so."

It took a moment for the smile to fade from Morgan's face; it had seemed like a joke at first. He was in India now, and he would have to do as the Indians did. His gifts were despatched via Masood, and thanks returned to him the same way. In this house—and in some others he would stop in—the closest he would come to a female presence was the sound of soft voices in a neighbouring room.

He hadn't expected this, but then nothing was the way he'd thought it would be. When Masood took him that first morning to see the Mohammedan Anglo-Oriental College which his grandfather had founded, Morgan was taken aback. In England, Masood had spoken of it rapturously as a centre of scientific excellence, where the finest of Western thought could be taught in an Islamic atmosphere; it represented, he'd insisted, the most modern approach to education. Yet when Morgan saw it, there was nothing very modern or inspiring about the disorderly scattering of reddish, ugly buildings, none of which seemed to have a single telephone in it, so that messages had to be carried around great distances by hand.

And there were other oddities, which for some reason had never featured in what he'd imagined. For one thing, though all the students were Mohammedans, wearing beards and fezzes, half of the teachers were foreigners. They seemed so stranded and out of place here, with their alien customs and their improbable accents, though they tried to pretend it was home. There were a lot of them, not only teaching at the college. At one moment he was rubbing up against a Kingsman, who was headmaster of the local school, or chatting to a German professor of Oriental languages; and at the next dining with a barrister called Khan, or discussing politics with a Persian professor of Arabic.

The atmosphere at the college, he would come to realise, was highly charged. There was a great gulf between the Indian staff and students on one hand, and the Europeans on the other. The two groups seemed to mix compatibly together, but when he found himself alone with one or the other, the conversation changed. The English staff in particular lamented that they weren't trusted here and seemed to live in fear that the Mohammedans would turn them out; the Mohammedans wrung their hands and declared that the Balkan War was the death-battle of Islam and asked why Sir Edward Grey should have been the very *first* to recognise Italian rule in Tripoli.

In these conversations, Morgan was never exactly sure where his loyalties lay; he experienced a complicated inner conflict which pulled him one way or the other.

"How do you manage it?" he asked Masood, on one of those early days. For his friend had always been adept, he saw now, at crossing the social frontier between East and West. For all his nationalist rhetoric, he was very much at ease in European company, yet he could drop all his Occidental ways in a moment, as if they were a piece of clothing.

"It is a skill," Masood told him. "Think of it as camouflage, in order to survive in hostile territory."

"What nonsense you speak. There are thousands of Indians who lack this skill, yet they survive perfectly well."

"Yes, but they do not flourish. They are always nervous, always anxious. They don't mix well with the paler types, can you not see it? Some strategy is needed."

"I am a paler type," Morgan told him stiffly, "as you may have noticed. You have never needed strategy to survive me."

"Can you be so sure?"

"Don't joke, Masood."

His friend smiled—still rakish and handsome, despite a faint fatigue that made his face puffy. He took Morgan's hand and instantly the bond between them was renewed. "My dear fellow," he said, "you must put all of it into your book."

"My book?"

He was genuinely nonplussed for a second.

"The one you came here to write."

"Yes, yes, my book. Of course."

He had almost forgotten his book. Although he had gone so far as to mention it to his publishers, it had ceased to matter as a reason for being here. His true reason was the one in front of him, still holding his hand, and telling him that an outing had been arranged.

"An outing? To where?"

Masood waved vaguely, looking bored. "Some villages," he said, "you will see. You will get material."

The outing was lovely—almost two full days, careering around the flat countryside in a *tikka ghari*, being fed and entertained by lowly Indian officials. But however much he enjoyed himself, it didn't provide material for anything except distraction.

He knew that his friend was fobbing him off. They had been speaking for years, in a feverish way, about being in India together and everything they would do there, but now that the happy day had arrived, Masood wasn't much interested. Morgan could see that he was preoccupied and morose. But when he tried to find out what the matter was, he was deflected with generalities:

"The future, the future . . . I have to make decisions."

"Decisions concerning what?"

"As I told you, the future. Don't cross-examine me, Morgan, I have enough of that in court. Would you like a mango?"

Even more distressing was the realisation that they wouldn't be spending much time together. Plans had been left blurry and undefined, but Morgan had hoped that Masood might join him as he travelled around. He quickly learned that it wasn't to be.

"I have to go back to Bankipore for work. I am not a free man here, you see, no, not at all. But I will go with you to Delhi next week and we will have a fine time together."

"And after that?"

"And after that you will travel. Oh, you will see many things, especially the Moghul splendour I have often mentioned. All of it will go into your book!"

"But when will we see each other again?" He tried to ask it casually, but his voice shot up into a higher pitch, giving him away.

"You will come to Bankipore to visit. I am returning there very soon. It is an awful place, I don't think you'll like it."

"You will be there, Masood. That is the point."

"Yes, of course, that is the point." But even now—or perhaps especially at this moment—his friend was looking out of the window, his eyes anxious and unsettled.

"And will we travel together then?"

"Perhaps so. Yes, perhaps by then it will be possible." His voice became fuller and more confident. "My life is simply too big for me at the moment, you must forgive me, my dear, it does not detract one tiny bit from my devotion to you, you know that."

When they moved on to Delhi a week later, things didn't greatly improve. They were staying with a friend of Masood's, Dr Ansari, whose wife was also invisible, though she sent continual little gifts of betel nut and scent. The house was very small, and Morgan and Masood shared a room. Not only with each other: a constant stream of visitors passed through, perching and squatting everywhere, while a cat and three dogs roamed about, and a shrieking cockatoo defecated on the mosquito net. Masood had recently had a cholera inoculation and spent most of his time in bed, worrying that he was sick, or that he wasn't sick enough. Now and then he reflected aloud that he was dying.

"But don't languish here with me, Morgan, my dear chap. I have organised a car to take you on some sightseeing expeditions. History awaits you."

"Won't you come?"

"I am too ill, my dear, truly. But you must go. I beg you, no, I *order* you, and if you don't I shall never, never speak to you again."

So Morgan went to old Delhi alone. He went to the Jama Masjid, and visited the Red Fort, where the spaces between the scattered buildings suddenly seemed very big and cold, overshadowed by the looming ugliness of the military barracks. He saw the great stone elephants, and the parapet where the English King and Queen had showed themselves to the crowd, but all the while unhappiness scratched at him inside. He had a headache, there was nobody to talk to, the grand sights left him disappointed.

Only on the very first morning did his friend accompany him, because they were visiting the Qutb Minar. The ruined remnants of Moghul times elicited Masood's highest flights of rhetoric, but it was hard not to feel the tension between these crumbling remnants of the past and the throbbing, smelly motor car that had brought them there. This same tension was especially evident at Humayun's Tomb, where a view out over a plain of broken forts and old mosques was undercut by modern Delhi in the distance, and the Marconi radio apparatus that was used for signalling at the 1911 Durbar.

At this Durbar, Morgan knew, George V had announced sweeping changes to the political system in India. The capital was to move from Calcutta to Delhi; the hated partition of Bengal had been reversed and the province reunited. The breeze of democracy had picked up a little, dispersing some of the noxious fumes that still swirled heavily after the Mutiny, nearly half a century ago.

Politics, back in England, had a leaden, immovable weight, as if history could not be altered very much. That wasn't the case here. In India, when people talked politics they were talking about the future—and it mattered a great deal. When Morgan spoke to Masood's friends about it, their voices took on a tense, knotted quality; their eyes became hooded. It was clear that they spent a lot of time thinking about their freedom, not as an abstract concept, but as a concrete and achievable goal. There was no little corner of life that seemed untouched by it, either in hope or despair.

Masood, too, could become excited on this topic. Back in England, his political musings had always had a theatrical quality, as if he were performing his beliefs rather than feeling them, but on a few occasions here the temperature of his blood did momentarily rise. One such moment came on Morgan's last night in Delhi, when Dr Ansari insisted on treating him to a nautch, a party with dancing girls. This couldn't be held in his own house, because his neighbour, an Englishwoman, wouldn't approve, so it was arranged in the home of a friend of his in the old city. But next door were the offices of *The Comrade*, a political journal run by the Ali brothers, who were friends of Masood's. Morgan had already looked through its pages in Aligarh and had been unnerved by what he found inside. It didn't seem untruthful to him, but it was so very angry, with an anger leavened only slightly by jokes and doggerel.

When they called in at the offices of *The Comrade* now,

Mohammed Ali was in an agitated state, and greeted them by announcing that he was about to commit suicide.

"What is it?" Masood said. "What has happened?"

"Oh, I am absolutely miserable. It is too terrible to think about. The Bulgarian army is within twenty-five miles of Constantinople." On the verge of tears, he swept into the next room, from which his voice carried out ringingly. "Let no quarter be asked, and none given now. This is the end!"

The emotion of this drama touched Morgan, though the history did not. He had already been exposed to these feelings among Masood's friends in Aligarh. It was clear that some sort of international Islamic sentiment was stirring Mohammedans in India. The fortunes of Turkey, which was facing defeat in the Balkan War, left Morgan indifferent, but it was hard to be unmoved when Masood became roused, as he did now. "This is the turning point of my career," he cried out dramatically. "We shall give the Turks all the money we have collected for the university!"

But ten minutes later, typically, all this high feeling had left Masood again. It became important to him that Mohammed Ali join them for the nautch. But Ali didn't want to go; he was steeped in his morose hysteria. "Nonsense, nonsense," Masood told him imperiously, "we can be serious again tomorrow," and he picked him up bodily and carried him out of the office.

The nautch was full of its own dramatic intensity. There was a small crowd of onlookers, all male, all—except for him—charged with glandular anticipation. He tried to be attracted to the dancers, even in a theoretical way, because he supposed it was expected. There was a fat girl with a ring through her nose, and a thinner one with a weak but charming face; both in truth frightened him, and though he tried to enter the spectacle through its noise and harsh emotion, he remained outside its ritualised exterior. There were moments when he almost glimpsed what this display might mean to an Indian, but in the end he was exhausted by it and the screaming did violence to his head. Alarmingly, it threatened to continue for ever, until he understood that only his leaving would end it. Dr Ansari tried to make him kiss the singers, but he slipped away with a quick hand-squeeze of the older, thinner lady. He was possibly not the only one relieved.

And then he was being seen off at the station at one o'clock in the morning and the first part of his Indian visit was over.

* * *

He knew he would see Masood again in a few weeks. But it was hard not to feel a sort of low-grade anguish, which was with him even in his better moments. He had hoped for more than he'd got, and the future might not deliver anything better.

Certainly there was some comfort at his next stop, which was Lahore, with the Darlings. It wasn't thinkable that he could come to India and not see them, though he wasn't yet entirely at ease with Josie, or her Tory politics. Still, here she was, and their little boy John Jermyn too, giving him hospitality and kindness, showing him around the vast, soulless distances of the city, introducing him to their friends. Very soon any underlying anxiety had been dispelled and he felt relaxed in their company. Malcolm had always been all right; he was good-hearted and filled with idealistic principles, which accounted for his exile to these parts, in a minor post in the Punjab. In truth, Morgan found him a little too earnest, but in certain quarters Malcolm was considered a dangerous radical and his efforts to befriend Indians had made him genuinely unpopular. There was a lot to admire about Malcolm.

In Lahore he was also reunited with Bob Trevy and Goldie, who had meanwhile been to Ellora. Goldie's presence in particular was a consolation, with his familiar dry intelligence shot through with flashes of nonsensical humour. Goldie knew

Masood, of course, and had some idea of Morgan's expecta-
tions. So when he asked how Aligarh had been, and Morgan
answered that it had been lovely, a deeper understanding
passed between them, which didn't need to be spoken.

"And Masood is well?"

"He seems to be, yes. A little preoccupied, perhaps. He is
thinking about his future."

"Ah," Goldie said, and nodded sagely. He had wasted years
of his own life on a fruitless love with a German man, who had
given him a lot of torment.

And Goldie too seemed unsettled. When Morgan asked
him about Ellora, he merely said, "Oh, it was fascinating. Yes,
fascinating." But his face tensed up, and when he added in an
undertone a moment later, "though it isn't England," Morgan
understood that something about the place had troubled him.

With Goldie and Bob, he went on to Peshawar for their
reunion with Searight. Morgan hadn't forgotten his shipboard
acquaintance or their remarkable conversations, though there
was no trace here of his other, secret identity. No, in this place
Searight was the very model of an English officer, aside from
one sly wink soon after their arrival. He was heartily pleased to
see them and hadn't forgotten his promise that he would show
them the edge of the Empire.

A day or two later, he took them a little way into the Khyber
Pass. They sat on a patch of grass at the bottom of a ravine and
watched tumultuous caravans passing in both directions, don-
keys and camels and horses and dogs and goats and chickens
among their human minders, the gait and attire regal, the faces
fierce and inscrutable, emblematic of unknowable lives. All of
it raised a brown screen of dust through which the stately pandemonium seemed to pass, at a great remove of time and distance, for a full hour and a half. The way was only open twice
a week, under armed guard, and each caravan was followed by
an escort of the Khyber Rifles. In the early afternoon the pass

was cleared again, and left to barbarism and bandits until the next caravan day. To the north and west, marked by impregnable peaks, stretched a no-man's land of hostile tribes; beyond was Afghanistan; and beyond that was Russia, with its secret imperial designs. At their backs was English civilisation, and one felt it nowhere so keenly as here, where it ceased. Nothing had ever seemed quite so homelike as the white veranda posts outside the Mess when they returned there in the afternoon.

That evening, Morgan managed to lose his collar stud and was ten minutes late for dinner. He imagined that everything would have continued without him, but only when he arrived did the band strike up "The Roast Beef of Old England" and the evening properly begin. It was a good hour or two before he shed his embarrassment on Searight's account, but nobody else seemed to mind very much. Most of the soldiers were young and rosy-cheeked—still almost boys—but even the older ones seemed full of a kindly forbearance that forgave all differences. After dinner, while the band played on, they danced *pas seuls* up and down the veranda in their scarlet coats. Searight, almost unrecognisably glorious in his full regalia, carried Bob Trevy on his back and then seized hold of Morgan and whirled him around in a drunken foxtrot. The cheerful comradeship that surrounded them was like a balm that cleaned away every bad impression he'd ever formed of the English abroad, and for the first time he understood a little of how Searight had made a life for himself in unlikely outposts such as these, where women were intruders and the only real love was between men. A couple of days later, when they said goodbye again, they promised each other they would meet many times in the future, and some letters did pass back and forth over the years, but in fact they would never be true friends.

He was parting again here from Goldie and Bob, who were

travelling on to Delhi, while he was going to Simla. They would meet once more in Agra in a few days, but meanwhile Morgan was on his own. He had wandered alone in Europe, and found it unsettling, but India had called something forth in him that Italy and Greece never did. A peculiar second nature seemed to have showed itself in him; a capable other Morgan, who traversed great distances and made decisive choices, often in the face of resistance. And as he moved about, it was hard to keep his mind from slipping sideways, off Masood and onto the landscape that contained him.

Over the two days of his journey up from Bombay to Aligarh, the strangeness, the distant otherness of India, had already marked itself on his mind. Even the light had seemed different, till he'd realised that the windows of the train had a darkened cast to them. Somehow, though, that bluish colouring still overlaid what also seemed familiar: certain pastoral vistas resembled Surrey, though particular details (the shocking brightness of a woman's sari, a cow blissfully chewing the cud on a station platform) tilted the world off its axis. Not even the Indian moon, with its power to evoke deep yellows and purples from the surrounding sky, seemed to match its English equivalent. And the sky itself had a hugeness, a blankness untextured by cloud, that could annul the whole earth beneath it.

The people themselves were a different sort of landscape and they claimed his attention too. Searight had not been lying about the legs, which were universally visible—the vigorous, toned, muscular legs of the lower classes, and their feet. Flesh, as Searight had said, was everywhere on display, usually toiling, and often on his own behalf. The figures he saw in passing seemed to move with a deliberateness, a distinctness, that made him notice them afresh. The Indians were inside their bodies, he decided, in a way that the British were not. His own flesh impeded his spirit. He was terribly excited, in the daytime, by the way young Indian men strolled about, hand in hand, or hung onto each other like vines; and at night he was stirred by erotic dreams of a sort that hadn't troubled him since childhood.

He had started to notice, too, the rigid hierarchy of the society around him. Among the Indians, the first division was between Mohammedan and Hindu. Beyond that, everything was stratified by caste: the Untouchables and the Brahmins were in adjacent, contiguous worlds. But the British, too, had succumbed to caste—or at any rate, as they usually did, to class. At the bottom of the heap were the Eurasians, those of mixed-race. Then came the non-official Europeans—professional men, railway employees, tea-planters and the like. Then came the army officers, followed by the smug government servants and the political players and finally, at the very top, floating in the high ethereal zone, were the Viceroy and his circle. Each was conscious of their place, and guarded it against incursions from below; yet they mixed socially at the club, of which every town had one, and where for the most part Indians were not allowed—though in some establishments the rules had relaxed enough to let the occasional Maharajah slip through.

From one level to the next, up and down the bewildering social staircase, Morgan passed. He was an outsider; he settled nowhere long enough to take a place. Yet he himself wasn't free, either of his skin or the designation it bestowed on him. And he had a shadow in tow, to remind him of the depths underfoot.

On board a ship in Greece years before, he had met an Oxford undergraduate by the name of Rupert Smith. They were very different types in temperament and in outlook, but they had maintained a touchy, long-distance friendship ever since. Smith was part of the Indian Civil Service, stationed in Allahabad, and he had organised a servant for Morgan, who had come to meet him off the ship. So Baldeo, in fact, had been the first person Morgan spoke to on Indian soil.

But Morgan was used to English housekeepers and maids and gardeners, removed from him only by class. A great deal more than that intervened between him and Baldeo: race and language and custom thickened the air, so that they couldn't see each other clearly, and therefore they had begun with a farce. After meeting him, Morgan had instantly forgotten Baldeo's face, and did not recognise him the next morning, sleeping outside his hotel room door. Instead he had searched everywhere for him, and sent messages, and suspected Goldie's servant of hiding him away, and all the while he had resisted the attentions of the strange, wizened, persistent man who followed him around, waiting for instructions. By the time he knew him again, he had humiliated himself and his folly hung over their subsequent relations like a debt that had not yet been paid.

Misunderstanding continued to dog them. Morgan found Baldeo's pocketbook, with all his credentials, laid on top of his clothes in his big travelling trunk. He was irritated, thinking it cheeky that this had been done without permission, but said nothing. Fortunately so, because he discovered some days later that as Baldeo's employer he was entitled to these papers. His servant had merely done the necessary, being ahead of him on every question.

He had come to realise that he could not manage without Baldeo. Like a familiar spirit, he was always with Morgan or, more accurately, just in front of him, going ahead to stations with the luggage, securing seats on the train, finding porters and tonga-wallahs, running errands, readying clothing and bringing hot water when it was required, cooking for him. Without Baldeo, India would have fallen in on Morgan, burying him in confusion.

Though it was true that much of what he did see confused him nevertheless. When he had first met Masood, his only knowledge of this country was a vague mix-up: elephants and holy men and hookahs and temples swirled around in a gauzy idea of a place. He had done a lot since then to educate himself and, once his visit was certain, he had read a great deal in preparation. Now all of that seemed useless. The reality he was passing through displaced many of his previous notions, and his notion of a novel too.

Insofar as he'd considered it at all, the book he'd imagined he might write would repeat his previous novels, where the chilly reserve of his English characters had broken down in the warmth and abandonment of Italy. Whatever their differences, surely Indians and their British rulers had their humanity in common, and he might place that at the forefront of his story. But how could these literary aspirations withstand what he was experiencing now? Every day served up a scene, a conversation, that was like two sharp edges grinding against each other. It was the meeting of the two worldviews, one way of life imposed upon another, which brought out the worst in both. In Simla, for example, he lived through the following, which was his first genuinely miserable vision of India's future.

He had been on several enforced jaunts already on his journey. There had been the outing in Aligarh, and in Lahore there had been a spiritless garden tea, featuring a cast of educated Indians making small talk. Such "bridge parties" had become fashionable in recent times, in an attempt to stem the rising tide of Indian nationalism. And it was in the same spirit, perhaps, that Morgan was taken now as a guest to what had been described, optimistically, as an "advanced" Mohammedan wedding.

It was a memory that wrung his heart anew each time he returned to it in his mind. The rationalist elements of the wedding seemed to have been put on for the benefit of the watching Europeans; certainly the Mohammedans were uneasy, muttering about how it was all contrary to Islamic law. The bride was unveiled, sitting with the groom on a sofa on a dais. The

Moulvi who married them read from the Koran in a desultory way, before a local poet recited overwrought poetry about Conscience singing like a bulbul in some metaphorical garden. But the saddest moment was an involuntary one: a gramophone at one end of the garden blared out "I'd rather be busy with my little Lizzie", while on a terrace at the other side a gathering of devout Muslim men performed their evening prayer.

The opened hands, the kneeling, the forehead pressed to the ground: he had seen Masood go through these ritualistic motions many times, and found them moving, perhaps because of what they meant to his friend; but it was impossible to feel anything except horror today. It was because of the whole straitened, strained gathering, and the awful song on the gramophone—which by chance came to its end at the exact moment the prayer did. To Morgan's eyes, the only loveliness in the proceedings belonged to those devout figures, now returning without a fuss to the milling crowd.

The wedding, rather desperately, was termed a success. The bridegroom's brother visited the next morning to thank everybody for coming and to tell them, emphatically, that all those who had objected yesterday had been pacified by the Moulvi's speech. But Morgan was more convinced by an Englishwoman, a Miss Masters, with whom he took an afternoon stroll later that day around one of the hills of Simla. She didn't mention the wedding, and perhaps hadn't even attended, but she launched without any preamble into a confession of how much she disliked Indians.

"I didn't used to," she told him. "I came out here with no feeling against them. But now I can't endure them. It is their own fault, really. Have you a bad feeling against Indians, Mr. Forster?"

Morgan murmured that he did not.

"Oh, it will come, believe me, in time. The change came

slowly in my case. Even the Indians expect it. They say all the English, but especially the women, change inside six months. And I think they are not wrong."

Morgan didn't answer. Simla was built on a ridge, so that views opened on both sides, and he kept his attention on a vista of mountains, rippling away.

"But one has to have servants, of course," she added quickly. "I myself have many. Have you any servants, Mr. Forster?"

He admitted that he did have one.

"You will hate him in due course," she said.

* * *

There had scarcely been a moment since he'd arrived in this country when he'd been alone, and he wanted to think about everything he'd seen. To escape from the humans for a while, he headed into the mountains. Baldeo was sent in advance with two coolies, carrying bedding on their heads, to the dak bungalow on the Tibet road.

He left Simla at noon with his lunch in a pack on his back, and walked for four hours to Fagu, with the wild road twisting through a wilder landscape, and the horizon splintered into a thousand jagged lines. He thought about his mother as he tramped. Time and distance had softened her outlines, so that he longed for her without ambivalence. Their alliance was occasionally sisterly, pinned together with cackling and gossip, and these moments had strengthened with her absence. Despite their difficulties, she had always been a good travelling companion and he imagined her beside him now, keeping pace in a rickshaw. Though he was very aware of his solitude too, through which the mountains pressed upon his mind.

He was still in the foothills; the Himalayas proper were seventy miles away, but the massive snowy peaks seemed to hang overhead. The air was icy and clear, and that night the stars burned with a close, cold fire. But their clarity was like a knife that cut too deep: Morgan woke in the small hours into a disturbing knowledge about Masood.

He saw his time in Aligarh properly at last, and understood what it meant. Masood had been affectionate and loving, as always; he had been happy to see Morgan and had made him feel welcome. But his distraction wasn't a temporary state, which would pass of its own accord. Indeed, it had always been the deepest aspect of his nature. Masood was slipping away from him; might, in fact, already have slipped. Now that he was back in India, his own country, where he belonged in a way that he never could in England, another kind of life had taken hold of him. He didn't need Latin lessons from Morgan any more; in truth, he didn't need anything. Morgan would see him again, of course, and they would probably have an enjoyable time together—and then Morgan would leave.

In the morning when he woke up, the mountains seemed somehow smaller than yesterday. Nevertheless, he might have travelled into them further, along the road to Tibet, if he had not arranged to meet Goldie and Bob in the other direction. Agra was the first place where local hospitality ran out and at last they had to check into a hotel. Bob was fretful and restless by now, not liking India, wanting to get on to China and then back home, and they hurried on to Gwalior.

The Morisons had given him an introduction to a Mr. Sultan Ahmed Khan, who had booked rooms for them at the hotel, met them at the station when they arrived, and then asked them to tea the following day. When they requested directions to his house he said, "Oh, no matter, I will send my servant to bring you. Simply wait." They simply waited, and no servant came. In the evening Khan appeared, with his English wife, and asked what had happened to them. "I invited a few of my friends and we have been expecting you, but you did not come."

"But you told us you would send your servant for us."

"Yes, yes, so I did, but as everybody knows where my house is, I decided the servant wasn't necessary."

Morgan was so charmed by the illogicality that he forgot to stay cross. Where else could this have happened but India? It struck him as revealing, though of what exactly he couldn't explain.

There was a great deal by now that he didn't understand, though mostly this amused him, rather than causing anguish. Goldie, however, was suffering. Morgan rode with the older man atop a painted elephant to see some Buddhist temples sprouting from a giant rock, after which they went down the other side to look at statues of naked Jain saints. These were very wonderful, in the sides of a deep chasm full of churning water and trees. In a certain light, if you came upon them unexpectedly, they might have been alive, something the earth itself had thrown up; and possibly it was this thought which caused Goldie to flinch and crouch, his face sealed against them.

In a general way, Morgan could see, Goldie wasn't happy. He had come to India in a spirit of enquiry and enthusiasm, and had thrown himself vigorously into the continent. Along the way he had delivered lectures and engaged in debates and tried to absorb what he saw. Goldie was a believer in the imperial project, which is to say, in the civilising power of social progress. But his visit to Ellora had left him troubled, and some of his unease came pouring forth now.

"We are from a Greek tradition," he told Morgan. "And that has nothing to do with India. Look at it! This mixture of religions, all in one place—what do we have in common with any of them?"

They were in the gorge, near a great stone figure blackened by dripping water, its face turned towards a tree. It wasn't unlike a Greek carving, Morgan thought, only perhaps on a different scale, but he thought it best not to say so. Instead, he pointed out:

"Religion isn't everything."

"But here it does seem to be. Have you attempted any rational conversations lately? Religion is always part of it, there's no escape. But not the sort of religion we understand. No, this is superstition and cruelty, and it can't be reformed. And let's not talk of the dirt and disorder! There is no closing the gap, whatever we do."

Morgan murmured, "Oh, come. I have seen many instances of whites and Indians getting on famously."

"Where have you seen it?"

The examples that came to mind didn't inspire, so he said, "Well, there is me and Masood."

Goldie stared gloomily at him. At last he said, "The unhappy fact is that the English are *bored* by the Indians. It gives me no pleasure to say so, but it's true."

Morgan was silenced by this idea, and the conversation tailed off. But it continued to flicker in the corners of his mind for days afterwards. He had always thought of Goldie as having the gift of midwifery, the ability to build bridges between different people and their worldviews, and this was the first time he'd seen it fail.

It was depressing for Morgan to be at such variance with the older man, when their accord was usually harmonious. He couldn't see India except through Masood's eyes, which made him understand things differently. It wasn't the Indians that had upset him so much as his own countrymen; he didn't like what the British had done, nor what they had become while doing it. Nevertheless, he had also had some conversations and encounters with Englishmen that he found surprisingly enlightened.

And unlike Goldie, Morgan found himself unexpectedly stirred by temples and mosques and roadside shrines. His reasons for rejecting Christianity didn't seem to apply here. He knew a little about Islam through Masood, and he had some feeling for it, but Hinduism remained an opacity and a mystery. He had read up on it before he came, but he soon discovered that the explanations had no purchase. Fire and water and smoke and incense and chanting and bells and butter and blood: this was a language whose syllables were translated into physical terms; a language of the elements. It was a language that he hoped might speak to him one day.

Meanwhile, he did his best to understand. He was soon to have an opportunity to observe the subject closely, when they moved on to stay with the Maharajah of Chhatarpur, to whom the Morisons had given him an introduction—for this man's every obsessive, fretful thought seemed to be about Krishna. Politics and the matter of running his state were relegated to the background.

The guest house where he put them up was outside the town, on a narrow ridge, and the view from the front veranda, looking out over forest and temples to barer hills behind, was soothing. Even Bob was pacified, and not so eager to move on. And for nearly a fortnight, the days unfolded with a certain regularity and routine. In the mornings the Maharajah's doctor (a fat Hindu) and his Personal Secretary (a fat Mohammedan) would come to take them on an outing somewhere. And every afternoon the Maharajah sent his carriage to fetch them. In this little decrepit landau, overloaded with ragged menials and stinking of grease, they were driven through the town, while everybody bowed. The palace wasn't overly large, but had been whitewashed into newness. After due protocol had been followed, they were escorted to a courtyard, where His Highness was waiting for them under a billowing umbrella.

The Morisons had described the Maharajah as an absurd creature. But he wasn't so—or not entirely; for there was certainly something foppishly ridiculous about the tiny, overdressed figure, living in the jungle with his retinue for company. An astonishingly ugly little man, his tongue stained bright red with betel-juice, wearing a dark frock coat, white embroidered knickers and socks, as well as earrings and a smear of yellow paint at the base of his nose, he could not receive them inside the palace, or even eat with them, for fear of contamination.

He was harmlessly eccentric, and his kingdom was too small to signify very much. In any event, he did not like the idea of ruling, and did so with scant enthusiasm. Accordingly, the minders sent to look after him were somewhat ludicrous too. There was a chaplain from the military cantonment, a foolish bounder who bullied the Maharajah tirelessly, shouting at him that he should be eating beef, that it would do him good. Whenever he left, the Personal Secretary would murmur to them that, "The Padre Sahib is a very nice man, he has no interest in religion, and that is very suitable for a clergyman." The politics were looked after by the Political Agent, a more sinister fellow who was nevertheless genial. A retired army officer and a Theosophist, he also liked to lecture the Maharajah in a nonsensical way. One afternoon, apropos of nothing, he suddenly declared that, "You must get rid of the Self and not expect a reward," and on another occasion that, "We should imitate the Infinite. If only we would, there wouldn't be this sinful outcry in England about conscription."

When Morgan and his friends were visiting, most of the talk was on spiritual themes too. The Maharajah decided early on that Goldie should be his main interlocutor. He lived for Philosophy and Love, and wanted to make them one: "Tell me, Mr. Dickinson, where is God? Can Herbert Spencer lead me to him, or should I prefer George Henry Lewes? Oh, when will Krishna come and be my friend? Oh, Mr. Dickinson!"

Goldie, whose stomach was in a terrible state, nevertheless brought his coolest Platonism to bear. Under the huge umbrella, the two men were gentle seekers together after truth. In these moments, perhaps, India drew almost within Goldie's grasp, human and tactile. Then the Maharajah would bring the meeting to an end by suddenly declaring, "But I will not tire you longer," and they would leave. Or else he would suggest a motor-drive. Then they would chug off peacefully somewhere, the three of them packed onto the back seat with His Highness, while next to the chauffeur in the front rode a silent "poor cousin", a wretched-looking man who carried with him his opera glasses, cigarettes, betel nut, umbrella, stick and State Sword, as well as a little bag of what Morgan suspected was food, although nobody ever saw him eating.

They would sometimes visit the Maharajah's second palace, Mau, which was a crumbling ruin on a lake. ("See, Mr. Dickinson, that balcony—did Hamlet climb up there to visit Juliet, do you think?") And then he would give the ruined palace to Goldie to keep in perpetuity, forgetting that he had given it to Morgan only two days before.

At night on a few occasions they were treated to a Miracle Play, danced and chanted by the resident acting troupe. The plays were often written by the Maharajah himself, and they usually portrayed some or other story from the life of Krishna. The troupe was funded from the royal treasury, and most of the actors were young and beautiful boys. His Highness never tired of watching them act out the themes of his spiritual devotions. But the little dramas were often incomprehensible and to Goldie this proved his point.

"You see," he told Morgan. "It's as I said. Everything comes down to religion, and it's dull, dull, dull."

"Religion is perhaps not the only element at work here."

"What do you mean? Oh, yes, I see . . . but even that part of it is dull. A mixture of rapture and cowardice. No action, but all that *quivering!*"

Chhatarpur was where Morgan had to part finally from his

friends: Goldie and Bob were going eastwards, and he was heading the other way. But religion also made it difficult to leave. The court astrologer was consulted, and bad omens were predicted for an eastward journey on a Monday. Bob and Goldie delayed in the end, but Morgan did not. He left on a Tuesday, which was unlucky for anybody travelling west, but he decided to take his chances.

* * *

He was soon to be in the company of another Rajah. He had arranged to meet the Darlings in Dewas, where they made a yearly Christmas visit to the palace. The ruler of Dewas State Senior was none other than Malcolm's charge, the young heir to the throne he had tutored just five years before and with whom he had remained close friends.

His Highness Tukoji Rao III, now twenty-three years old, was a very different figure to his counterpart in Chhatarpur. He was both more serious and more light-hearted, not being plagued by inner doubts. He ate food with his foreign guests, unfussily, and his conversation was not exclusively about his soul.

Morgan's first meeting with him took place in the most unlikely of settings. He had made his way by degrees, via Jhansi, Sanchi, Bhopal, Ujjain and Udaipur, to Indore. His next destination was to be Dewas, but meanwhile he was stopping with a Major Luard, whom he'd met through Goldie, and he'd been taken down to the club for a drink. He was introduced around and at the sound of his name, from an armchair nearby there sprang up a tiny, shiny little Indian man, wearing a turban, who grasped both his hands and twisted them delightedly.

"I am the Rajah of Dewas Senior," he announced, "and you are Malcolm's great friend. You are to call me Bapu Sahib."

Only a very few clubs had started to open their doors to

Indians, and then only to men of the highest breeding. Morgan was delighted, and suddenly he didn't so much mind the depressing rabble of Englishmen eating chip potatoes and drinking whisky and soda.

Bapu Sahib was there, he told Morgan, to compose a telegram. It was a moment of crisis, and he was writing to the Viceroy.

"Perhaps you can help me with the wording," he said. "I wish to convey my outrage and loyalty after the terrible incident in Delhi."

Morgan knew, of course, what he was referring to. The white community had been speaking of little else for the past three days. At the official transfer of the capital from Calcutta to Delhi, a homemade bomb had been thrown into Lord Hardinge's howdah as he rode in the procession. The mahout had been killed, but the Viceroy and his wife had escaped with only minor injuries.

The political reverberations from this incident were huge, and they moved out in concentric rings across the continent. Josie and her son were already in Dewas when Morgan got there the next day, but it was only when Malcolm arrived a little later that the news from the capital was freshened. Malcolm had been in the Punjabi procession, just ahead of the Viceroy, and was deeply shaken.

"It was terrible, Morgan, and it's going to cause a lot of trouble. Already there are people saying revenge must be taken. I heard some talk, from top officials too, about turning the Tommies to fire on the crowd. And there are some who would, I can tell you." When Josie and the other women were out of earshot, he added, "I also heard it said that it's a pity Hardinge didn't die, because then they could really have done something drastic. These thoughts are actually being spoken."

"But not acted on so far."

"No, but they might."

The common perception was that the bomb had been thrown by a Hindu, protesting against the capital being moved to Delhi, a predominantly Muslim area. The outrage had happened in Chandni Chowk, not far from where Dr Ansari had his offices. Morgan could imagine how Masood would be lamenting—and there it was again, that inward turmoil, the double frontiers of loyalty.

He was depressed by politics, and by Indian politics especially. He couldn't see through events to the people behind them, and felt he'd lost his way. He had a small breakdown just a few days later, while he was out for a walk with Malcolm and Josie, and they told him casually about some of the schemes and plots of the Maharajah of Gwalior, who was the Rajah's uncle and rival. The information churned suddenly in his gut. They were under a soft evening sky at the time, walking up some gentle hills not unlike the Sussex Downs, but in an instant the very soil underfoot seemed hard and treacherous. There were holes in the earth, concealing scorpions and snakes; a crow flying overhead cawed with an awful, raucous voice, like the land itself berating him.

"Oh, do stop," he implored them. "I don't want to hate this country."

In that moment, he felt he did. He hated India. It made no difference whether it was English or Indian, all human interaction was power; under the plumage and finery, people circled each other with poisonous intent. Every conversation jumped continually between subservience and rudeness, with no possible middle ground of genuine emotion.

In the morning, he felt better. History receded as the present took hold. He was staying in a luxurious tent pitched next to the guest house at the edge of a lake. In the still silver water, the reflections of flying cranes mirrored the real birds overhead. Baldeo was crouched down, singing, while he washed clothes. On the far side of the lake a series of small tombs mimicked the larger shape of the hill of Devi, which overlooked the town.

He walked up the hill a while later. It took less than half an hour to reach the summit. From there the whole tidy little town was visible, all its buildings and people and their doings mild and far away. Human divisions were reduced to their usual scale, minimal in the larger picture.

On the ground level, however, the divisions were more significant. He had heard from Malcolm, in his letters, about how Dewas State had been split into two branches, Junior and Senior. Bapu Sahib was Rajah of the Senior branch. It seemed that a previous Rajah, in the last century, had given his brother a share of the government, and this generosity had been extended to subsequent generations. When the British came, they had made the split official. Now the two kingdoms lay intertwined: one side of a road might belong to the Junior branch, while the Senior laid claim to the other. Each ruler had his own court, his own tiny army, his own palace, his own waterworks and tennis club, and the mountain of Devi had been divided between them, so that each might ascend to the summit by a separate footpath. For a time even the flagstaff on the top of the mountain had been jointly owned, with the flag flying exactly at half-mast.

It was surreal, fantastic—like no other kingdom Morgan had ever heard of. Malcolm had spoken of it as *Alice in Wonderland*, but for him it was more out of Gilbert and Sullivan: a quaint alternative universe where everything seemed accompanied by a tinkling piano. The Rajah of Dewas Senior was merely a colourful character trapped in his own outrageous set.

* * *

Afterwards, he decided that his friendship with Bapu Sahib really began on the evening that His Highness hosted an

Indian marriage celebration for the Goodalls, who were friends of Malcolm's and also staying in Dewas.

Morgan was in his tent, dressing in his English clothes for the occasion, while Baldeo hopped around him, trying to snip his frayed cuffs. From behind a curtain a voice called, "May I come in?" and the Rajah entered with a handsome young courtier, carrying a pile of Indian clothes.

For almost an hour Morgan became the centre of attention, while Baldeo and His Highness and the courtier all dressed and redressed him. When he emerged, he was unrecognisable in white muslin jodhpurs, a white shirt, a gorgeous waistcoat, a claret-coloured silken coat, trimmed in gold, and atop it all an oversized Maratha turban. The other guests had been similarly dressed in Indian style. The Goodalls toiled towards the New Palace, not half a mile distant, on top of an elephant, while the others followed in carriages with sirdars in attendance, all of it surrounded by torches and a band playing lustily. At the palace they were treated to a lavish banquet, and then they went up to the rooftop for champagne and dancing. In the middle of all this, a message came from the Rajah's wife, the Rani, that she wanted to meet them.

In his Indian travels so far, the wives and mothers of Morgan's friends had all stayed invisible to him. In Bhopal, the only native state ruled by a woman, the Begum herself— despite his official introduction from Theodore Morison—had kept herself hidden. So he was especially touched by this unexpected midnight summons. The Rani was extremely lovely, wearing a filmy white dress. She had molten doe-like eyes, from which she stared at them in friendly fright as she clutched to the doorpost, while Malcolm tried out a few words of Urdu, in vain. The meeting lasted only a few moments before they retreated downstairs once more. Morgan would never see her again in his life.

His Highness pretended indifference for a while, but couldn't sustain it for long. He leaned towards Morgan and asked, "You met my wife?"

"Yes, we did. She is very beautiful."

He nodded to himself, in agreement or approval. "I am glad she sent for you," he said at last. "I wish to make her modern, but she longs to remain wild. She is the daughter of the Maharajah of Kolhapur, you know, and the marriage was a good alliance. But I love her too." Then he shook his head, and his love for her was evident in his tiny, happy-sad face. Morgan liked him very much in that moment.

* * *

For a little time, while he was in Chhatarpur and Dewas, Morgan had left the poisonous atmosphere of colonial rule behind. The princely states were like tiny enclaves, apart from the rest of India; although the British maintained control, their government was nominally Indian and the atmosphere that prevailed was unnatural. The English were loved and revered there, and Indian nationalism was an affront. It was a tender illusion, and for a while it had almost seemed real. But he was awoken rudely from the dream when he arrived in Allahabad.

Almost as soon as he got there, word reached him through Baldeo that Rupert Smith was on the far side of town, staying with the Collector. Morgan immediately went to see him, and was invited to stay on to dinner. Smith was by now a Junior Magistrate, not a post he was likely to hold in London. Brittle and oversensitive, he managed to seem both more and less at home in India than he did in England. Not unnaturally, they talked about Baldeo. Had he been a satisfactory servant? He had been excellent, Morgan replied; he'd given full satisfaction.

In truth, his relationship with Baldeo had become a wordless complexity at the heart of his travels. On the one hand, the servant was a great help, a companion who knew all the cryptic codes of India. On the other hand, he cheated Morgan continually, small amounts of money that mattered very little in themselves, but which required ritualistic scenes of confrontation and remorse. And he tortured Morgan with tiny requests that verged on being demands, pricking his conscience expertly. In Bhopal, for example, Baldeo had wanted a bolt of cloth with which to make a new jacket, having admired Morgan's. This he had received, but then he wanted more cloth for a pair of trousers. Morgan had refused, because he liked Baldeo to wear a dhoti; it was simple and genuine, and he wanted him to keep it. But Baldeo had seen Goldie's servant in trousers and had set his heart on them. The subtle, intense wrangling that had gone on over these trousers had been exhausting, and though Morgan had won, he felt somehow that he'd lost.

Though Morgan said none of this, Smith smiled knowingly at him, one eyebrow lifted, and smirked. "Beginning to understand how things work out here, eh?"

This line of conversation had continued at dinner. The Collector's wife, Mrs. Spencer, did not try to disguise her contempt for anything Indian. Purdah parties she disliked especially, but then she seemed to dislike everything on principle. Mr. Spencer tried to blunt her edge at first, saying, "Oh, it's not that bad, is it, my dear," but then he lapsed into the frank admission that he despised the native from the bottom of his heart.

After a moment's silence, Rupert Smith—perhaps aware of Morgan's internal sigh—murmured, "I haven't quite got that far yet."

But Smith, Morgan thought, had got that far. So had almost every English official he'd met. It was awful. From practically his first conversation on board ship, he'd been aware of his own discomfort, which turned at certain moments into torment. So this particular evening became part of a general impression, a series of interactions with the English in India, in which his hosts and their friends were never less than generous and kind and welcoming to him, and yet he felt removed from them, watching from a great distance.

He could never live here, he thought. Not as these people did. Even if political affairs were never discussed, he experienced his remoteness from his white kin as almost a physical difference. This was a vigorous, outdoor world, full of sports and guns. If you didn't join the club or play polo or shoot tigers or subdue barbarous tribes on the borders, you were immediately an unsound quantity; the more so if, like Morgan, you lived in your mind a great deal and wrote books. Of what earthly use were novels? How did they *help* anybody? No one had actually put the questions to him, but they had let him know, in their tone and their turn of phrase, that they found him not quite pukka.

What made it worse was that, although his sympathies were usually with the Indians, he couldn't always like them more than he did his countrymen. Whatever he did, he was always to some extent a Sahib, and the room for antipathy was vast. On those scattered occasions when a true understanding was reached, he always felt disproportionately grateful.

Allahabad offered him one such moment. He had already joined up the previous morning with one of Masood's friends called Ahmed Mirza. He had met Mirza in London, where he had studied engineering, and they had liked each other in a tentative, careful way. Now, however, on the other side of the world, a curious closeness sprang up between them. They drew together with a strange, magnetic attraction, not entirely comfortable.

They arranged to meet again, and while they toured around the depressing fort, Morgan mentioned the Bathing Fair, which he was planning to come back to see. Mirza immediately suggested that they go out on the water. "We can bicycle down to the Jumna and take a boat," he said. "We can row out to the Sangam. That is the holy joining place, where the Ganges and the Jumna meet. Then you will see the place without the millions of bathers, before you come back next time."

Morgan said that he would like that very much.

"Perhaps you haven't heard this," Mirza went on. "But there is a third river also. At least, the Hindus like to believe it. At the Sangam, they say another river comes up from the centre of the earth."

"Have you seen it?" Morgan asked, intrigued.

"No," Mirza said sadly, then added, "it is not a real river, I think. It is invisible, unless you believe in it."

Morgan was sensitive to metaphors and this idea took hold of him. As they were rowed across the sluggish green surface of the Jumna, hacking their way through thick weeds, it came to him that certain human relationships were like two rivers meeting, causing a third river to spring up. He had glimpsed it himself at exceptional moments.

But today, in the real world, they were having difficulties finding even a second river. An old man and a boy were rowing them, though they seemed too weak to contend with the oars. When Mirza challenged them, the man said crossly that it was a long way to the Ganges.

"Well, we want to go there," Mirza said, but in English, so it wasn't understood. To Morgan, he went on, "I am so miserable, living here. I don't have a single friend of my own age. I grew up in Hyderabad, and then I lived those years in England, and now I struggle to find myself."

"I'm sorry to hear it."

"It is the lodgings, you see. I can't live with Hindus, because they won't let me eat meat. I have tried to live with the Eurasians, but I hate them, and they hate me too. I am very much alone." Suddenly wretched, he spoke harshly to the old man, who spoke back at length, gesturing over the water.

"What does he say?"

"That we are in the Ganges already." He stared out fiercely towards the bank. "But we aren't, he is lying, we are in the same river."

To soothe him, Morgan started to share some of his own feelings. He too felt alone in India, he said; he found it hard to speak, truly speak, to either Indian or English. The latter especially, and the women in particular. There had been moments since his arrival, he said, where he had felt utterly unmoored from the world around him, as if he might drift off and float away.

"Yes, you have said it exactly," Mirza said. "That is how my country makes me feel."

They looked at each other for a moment, united in sympathy. Then Mirza became embarrassed, and spoke rapidly to the old man again.

Afterwards he told Morgan, "He says the Ganges is too strong, it would carry us away. And that it is too late now, we should turn back. He is a liar, we should not pay him any money."

But the fight had gone out of him; they were already turning on the water. They moved without speaking through the twilight, mist half-obscuring the Ganges bridge, ducks honking mournfully overhead.

The next day, Morgan visited Mirza's lodgings: two bare rooms, not quite a bungalow, miles away from his work. A sad kind of home. But although he understood his new friend, no third river sprang up between them. For that, understanding isn't necessary; only deep affection is required.

* * *

He would be seeing Masood again in ten days. He was supposed to feel excited at the prospect, but his stay in Benares was unhappy. It was the most thoroughly Indian city he had visited, yet somehow he didn't see it properly. The sadhus, the broken-down ghats, the burning bodies and the devotees at the river—all of it felt remote from him. His attention was elsewhere and nowhere, and his anxiety grew as the date of his departure drew nearer, though he wasn't even sure what he was anxious about. He only knew that he wanted to be happy, but wasn't.

At Moghulsarai station, on the way to Bankipore, he saw the following message inscribed on marble blocks:

Right is Might. Might is right. Time is money. God si love.

The words of the last statement lingered with him, losing their charm and taking on an unexpected significance. The reversed letters made you see the original idea differently. It meant nothing, really, *being* love. Love was felt, love was acted upon, or it meant nothing. That was the heart of the matter, and it was what his friend had never understood.

Masood came to meet him at the station. They greeted each other with unfeigned delight, and for a short while it was as if his Indian travels had only just begun. In the carriage on the way to his house Morgan spoke, a little overexcitedly, about everything he'd seen since they'd last parted—but he could tell that his friend wasn't listening and he fell silent. The silence continued while they both stared out at the endlessly passing hovels at the edge of the road.

"I'm sorry," Masood said at last. "I really was paying attention to you, my dear fellow."

"I'm speaking too much. I haven't had anybody to talk to in quite a few weeks."

"I'm very tired. You must forgive me. I have been working hard."

"That means business must be going well, at least."

"I have a lot of clients, yes. But . . . " He gestured out of the window, at the low shape of the town. His face was twisted into an expression of despair.

In just a day or two, Morgan would begin to understand

that expression better, and to have some sympathy for it. The view from the carriage was everything. That was it: Bankipore consisted of that road, fourteen miles long, with its fringe of dirty dwellings. Nothing else to it and no way out. Morgan borrowed Masood's bicycle on one of his first mornings and tried, but there were rice paddies on one side and on the other, out of sight, the Ganges. It was like a huge hand taking hold of him when he did eventually find a way down to the bank: standing on black, smelly mud, staring out over the roiling expanse of water.

Masood's house was bare and big and pleasant, and at first he hardly left it. The back windows showed a prospect of open space, though it didn't extend far. That illusion could be reproduced from the roof, where you seemed to look down into green gardens on either side. Curiously, Masood had never been onto his own roof before Morgan found a way up, nor did he know that the turning beside his house led down to the water. Something in him had been blunted, or frightened, by his life here, so that he didn't look too closely at anything.

"And the worst of it," he declared, "is there's no tennis. Except at the club, where they won't let me in."

He said it with a smile, but he may not have been joking. A memory came back to Morgan, from a visit to Oxford, of Masood prancing about in his tennis whites, performing for his admirers. He had always been a showman, at his best in front of an audience. Perhaps there were simply not enough onlookers here.

In just a few days, Morgan himself would be beset by boredom. Bankipore was horrible, and offered almost no distraction. He was here for only two and a half weeks, which felt both too short and too long. What would ever happen in this place? There was nothing to do, and very little to think about. The only open space was the Maidan, some distance down the road; between it and Masood's house were the Library and the

Law Courts. These buildings weren't much better than the hovels that surrounded them, and on the dusty ground between them squatted litigants waiting for lawyers, while inside the courts, lawyers waited for litigants. That was the sole entertainment.

He was in touch with one Englishman he had known from King's, but he preferred spending time with Masood's friends. Two in particular became his escorts and companions. In the morning, while the rest of the household was still asleep, he would bicycle over to the house of one or the other, and they would accompany him for a few turns about the Maidan. Then he would return home for breakfast with Masood before he left for the courts or consulted with clients in his office. There were many hours spent alone in the middle part of the day, until evening and more conviviality came along.

One afternoon, while Masood was out, three young men came to call on him and were treated instead to Morgan's company. He found himself holding forth to the visitors on politics: he spoke about English foreign policy and the complicated, contradictory interests of the Empire, emphasising that much of what Britain did was based on fear of Germany rather than hatred of Islam. The youths listened eagerly and when they left one of them delivered an effusive speech about their good luck in meeting him and how the Empire could go on for ever if it produced wonderful gentlemen like him.

It was only afterwards that Morgan reflected, with amusement, that everything he'd said had sounded credible only because he happened to know a little more than the young men did. And yet there was something about the exchange that reassured and pleased him. If people could only sit down together and speak—or perhaps more importantly, *listen*— then many intractable problems might disappear. Everything of significance in his own life had come about through the simple act of open-hearted conversation.

Yet that could be the most difficult thing in the world. Sometimes the better you knew somebody, the more impossible any real talk became. That, at least, was how it felt to him. Here he was, in the home of the man he loved, on the other side of the world from his own constricting life, and what truths could be spoken between them? They talked about food, or the weather, or problems of justice, but they didn't speak about anything that mattered. Everything was jest, or chatter, or deflection, and all the while the days were passing.

Of course, some important things were said, though more by accident than design. There was the moment, for example, when Masood mentioned that he thought he'd made a mistake by going into law and that he was considering a change.

"But to what?" Morgan asked.

"I am thinking of education. It is a very necessary field."

"Of course, but you've spent years, studying in England . . . "

"Yes, yes, but the time wasn't wasted, whatever happens. I have met you, apart from anything else. Just look—here we are, six years later, sitting together in India."

Morgan couldn't help himself; he was overcome with pleasure at the words. It did seem miraculous that an appointment to teach Latin in Weybridge could have carried him such a distance. The talk about Masood's career became forgotten.

But it was followed by another conversation, possibly the very next night, when Masood mentioned casually, as if it didn't matter, that he thought he might marry soon.

"Oh?" Morgan said. A bolt of pain fell cleanly through him, then vanished into the floor. "Do you have somebody in mind?"

There had been no women evident, not even in their idle chatter.

"Yes, yes," Masood said impatiently. "You remember in Aligarh, you met my friend Aftab Ahmed Khan, we had dinner together . . . "

"Yes," Morgan said vaguely. There had been so many dinners, so many meetings . . .

"I am considering marrying his daughter." As if there had been some objection, he added, "These things are arranged here in India. We do not pretend to follow the English example. Our tradition is different."

"By this time, I should hope I know that." And both of them laughed and put the subject away hurriedly, as if it were somehow shameful. But the thought of it kept Morgan awake that night and it was the first thing in his mind when he woke the next morning.

Masood getting married; a door closing deep inside somewhere. He could be miserable if he thought about it too much. Though it wasn't as if it came as a surprise. Marriage was inevitable here, far more so than in England; he'd known it would happen one day.

Still, he struggled to contain a sensation of rising dismay. He was at the midpoint of his time in India: three months behind him and three in front. Nor did his friend seem troubled by that fact. There had been no mention of seeing one another again. And when Morgan brought it up, Masood waved the matter away.

"I am very busy, my dear chap," he said. "You see how my days are. Of course I would love to travel around with you, but I don't know how it's possible. Not at the moment. But the next time you come—certainly then, oh yes, we'll tour about and I'll show you everything. Oh, I look forward to that hugely."

"The next time. When will that be?"

"I don't know, Morgan, that's up to you. But you'll come back, of course you will. Now we're not going to be depressed, are we, and spoil our happy days together? That would be too dreary." And he went off, singing a ghazal, to shave before work.

In the end, Bankipore seemed to fall past him, so swiftly did his stay run out. And his memory of it afterwards was filled with Masood's friends, rather than Masood himself. As the days converged on his departure, his anguish rose invisibly, not uncoloured by resentment. Why had he come here—to India—at all?

* * *

And then there were the caves.

"I have organised a little expedition for you," Masood mumbled at him on one of his last mornings, as they took breakfast together on the roof. "Before you go to Gaya, I think you should see the Barabar caves. I am sending you with a friend, and you will have a picnic breakfast."

"That is very kind of you," Morgan said, "very kind," but his teeth clinked painfully on the edge of his cup. "Are they wonderful, these caves?"

"Oh, yes. Famous caves." After a moment he conceded, "Well, they are not so wonderful. But you should see them." And after a further pause: "I have arranged an *elephant*."

Morgan, staring down into the complicated trees, tried to be impressed by the elephant.

The last day was the worst. Time seemed to swell, becoming waterlogged with emotion. He thought he would get through it all right, but then in the middle of the night, when they'd said goodbye, his sadness had become too big and he'd gone back through to Masood's room and done what he'd done. The attempted kiss, the pushing away, the tears: all of it had shamed him deeply, so that he couldn't consider the memory too directly. And he had taken those feelings—of sadness and longing and shame—to the caves with him the next morning.

It was true: the caves were not so wonderful. They were small, with almost no ornamentation, no visible history. And they were spread out so far, in such a remote place, that he found himself retreating afterwards with a low, persistent headache and his deep melancholy unassuaged.

But despite their ordinariness, the caves lingered in him. He carried their hollowness inside, their negatively asserted shape. In Bodh Gaya, in the sunken garden where the Buddha had supposedly attained his enlightenment, he was less stirred by the prayer flags and the pilgrims than the memory of a glassy smoothness under his fingers, and that echo.

That echo. It played in his head at unexpected moments, repeating certain sounds and making nonsense of them. But could you remember an echo? Memory itself was like another kind of echo, everything duplicating endlessly, in shadow versions of itself.

Something had happened between Masood and himself, he felt, in the caves. Which was nonsense, because Masood hadn't even been present. Though that was exactly the point. That was what everything between them had come down to: Masood still abed, while his friends, Agarwala and Mahmud, were at the station to see Morgan off. And wasn't that always the way of it? Hadn't his association with Masood, under the elaborate filigree of language, hadn't it always been about this deferment, this selfishness, this veil drawn over the obvious truth, which was that Masood simply did not care enough? Morgan could not look at the possibility for long, but at least he could look at it, and over the coming days he took it out and hurt himself with it at particular moments when he was alone. He had always been slow to comprehend his own feelings, and it came only gradually to him how disappointed he was. He had hoped for a great deal in making this journey and none of it had come to pass. Now he was left with time and an immense amount of space, and nobody else to keep him company.

In the weeks that followed, Masood, bewildered or lazy or unable to help himself, continued in his apparent indifference.

The promised letters did not arrive. Morgan wondered: would they ever see one another again? And would it matter if they didn't? His mood, which seldom left him, was like being under the sea, in aquamarine light. However bright or loud your surroundings, you were somehow always alone.

Even in the middle of the vastest tide of humanity he had ever seen in his life—at the Magha Mela, the Bathing Fair in Allahabad, which Rupert Smith had invited him to—he felt profoundly singular. He was in a tent again, pitched in the middle of a mango grove. Nearby, the crowd seethed. A million people, Smith said. It was like a small nation, in which certain details could suddenly become apparent. People praying to idols with frighteningly painted faces. A sadhu hanging over a fire, his head in a black bag, being pushed back and forth by another sadhu. Long lines of pilgrims, waiting to have their scalps shaved, except for the one lock by which they hoped to be pulled to heaven. Their shorn hair piling up, to be taken to the water.

For the most part he watched it from an observation platform, astounded at this epic display of faith. The scene was especially remarkable in the early evening, when the air was blurred with dust and smoke, and people became like tiny animals crawling on the bottom of the sea. The junction of the two rivers kept changing overnight, according to how the Ganges wandered in its bed. This must have been the reason that he and Mirza had been unable to locate the spot, yet other people now were finding their way.

His journey had lost some of its velocity by now, though its form continued to hold him. He went on to Lucknow, where the Residency, the site of the Mutiny siege, had been preserved as a museum, through which he stumbled by the light of a golden afternoon. It was very still and weirdly beautiful, the wide, garden-like spaces with their bougainvillea and bursts of orange creeper, shaded by tall banyan trees, and then the broken buildings, punched and pocked with the marks of cannon balls, looking like much older ruins already. In one place the besiegers were only the width of an alley from the residents, whose presence still trembled on the air, in the form of heat ripples rising from the ground.

He fled from them, back to Agra, Muttra, Aligarh. It was a measure of how much he'd seen that Aligarh, and the college, now seemed like a place where relations between the races were good, even kind. He went to call on Masood's mother, who still would not see him in person. But Mirza had coached him in the right words to convey. *Give my salaams to Begum Sahiba and say that I have been at Bankipore and that Masood is very well.* All true, of course; but he began to wonder whether his entire Indian visit might not dwindle to those bare facts.

Injury had transformed slowly into anger, inseparable sometimes from the landscape he was travelling through. He had begun to voice this emotion in letters, in a way he'd never done before. *You can now go to hell as far as I'm concerned . . .* These words, to Masood! *You didn't work at law, you don't write anyone letters, you can't even stop yourself getting fat by taking proper exercise. Soon you'll be too slack to trouble to keep your friends and will just drift about making casual acquaintances with the people you find handy. I do think that is beastly of you.*

Such sentiments would have been inconceivable just a few weeks before—to say nothing of signing off without love, which he now pointedly did. Love was still there, of course, but to refrain from declaring it was a declaration in itself.

* * *

In the first half of his journey, everything had seemed to fall past him at dazzling speed; nothing was still or fixed. But now that Masood was behind him, the end of his stay had become visible in the distance. All of this would finish. The world that he was passing through was not so new or shiny any more; it had taken on solidity and weight.

He found himself noting little moments, or particular people, with an eye to using them later. He didn't really know what he would do with them; only that they were part of a fabric he'd begun to weave. His mind was especially receptive on a return visit to the Darlings in Lahore. He had enjoyed his previous stay, but it was only now that he fully appreciated how unusual the Darlings were in British India. Every week there were several gatherings involving a mix of Indians and Europeans, and at an evening party Morgan met an elderly gentleman, whose name made an impression. After the party ended Mr. Godbole strolled with him through the public gardens, discussing ragas. Different scales were applicable to different times of day, he told Morgan, and to illustrate the point Mr. Godbole sang to him a little in C major, which was appropriate for the evening.

The old gentleman was not, in the end, especially memorable, though his name did linger behind him. It was perhaps usable if bestowed on a minor character, a walk-on part that nobody would remember. But the trouble with Mr. Godbole, and all the other bits and pieces he was gathering, was that they remained loose strands—little pieces of talk, or momentary impressions gleaned in passing—with nothing to knot them together. In writing his previous novels, there had always been something at the middle of the narrative, a thickening into solidity, around or over or through which the story had to pass. Everything would lead up to it, and then everything would lead out of it again. Without that obstacle in his way, he couldn't even begin. But although his mind had been preoccupied with his Indian book for quite some time, he still had no sense of what that central density might be.

Well, it would come or it would not come; that was all. If

the Big Event didn't show itself to him, there could be no book, nor did he think the world would be much poorer for it.

In the meanwhile he remained a traveller, and India continued to strew events and places in his path. In Delhi, Malcolm had arranged another meeting with Bapu Sahib for him. Morgan was very keen to see His Highness again, who had begun to loom in his mind as the Indian he knew and liked best after Masood. No sooner had he located the royal party than Bapu Sahib ran up behind him and put his hands over Morgan's eyes; this happy greeting set the tone for the two days of his stay.

His Highness was there—with the Rani and their child, his brother, the Prime Minister and sixty-five attendants, all of them staying in the same hotel—to attend a Chiefs' conference. On his last day in the city Morgan accompanied him while he made official calls. When his duties were done, Bapu Sahib became boyish and boisterous, bouncing delightedly on the cushions. The royal carriage took them into the city, where they chanced to meet his brother and other members of the court who had been shopping. The squabbling, noisy, happy party—ten of them—pushed into the carriage too, along with their mound of purchases. Morgan found himself between His Highness, who was adorned with a large pale-yellow turban, and his brother with a purple one, the doctor in a red Maratha head-dress opposite, while nearby lolled a secretary who appeared to be wearing an orange cup and saucer, next to the court buffoon, who held a wheezing elderly pug on his lap. Outside the carriage hung the coachman, an attendant, a footman and a groom. As far as Morgan could tell, nobody in the street paid them the slightest bit of attention.

This ride put him in a good humour again, and it lasted all the way through Jaipur, which he disliked, and Jodhpur, which he did not. Mount Abu cheered him further, with its valleys and trees and temples, and it was in almost victorious mood that he arrived in Hyderabad, far to the south. After a few days, when he moved on to Aurangabad, he was nearing the end of his time in India; he could feel it all closing on a final, finite point.

Morgan had scarcely arrived at the dak bungalow when Saeed, Ahmed Mirza's younger brother, swept up in a flurry to take him off and he was settled instead into quite the loveliest quarters he had seen in this country: a large hall divided into two by exquisite blue arches, its side open to a garden of trees whose presence crowded into the house. The air was heavy with the smell of flowers. Before he slept each night he went out to look at the house from the other side of a rectangular tank, full of fish, and the sight reminded him of the Loggia de' Lanzi in Florence.

Saeed and his housemates—a Municipal Inspector and yet another barrister—lived in an ugly dwelling in the yard, and on his second night they all ate together, and afterwards shared a hookah and conversation. They recited poetry to one another in Persian, Urdu, Arabic and Greek, and talked about astrology and the shortcomings of Englishmen. It was a clear, calm evening and for a moment Morgan had the impression that he had been carried back in time, to one of his early visits to Masood in Oxford, when everything was still new between them.

He had known Saeed a little from London, but this young man had grown very dashing since then. He was a Munsif, a Junior Magistrate, and Morgan visited the courts with him on various days. In the sub-judge's room, he observed a civil surgeon giving evidence in a case of murder, while a punkah-wallah, a superb, bare-chested, sculpted youth, in whom graven idol and flesh became one, fanned them rhythmically, pulling his rope impassively as Atropos.

It was becoming clearer to Morgan that his novel might turn on an incident of some kind, which would play itself out in a courtroom. The idea was connected to his experiences in India generally. Most of the educated class of Indians he'd met—Masood and his friends—were barristers. On the other hand, many of his English acquaintances worked for the Indian Civil Service and had been employed as magistrates. He had found himself very exercised in Allahabad when he'd gone to watch Rupert Smith presiding over a court in session. Smith himself had already been marked in Morgan's mind as the embodiment of a certain type, but now the setting had taken hold of him too. It had become more and more troubling to Morgan, in a personal, discomfiting way, that these two classes—the finest minds that each side could offer—seemed to regard each other with suspicion and contempt. The Indians felt that they were abused and mistreated; the English officials said that the educated Indian was a drop in the ocean and meant nothing. Even justice, it seemed, was cracked down the middle.

This crack, this deep divide, would run through his book. Two nations, two distinct ways of doing things, were in endless friction with each other. And it was everywhere obvious. The conflict was in him and around him, and wanted to be worked out on the page.

* * *

Home was beginning to loom ahead now, not only as an idea but as a fast-approaching reality. In just one week he would be boarding the ship at Bombay. Because it was on his mind, he mentioned England more than usual in conversation, and it sparked an outburst from Saeed.

He and Morgan were riding on horseback to see a nearby Maratha village. It was evening, and Morgan had an upset stomach from a banquet he'd been treated to the previous night. He'd fallen off this same horse a day or two before, but thankfully the animal played no tricks today. Instead it was Saeed who was fretful and skittish.

"What do you English imagine?" he cried. "That you will rule us for ever? Do you not know that already your days here are ending? Clear out, you fellows! The Raj and you will be defeated. It may be fifty or five hundred years, but we shall turn you out."

His face became quite distorted with fury. It was a sharp-edged, nasty little moment, which Morgan was glad to leave behind. As they rode on and a happier conversation resumed, he thought: *he hates us. He hates us far more than his brother does.*

Their friendship had become fraught, as every one of his Indian friendships seemed to in the end. Even so, by the next day the difficult talk was forgotten as Saeed accompanied Morgan to visit the caves nearby at Ellora. On the way they stopped in Daulatabad to visit the hill-fort. This unlovely creation had the power of impregnability: one entered across a bridge that spanned an excavated moat, and then ascended a spiral tunnel through the hill. From the very summit, above all the guns and fortifications, the Deccan plateau simmered bleakly in the heat.

Saeed flung a stone over the edge as they went back. He said, "When I look down on walls I thought big below, I despise them."

For his part, Morgan thought, *what should I do with such a kingdom?* The temptation to power had no purchase here, not for him. People like Saeed wanted to rule, but they didn't seem to know what that involved. It was a great labour and a great burden, he had glimpsed that in the last weeks. Power both amplified and diminished those who wielded it.

After lunch they walked around the outside of the moat, stepping carefully through a rocky landscape that baked and shivered in the sun. The heat and immobility and silence were preparation for what awaited him at Ellora in the evening. He had been to so many forts and temples and shrines and tombs over the past six months that he didn't believe he had any reserves of awe left. But the Kailasa cave, seen in the last bloody rays of the sun, amazed and astonished him.

Cut out of a single vast rock, it was a temple complex with many levels and galleries and courtyards, covered in sculptures and friezes of an arresting intensity. The shrine at its heart, built around a gigantic lingam, made impression enough, but what stayed with Morgan afterwards were some of the animal images, charged with spiritual hostility, and the terrifying blank indifference of a goddess while she casually inflicted cruelty. He returned alone at sunset, and again the next morning. By now he had made up his mind that the inspiration behind the Kailasa wasn't godly, but diabolical. Many, many hands and years had made this place; it gave expression to three different kinds of religious thinking. Nevertheless, whether Buddhist or Hindu or Jain, the caves did not exude a good feeling. They weren't beautiful, and their grandiosity was of a frightening kind. They had been carved as shrines to an ancient and primitive fear in people; they had certainly touched that place in him.

He found himself thinking now about those other caves, in the Barabar Hills far to the north. He had returned to them often in his imagination, like a hard hollowness at the centre of his journey. They were nothing like Ellora or the Kailasa, of course; they were vacant and smooth, without idols. Nevertheless, they had become larger and more numerous in his mind, more perfect in their emptiness.

They could be made significant, he thought, even if the reality had been disappointing. Those caves could be touched, he saw now, with some of the dread and darkness he'd felt in Ellora. He didn't need the busy, alarming carvings, nor the scenery or the scale. No, absence and silence were his material . . . broken only by that echo.

He had it now, he thought. What he had been searching for till now: the heart of it, the central, engendering event. Something happened in the caves. He knew that much, at least. A terrible incident, a crime of some kind. But when he tried to focus on what it was, it became unclear, all of it retreated from him. It had been too dark to see properly; the echoes had been confusing . . .

* * *

Saeed was wholly his friend again when he came to the station to see him off. The Station Manager had to delay the train by ten minutes while they went through their farewells. Hung ceremonially around the neck with three garlands of jasmine and marigolds, Morgan was abashed, honoured and inadequate all at once. "But I have no gift for you," he murmured. "And you have been so kind . . . "

"The accounts of friends are written in the heart," Saeed told him, smiling, as he stepped back to watch the train depart. It was a line Masood might have spoken in one of his more insincerely lyrical moments. But Morgan liked Saeed, and really had wanted to thank him properly. In any case, he would be able to buy some confectionery for him in Bombay.

Though, as it happened, he couldn't. India was to finish for him in confusion. The boat, he discovered, was leaving twelve hours earlier than he'd been told, and there was no time for anything that he'd planned—to visit Elephanta Island, or eat mangoes, or buy cakes for Saeed. He couldn't even repack his luggage properly. It was all he could do to make the ship, and he wasn't sufficiently collected even to feel the loss as the shoreline receded behind him.

In the end, after everything that had happened and all the people that he'd met, it was only Baldeo who stood at the quayside to watch him go—ageless, inscrutable Baldeo, whom he did not hate after all; no, not in the slightest. They waved to each other just once, without apparent emotion, and then the intervening distance grew greater and their futures cleanly diverged.

He had brought gifts for his mother, mostly bolts of expensive and gorgeous cloth, which on his first morning he laid out in the dining room amidst burning sticks of incense. When he called in Lily and the maids to look, they cooed and cried out in delight, and for a brief instant he saw through their eyes the spectacle of strewn silk. It was all there: the smell, the colour, the awakened glimpse of a far-off place. And then it was put away, the cloths folded and stowed in packing-cases, and never brought out again.

He felt lost for a while. The old rituals and habits were insufficient. Nothing was quite bright or beautiful enough; everything was too known. He thought constantly, obsessively, of India—but there was nobody in his circle who shared his interest, which made it worse. He returned there continually in his mind, often to quite arbitrary impressions and textures. In his more fanciful moments he imagined that he had fallen in love with each and every one of its millions of inhabitants.

In fact, only one of them truly mattered. He missed Masood dreadfully, and wished he could see him again. But his anger hadn't abated. Time and distance had softened its sharpness, but Masood kept forgiveness at bay by writing only every few months, and with no real news. He was aware of Morgan's feelings, which hadn't been subtly expressed, but it seemed he couldn't help himself. Silence or empty posturing were all he offered in response.

But in one of his letters soon after Morgan's return—and

perhaps only out of guilt—he did yield up a genuine revelation. He approached it in a roundabout way, not quite saying what he was saying, though his meaning was clear enough. His father, he thought, had been a minorite.

Oddly, this didn't come as a complete surprise. Something in the way Masood had talked about his father, and the tales of distressing behaviour that he'd recounted, had planted the idea in Morgan's mind. There had always been some great unhappiness there, some knot of unspoken torment, suppressed through drink. But now that the words had been set down on paper, they loosened a flurry of emotions in Morgan, which tolled like a bell through his life, back to his beginnings.

He was thinking about his own father. He had never known Edward Forster, except through family anecdotes and stories, especially Lily's. But these had been enough to create a disturbing question, never sufficiently clear to be spoken aloud. There was always an antagonism, a disappointment, in Lily's voice when she mentioned him, and it seemed directed at something fey and weak and unmasculine in his character. Morgan had sensed this early on, and tried to adjust his own nature accordingly.

But something else came to him now, something he'd always known but never pondered. Morgan had an appointed guardian, a Ted Streatfeild, a very dear and close friend of his father's—so close, in fact, that he had accompanied Lily and Eddie on their honeymoon to Paris. Lily had told him this only once, many years before, in his childhood. Something acidulous about her tone had made him feel unhappy, though he hadn't understood why. And then his mother's face had closed over, and the subject was dropped and never picked up again. Just as, after his father's death, long before Morgan could even form a memory of him, Ted Streatfeild had disappeared from their lives and his name was barely mentioned.

What was one to make of this? Certainly he could never ask

Lily. It felt like a private sadness, something she had been through that didn't include him. Yet it troubled him now, like a ghost that had come in an envelope from India, uniting and dividing him from his friend.

He didn't tell any of this to Masood. Their lives were no longer joined in the same way as before. Never had this been clearer than when, on a visit to the Morisons, he discovered that Masood had announced his engagement. He was hurt to learn of it like this, though a letter did follow from Masood soon afterward. He was going to marry Zorah, the woman he had mentioned, the daughter of the barrister Morgan had met in Aligarh.

It was hard to reply as he had to. *Your welcome news has moved me. I am thankful it is settled, and very happy. I have always wanted it. I suppose I* must *love you as myself if I desire a new person—not me—to come into your life. I do desire it, as with my own heart.*

The words were both true and false. And after his announcement, which had perhaps been difficult to make, Masood went quiet for a while. There were almost no letters, and Morgan was left with his longings, which sometimes threatened to undo him.

He found himself behaving in ways that were potentially dangerous, without quite knowing what he was up to. On one or two occasions he loitered in public lavatories, hoping for some offer to present itself. Open spaces, especially those in Hyde Park, excited him with possibility. But there was only ever a glance, an accidental collision, which left him turbulent with fantasies. To act out of lust, even without any tender accompanying feeling, would be less damaging, he felt, than these corrosive bursts of desire that went nowhere. He took himself to see Nijinsky dancing almost naked in *L'après-midi d'un faune* and the utter abandonment of that human body alarmed and delighted him, like an enactment of everything which roiled invisibly inside. Afterwards he longed to miss his train home and give himself up wholly to adventures in the foliage somewhere, though he wouldn't have known where to go.

His own sterility was apparent to him and would soon, he felt sure, be visible to others. Curiously, he didn't feel depressed at the prospect. He was almost intrigued by the idea of giving in to his oddness, turning into one of those remote, ineffectual creatures so warped by their solitude that they became distasteful to normal people. He had seen the type before.

* * *

A month after getting home, he'd told Masood in a letter: *I don't know that I shall ever be able to write about India—when I begin I seem to dislike you all equally. But it is certainly waiting for a great novelist. Produce one yourselves.* This declaration was so convincing that he was mildly surprised to discover himself, soon afterwards, ascending to the attic and sitting down at his desk.

He had chosen a green ink, not a colour he'd used before, to set the book apart from the others, even if only in his mind. And at first the green words fell out of him, in a decisive and rhythmic torrent. Though much, he also sensed, remained unformed.

Through the last weeks of his Indian travels, but especially on the voyage home, he had begun to conceive of characters in a particular setting. The place that suggested itself was very like Bankipore. The river, the mud, the oppressive awfulness—all of it was there, but also the greenery visible from the rooftops, and the pleasant regularity of the Civil Station. It was a way of returning to it in his mind, and of re-joining Masood . . . though Chandrapore was also composed of all the other little towns he'd seen and passed through over the last six months.

The people he imagined were likewise made from those he'd encountered in India. Nobody was precisely anybody: he built them from aspects and shards and impressions. He had learned, with his earlier novels, that if you screwed up your inner eye when looking at somebody familiar, you could glimpse a new personality, both like and unlike the original. Once this outline had taken shape, you could fill it with traits that in turn had been borrowed elsewhere.

Mr. Godbole, for example, had survived the voyage, and had taken up residence in a corner of Morgan's mind, seated with arms and legs impossibly neatly folded. But he had shed his comic veneer and was chanting a sort of obscure wisdom. Nor did he resemble—except in his singing, and in a certain composure of temperament—the old man encountered in Lahore. A name, a quality, a way of behaving: these came together to suggest a person.

Or, more exactly, many people: the world, for Morgan, had always been a throng. You couldn't tell a story without two people, at least, at the centre of it. Accordingly, he had imagined a friendship at the heart of the story which echoed his own with Masood. It wasn't thinkable that he could write a book about India without also writing about this, the great affection of his life. It had been the fount and the source, and it continued to haunt him, even now. But of course he couldn't write it down directly; he had to camouflage the known.

In the case of Masood, he could successfully mingle his qualities with those of Ahmed Mirza, as well as Mirza's brother, Saeed. He saw a young man, passionate, intense, full of pride and injury—exactly the sort of person Morgan responded to. Masood's bluster and febrility were in there, too, as well as the emotions that coloured certain Indian conversations. Out of such elements, Aziz had very quickly taken on his own life; he was the character who had most completely arrived.

Harder to do was the Englishman, Fielding. He couldn't be like Morgan exactly; he didn't think of himself as heroic. But Malcolm Darling did provide the mould for a certain kind of man, a vessel into which Morgan might pour himself—a person he could have been in a different life. And he drew on Leonard Woolf, too, with whom he was recently becoming more friendly. They had known each other a little at King's, but it had only been in the months before he'd left for India, when Leonard had taught him horse-riding, that a closeness had crept in. He'd been thinking a great deal about him lately: Leonard, who had spent years in the Civil Service, alone with his high principles in the jungle in Ceylon. But there were not a great many other Englishmen, not among those he'd seen in India, who might think or feel the way that Leonard did.

This was distressing to him. Indeed, when he dwelt for any length of time on his Indian experience, it was unpleasant to realise how difficult it had been. Yes, the place had hurt him, in complicated, contradictory ways. He couldn't stand too much ugliness, and there had been a lot of that. Worse, it was in human relationships that the ugliness had showed itself. In the relationships between Indians, or even between Indians and himself, there was no essential problem, but in the treatment that the English meted out to the local population he hadn't found much cause to be proud.

He was angry about it, and the anger showed in his writing. This was something new for him. His previous books had a lightness, a humour, which he struggled to find now. Over and over he kept returning to the subject of power, racial power, and then the ugliness appeared again. He wasn't an especially political person, and he didn't like what was coming out of him. Yet it was what he had seen and felt, almost from the moment he'd boarded the ship in Naples, and he had never raised his voice against it. He had murmured and muttered, it was true, and he had tied himself into convoluted knots, but that was the extent of his protest. Now his spirit wanted its say.

The story that was forming would turn around a young woman, rather a lost, dry creature, on her first visit to the country, eager to get to know Indians. Not unlike himself, in other words, and maybe that was why she was giving him trouble. He couldn't even settle on her name: at first she was Janet, then she became Edith, but neither struck the right tone. Much would depend on what exactly happened to her in the caves and, until he understood that better, her nature would stay inscrutable.

The closer he came to those caves, the more he began to falter. He knew that something took place in the dark, a sexual attack across racial lines. The caves held that kind of power. But it wasn't simply a question of the action; it was what the action arose from—what it meant. The problem was fundamental. No matter how he tried it, the words sat on top of the deed; they had no soil and no roots. There was something wrong with how he had imagined it, something essentially dishonest and out of balance, and as his narrative crept toward the threshold, the rock refused to open for him.

So he had already lost momentum when something else happened to throw him off course completely.

* * *

Lily's rheumatism was still bad, and in September of 1913 she decided to take a cure at Harrogate, in the north. She planned to be there for a month, and Morgan was to stay with her for much of the time. But Harrogate was in reach of Millthorpe, and Millthorpe was where Edward Carpenter lived.

He had heard Carpenter's name many times. They had some acquaintances in common, Goldie most notable among them. Many years before, when he had been an undergraduate and in love with Roger Fry, Goldie had gone to stay in Millthorpe Cottage and had retained a glowing enthusiasm for the place and for its owner. He had urged Morgan to visit and had provided him with written introductions, but he had never taken up the suggestion. It was always the wrong time, or the journey was too inconvenient—though in truth he was simply afraid.

Carpenter had a reputation. Or perhaps it was more true to say that he had many reputations. Born thirty-five years before Morgan, he had long been vocal in support of different but related causes, from socialism to vegetarianism to women's rights. This had made him famous, not to say infamous, in certain circles, though it was a different campaign that had ensured his notoriety.

Carpenter was a minorite. But unlike Morgan and Goldie, he had spoken out about it, publishing two books and delivering speeches and generally behaving in a brave and brazen way. True, he had hidden what he believed under a veil of mysticism, and he had always been careful to take cover behind a general openness in sexual matters. True too, he picked his language carefully, speaking about love between comrades and invoking a tradition of male companionship that went all the way back to the Greeks. But he hadn't shrunk from living what he believed, and it was well known that he shared his home with a much younger, working-class man. They had been together, Goldie told him, for more than twenty years.

Morgan had read some of Carpenter's writings on what he called "Homogenic Love". They had excited him, and echoed many of his own feelings. But he had been wary of drawing closer to Carpenter in person, for fear of what it might lead to. Since his visit to India, however, he had felt more daring and courageous, and when this opportunity was presented he knew he should take it.

It was not an easy expedition. For one thing, he couldn't tell Lily where he was going, so he had to cover himself with vagueness and excuses. For another, Millthorpe was not on any regular rail connection: from the nearest station he had to walk for miles through the countryside. And he was nervous that, when he did finally arrive, he and the great man might not hit it off. But these were small concerns in the end. When he stood shaking Carpenter's hand at last, it felt like a significant moment, long overdue.

"*Ee Em* Forster," his host intoned, smiling through his beard in gentle irony. "What coy initials to hide behind. What is your *name*?"

"Edward, like yours. But everybody calls me Morgan."

"And are you like me in other ways?"

"Possibly I am, but I don't know you well enough to say."

"Soon you will know me better. You are very welcome here. I should measure your feet."

"I beg your pardon?"

"For sandals. I'd like to make some for you. You are in need of release, your poor feet cannot know the earth in dreadful shoes like those." Carpenter's own feet were sandal-shod, and both of them looked down for a moment at his long, gnarled, brown toes. "My first sandals came from Kashmir," he told Morgan. "My dear friend Cox sent them to me."

"I have just recently returned from six months in India."

"Ah, India, India! It is the most marvellous, extraordinary place! Though in fact it is many places. I spent some months there, oh, twenty years ago now. You must tell me all about your experiences, but first please come inside."

The stone cottage was plain and regular, built in rigid lines. There was no passageway linking the rooms together, so that they simply followed on from one another, in an abrupt and linear way: kitchen to scullery to wash-house to stable. The sitting room, where Morgan was allowed to settle himself, resembled a bare, bureaucratic space, but the view from the windows—of a leafy, private garden—was pleasant enough. And the starkness of the distempered walls and wooden floors had the effect of amplifying Carpenter's presence, once he had seated himself opposite Morgan.

There was no denying it, he had a strange, internal power. Tall and thin, wearing tweedy country clothes, he had a way of facing the world that was very upright, very open. Although he was nearly seventy, he listened and spoke with the same open, intense directness. It was both unnerving and uplifting.

They talked about India, and for the first time Morgan felt he'd met another Englishman who understood. Carpenter wasn't interested in colonies or conquest; he cared about people, the simpler the better. He had spent much of his time in India and Ceylon among ordinary workers who did unimportant jobs. It was his belief, he said, that England would either have to grant more freedom in India or quit it altogether, unthinkable though that might be. He had also, to Morgan's great surprise, visited the Anglo-Oriental College in Aligarh, and had been hugely impressed by what he'd seen.

This led him to tell a story that startled Morgan, about two Muslim men, students at the college. "They loved each other so much," Carpenter said, "that when they were forced to part, they killed themselves. Yes, yes, it's true. The one drowned himself and the other, if I recall correctly, lay down in front of a train."

A silence followed, while the two men contemplated dying for love. Morgan glanced around surreptitiously, looking for Carpenter's companion, who had so far not shown himself. There were other people nearby, he could hear them, and a female figure had passed the window at one point, but nobody else was in the house. Stirring himself, Carpenter asked, "What of you? Do you have a . . . special friend?"

Morgan replied that he did not. "I am alone."

Carpenter snorted. "Nobody is alone. We are all part of a great world community. If the world only knew it."

"Yes, yes, quite so, but I—"

"Come into the garden and meet George."

Morgan trailed behind his host across the grass, towards a small stream that burbled happily over stones. A shirtless man, perhaps ten years older than Morgan, was dancing from one foot to another in the sun. George Merrill's whole body seemed to aspire upwards, though his moustache, and his eyelids, drooped. He did not cease from dancing, even as he clasped Morgan's hand. "The water is wonderful," he told their visitor. "You should undress and have a bathe."

"Perhaps another time. It's a little chilly for my taste."

"Nonsense, nonsense," Carpenter cried. "You are merely inhibited. What are your thoughts on nudism?"

This was another subject close to Carpenter's heart; clothing, like many social habits, concealed what was natural and lovely in human beings. A little desperately, Morgan repeated, "I should like to bathe another time. At this moment I want to see the grounds."

For the most part, the place had been left to grow wild, aside from a kitchen garden that was as geometric as the house. But there was a real charm to the view down the valley, with hills and hedgerows and flowers all around. At some point during their stroll, George caught up with them, still tucking in his shirt. While Carpenter spoke about what Millthorpe meant to him—the Utopian vision of returning to the land—his special friend kept glancing sideways at Morgan, and once he winked in a knowing way.

Morgan was perturbed by this, but only a little. People conducted themselves differently in this house, he knew that. Carpenter and his devotees were trying to live out a revolutionary view of life, in which all the normal rules were thrown aside. From a distance it could seem absurd, even frightening, but from close up, what he sensed more than anything else was kindness—kindness of a human and immediate sort. It was surprising how very radical this simple emotion could be.

This feeling persisted through the hours that followed. While they wandered outside and afterwards, while Morgan sat in the kitchen and watched George prepare lunch, he kept thinking: *why not? Why not live like this?* The thinnest of veils seemed to separate his own life, as it was now, from this alternative vision of how to approach everything. There was no reason why he should not lift the veil aside.

Well, there was Lily. He could imagine his mother's face if he told her he was giving up meat and alcohol and going to live off the land and make sandals. Not to mention homogenic love. The veil might be thin, but in certain cases it was insurmountable. Though Carpenter might not agree. Carpenter himself had come from an upper middle-class home in Brighton. He had also gone up to Cambridge, on some sort of religious scholarship, before casting religion and the academic life aside.

It couldn't be for everybody. Goldie had also tried this lifestyle, Morgan knew, when he was a young man. Goldie had had a spell of living on a farm, among working-class people, trying to embody the new philosophy, but it had turned out to be disastrous. It was only as a thinker that Goldie could find his place. For some people, Morgan among them, the only possible life was the life of the mind. And what was wrong with that? Carpenter himself had been influenced by F. D. Maurice, the theologian and Christian socialist, during his Cambridge years. Maurice had inspired the creation of the University Extension Lectures and, along with Goldie's father and some others, had founded the Working Men's College in London. Morgan and many of his friends had taught there, and had formed some lasting connections with men from the lower classes.

They talked a little about Maurice while they ate. Carpenter could do an amusing impression of the great man, closing his eyes and smacking his face with his fingers while he formulated thoughts incoherently. Yet those same thoughts had radiated outwards and down the years, leading perhaps even to this cottage and Carpenter's way of life. Maurice had believed in the power of personal relationships, of love between people, beginning with the family and extending to society. Where was that power on more evident display than here, in this room, where George, the working-class boy from the Sheffield slums, had moved his chair next to Carpenter's and was running his hand through his older lover's hair?

Only connect. The gap had closed, or vanished, for those who chose to ignore it. Class and age and background could be pushed aside by a gesture of human affection. *God si love.* For a moment, this little tableau was everything. Perhaps much of Carpenter's life was beyond Morgan; he could not live in this rough, rude way. But to be sitting next to a man of a different background, touching him gently, casually, with no thought of wrongness—why was it so impossible? He wanted it, he could have it, if he would only *do* it. The choice seemed suddenly so obvious and uncomplicated.

Then George was pushing his chair back and clearing plates from the table. It was the middle of the afternoon already; Morgan still had to return to Harrogate this evening. He ought to be readying himself to move. In a half-polite, half-distracted way, he tried to help. He wasn't used to carrying crockery, or to the intimate gloom of the kitchen; it wasn't his usual part of the house. Looking for a clear surface on which to set down the plates, he was aware of George's closeness behind him, and of the sound of his breathing.

"Is this all right?" he asked. "Here?"

"Let me see. Yes, that's all right. Just put them down."

He put them down and stood, not moving. He could still

hear the sound of breathing, close enough to be intrusive. Then he realised it was his own.

"Oh," he said, surprised.

And then a little frightened.

Because George was touching him.

It was merely a hand, in the lower curve of his back. The contact was suggestive, though the fingers didn't move. Perhaps it was the talk they'd been having, or the thoughts he'd entertained, but there was something subversive about that hand. Something flowed out of it, transmitted through the palm: a presumption of equality, or worse—of ownership. Yes, this must be how it felt, to be touched by a lover. He could feel the heat of it, the possessive certainty of its contact. Then the hand dropped down, to his bottom, wavered there for a moment, and came to rest a little above his buttocks, at the base of the spine.

It was astonishing. Something had happened to him. He wasn't quite in the kitchen any more, not quite in his own body. His mind had flashed away from itself, to some inner place where the events of the day were still being arranged. Now they were arranged differently.

"Yes," George said again. "That's all right, there."

Carpenter's voice called outside, and the hand fell away. Not a weighty moment after all. But on the long walk back to Totley station, with the afternoon shadows stretched long and pale across the ground, Morgan's mind was digging in the sand. He was excavating an outline, a form that had become imperfectly plain to him.

He had a story, a new story. Afterwards, it would seem to him that it had arrived whole and entire, rushing in somehow through the small of his back. But in fact it was in the aftermath of that touch, especially in the ride on the train, that he had assembled its disparate parts. They had been lying around in him for a long time, like bits of shattered statuary, and something had happened to make the fragments fly together. When he got back to Harrogate, he made his excuses to Lily and retreated to his room. He had a terrible stomach from George's cooking, but he also had paper, he had his pen. Between frequent visits to the bathroom, he started to write.

* * *

One book displacing another: his Indian novel was forgotten. Instead he was writing about being a minorite. A homosexual story! For all his life he had had to imagine the opposite, the joining and unjoining of men and women, while secretly longing to speak about himself. Now a chance touch at the base of his spine had let loose this other, buried narrative. In one moment, as if lit up by lightning, he had seen the whole arc of events, the three characters at the centre of them.

Of course, he could never publish it. He couldn't even show it to most people he knew. There were some, naturally, who would understand, and he wrote for them, or for himself. Anyhow, some idealised reader who would accept everything, and forgive.

The feeling of release was huge. An enormous pressure had built up behind the words, years and years of silence, which now pushed into the open. Few things are more powerful than confession, and he told it all to the page. The uncertainty, the doubt, the slowly dawning realisation: he could let it spill. He travelled back in his mind to the unfolding of his spirit in Cambridge. Though some concealment was necessary.

He plucked the name of Maurice from his afternoon with Carpenter; it would do as well as another. And to separate Maurice from himself, he made him vigorous, athletic, extroverted—Morgan in another life! Hom was closer to the truth in the form of Clive Durham, and what had happened between the two of them was also present, in altered form. But the family details and the lesser characters, all this was disguised, in case the wrong eyes should fall on it.

It was hard to keep away from the work in the beginning. It was all so vital, so necessary, that the act of writing took on an electrical charge. There was so much to be conveyed, so much of it rooted in his own life, that the enjoyment felt private and personal. He even began to dream about it. Thinking about his past had raised it close to the surface; he was remembering images and sensations and events from long ago. The years at Cambridge were one thing; they had been his awakening. But his minorism had begun much earlier, of course, when he was very young.

His first sexual feelings had had no object. He had liked to climb the trees at Rooksnest and stimulate himself against the branches. Then later he had been terribly excited by the various garden boys, especially Ansell and the tickling in the straw. And the fat, dark Irishman, Mr. Hervey, who had been his tutor at Stevenage for a while, when Morgan was eight. He'd had a very disturbing dream about Mr. Hervey's penis, which had been like a long, white snake that filled the whole hall and dining room, winding Morgan in its coils. He'd believed the dream to be absurd, because he, Morgan, was the only person in the world to have a penis.

The first conscious moment of choice had come later, when he was eleven. On holiday in Bournemouth with his mother, he had been preoccupied by a sense of the future as a territory of many forking paths. He would have to find a way through this unknown, twilit landscape, and the decision he made at each split in the road would define his whole destiny. It was a cause of great anxiety to a little boy and, looking out of the hotel window, he decided to leave the biggest choice to fate. *It all depends*, he thought, *whether a man or a woman first passes*, and then he had waited fearfully for what the empty street might deliver. When a man with a brown moustache appeared from the right, he had experienced a rush of relief.

A line of uneasy wanting—though of what exactly he couldn't say—had run through all his school years. At Kent House in Eastbourne, the sourish smell of the public baths had lodged permanently in his nose, an accompaniment to all the naked boys leaping in and out of the water. Underscoring the flickering, innocent skin around him, the mingled roar-moan of the sea, connected to the baths by a subterranean passage, was a reminder of a larger, more frightening world outside the dripping walls. He always remembered this weekly event with a sensation that was half-thrilled, half-sick, though nothing of importance had happened to him there.

Genuinely important, though probably best forgotten, was the actual, ordinary man, without a moustache, but wearing knickerbockers and a deerstalker, whom Morgan had found defecating on the Downs above Eastbourne one midwinter afternoon. That was shocking enough, but meaningless by comparison with what followed. The man had drawn him aside, among bushes, his flies still undone. *Pull it about*, he'd said. *Dear little boy, pull it about.* Morgan had pulled it about, till some kind of white fermentation had taken place. Then the man had grown bored and offered Morgan a shilling, which he refused. The reporting of this incident, first to his mother, then, on her instructions, to the headmaster, had sent out waves of shock and consternation, centred on him. He understood that something awful had taken place, for which, it was implied, he might be partly responsible. Nevertheless, at the age of eleven, it had made him feel powerful. With indignation, he had told the horrified headmaster, on their way to the police station, that the man's bowels had been diseased. When he received counsel, in return, about the dangers of accusing the innocent, he had said: *We shall know him, sir, by this disease.*

He did not put any of this into his book. He wanted to write in an altogether more positive, more uplifting way. He wanted to do everything, in imagination at least, that his life would otherwise not allow him. Above all, it would end in love. Two men from different classes would live together and love each other, in a sublime, suspended, fictional state.

The first half of the book proceeded from him with a steady, effortless ease. Cambridge and thorny Platonic longings—all of this was close to home; there was no artifice required. Shadows and allusions, always on the verge of action: it was the stuff of his life. But then he came to Alec Scudder, and he was no longer so certain. He had only dreamed this part, not lived it. Knowledge had been replaced by fantasy, and the novel had become a little slippery in his hands.

At the same time he made a visit to Goldie, whom he hadn't seen since India. The memory of the journey brought them closer, though Morgan still deferred to the older man. They talked about what had happened since they'd parted, and then Morgan told him about visiting Millthorpe and the book that had come out of it.

Goldie's face was pinched. "But what is the purpose," he murmured, "if you cannot publish?"

"The time may come when I can."

Between them, the future shimmered for an instant.

"Do you think so? I hope you may be right. Well, in the meanwhile, I should like very much to read it, when it is ready."

Morgan hadn't brought the manuscript with him, or he might have shown some pages. But there was something else to hand. "You could take a look at this, if you want to. It's a short story I wrote a month ago. A gesture in the same direction, you might say."

He meant in the direction of the flesh. He was giving Goldie one of his erotic short stories, which he continued to write intermittently. They were not love stories. But of everyone he knew, he thought Goldie was the person most likely to share his sort of fantasy.

He was wrong. In the morning at the breakfast table a very awkward conversation took place. Goldie, it turned out, was horrified by the story. More than that, he was disgusted. Such things, he thought, shouldn't be written; they demeaned the reader as much as the writer. He told this to Morgan with pained frankness, looking down obliquely over his teacup at a patch of spilled sugar on the tablecloth.

Morgan was profoundly set back. He hadn't expected this reaction at all. "I showed the same story to Hom recently," he said. "He wasn't upset by it."

"Perhaps Hom thought it would be too *ordinary* to be upset." Goldie's lips had stitched primly together. He stacked Morgan's story very exactly and slid it back to him over the table, then busied himself with the tea cosy. Both men understood that the matter had been put away and wouldn't be referred to again.

Nevertheless, Morgan was badly thrown by the exchange. The most troubling thought was that, if Goldie could respond like this to a mere sexual bagatelle, how might he feel about *Maurice*? For the first time since he'd started working on the book, Morgan had doubts. Was he base and crass to be exposing himself in this way? Was he making an exhibition of his perversity?

He paid a return visit to Millthorpe, hoping to rekindle the fire. Though he took away the same joy afterwards from his encounter with Carpenter, George Merrill didn't touch him anywhere. He kept picking away at the book, but his work was slow and worry inhibited his pen. He was drawing closer to the heart of the story, i.e. the union of Maurice and Alec, but how could he describe it? How could he, when he hadn't lived it yet himself? He was thirty-four and virginal and would perhaps be virginal all his life.

And in the only fertile area so far—his writing—he had become sterile too. Here he was, stranded on the threshold of middle age, with three unfinished novels in his hands. He hadn't touched *Arctic Summer* in a year. His Indian book was in trouble, stalled somewhere in its deeper mechanism, and now *Maurice* also seemed to him a morally questionable exercise. Maybe he would never complete anything again. Maybe his power had left him.

* * *

In March of 1914 he went to stay with Meredith in Bangor. Hom had sunk so far into his married life that only his eyes showed. But there was still a spark and a freshness between him and Morgan, so that it seemed natural to hand over a batch of pages.

"It's my Uranian romance," he said. "Some of it may seem familiar."

Hom grunted in vague alarm and carried the manuscript off with him. But he didn't mention it again. Morgan was stopping for a fortnight and on his last morning he asked whether his friend had had a chance to read it.

"Well, I glanced at it a little." He pulled a face, which left no doubt about his feelings.

"You didn't care for it."

"Not much, to be honest. I'm not sure what you're trying to prove, Morgan."

"I'm not trying to *prove* anything, I'm sure. Just to, to . . . tell the truth, I suppose."

"The truth? Well, perhaps there is some truth in it. What I don't understand about your type is that you want to emulate the other side. You kick up such a commotion about being different, and all you want is to be the same."

"To be *treated* the same. Is that so terrible?"

"Yes, it is, if you only knew it. What you want is to live with a man in a happy home. But you don't know how trivial it is.

Marriage is emblematic of modern life. The way men and women are together—it's a silly business, it has no nobility. I wish you could see that, instead of romanticising it."

The remark hurt Morgan deeply. It was Hom's indifference—or the idea that his indifference didn't matter. He'd thought that the story belonged to both of them; now he saw that it might be his alone. *Your type*: he had been set aside, and could only accept his new place.

The great friendship with Hom, which had once promised so much, had run into the sand. Too much time, too little nobility: it had grown between them like a barrier. He could be unmanned by thoughts like these, but it didn't last long. He felt that he had changed in some profound sense. India had done it to him—had shifted him from one base to another, had angled him somehow differently. He didn't depend so much on the good opinion of others to feel complete. Nor did he expect happiness as his right any longer; he knew it was only for the strong.

* * *

Goldie was his first and most frightening reader. After his reaction to the short story, Morgan expected judgement on a larger scale. But when Goldie responded, it was with warmth and admiration. For the first time, Morgan felt, he and the older man had become true comrades. His little book had done that for them.

Morgan wondered whether Goldie wasn't compensating for his harshness over the short story, but in the months that followed he kept mentioning *Maurice* again, and on one occasion his eyes filled with tears. "You may not have intended it," he said. "But you spoke for me, as well as for yourself."

Encouraged by this reaction, Morgan showed the book to a few other friends. Forrest Reid, Sydney Waterlow, Florence

Barger—all of them approved. With trepidation, he even gave it to Lytton Strachey to read. Amazingly, Strachey liked it—and he especially liked one aspect.

"Tell me," he said. "Do not dissemble. Risley, *c'est moi*. Yes? Confirm!"

The character was not flattering, and Morgan had hoped the resemblance would pass unnoticed. But he had seen a certain gleam in Strachey's eye and after a moment he nodded.

"I knew it! I knew it!" The delight was unmistakable. It was Strachey's voice, above all other signs, which conveyed most completely his feelings on any subject. You couldn't mention Edward Carpenter's name, for example, without eliciting a stream of high-pitched squeaks, like a bat in flight. Now his voice rose in a muted shriek of triumph: "My dear, immortality is mine! The title must obviously be changed. No more mention of Maurice. It is Risley, Risley, Risley! This is my only criticism."

Of course, Strachey didn't have only the one criticism to offer. In a long, perceptive and pertinent letter that followed, he made it clear that in general he admired the parts dealing with the Cambridge set, but he remained unconvinced by Maurice and Alec Scudder. Nor did he think a relationship across classes like that had any chance of lasting. Six months at the most, he gave them. But his most memorable comments had been those about sex. The whole attitude to male copulation, he said, struck him as diseased. The matter of Maurice's tortured chastity, followed by the elaborate internal contortions he went through before going to bed with Scudder: there was something very wrong, he felt, with how the book treated intimacy between men.

Morgan was given pause by this idea. Writing revealed one to oneself, of course, more damningly than any confession, but he hadn't considered this particular question till now. Worse, the comment made something else clear: namely, that Lytton *knew* about these things first-hand. It was bothersome that this unattractive, bizarre-looking man, with his undisciplined limbs and his extraordinary voice, should have engaged in love and carnality when Morgan didn't dare to.

* * *

If he had imagined that writing *Maurice* would free him elsewhere too and that he would go back to his Indian novel with fresh vision and enthusiasm, he discovered now that it wasn't the case. Reading over the pages of green ink, they looked stale to him, without blood or breath. He was still stuck in the caves, still vexed by what did or didn't happen there, and what it meant. Now that he had written so much more personally, he felt suddenly very far from India and he didn't think he could return to it.

And in the meanwhile other happenings had unfolded which made India seem not just distant, but unreachable. The very idea of war seemed impossible, outrageous. And yet the word was coming up suddenly in every conversation, growing and thickening till there was no other topic. Nor was it often mentioned without fervour.

When England officially joined the conflict, Lily became restive. "I think you ought to do *something*, Poppy," she told him. "Everybody else is volunteering."

He would not join up; he would not fight. He knew this with calm certainty, in the same way that one knew one's own character. Just the day before he had seen some white-faced boys guarding the railway line, as if it might be in danger—he could do something meaningless like that, or perhaps there might be work in a hospital somewhere. He was happy to mop up blood, just not to shed it.

Only a few days later, there was a solution. One of his Weybridge acquaintances, Sir Charles Holroyd, was Director of the National Gallery. He sent a message that Morgan should come to see him, and then offered him a post as a cataloguer at the Gallery.

"It's only four days a week," Sir Charles told him. "And a night of fire-watching here and there. Nothing very taxing, I can assure you. In any case, we are putting the more important paintings in storage, until this unpleasantness is over. One never knows—bombs and whatnot."

"So if I die there, it'll be among second-rate masterpieces. How fitting."

Sir Charles stared at him with open mouth for a moment, then guffawed when he understood the joke. "You won't die *there*," he said, then spluttered. "I mean to say, I hope you won't die *anywhere*."

His mother agreed completely. "Now you will be able to do your bit," she told him, "and still come home for dinner in the evenings."

So life continued in a semblance of its old form for a while. One didn't have to consider the War too closely, although it ran through everything like the vibration of a distant earthquake. Perceived from home, it was a great concentration of calamity, but out of sight, over the horizon somewhere. He secretly suspected that it existed merely on his account, to teach him some kind of moral lesson. If he died, it would cease to be there, it would be cancelled.

But in his normal life it showed mostly as a deep change in the attitudes around him, very alarming to a sensitive disposition. The Defence of the Realm Act, for one thing, with all that it allowed, including censorship—though what bothered him much more was the *acceptance* of these changes by everybody. People believed it was necessary and somehow *good* to be altering their priorities in radical ways. A new mentality was taking hold, a mentality of crowds and slogans and mass emotions, in which he felt queasy and afraid.

He visited the Morisons more frequently than he wanted to, in order to get news of Masood. Theodore Morison had been knighted a few years before and—though he remained humble about it—his wife had taken on great airs. He was startled one afternoon to hear from Lady Morison the sentiment that war lifted people to a higher plane.

"A transfiguration takes place," she told him, "when a man picks up a gun. A spiritual renewal, very mysterious. It is almost like a light, shining from within. Do you not agree?"

So surprising was this idea that he believed, for an instant, she was being ironic. Then he saw that her face had its own shining light, and set down his teacup.

"No, I'm afraid I do not," he said firmly.

"You must have observed it. Surely."

"I have observed a base instinct take charge," he said. "I have observed European civilisation being set back by thirty years. That is all."

"Indeed." The light had switched off in her now, to be replaced by coldness. "Of course, you are entitled to your opinion, though you mustn't expect patriotic people to agree. But is that the time? I hadn't realised it was so late, I'm afraid you will have to excuse me."

These little clarities didn't last. He couldn't rest too smugly in his own convictions, not when doubt continually gnawed at the extremities. Morgan wasn't immovable. Though the idea of killing was awful, he found something distasteful, too, about the lofty isolation of those who refused to fight.

Was he a conscientious objector? The description didn't fit comfortably. The principle of abstaining didn't ennoble him, any more than bloodshed would. Both sides had their idealism, which he heard everywhere he went, till he felt that he might choke. What was most distressing was the ability to understand both viewpoints while being able to follow neither.

* * *

At the start of 1915, his spirits were briefly lifted by a new acquaintanceship. He had known Lady Ottoline Morrell for a few years, though he had always resisted being drawn too fully into her social stratagems. Many people in his circle, especially Lytton, were regular visitors at her Bedford Square soirées, but she alarmed Morgan slightly, with her jutting jaw and her horsey teeth, to say nothing of her outlandish outfits when the eccentric mood struck. But now Lady O had taken it into her head that he, Morgan, would get on *extremely* well with her new protégé, a young novelist by the name of David Herbert Lawrence.

Nor was she wrong at first. Morgan was seated next to Lawrence at the dinner party held in his honour, and they took warmly to one another. Lawrence did hold forth somewhat emphatically, it was true, and his new German wife was afraid of being overlooked, but the impression they left behind was of passion rather than egotism. The very next day, however, at Duncan Grant's studio, the mood was decidedly different. When Lawrence launched into a heated diatribe against the *evil* he detected in Duncan's paintings, Morgan thought it best to make his excuses and slip away.

An exchange of letters followed. He found himself accepting an invitation to Greatham in Sussex, where the Lawrences were living. The visit was pleasant to begin with. He was stopping for three days, and on the first afternoon he and Lawrence went for a long walk on the Downs. While they walked, they talked of a topic Lawrence had already raised in his letter—namely Rananim, his projected Utopia.

"And you will always have a place there, Forster," his host assured him. "You and your woman."

"Well, that is very generous." Not keen to linger on this topic, he asked quickly, "What exactly does your Utopia consist in?"

"It is an island. Not part of the existing world. That is all you need to know."

"But how does one live in it?"

At this, Lawrence became so voluble that he lost coherence. It seemed to be a place without class or division or money, where people who were already fulfilled might fulfil themselves further.

"Not unlike Edward Carpenter's little cottage," Morgan ventured to suggest.

"Carpenter? That old outdated mystical fraud! No, Rananim will be nothing like that."

Morgan laughed uncomfortably, but the remark about Carpenter would stay with him. It would take on an extra sharpness the very next afternoon, when Lawrence suddenly, without any apparent reason, launched a ferocious attack on the English political system. A revolution was needed! The land, industry and the press should immediately be nationalised! Morgan murmured mildly that he couldn't quite agree and suddenly the mood changed. Like the hot beam of a lighthouse, he felt Lawrence's angry attention swing round upon him.

It began quietly, though the tone was earnest, and soon became an unfettered rage. It was astonishing to realise that *he* was the object of so much displeasure: his person, his lifestyle and his writing. All of it, apparently, was unacceptable. Why was Morgan content to live in such a cloistered, limp, ineffectual way? Why did he shelter himself from his own primal being? He should *act*, he should engage his basic appetites and live them out! He should find a female counterpart and dig down to his volcanic base material, instead of fossicking about with love stories set in Italy, in between his knitting and visits to the opera. His books were proof enough of his sterile preoccupations. The characters that interested Morgan were all, without a single exception, types that belonged to a suffocating and futureless world, which he, Lawrence, longed to tear open like a placenta and emerge from, newly born and blood-ied and crying . . .

Morgan interrupted this tirade to say primly: "I don't knit."

Lawrence scowled and flung a stone at a tree. "In your soul, you do," he said. "If you want to come to life, you must change your whole existence. All of it!"

"How do you know I'm not dead already?"

"You see, that is precisely the kind of remark I mean. Your idea of the future is a return to the Greeks. Your idea of God is Pan. But Pan is the source, not the end. No plant grows down to its roots! We must struggle upwards, we must put out shoots, even if they have thorns on them! Do you not see?"

"Perhaps I don't."

Lawrence, who had just begun to calm, became excited again. On and on, quite literally for hours, until he was hoarse, he called his guest to account for all his multitudinous short-comings. When eventually a silence fell, Morgan ventured to ask:

"And really—nothing in my books interests you? Not one of them is worthwhile? Or, not even that . . . nothing *in* them is worthwhile?"

"Well, I speak harshly. I speak in absolutes, because I . . . all right, yes. Leonard Bast. I give you Leonard Bast. That was courageous."

Frieda Lawrence, who was seated nearby, tossed her head and laughed. "*Ja*," she said. "Leonard Bast."

It was by now fully dark and they hadn't eaten, but Morgan decided that he was indignant. "The two of you," he said, his voice sounding even to his own ears like that of a maiden aunt, "I'm not sure you're both not just playing around my knees." Then he stalked off to bed without saying good night, feeling sure for some reason that his hosts would soon be rutting like rabbits.

It was all so big, so final—surely the horrible demise of a friendship. But the next morning Lawrence was in an equable mood again. When they said goodbye, he told Morgan, "I hope you know I like you very much. And I also hope you will visit us again soon."

But Morgan didn't ever go back. He was attracted to the man as much as repelled by him—all the hot, sandy-coloured, working-class vehemence of him—but there were only certain intimacies one could hope to survive. He would never inhabit Rananim, and in the meanwhile even Greatham seemed beyond him.

In the end, it wasn't Lawrence's fanatical certainties—either in conversation or committed to paper—that put Morgan off. Finally, when he reflected on it, the remark about Edward Carpenter had done for their friendship. An outdated mystical fraud? No, no, no—anybody who saw the old man that way was on the other side of some deep divide. Whatever his shortcomings, Carpenter was the future, and nobody could speak against him.

* * *

On a visit to Goldie in Cambridge, an incident occurred which made it clear how English life had broken into two. A group of Welsh soldiers, upon encountering the sight of an undergraduate in cap and gown, had collapsed in wild laughter—they had never seen a creature so outlandish. But the outlandish creature was a tradition that had given rise to Morgan, and he was appalled to have it laughed at.

When it was suggested to him that he might join an ambulance unit in Italy, the idea of trying to staunch wounds, repair broken bodies, pulled powerfully at him. George Trevelyan was working there and would take him on immediately. But Lily became querulous and morose. "It sounds *dangerous*," she told him.

The danger was what attracted; it might justify his continued existence.

"Italy could never be dangerous. Don't you remember Florence? A nation that produces such wonderful art could never harm me."

"Don't talk nonsense, Morgan. Not everybody was meant to fight. The idea of you killing people is simply ridiculous. You know it isn't in your character."

"What is my character, do you think?"

"Why don't you stay at home and write?"

It was writing that felt most impossible then. Or more precisely, it was novels that were out of the question. To invent lives and dialogue, to dream up the unreal, when reality had taken on so much weight and ugliness: it would be like defying gravity.

Then he overheard a conversation between two nurses in the train. It seemed people were needed as searchers for the Red Cross in Egypt or Malta. "Searching", as far as he understood it, meant interviewing the wounded in hospitals for information about those who might have gone missing or untraced. It sounded like work that he could do and could respect himself for doing.

He had to arrange an interview with Miss Gertrude Bell, who, despite her fame, turned out to be a severe and maudlin presence behind a desk. She brought with her the aura of deserts and disdain, not bothering to look closely at him after her first weary summing-up.

"I don't think you are quite suitable for this kind of work," she said. "What are you doing at the moment?"

"I'm a cataloguer at the National Gallery."

"I think that is far better for you. I think you should stick with it."

"I very much want to go to Egypt."

Miss Bell quivered. "*If* I can find you a place," she said, "*then* I will get in touch with you."

In the end, he had to pull strings with an old Cambridge

acquaintance to get her overruled. To round off the whole business, he found himself in front of her again, to have his papers approved and signed. She was resigned to him now; his persistence had triumphed.

He leaned towards her to ask, "What are they like, the inhabitants of Alexandria?"

"You will have no opportunity to find out. You will only see them in the streets, in passing, as you go to and fro on your work."

His visit to India emboldened him to say, "In foreign places, I like to mix with the locals."

"Not in Alexandria. There are parts of the city that will shock you."

"Those are the parts I want to see."

"No," she said, glancing sharply up at him. "I suggest you look neither right nor left, only keep your head down, and walk directly to where you are going."

Her tone was very strict. But she did give a tiny dry smile, and he decided that he liked her after all.

CHAPTER FIVE
MOHAMMED

The two men were angled slightly past each other in their armchairs, sipping cheap whisky, and their conversation hovered a little above the surface of the earth, never quite touching anything. They spoke of Mediterranean civilisation, especially the Greeks, but the talk was desultory and drifting, and there were occasional silences.

It was only their third meeting. Previously their encounters had been in public, at the Mohammed Ali Club, and both gentlemen had studied one another courteously, from a distance. But tonight a gesture had been made; Morgan had been invited, with two friends, back to the poet's home for a drink. The friends had long since departed, and now only Morgan remained. There was a brief moment of awkwardness as both of them adjusted to the new situation, but then it passed. He liked his new acquaintance, about whom he'd been hearing for some time, and was keen to deepen their relations. More immediately, he was curious to see where Cavafy lived.

He hadn't been disappointed. The Rue Lepsius was in the Greek quarter and had perhaps once been a good address, but it had obviously fallen on harder times. Below Cavafy's flat was a house of ill repute, which men furtively approached at all hours. "I have watched them from my balcony," he told Morgan, "and there are many monsters, oh, many! But not all of them are bad. There are some young men, whose faces, believe me, are angelic."

Like the street outside, the interior of his flat, too, had an

air of dilapidated grandeur. The large salon in which he entertained Morgan on that first occasion was cluttered with furniture and vases and hangings and ornaments, none of it very
clear in the light of the petrol lamp. But the effect was of relics
and remains, the traces of a better, higher life that had now
fallen away.

Or perhaps that was merely his reputation. Morgan had
heard too many stories about the poet by now, little flashes and
fragments from different sources. In the miniature world of
Alexandrian cultural life, Cavafy was famous—which was to
say, people *talked* about him, sometimes admiringly, sometimes
in low-voiced asides. It was well known that he came from a
good family, originally from Constantinople, which had lost its
fortune through bad luck and worse investments. One by one
the various progeny had floated away or died, leaving the
youngest son, now middle-aged and alone, among the lingering left-over debris of their lives. And there were other little
anecdotes, about the shadowy corners of his life, which stirred
envy and disgust in different quarters.

The night was cool. Cavafy had a half-cigarette in his
holder, unlit, and he was waving it about as he talked in a long-
suffering tone about his employment in the Ministry of Public
Works. His department was the Third Circle of Irrigation and
he was pained by the stupidity of his colleagues. "I have to
check their grammar," he told Morgan, "in every memoran-
dum, every letter. And no matter how many times I explain the
correct use of the comma, they simply repeat their mistakes.
And let us say nothing of the apostrophe! But I do not give up.
I call them in and explain it all again, in the hope that one day
the light may dawn. What a happy day that would be! But I
doubt it will ever come. There is no atom of poetry in any of
them, not one."

The mention of poetry seemed to trouble him; he reflected
for a long moment, then looked mournfully at Morgan through

his spectacles. "You have not asked to read my poems," he said.

"I haven't presumed. But I very much want to read them."

"They will all be Greek to you, precisely because they are written in that language. But more than that . . . " He gave a shrug that was half a sigh. "My concerns are not those of most people, I am an unusual man. I am drawn to the past, you see, the very old past, or else to the margins of current life. I am . . . oh, what is the use?" His eyes had left Morgan and were roaming beyond the corners of the room.

Morgan said again, "I very much want to read them."

"You could never understand my poetry, my dear Forster, never."

"Perhaps I might. You should try it on me at least."

"No, no, no. What is the use?" This seemed to be final, but he abruptly stood up. "Please wait," he said, "I am going to the bindery," and he disappeared into a back room.

When he reappeared soon afterwards it was with a loose-leaf folder under his arm, in which Morgan could see pages hand-written in red and black ink. But the poet didn't return to his chair. "Let us move to the red salon. The light is much better there."

The light was not better in the red salon; it was the room itself, the furnishings, that were of higher quality. There was no oil lamp here, only candles, which Cavafy began to move about in accordance with some private design. He finally appeared satisfied when he had enshrouded himself in shadow and Morgan was near the window with a fitful yellow glow to read by.

The visitor was aware of being tested. Cavafy had become bored and indifferent, which could only mean he cared deeply. But Morgan's Greek, unexercised since his days at Cambridge, didn't feel up to the task. He was imperfectly aware of the meanings he held in his hand and after a few frowning, peering minutes could offer a mere paltry observation. "There are some coincidences, perhaps, it seems to me . . . between this Greek and public school Greek. I might be wrong . . . "

The effect was instantaneous. Cavafy snapped upright in his chair, alert and awake in a moment. "Oh, but this is good, my dear Forster, very good indeed!" He began to call fretfully for his servant. "Mirgani! Come here immediately! Mirgani!"

Mirgani came and was told by his master to bring whisky.

"My glass is not yet empty," Morgan said.

"Yes, but that is the Palamas whisky. Poetry requires something better. In the red glasses, Mirgani!"

Mirgani brought good whisky in red glasses, as well as a plate of cheese and olives. Candles were being snuffed out and others lit in a fresh configuration; it was Cavafy now who was visible and his guest who had sunk into shadow. The poems, too, had changed hands.

Morgan understood that his station had altered, now that he had proved worthy. The red salon, the red glasses: they signified an uptick in esteem. He tried to disport himself accordingly. But in a moment, when the poet began to read, there was no need to pretend.

Cavafy's voice, with its cultivated English accent, was soft and certain. He was translating as he went, but it was clear that he knew his own words very well and the paper was almost unnecessary. The long, pale face, with its saurian eyelids, its air of melancholic delicacy, seemed to vanish in a moment, into a mist, through which Morgan was led, down a winding passage that took him to an image of a midnight procession, ghostly but beautiful, passing out of the Alexandrian city gates, in a time long ago that might have been no time at all.

The poem was short and its meaning out of reach, until Cavafy laconically added the title, almost as an afterthought. "The God Abandons Antony."

"From Plutarch?"

"Yes, exactly. Oh, excellent, Forster." Again there was the

note of renewed energy and interest; his guest was pleasing to him tonight. "Would you like to hear another?"

"Very much."

Another poem was read, and then another. In each of them a visit was paid to the ancient world, either through history or mythology. And in each of them the lost past was reclaimed, brought back—through an image or a sentiment or a longing—to the present. The voice of the poems, like that of their author, was restrained and spare, cold and warm at the same time, quivering with irony. Their beauty was unmistakable.

The Greek quarter, where the poet lived, was to the northeast of the main square, where Morgan's hotel was. Walking back alone through the streets later that night, Morgan felt for the first time how old the city was. It was a new awareness for him, and he hoped he wouldn't lose it. Until now, Alexandria had felt like a transient, impermanent outpost, a place for travellers and visitors and invaders, and even now—after midnight—the streets were filled with well-dressed people rushing from nowhere to nowhere. But under their feet, and around them, there wasn't much trace of ancient history to be seen. Everything was being continually smashed down and rebuilt. This was the city founded by Alexander the Great, the home of Callimachus and Theocritus, the death-place of Cleopatra. It didn't seem too much to expect remnants of the past to be standing about, as they did in India. But instead it was simply a modern cosmopolitan town, built along a limestone ridge, with sea on one side and salt marshes on the other.

Alexandria had come to seem ordinary and banal, in the way that stones and water often did. In the end, one couldn't even hate it properly.

* * *

He'd wanted to come to Egypt because it had felt like the

East. But it wasn't; it was merely the pseudo-East. He had been here for four months already, and from almost the first moment he'd arrived, the landscape seemed flat and unromantic to him, with no sense of mystery. Only at sunset did something inscrutable occasionally enter in.

Nor was he especially drawn to the Egyptians. They didn't excite the same sympathy in him that the Indians did. Everything about them—their movements, their dress, their customs—kept him at a remove rather than pulling him closer. There had been only one or two occasions (a young man on a tram, touching the buttons on the tunic of a soldier as he said goodbye) when his sexual interest had been stirred. For the most part, he felt a physical distaste for the natives. But at the same time, these feelings were repellent to him. They reminded him of nothing so much as the English in India. Who could have known that it was in him, too, this racial arrogance, this contemptible contempt? It was worse than any mud, and it unsettled him badly.

On his first arrival, there had been some talk of an invasion from Turkey, and he'd felt a little brave in consequence. But that had quickly faded, leaving only duty and routine behind. His work meant travelling around the various hospitals in Alexandria, drifting through the wards, speaking to the wounded men. He listened to their stories and made notes. Every night, at the Red Cross offices on the Place Mohammed Ali, he would type up a report to be sent to London. From there, he supposed, further steps were taken to inform families of their dead, or about where their missing sons and brothers were. His reports were dry and factual, and no doubt helpful. But it was the voices behind the reports which told a truer story:

There was this dead Australian, see, who was in the way when we were making a parapet. So we cut him at the neck and knees and fired through him.

That time we made a charge, they gave fourteen spoonfuls of rum instead of two, so we weren't afraid of anything. But the worst is when there's some delay and the mood passes. Then your heart thump thumps against the ground.

His own heart thumped as he imagined. They were so very young, most of these men, almost boys still, with a vulnerable and innocent quality. Any of them, he was sure, would have ended the fighting today if it was in their power. They had seen terrible things and perhaps done terrible things too. ("We fought every inch as dirty as the Turks did," one told him, and he knew that it was true.) More to the point, all of them, in one way or another, had had terrible things done to them. That was why they were here. Some of them had been wounded in vicious fighting, some were just very sick. Blood and pus and puke and shit: never had he been ground up so hard against the human body, its failure and breakdown and decay. He tried not to avert his eyes, but the strongest certainty he carried away from those wards was that suffering like this should be stopped now, immediately, at the cost of any humiliation.

It was not a view widely shared among other Englishmen. From his fellow Red Cross officers he heard that there were worse things than war, and that Britain's debt to gallant little Belgium had not yet been discharged. One especially offensive colonel, after listening to Morgan for a while, said sneeringly, "Well, you are clearly not cut out to be a soldier. Best you keep on with searching. You are such a wonderful *sticker*."

In fact, no staying power was required: speaking to the ordinary soldiers gave him pleasure. His Red Cross insignia provided a cover for tenderness that might otherwise have been suspect. Their talk was frank and unvarnished; idealism had been scraped off the bare facts. They had been sent to face the guns, while the gentlemen-officers, like the awful colonel, tended to linger in the rear. He thought of them as the real England; once snobbery was set aside, you saw the true qualities. He spent far more time than he needed to in their company, playing chess, writing letters for them, reading aloud or entertaining them on the piano, a couple of times even taking their watches away to be repaired. But mostly he simply listened to them, in his murmurous sidelong way, while they talked and talked about the War.

* * *

At work, he was answerable to a Miss Victoria Grant Duff, the head of the Wounded and Missing Department. She was perhaps a decade older than Morgan, and a trifle shrill and nervous, but friendly enough. They had found a common talking point in India, because her father had once been the Governor of Madras. More importantly, though, she felt enthusiastic about his reports. She had called him in after two or three weeks to tell him that London had cabled to say how good they were. "You are by far the best of my searchers," she announced.

"I am glad to hear it."

"But don't tell the others I said so."

"No, of course not."

The idea of being the best was amusing, because there were only four searchers in total. One was at the Majestic Hotel, too, where Morgan was living: a fellow named Winstanley, who told him the other searchers did almost no work. The competition couldn't be described as fierce.

Nevertheless, his position felt secure. He had already been here much longer than he planned to, and had no thought of going anywhere. He could wait out the War on the sidelines, contributing without taking part. So it came as a profound shock when—not long after his meeting with Cavafy—there was a crisis at work that nearly upset everything.

Word came through from higher up that Red Cross workers were required to attest before a military commission. What was wanted was a declaration that every able-bodied man was willing and ready to serve. It wasn't quite conscription—though that had been introduced in England three months ago—but it was a first step in that direction.

By coming here, Morgan had believed he was leaving this particular quandary behind, but now it had followed him. His own cousin, Gerald Wichelo, had recently declared himself a conscientious objector, and was prepared to go to jail in consequence. Morgan didn't know if he was quite that committed.

The crisis passed, but not before he found himself in front of Sir Courtauld Thomson, the Chief Red Cross Commissioner, stating his beliefs. This was difficult, because he wasn't quite sure what they were. Nevertheless, he found himself saying that the idea of killing another human being, whoever it might be, was the most horrible notion he could contemplate. There was nothing *religious* about this sentiment, he added; the only word he could find for it was "conscience".

After due consideration, Sir Courtauld told him, "I'm afraid conscientious objectors cannot be considered at all."

"I see," Morgan replied. "They don't exist?"

"That is not what I said." The face of his superior had grown heavy with blood.

There was every prospect, at this moment, that he would be shipped back to England to face down the issue along with cousin Gerald. But his medical examination, which had first declared him fit for service, now changed its mind. And Miss Grant Duff argued strongly on his behalf, because nobody else would do his job half as well. When the upset finally passed, instead of feeling he had courageously defended his principles, it was his cowardice that had been reinforced, at least in his own eyes. Nobody would know how, alone in his room, he had thrown himself against the furniture in despair, and once even fallen to the floor in a tantrum, or a faint.

Nevertheless, he had prevailed. He was still here. He was an artist, and artists didn't fight. They didn't harm other people. Though what they did do wasn't always clear, least of all to themselves.

* * *

He had brought his Indian novel with him and every now and then he would take it out and pick over it, moving a few stray words around. He had even read sections of it aloud to a few of his new acquaintances, hoping to rouse something in himself. But the effect was the opposite: he felt bored by what he'd imagined. The idea of sitting down to it again, in the sustained way needed to finish, was impossible. For that, he thought, he would have to go back to India.

But India had taken on an unreachable quality, like a place seen in a dream. And never more so than when—suddenly, unexpectedly—it offered itself to him.

A cable came from Dewas. His Highness, Bapu Sahib— who had been promoted from Rajah to Maharajah—needed a Private Secretary and was Morgan interested in the job? Of course, he would have to drop his war work and get on a ship immediately . . .

The invitation churned him up internally. Should he go? For a little while the temptation was immense. And in theory it was perfectly possible. He was close to Port Said, where he could pick up a passage. And the idea of moving on, eastwards, had been at the back of his mind from the outset. He had been thinking of India frequently, with soreness and longing; in his room he kept the reproduction of a Moghul miniature painting, which he often picked up and stared at, and secretly wished upon.

He didn't waver for long. He would go back to India one day, but not in the current situation. The War made it impossible. He had obligations to the Red Cross in Egypt, and to his mother back home in England.

Behind this reasoning was something he couldn't tell anybody. His relationship with India was his relationship with Masood; it was difficult to separate one love from another. He'd been feeling far from his friend lately, whose sentiments would be with Turkey, he knew, in the fight against England.

He had been very hurt by Masood in recent months. There had been almost no communication between them in a long time, and then he had learned—from his mother, of all people, who had learned it from the Morisons—that Masood had become a father. When Masood did eventually write, months after the fact, it was to apologise in his florid and evasive way for not having named the boy after Morgan, but saying that he felt his son belonged to him anyway and asking whether he would like to adopt him.

It was all so jocular and offhand, as if none of it mattered. But nothing since that terrible midnight rejection in India had undone Morgan quite so badly. He felt offended, and it took him a while to discover he was furious. He had been disappointed in Masood, but indifference and silence had now been added to the mix. He still loved his friend, and knew that he was loved in return, but what did love *mean* if it was doled out so carelessly, with no thought of consequence?

No, he couldn't return to India now. He wouldn't be going back for the sake of Bapu Sahib, but for somebody else— somebody who had become remote to him. By now Masood had left the practice of law and gone into education, and this change, Morgan knew, would distract his friend further. If they were to meet again it would have to be later, much later, when the War had run its course and the world had returned to itself. In the meanwhile, he was fated to be in Egypt, and he would have to make it his own.

* * *

For all his dislike of their company, most of his time outside working hours was spent with English officers. Every morning he walked from the Hotel Majestic on one side of the square, where he was staying, to the Red Cross offices on the other. To visit the hospitals, he travelled on the new electric trams. But he hadn't dared venture into the maze of crooked streets outside this narrow grid, where Egyptian life took place.

The long reach of Cambridge extended even this far: the person he knew best in Alexandria was Robert "Robin" Furness, whom he had met long ago at King's. Robin was head of the Press Censorship Department and Morgan had got in touch with him almost as soon as he'd arrived. The few friends that he'd made here had come to him through Robin. But his social circle remained small, and resisted his attempts to venture further.

What he really wanted was to be introduced to the more squalid precincts of the bazaar. Robin could help, if he'd wanted to; he had lived in Egypt for many years and knew most of its secrets. Before the War he had been part of the Civil Service and was fond of alluding to all the moral delinquency he'd witnessed. "Oh, oh, oh," he would sigh, covering his face with his hands. "It's beyond description. You don't want me to tell you."

Morgan *did* want him to tell, but Robin resolutely refused. Through Lytton, who interspersed each revelation with a keening castrato wail, Morgan had heard about a letter Robin had sent to Maynard Keynes from Egypt nine years ago. Robin had been an Inspector of Police then, and had spoken, Lytton said, of "various *debaucheries*. My dear, he talked of peering into catamites' anuses, if you can conceive of anything more wonderful. To say nothing of stabbed Circassian whores and conducting inquests upon worm-eaten beggars. It sounded very

heaven, let us book our passage to Alexandria immediately!"
And he shuddered in rapturous revulsion.

All this Robin would acknowledge, and remark on dryly,
but he wouldn't actually *show* any of it. The most he would do
was to take Morgan to visit the Generah, an area of the city
where prostitution was concentrated. The dark, narrow, piss-
smelling entrances, with the calling, clutching women, some of
them old and haggard, and the men skulking and prowling and
occasionally fighting: it was impressive and operatic and somehow timeless. But there was nothing here that catered to his
tastes. One particular doorway had made him hopeful,
because of the sensual lips on two young men standing outside,
but he'd been let down again. Alas, if these were the depths of
sin, he couldn't respect them much.

Through Robin, however, he made a new acquaintance, an
Egyptian man who worked for the Police Service, and this lead
was more promising. When Morgan asked to see the real
Egypt—"the dirty side of things"—the response was encouraging. Would he like to visit a hashish den one night? Yes, he
most certainly would.

In India, in Lahore, he had been taken by an American mis-
sionary to see an opium den, and had been left unsatisfied. The
place had seemed clean and ordinary to him. He expected
something similar here, but from the outset, as they left the
European quarter behind and started tacking through intricate
backstreets at the heart of a slum, the experience was gratify-
ingly sordid.

Up an unlit flight of stairs, scratch-knocking on a filthy
door at the top. It was opened just a crack by a one-eyed
Maltese man, speaking Italian. A hash den? No, he knew nothing about it; he was not even sure what the word meant.
Morgan's Egyptian friend was having none of it. They pushed
in through the door, into a long room, filled with a calm, quiet
company, all of them puffing on pipes that sent sweet smoke

coiling into the air. A tired Arab girl wandered about barefoot and on various beds and divans against the walls lounged a retinue of Egyptian youths—attendants, it seemed—who were playing cards.

Morgan and his companion settled themselves. The Maltese man, who was clearly the proprietor, came to offer them a pipe. Morgan hesitated; he wasn't averse to falling over the edge. But his friend made a sharp, dismissive gesture, and the offer went away.

Time had thickened in the dim room; nothing much happened, and it happened slowly. A tray went past with tea, another pipe was lit. Everything was sleepy and languid, yet Morgan's perception became sharpened. He was suddenly aware of closed doors nearby, from behind which inexplicable sounds drifted out, and in this moment one of the young men made a sign to him. It couldn't possibly mean what it seemed to and he didn't respond.

The young man got up and came and sat close by. He was distinctly beautiful, wearing galabeya and tarboosh, with a soft face atop a hard body, and Morgan was full of confused desire. But when he tried to speak to him in Italian, the reply came in Arabic, and they shrugged helplessly at each other. Some of the other young men, noticing their exchange, also made cryptic signs at him. But his companion, the Egyptian police official, sat in rigid puritanical disdain, and he didn't feel able to pursue his vices.

Worse, their aloofness appeared to have infected the gathering. There was a palpable air of anxiety that centred on them, made manifest in whisperings and watchfulness. When three new customers came in—Italian shop assistants, wearing straw hats—some of the boys tried to sit on their knees, but were pushed roughly away. Everybody smoked, and a slack, smiling inertia filled the room.

Then his companion stood up and, with a jerk of his head,

indicated that it was time to leave. As they descended the dark stairs, he said, "Now you have seen it. The bad life of Egypt."

Yes, he had seen it—but he hadn't tasted its badness, and he wanted to. If he'd been alone, he would have smoked; if he'd been alone, a boy could have sat on his knee. He hoped wildly for a moment that he might be able to find a way back to that room, but in the warren of streets outside he was almost instantly lost. Without a guide, he could never return.

He told Robin Furness about it a day or two later. "You see," he said, "I am reduced to doing research on my own. If you would only help me, all these secret doors might open."

Robin smiled wryly. "Well, that particular one won't. Not for you or anybody else."

"It has a regular clientele, from what I saw."

"Yes. But I heard that the proprietor of the den has been reported to his consulate. He is from Malta, I believe?"

"Yes, yes."

"The place has been closed down. The man will most likely be deported."

Morgan was sorry to hear it. He had felt curiously at home in that haunt of vice, though he had merely been a witness. And when he took his Egyptian friend to dinner a few nights later, he told him the news ruefully.

"Yes, I know," the man said, smiling with false modesty. "It was I who made the complaint."

"*You* did? But why?"

"Oh, yes, you see, it was my duty. I am a private gentleman in the evening, but a member of the administration by day. I keep the two apart."

Night selves and day selves: Morgan was outraged. He cut the evening short with an excuse and soon afterwards brought their relations to a halt.

* * *

He told Cavafy about the hash den, and the attractive young attendant he'd seen there. He chose his words with circumspection, not giving too much away, unsure of the response. He was especially careful not to describe his own feelings, though he watched the poet's reactions as he spoke. But Cavafy merely smiled gently, closed his eyes and said, "Ah."

Morgan had returned to the Rue Lepsius from time to time, for more whisky and discussion and poems. He encountered the poet sometimes in the street, on his way to or from work, and his newfound friend would always launch into an eloquent soliloquy, often on some classical theme, which seemed to presume an intimacy between them. But when Morgan attempted to build upon this closeness, he found himself kept at a distance. Cavafy was friendly and scrupulously polite, but he would never disclose anything that reflected upon his private habits. And Morgan in consequence didn't feel free either to speak about himself in too loose and easy a way.

Their evenings sometimes concluded with a reading of a poem or two, Cavafy translating with one hand raised in the air. Tonight seemed no different as Cavafy began to read, his voice perhaps a little drier than usual. But what he heard made Morgan shift in his chair. It was an account, in the first person, of an erotic encounter on a bed in a dingy room above a squalid street. There was a delicacy to the language that refrained from being too specific, too physical, and yet it was obvious that the poet was writing down a memory, or perhaps a longing. It was also almost clear that the object of the encounter was male, hiding coyly behind an absence of pronouns.

Morgan knew, of course, about Cavafy's minorism. It was evident in his fussiness, his over-refinement, but there were also rumours that the poet frequented the questionable Attarine quarter. So there was nothing especially surprising in what was described, except for the fact that it broke an unspoken agreement between them. Neither of them had mentioned, until now, what they had most deeply in common.

Cavafy cleared his throat. "And here's another," he said. "But I am still working on it. It is not yet perfect."

And he read an account, in the third person this time, of a young man going down a street, dazed from an illicit pleasure he has just enjoyed. It was a very short poem, but it seemed to press down with great force on a sore place in Morgan's mind.

A long silence followed, in which the evening bell of the nearby church could be heard. Cavafy occasionally joked that his funeral would be held there one day, but for now St Saba was merely a faint, silvery sound, already fading on the air.

Morgan said, "I should like to ask you about those poems."

His host immediately began to cough and wave his hand. "Oh, that is enough for one night," he said, laying the pages aside. "I must be boring you." And he set off on a sideways line of musing about the fall in the price of cotton that had just affected the market.

That was all. At the end of the evening, as he was readying himself to leave, Morgan had the sense of words that would not come. But he also understood that the two poems were a reply to what he had—almost—said. Cavafy seemed to be looking at him with dry amusement, or perhaps he was merely tired. The two men shook hands, and Morgan stuttered for a moment before heading into the night.

For days afterwards Morgan was tormented by the idea that, if Cavafy had visited the hash den, he would have taken that young man by the hand. They would have lain on a bed together in one of those back rooms, and afterwards the young man's beauty would have been celebrated in verse.

* * *

His loneliness was now so big that it had become his life. With it there had grown a sort of finicky distaste, so that if the experience for which he longed had actually been offered to him, he feared he might refuse it. At times, when he leaned over the soldiers in their hospital beds, the fancy came to him that if some of these men, who were good and decent sorts, only knew of the distress he was in, they would want to help him. But he could not speak, of course; he could only listen.

The earth is full of dead men. Their arms and legs stick out of the ground.

Even hearing it second-hand, the pictures became vivid to him.

When a mine explodes, they get so mixed sometimes you have to cut through corpses.

Terrible. Terrible, even to think of it. Which was as close as he would come to that reality. The theatre of war was nearer now, but still far off.

They lie between the trenches after a charge and the smell of them is awful when there's a hot sun and a bit of wind.

He thought of the bodies burning at Benares. The multiple fires, the heat of them palpable from a distance, and the smell of sandalwood and sizzling flesh: it had made the air close and unwholesome. No matter how impartial you tried to stay, your eye was always drawn with uneasy fascination to the simple, brute fact of the shrouded figure at the heart of the fire—one of which, he remembered, as its muscles contracted, gave a last animated spasm in the form of an arm lifting skywards, till an attendant beat it down with a stick.

It was no good dwelling on the dead in this way; better to fix upon the living, which even these broken soldiers still were. Most of them were here only for a week or two, and would then be shipped back into the inferno; but at least for this time they were set apart, looked after and cared for, kept between sheets. Morgan was glad to let loose his more brotherly—or were they motherly?—instincts upon them. In return, one afternoon, he was given a glimpse of something celestial, just where he least expected it.

The hospital at Montazah, out on the eastern edge of the city, had once been the Khedival palace, and it had an elegant grandeur which always pleased him. One approached from the station through avenues of flowering oleander, discovering anew each time the pleasing configuration of tiles and pergolas and Moorish arches. It was set in a garden of roses and pepper trees and groves of tamarisk, on the verge of a rocky cliff, and from the terrace of the Selamlik, the men's quarters behind the palace, was a view of the curved bay it overlooked, with its ravishing reefs and promontories and breakwaters.

He was so charmed by this prospect that it took him some time to discover the stairs in the rock that led one down. He was amazed to descend into a littoral Eden of grottoes and stones and sand, peopled by men in various stages of undress. There were hundreds of them, a small benevolent army, bare-chested and bare-legged, many of them completely naked, playing games, swimming, fishing, wrestling, talking, listening to little impromptu bands play music, swinging in hammocks, some of them—like him—just wandering aimlessly. None of them paid him any mind; they were too much inside their own bodies. It was a paradisal vision, and he was most stunned by it when, at sunset, he came to the crest of a wooded knoll, a vast ring of men encircling it like a crown. Among the purple shadows and the orange flecks of light, their brown skin glowed like a heated metal, accentuated by the blue of their linen shorts, the delicate mauve of their shirts.

He returned soon afterwards, and soon after that again. The place never failed to astonish him, but was always most exceptional in that sunset hour, when its colours bloomed fully.

On one such occasion he was alone on the deserted beach and felt sufficiently emboldened to set his uniform aside. So he found himself standing waist-deep in the water in his drawers when a young soldier rode up on a donkey and stopped near him to undress. Morgan watched as the naked man strained to pull the animal into the water with him, while it pulled the other way in resistance. The donkey won, but from the trembling tension of their equal moments he took the memory of red light on muscle, and ripples like feathers on the sand. It was a painting, a nude that had come to life, its beauty created solely for him.

* * *

On a breakwater there one day he overheard a snatch of conversation that gave him pause. After a few steps, he returned.

"Which of you is from the Royal West Kent?"

"All of us, sir."

"Do you happen to know Kenneth Searight?"

An instant clamour of approval. Yes, they knew him! The friendliest officer in the regiment by far! The other officers weren't nearly so kind to the men, not like he was! He was a fine fellow!

"He's not here with you, by any chance?"

No, no, he was in Mesopotamia. He was safe in Mesopotamia, causing trouble. They themselves had been fighting in Turkey.

One of the men, who had been watching slyly from the side, asked him, "Where do you know the captain from, sir?"

"Oh . . . We met on board ship once. On the way to India . . . "

His voice trailed off, into a memory of that conversation: the sea shining in the background, the smell of Arabia in the air. And the words; the unlikely words. *I blame it on the heat.* And Morgan had gone to India, and the heat had not undone him. He had remained respectable.

He thought now of having to admit this to Searight, if they were ever to meet again. Other people might have to confess their sins, but he, Morgan, could only confess their absence. It was a strange involution, and one which caused him peculiar shame.

With this on his mind, he stumbled on from the friendly colloquy on the breakwater, into the more opaque complications of the bay. It was near the middle of the day and the heat was intense. The rocks, the trees, could be an obstacle here, especially at high tide. What he'd thought of as a passage turned into a cul-de-sac and he was just considering turning back when he saw that he wasn't alone.

A young man, a soldier—his arm tied in bandages—was urinating against the base of a tree. He was wearing short trousers, which he had opened for the purpose, but he didn't quite close them when he was done. He engaged Morgan with a stare that might have been hostile.

"You spoke to me," he said.

"I beg your pardon, I didn't say anything."

"In the ward, the other day, you remember?"

He was so far out of his normal world that it took a moment to return: of course, he had interviewed this man the previous week. He couldn't quite recall his story; the fellow hadn't made much impression. Mackenzie, was it? Or Dodds? Injured in a charge? There were some you didn't notice—though the man was noticeable now, standing so tense and still, looking angry.

"What are you doing here?"

"I was trying to find a way through," Morgan said.

"No way through here."

"Yes, I see that now."

They regarded each other silently for a moment. Dodds, or Mackenzie, had a sandy look to him, his hair short and gingery, face smattered with freckles.

"And you?" Morgan asked.

"What about me?"

"What are you doing here?"

"Oh, I'm looking about, looking about."

"Looking for what?"

"Looking for trouble," the man said, and smiled. He seemed less angry now, or perhaps it was just a softening of the light. "You'd be surprised at what you can find. Come and see."

Morgan followed him, into a twist and curve in the rock, to where the sea and the bend of the bay were out of sight. It was dank and cold here, in this cleft, and there was no sign of the trouble the man had mentioned—unless it was in the way he had turned and was plucking suddenly at the front of Morgan's tunic.

It was distinctly alarming, and one's voice did not hold steady. "What do you *want*?"

"Only what you do."

"I don't understand."

"No? Really not? Because . . . when I saw you . . . in the hospital . . . I thought you did. I thought I could see . . . in your eyes . . . "

He was searching Morgan's gaze now, as if to find again what he'd spotted there. But the real discovery was lower down, in what his flickering fingertips confirmed.

"Yes, that's better. I knew I wasn't mistaken."

"Oh, I see. Dear Lord."

Both of them saw now. There was no more doubt. With renewed certainty, the man was pushing Morgan's shoulders down, so that he could face the problem at eye-level.

The long curve of the bay, bathed in clear light, had always seemed innocent to him, so that his own desire was the enemy, an intruder who had slipped through in disguise—yet here it was, reflected back at him in the body of another. It didn't seem possible that he was holding a penis, not his own, in his hand. The heat and feel of it were shocking; and its primitive, root-like appearance seemed inhuman. The world was suddenly removed from him, abstracted, dreamy. He knew at the same time that this was the realest moment of his life.

There was no doubting the direction the man's hands were pushing him in, and he didn't resist, though for a second he wanted to, while his brain threw out schoolboy words that named, and could not name, the thing that was now in his mouth. Touching himself, as a child, he'd called his *dirty trick*, and he'd prayed every night to be rid of it. He thought about his mother and then his mind flew back to the baths in Eastbourne, jostling against the rubbery bodies of the other boys, the mockery they'd flung at him. *Have you seen Forster's cock, a beastly little brown thing.* The jeering had felt like a judgement, infusing every moment of desire since, so that he stood apart from himself and couldn't act. That wasn't the case now. No, his body had taken him with it, he'd failed to subdue its will, it was a creature with a life of its own—and never more so than at this present moment, when it was flooded, very suddenly, with an unpleasant taste, sharp and medicinal and strange.

All over in a moment. Then the man was buttoning himself and moving away, half polite and half fearful, saying, "Thank you, sir . . . if you'd just wait . . . let me go first . . . "

Leaving Morgan staggering to his feet, his khaki trousers soaked to the knees, scooping up salt water to clean out his mouth. If they could have seen him doing . . . what he'd just done, his mother, oh how terrible, or Maimie or Aunt Laura, any of the old, powdery, frangible halo of women who encircled him, there would be no words. All of them would understand, as he did now, that he had crossed a line in himself, he had left their world behind, the decent world of tea parties and suburban witticisms. Of *telegrams and anger.*

When he reeled out again, into the sunlight, he was certain that everybody would be staring at him. Everybody would *know*. It was a second, slow shock to discover that the universe had continued in his absence, indifferent to his transgression. Some men were throwing a ball to each other and when it landed near him he picked it up and tossed it back to them. Not one of them gave him a second glance. At the base of the stairs that went up the cliff he saw somebody he recognised, and they greeted each other in a friendly way. Nobody called out his name; nobody pointed at him; nobody accused.

Nevertheless, the fear he hadn't felt in the moment came to him now. Halfway up, his knees wouldn't bend properly and he felt a little faint. He began to perspire heavily. Crouching down to recover, keeping his head low, he whispered it to himself, not quite believing it was true: "It has happened . . . It has happened . . . "

He was thirty-seven years old.

* * *

In the days that followed, the strongest residual feeling was sadness. There was no remorse. If he had only been able to take this step, he thought, at the normal age—when one was young, excited, eager—he might have had remorse and more happiness. But by now something had run its course in him; he was tied to a life of the spirit, a cold, lopsided, inward life, rather than the body. (Why did people believe it was only the flesh that binds?)

In any event, the hunger wasn't satisfied. Even in one's most physical moments, the real craving was for love. Those few fumbling seconds at the edge of the sea: they had given him something and then immediately taken it away. There had been no opportunity to converse; for God's sake, he didn't even know the man's *name*.

Nor did the sadness depart. It shaded off into a general gloom, a vague feeling of incompetence, which took specific form in a bout of vomiting at a dinner party. Thankfully, this could be diagnosed: he was told he had jaundice, and he was sent to stay at the officers' quarters in the General Hospital to recover. But although the sickness passed, the spiritual malaise did not.

He had been in Egypt for a year and a half, but he still hadn't learned to like it. There were some nights, coming back to his room alone, when a weariness seized hold of him. *Will it always be like this?* he wondered. Day after day, the level sameness of events. A numbing round of habit with no feeling inside it. He feared at certain moments that the only new knowledge he would take away from this country was learning how to swim and use the telephone.

By now he was in lodgings; through a friend, he had been put in touch with Irene, who was Greek but spoke Italian, and owned two boarding houses in Ramleh, in the east of the city, where most of the expatriate community lived. His work had taken him there almost daily, because some of the larger buildings had been commissioned by the Red Cross as hospitals. Now his journey was in the other direction: back to St Mark's Square, where his reports had to be written and handed in.

Riding on the trams was mostly tedious: lost time, which would never come back. But on one of these journeys, going home on a cold night in January of 1917, he lifted from a murky sea-bed in himself to an awareness that a young man was leaning over him. He was wearing a conductor's uniform and Morgan began searching for his ticket, but the man held up his hand.

"Excuse, please," he said. "I am asking you to rise."

"I beg your pardon?"

"My coat is under your seat. I am sorry to disturb."

He got up hurriedly, so that the young man could retrieve his coat. As he put it on, Morgan said to him, "Yes, it's cold," and they smiled at each other.

They were almost at Saba Pasha, where his journey would end, but in the remaining minutes Morgan realised several things. He was the only passenger left and he had been so sunk into his mood that he hadn't recognised his new acquaintance, but now he remembered that they had seen each other before. The first occasion had been half a year ago, when from the platform he had noticed a handsome dark head passing, a white flash of teeth under a red tarboosh, and thought: *nice*. The morning had been sunny and its freshness enlivened by this transient glimpse of beauty.

He had looked for the young man since, and had noticed a delicacy to the way he performed his duties: stepping between the feet of the passengers, rather than treading on them as the other conductors did. There was a delicacy, too, to the moment when he was saying goodbye to a soldier-friend at the terminus. Framed in the doorway of the tram, the farewell had taken a sensual form: the conductor had lingeringly touched each button on the soldier's tunic, almost as if he were playing an instrument.

Thus a particular face rises out of a crowd. What Morgan felt couldn't be spoken; instead he'd felt the need to speak in crass generalities. He was with Robin Furness at the time, and had said to him, "That boy has some African . . . that is, negro blood."

Robin nodded slowly, looking sidelong at his friend. "Yes," he said thoughtfully.

These memories, slightly shameful, returned to Morgan now, along with a new awareness of the face in front of him: young—perhaps still in his teens—with a well-shaped round head, full lips and emotional dark eyes. It is always an attractive moment when curiosity takes hold and he saw that happen now, at the same time that it happened to him. But there was nothing else he could think of to say, so they merely nodded at each other before the young man went to rejoin two other conductors riding on the footboard. Once or twice they glanced towards each other, before looking sharply away.

The next day Morgan waited for his new acquaintance at the terminus, a copy of *Punch* under his arm. He had some half-conceived plan that the pictures inside might start up a proper conversation between them. But he couldn't find him, and it was only a few days later, in a press of people, that they happened to pass again. The Egyptian half-saluted, it might have been ironically, and the Englishman half-waved in return.

Now his interest was truly awoken. He loitered at the terminus for hours, waiting for an opportunity. But he had no luck, and it was only by chance that he found himself riding the right tram again one evening. They immediately watched each other. When Morgan tried to pay his fare, a hand was held up in refusal. "No, no," he was told. "It cannot happen."

"But why not?"

"You shall never pay. If you do not want that piaster in your hand, throw it into the road or give it to some poor person as a charitable action. I will not have it."

"Why are you being so kind to me?"

"I like your good manners. The way you have thanked me, I am gratitude to you."

Morgan could not remember ever thanking him, but he didn't say so. "What is your name?" he asked.

"I am Mohammed el-Adl." It was said with a sort of defensive pride. Morgan waited for the same question to be asked of him, but it didn't come.

"You talk English," he said at last.

"A little, only. Practice makes perfect."

"Well, you are far better than me. I have no Arabic. I wish I could talk Arabic."

"Why?"

He didn't know what to say, and picked a reply at random.

"To read the *Elf Lela wah Lela*." The Thousand and One Nights.

"Oh, they were written by a famous philosopher. Am I right?"

He was wrong, but it was their first conversation, and Morgan felt disinclined to correct him. The encounter stuck into him like a splinter, a small, sharp, persistent pain. Out of all the nameless crowds around him, there was one Egyptian now who had been singled out.

He began to stand amidst the roar and the rumble at the Ramleh Terminus, sometimes for almost an hour, till the tram he was waiting for drew into the swirl. It gave him a mix of excitement and panic to see the head of Mohammed el-Adl bowed over his account book as he went into the office, and to notice his number, eighty-six, on a little white-and-blue oval plaque that he had to present inside.

When he contrived to bump into his new friend again, he was asked, "You are looking for me?"

"Yes."

"I will tell you exactly." And all the necessary information was conveyed—which tram routes, what times of day. "But if you ride with me, you shall never pay!"

* * *

The question of payment didn't go away. Soon afterwards, riding the tram with Mohammed, Morgan offered him a cigarette. "I seldom smoke," the young man said, gently accepting. "My Ministry of Finance does not permit me."

He had spoken with humour, but the words bothered Morgan. They seemed to conceal an opposite suggestion. Did he want money? Did that account for his interest in the first place?

"Today," Morgan told him, "I am paying for my ticket. And you must keep the change."

But Mohammed closed his hand. The coins fell and scattered on the floor, and it was Morgan who ended on his knees, retrieving them. This time the young man accepted them, and they jingled in his pocket as he rode sulkily on.

"There you are," Morgan said. "Now you can buy yourself an English book."

"The sum is too small for a book."

This reply obscured the matter further. There was obviously a great financial gap between them, and Morgan was on the better side. The next time that he took the tram and Mohammed refused his fare, he accepted the kindness with a nod.

On the way to the Red Cross Hospital one morning, the young conductor said, "I want to ask you a question about Mohammedans, which please answer truly, sir."

"I'll try."

But the tram was already arriving, and the rest of the conversation was delayed till the evening.

"I want to ask you this. Why do English people hate Mohammedans?"

Morgan saw another face—Masood's—in front of him for an instant. "But they don't," he said.

"They do, because I heard one soldier say to another in the tram, 'that's a mosque for fucking (I beg your pardon) Mohammedans'."

"They were joking, I think."

"You think. You are not sure."

"No, I am sure." It seemed a good moment to make a point. "One of my greatest friends is a Mohammedan. I went to India to see him."

The conductor nodded carefully. "That must have cost much money," he observed, then added: "With what you spent seeing your friend, you could have bought many friends in England. You can get friends if you have money—except one or two."

Money again. The young man seemed to be genuine, but what if his affections were for sale? It would tarnish every word that had passed between them.

An incident which occurred soon afterwards, however, pushed Morgan's doubts aside. An inspector climbed onto the tram a little while after he did and asked to see his ticket. Mohammed spoke to the man in Arabic, and a heated exchange followed. When things cooled down again, Morgan asked what was happening.

"I have told him you have authorisation from the Station Manager."

"But that isn't true."

"I find a certain amount of lies necessary to life."

This reply silenced Morgan, but at the next stop the inspector halted the tram while he climbed down and telephoned back to the station. Another explosive row ensued before the man waved the tram on, leaving Morgan alone with his friend.

After the shouting, the silence seemed big.

"Is everything all right? I knew I should pay for my ticket."

The dark eyes of the conductor were a little darker, but otherwise his expression was serene. "I am to get the sack," he told Morgan.

"What?" He peered into the young man's face, hoping that he was joking. "But this is too awful, too appalling . . . "

"Why so? I have performed a good action."

The answer was given with perfect sincerity. In a moment Morgan saw his new friend differently. Mohammed stood to lose his livelihood, and he wasn't appealing to the Englishman for help. On the contrary, he seemed to want to comfort him. Seeing Morgan's distress, he said innocently, "Please answer me one question. When you went to India, how many miles was it?"

"I don't know or care!" His mind was scrabbling for purchase in a new, uncharted territory. "Whenever shall I see you again?"

The conductor thought the question over. "I might try to meet you one evening. In my civil clothes, perhaps."

Flustered, feeling dizzy, Morgan alighted from the tram. Watching it recede from him, carrying the small, dark figure that stood out now from all others, he was awash in emotions, none of them happy. What had he been playing at, accepting charity from somebody poorer and weaker than himself? In a whimsical, half-asleep way, he had brought about a great calamity for this young man, whose welfare he'd wanted to care for.

He went to see Robin Furness the next morning. Furness knew a great many people; if anybody could suggest a solution, it would be Robin. Though it had to be approached delicately. A great deal between the two men was understood, but not explicitly. One could easily be too blunt about these matters.

So Morgan spoke about the fine young fellow he'd met on the tram, and how much better he was than the usual examples of his class, and the kindness he'd tried to show by not letting him pay; and how he, Morgan, had taken an interest—perhaps misguidedly—in him, though not of course in any inappropriate way; and how the best intentions had somehow gone awry and led to this terrible misunderstanding . . . And when the situation—haltingly and evasively—had been made plain, Robin nodded.

"As it happens," he said, "I know the Station Manager and I'm going to be seeing him later. Even better, he owes me a favour. I'll speak to him and let you know what he says."

"Oh. But that's splendid. Perhaps it can all be settled then."

"Perhaps it can." Robin shifted behind his desk, not quite meeting Morgan's eyes.

By midday, a note was brought to Morgan at the Red Cross offices. All was well, it told him; but in any event Robin would like to see him that evening at the club to talk the matter through.

Morgan was elated. He had done something for his new friend! And his gratitude to Robin was correspondingly voluble. It was such a kind deed, and really it was a favour to Morgan, not to the tram conductor, whom Robin had never met, and if there were ever an opportunity for him, Morgan, to repay the generosity, Robin had only to say the word. The British Empire was at its best under men like him, and all its injustices were somehow made invalid when the right thing was done . . .

Tall and dry, composed of jointed segments like a large, untidy bird, Robin seemed always uncomfortable, but more than usually so at this moment. "Yes, yes, quite so, it's good of you to say it." He waved a big hand in dismissal. "However, Morgan . . . "

"Yes?"

He had become serious. "It's not for me to advise you, of course. I'm sure you can take care of yourself. But in matters like these, where there is such a difference in every way, you know, class and worldview and all that, I'm sure you understand . . . "

"I'm sure I do."

"One can't be too careful. People talk, you know, people notice. One has to observe the proprieties. I'm as enthusiastic as you are, naturally, about somebody like this fellow, who tries to rise above his position. But you can't always believe what you're told. He was never going to get the sack, for one thing. He was merely going to be fined."

"I think that's a problem of language, Robin. His English isn't excellent."

"Yes, perhaps. But how do you know he wasn't deceiving you?"

"A fine for somebody in his position is bad enough."

"I take your point. But do you take mine? I'm only saying that perhaps you ought to find out more." He considered

Morgan over the rim of his brandy glass. "Perhaps you ought to learn a *lot* more about him before you think of . . . showing an interest. One knows nothing about these people. They present a friendly face and one wants to believe it, but, you know, a situation can develop. Like this one, which has happily been resolved, of course, but next time . . . "

"Next time may not be so simple."

"Quite so. I do hope you understand that I speak to you as a friend. At the very least, Morgan, I think you should refrain from travelling on this man's tram. You have got him out of a tight spot and that's enough. Perhaps later you can resume the acquaintance, but for the moment . . . "

He felt sobered by the warning. And for a few hours afterwards, he contemplated its implications. Robin had got the wind up, and had put the wind up him.

But he felt this way only briefly. The next day, through all his hours of work, he kept thinking about Mohammed, remembering the calmness of his face as he'd said that he'd performed a good action. The qualities he'd seen in him didn't belong with Robin's warning. No, Mohammed wasn't a deceiver; he was the missing piece of Egypt that Morgan had been longing for and, if he gave in now to his fears, this one chance would pass him by.

So it was with relief and a curious sense of pride that he boarded the tram that evening. The two of them looked at each other and smiled; something had been agreed between them.

"Did you speak to the Manager?" Mohammed asked immediately.

"No, I didn't."

"But the problem is disappear."

"Yes, I know."

Mohammed might have asked more, but there were a few other passengers and he was kept busy for the first part of the journey. When the car was emptier, he moved towards Morgan and sat on the seat beside him. Their thighs, in their respective khaki uniforms, pressed momentarily together.

"I want to see you after work," Morgan said. "Will you meet with me?"

The reply was soft but vehement. "Any time, any place, any hour!"

Six words that struck him like a slap. He was so filled with feeling that he got off the tram at Sidi Gaber, several stops early, and had to stumble home on foot through the dark.

* * *

It was with deep anxiety that he waited on the Sunday evening in Mazarita. He kept taking out the tram ticket, on the back of which he'd written directions, in order to read them again. People were pushing past, and a minute of confusion followed before he understood that the quiet, smart figure standing close by was Mohammed.

They hadn't recognised each other because for the first time neither was in uniform: Morgan wore tennis whites, which for some reason had seemed appropriate, and the Egyptian a dark coat, white flannel trousers and gym shoes. He also had on a pair of spectacles, which changed the shape of his face. They had stepped outside the world in which they'd met, and both of them were curiously shy.

For the first few moments they didn't know where to go. Then Mohammed said, "Let us go and sit in Chatby Gardens." As they started to walk, he added nervously, "I call them Chatby Gardens because they are near Chatby. I give them that name— it may not be their name. I give all sorts of things a name."

They were only the Municipal Gardens. It was a good place to be, because it was unlikely that other Europeans might see them there. Both of them were scratchily uneasy to begin with. They pretended to be interested in the pink Ptolemaic column at the western end, and the lion-headed statues beside it. But as they walked in the last sunshine, between the remnants of old Arab walls, a genuine lightness took hold of Morgan. Why couldn't life always be this easy and this free? If you wanted to meet your friend, you simply met him, and what did it matter if he was from another race and class, and the social gulf was huge?

But of course it *did* matter, and when he took out a bag of sticky cakes he'd bought, thinking them a nice gift, Mohammed became sullen and suspicious.

"I don't like cakes," he said, tasting the edge of one nevertheless. "What did you pay for them?"

"I really don't remember."

"No? How many centuries ago did you buy them?"

"Why does it matter what I paid?"

"Because next time you will put me to similar expense."

"There is a Greek proverb you should know. 'The possessions of friends are in common.' I believe that."

"I do not. I have many friends, but what is theirs belongs to them. You cannot have everything."

"You are angry today."

"No, I am not angry. I am only different to you. You are a gentleman, but look at me. Even a butcher's son . . . " His voice trailed off. It was almost dark by now. As they settled themselves on a bench at the edge of a pond, Mohammed told him, very seriously, "I am still only a boy."

By now Morgan had sensed his fear: sensed it almost with gratitude. They were not so unalike, after all! Butcher's son and gentleman—they were both human and afraid, and enjoying the warm evening together.

"Well," Morgan said. "You are a *gentle* boy."

Mohammed smiled. The right words had been spoken at last, and they began to converse in a more natural, less guarded way. On the last few occasions they'd seen each other, on the tram, Morgan had been overcome with sensual feeling, but it wasn't like that today. He was fascinated instead by his friend's character and talk. Desire was shading off into interest; the two men turned gradually towards each other on the bench, shifting a little closer.

Then Mohammed seemed to make a decision. He said suddenly, "Do you want to see my Home of Misery? It will be *dreadful*."

Morgan fetched up one of his deeply wrung laughs, a spasm more like agony than mirth. "I would like that very much."

On the tram ride Mohammed was in festive mood, doling out the sticky cakes to the other passengers and joking with them. But in the narrow, dirty streets of Bargos, his neighbourhood, he became quieter. The Home of Misery turned out to be hardly more than a room, very bare, very basic, with a bed and a wooden trunk. A lamp threw big rippling shadows on the wall. Mohammed looked anxiously at his guest, but Morgan was cheerful. "I see no misery," he said.

"You are lying, I think."

"What did you say to me on the tram? A certain amount of lies . . . "

" . . . is necessary to life. Yes, please, sit."

They sat on the bed. A plate of food—dates and bread—was produced and set down between them. As they chatted and ate, Mohammed slowly relaxed. Questions at this stage were all from the English side, but the answers became fuller and less reserved. Morgan learned that Mohammed was about eighteen, but his parents were illiterate and the date of his birth had never been recorded. He'd been taught English at the American Mission school. His family continued to live where he'd been born, in a town in the Nile Delta called Mansourah. He spoke warmly about his mother and brother, but he was frank in his dislike of his father, as well as his father's new wife and family.

"I have always ate apart and lived apart and thought apart. Perhaps I am not my father's son."

Morgan smiled. "That is always possible. But you will find out in time, if you inherit your father's face."

"Hmm, perhaps, but I do not find rules useful. All is exceptions in men as in English grammar."

Morgan was charmed by these eccentric phrases, their oddness renewing the sound of his own language for him, as well as illuminating their speaker. He was beginning to see Mohammed differently. He hadn't expected the intelligence or humour he was discovering, nor the honesty that now suddenly showed itself.

"I will tell you something. Until this moment I did not trust you. But my mind is change, I want to show you everything."

He jumped up to his feet and flung open his little wooden trunk. He began to throw out his belongings, item by item, onto the bed, naming each one as he did so, sounding almost angry.

"My notebook, my pen. My bible, although I do not follow religion any more. My father told me it would be shameful to leave the religion in which I was brought up, but I did not refuse for so foolish a reason, but because I did not like Christianity. And here are my clothes. Not many of them. Here is my conductor's badge, which you have seen already many times. Here is my needle and thread. And this is lip salve."

He tilted the trunk so that Morgan could see it was empty.

"Not much, but all clean," he said defiantly. "Now I have shown you all there is to show."

* * *

It was only at the end of their second meeting a few weeks later, as they parted at the station, that Mohammed said, "I have the honour to ask your name."

"Edward Morgan Forster."

"Forster. I am happy to meet you."

From that moment on, Mohammed called him by his surname. In the beginning it seemed like a liberty, and Morgan was almost offended. But then he decided that it was a sign of equality between them, and he became pleased.

Thus far, relations between the two men had followed a familiar pattern. Raw physical yearning had been covered over with restraint, and their meetings were in danger of becoming permanently respectable. But Morgan was more preoccupied than ever by sexual thoughts, which disordered the normal workings of his mind. He wanted to live like one of the young men Cavafy described in his poems, who indulged his desires without guilt. He was very far from everything that mattered, on the fringes of events; there was nobody to see him, to report him to his mother or cause a fuss. But if he didn't *do* something, their friendship would remain forever frozen like this between decorum and fear.

The trouble was, he didn't know how to go about it. In his mind, he dwelt often on the encounter he'd had on the beach at Montazah. But that had happened wordlessly, in accordance with laws that he didn't understand, and he couldn't approach Mohammed in the same way. For one thing, at the Home of Misery he felt too out of place, too uncertain of himself, to try to set a seduction in motion.

The best option might be to attempt something in his own rooms. Though that, too, was not a straightforward proposition. His landlady, Irene, could be overbearing: she continually thrust her head around the door to see what he was doing and was full of intrusive advice about what sort of people he ought to be mixing with. She liked Morgan and thought well of him and the idea of disappointing her was overwhelming. It was unthinkable that he should bring Mohammed there when Irene was at home.

But after a while, fate threw an opportunity in his path. Irene had two boarding houses, in Camp de César and in Saba Pasha, and it was her habit to move from one to the other, according to the whim of the week. She liked Morgan to accompany her each time, so that he sometimes felt like a doll being carried about. But on this occasion, when she tried to get him to move, he refused. There was a small crisis between them, till eventually she gave up.

Immediately he invited Mohammed to visit him at home. It was so simple, so easy, yet once the arrangement had been made, he suffered through waves of apprehension and longing. It wasn't enough only to have the opportunity; he now had to act on it.

On the evening in question, nothing felt sure any more. He met Mohammed at the station and walked him to the house and, as they drew closer, Morgan began to worry. By the time they came to the front door, he was almost stammering with anxiety.

Once they were indoors, he calmed. Nobody had seen them, and the world outside continued in its usual way. In the end they were just two people in a room.

"*My* Home of . . . I don't know what." Morgan had always thought of it as spare, but from the paintings on the wall, to the carpets on the floor, to the view from the window, there was nothing miserable about it. "Comfortable loneliness, perhaps."

"You are loneliness?"

"Sometimes."

Mohammed seemed unable to settle, wandering around the room, picking up objects and setting them down again. He was frowning.

One of the objects, at least, provided a way forward. "Do you play chess?"

"A little."

"Shall we have a game then?"

They settled themselves on the red bedspread with the board between them. Morgan kept looking at his friend. It seemed astonishing that he was here—a young Egyptian tram conductor—in his room. The game was an abstraction; it was this other presence, lying close by, that had substance.

He felt both cold and hot with fear. It was clear to him that the first move had to be his. The difference in their social standing, combined with Mohammed's pride, meant that nothing would come from the other side. Though he thought that the Egyptian might respond to a physical overture. When they had bumped against each other accidentally in the past, Mohammed hadn't pulled away. More interestingly, he kept his hands in his pockets for the first few minutes whenever they met, and Morgan suspected that he was concealing his arousal. So the signs were propitious.

This was the moment. He had to take steps, but he didn't know what they should be. How did other people—Cavafy, Searight, Carpenter—how did they know what to do? What the right words were to speak? It was probably best simply to submit to desire, and let the body follow. Even if it was trembling, and its heartbeat seemed to fill the room.

Now a peculiar ritual started, not unlike the strategic dance of the pieces on the board. In reaching for a pawn, Morgan touched his friend's knee and let his fingers linger. If there had been the slightest recoil, the smallest shrug, he would have withdrawn, but instead Mohammed inclined towards him. It was all right; he could proceed.

He lifted his hand to stroke Mohammed's hair. The feel of it was very distinct, as if his sense of touch had been magnified. He was frightened, because he couldn't pretend that his interest was casual. If there was cruelty, it would come now.

Mohammed said something.

"What was that? I didn't hear you."

"I said—short hair. But crisp."

His voice sounded strangled. "I like your hair."

"No. Yours is better." Mohammed's hand lifted now, to touch Morgan's head in turn. Barriers were falling down; huge distances were vanishing. "Beautiful hair," he said.

"No."

"Yes. I'm happy . . ."

"And I."

They were sinking down now, into a simulation of tiredness, though Morgan had never been so awake. He found himself lying on Mohammed's arm. It was clear to him that this moment had always been waiting for him, just below the surface of his life, pulling him towards it through all his empty years. He was blank with terror, yet nothing was required of him except that he follow the actions that had long been prepared for him and had been stored here all this time, ready for him to take them up. Leaning forward, closing his eyes. Pressing his lips against those of his friend. Becoming aware of sensory impressions: the faint taste of tobacco. The dry texture of skin. Thinking: *not since Hom. Not even close. Kissing.*

He was kissing Mohammed.

As if this were entirely natural, they pulled back from each other a little and smiled. But excitement overran all his reserve and Morgan couldn't hold himself back. He shifted his position and the chess board overturned, all the pieces sliding and skidding.

"What are you doing?"

"How fond of me are you?"

"What do you mean?"

Feeling dizzy, he reached down to unbutton his friend's trousers. There was no resistance at first and they both looked down, almost in shock, at the shape of his erection, straining under the thin cotton layer of an undergarment.

Morgan was unbuttoning his own trousers now.

"Hmm," Mohammed said. His hand had moved to cover

himself. "My damned prick stands up, whoever it is," he said. "It means nothing."

He sounded almost bored and had started to do up his buttons again. Morgan reached to stop him and he made a sudden movement, its vehemence at odds with the calm tone of his voice.

"You hurt my hand."

Mohammed didn't answer. The mood between them had changed into crossness and bafflement. And the pain in Morgan's hand wasn't small. But more painful was the idea that this moment had closed to him and would never open again. He tried to reach for his friend's face and the defensive movement, so sudden and violent, was repeated. This time he felt a fingernail catching on something.

"Now you have hurt me too."

"It wasn't intentional. It was you who . . . Oh, you're bleeding."

He had torn a soft place close to Mohammed's eye. The nick was small, but the blood flowed freely. It gave a new focus to the two men, who might otherwise have become knotted up in embarrassment. They got off the bed and fussed around the wash-basin. All the tenderness of a few minutes before had become displaced into clinical ministrations with water and cotton wool. Neither of them mentioned what had happened and, not long afterwards, Mohammed said that it was best for him to go.

Morgan walked to the station with him and though he tried to make jolly small talk along the way, a silence had set in. Their parting was polite and the resultant misery immense. On the walk back to the room, Morgan noticed, as he hadn't for some time, the hugeness of the sky overhead, the prominence of the stars. You would never see a sky like this in England, and he experienced anew his dislocation from home.

It was finished; he was certain of it. He'd made a hash of his seduction attempt, and everything was ruined. He thought of

Mohammed as superstitious and no doubt the fact that he'd drawn blood would count against him. It remained only to make his apologies and afterwards to keep his distance.

* * *

But when he climbed onto Mohammed's tram in the morning, there was no trace of last night's heavy emotions. He was greeted with a smile and, once the tram had emptied a little, the conductor came over to sit with him.

"How is your hand?"

"My hand is bruised still, but it will heal. How is your eye?"

He turned his head to show Morgan. The scratch was still visible, but in daylight it didn't look like much.

"I am very sorry I hurt you."

"It is nothing. Do you want to meet at the Nouzha Gardens on Sunday?"

It was as if no mishap had occurred. Indeed, the agreement between them appeared to have taken root.

Over the weeks that followed, they didn't see each other often. Because of the long shifts that Mohammed worked, at most a couple of hours a week were possible. When they met in public they always travelled separately to and from their rendezvous, and always in civilian clothes. These precautions might not save them, but they minimised the danger of detection. They were both aware of breaking a powerful rule, and it made Morgan feel guilty and excited.

And yet, he wondered in frustration, what were they actually *doing*? Even in their few moments alone, their crimes were not great. Sometimes they caressed each other; occasionally they kissed. For some reason, these demonstrations of affection were acceptable to Mohammed, though the sexual ones were not. But what felt like the most flagrant offence didn't lie in any specific action rather than in what was underneath it.

That they cared for one another, that they enjoyed each other's company and spoke openly to one another, without awkwardness or barrier: that was the great sin. No emotion was supposed to cross the great divide of class. Affection could erase all hierarchy; in this was the danger, and the delight.

A moment that moved Morgan deeply, for example, came when Mohammed criticised his clothes. Taking him disdainfully by the sleeve, he turned Morgan around for his inspection, tutting all the time. "You know, Forster, though I am poorer than you, I would never be seen in such a coat. I am not blaming you, no, I praise, but I would never be seen . . . and your hat has a hole and your boot has a hole and your socks have a hole."

Morgan was thrilled. "I shall try to do better," he said.

"No, no. Good clothes are an infectious disease. I had much better not care and look like you, and so perhaps I will, but not in Alexandria."

Why did this admonishment make him so happy? Because it was true—but truer still was the warmth of feeling from whence it sprang. Here at last was the brother for whom he'd longed, finding loving fault with him.

More tryingly, the matter of sex continued to eat at him. He was allowed to caress his friend, but when his hand wandered too low, or too high, it was instantly stopped. "Never! Never!" Morgan was made ashamed by these refusals, because he assumed that Mohammed was nobler than himself.

So he was astonished to find out in casual conversation one day that his friend had engaged in physical relations with men in the past.

"Friendship can make me excited," he said simply. "Or if I am feeling kind. Usually I do nothing, but if the other person is beautiful, or I start to imagine, then sometimes I do more." After a moment, he added, "And sometimes I have done it for money."

"What do you mean?"

"You know very well what I mean. There is no need to explain. Older men will pay for enjoyment. And sometimes, if it is a secret, it is easy to ask for money."

"You're talking about blackmail."

"Yes. I did this in my younger years. But for some reason, I started to imagine myself in other people's place. And I addressed myself, saying, 'you would not like it if such things were done to you.' So I stopped."

In the silence that followed, Morgan felt mystification, not jealousy. Finally he asked, "But then why will you not, with me . . . ?"

"Oh, Forster, Forster. Do you not understand?" Mohammed turned his head away. His voice became very soft. "I want to ask you a question. Do you never consider that your wish has led you to know a tram conductor? And do you not think that a pity for you and a disgrace? While answering my questions you are not to look at me."

Morgan turned his head away. He did, finally, understand. Mohammed respected him, and his physical desires made him abject in his Egyptian friend's eyes.

The two men lay next to each other, gazing in different directions.

"I don't care that you are a tram conductor."

"Do you only like me because I am a boy?"

"I like you because you are Mohammed."

* * *

There was no point in deluding oneself. Mohammed wasn't a minorite, but he was open to the possibility of romance, in a way that no Englishman could ever be. And though he argued the body's case with his friend, Morgan was hardly indifferent to romance. From that first evening in the Home of Misery, what he remembered more strongly than his excitement was the soft sensation of Mohammed's arm under his head as they sank down onto the bed. Yes, when he thought back on their meetings, it was the embraces and caresses that stayed with him, not his lust, which was like a question without an answer.

It was only now, he realised, that some form of equality had really opened up between them. They had only been playing at it before, shouting across a gulf that there was no gulf between them. But now he had begun to experience the Egyptian world through the skin of his friend, and it didn't resemble the one he lived in. Distantly, imperfectly, he thought he grasped a little of how it might feel to be an Egyptian working under English control, and the flashes of humiliation and anger it might involve. When Mohammed was hit in the jaw by a drunken sergeant-major, or whacked on the leg with a cane by an irate officer, it was as if the blows had landed on Morgan's own flesh. And he was outraged on Mohammed's behalf at the salary he received: only two bob a day, barely enough to get by on. To say nothing of his hours of work, which left him with almost no leisure time.

"And I am always in a temper," Mohammed added, "which is bad for my health."

Despite all this, he wasn't sorry for himself, which had the effect of making Morgan more sorry for him. But there wasn't a lot that could be done. This wasn't England in peacetime, where friends and opportunity were plentiful.

A little desperately, he sent Mohammed with a letter to the lady who ran the Government Employment Bureau. There was no job on offer at the time, but she wrote a warm appraisal of him, and promised that she would call him up soon to be a clerk. At five shillings a day!

"As your income increases," Morgan told him, "so will your wants."

"To have wants is to understand life."

"That is unsound thinking, even though it's true."

The job never came, and he continued to fret over Mohammed's circumstances. The more he came to know the young man, the more threadbare his wardrobe seemed, the more limited his prospects. By now Morgan felt acutely the difference between their stations. There was simply no way to close up the gap. It was a quirk of destiny, nothing more, that had decreed Mohammed to be poor and unskilled, a tram conductor, while Morgan was a well-fed fellow with uncalloused hands. He would have changed places if he could, but the most that he could do was try to utilise his power.

That meant Furness again. After their previous conversation, Morgan was abashed to approach him a second time, but he could see no other way to do it. "It's that young man I spoke about before, the one who works on the trams . . . "

"Him again! I thought you weren't going to see him any more. What's he got up to this time?"

"It isn't like that. He hasn't done anything. I was just wondering whether some position might not be found for him, a job that offers a better salary."

Robin sighed. "Morgan," he said, "will you not listen to reason?"

"Is it unreasonable to try to help a friend?"

"No, of course not. But how much of a friend can he truly be? He's a native after all, and I did try to tell you . . . " He shrugged his bony shoulders and threw up his hands. "You will get yourself into trouble, you know."

"No doubt. But not over him. Please trust me a little, Robin, I'm not an utter fool."

"I'm not so sure about that." He shook his head in exasperation, but there was amusement in his disapproval. "I'll ask around," he said at last, "and see what I can do. I make no promises."

* * *

In recent weeks, there had been news from home that he couldn't ignore: Maimie Aylward, his mother's old and dear friend, was dying and Aunt Laura, his father's sister, was very sick. He was roiled with notions of duty and obligation. Should he give up Egypt and return?

He was under no illusions about what this meant. If he left, this golden moment would be lost to him. There would be no coming back to Mohammed and to this time. And it was a choice he had to make almost alone: he couldn't explain any of it to Lily or to Aunt Laura.

Whom could he tell about his love? He wrote about it to a handful of people at home, but he was aware of how absurd, how ridiculous, it sounded. Certainly nobody in Egypt would understand. Nevertheless, that it was love was no longer in question. There had been no definite defining moment, as with Masood in Paris. It was more as if he'd fallen *into* love through Mohammed: into a small circular space in the very centre of his life, where almost nothing threw a shadow.

A failure to decide is a sort of decision. While he hesitated, time fell away, and the resulting fugue was not unpleasant. But his crisis was put into proper perspective when a message came that Mohammed's mother had taken ill and died.

Morgan had experienced before how it felt when somebody close to him suffered. But with one's English friends, there were social rituals to demonstrate one's concern. That didn't apply here. He couldn't accompany Mohammed to the funeral; he couldn't share with him the difficulty of facing his father and his second family. He could only hear an account of it from afar, in the form of a brief letter, and wait for Mohammed to come back. When he did, he seemed to have taken on more weight and substance; sadness had made him heavy. He had loved his mother very much.

He felt both nearer to Mohammed through this event and further away. He understood his friend better, but had been reminded of how separate their lives were. And that separation was deepened by a new presence in the Home of Misery: Mohammed's half-brother had returned with him after the funeral and squatted now in the corner with glowering, mute malevolence when Morgan visited.

At the same time, there was a setback at his own rooms. When Mohammed came there one Sunday, to talk and play chess, Irene unexpectedly put her head around his door and gave an involuntary little shriek when she saw the two of them on the bed.

He spoke to her about it afterwards, of course. "He is somebody I met through Robin Furness," he told her untruthfully. "A very decent young man, I promise you. I am giving him English lessons."

"But you cannot trust them! Even when you think you can. No, you must not be gullible! I have many valuables at home . . . "

"I will be answerable for your valuables," he told her, and eventually she was pacified. But he thought it best not to bring Mohammed there again.

Their life together had always been small, made of spare, left-over moments. But even this tiny island was shrinking. There was nowhere to meet in private and the public opportunities were dangerous. Mohammed—more used to intrusion—was philosophical, but Morgan felt despondent. So that when an offer came that changed everything, it didn't seem too terrible.

Furness hadn't forgotten his request and had been making enquiries on his behalf. Within a few weeks, he told Morgan that he might have found something.

"It's with military intelligence," he said. "Work connected with the War, you know. But there is a drawback, at least from your point of view. It's in the Canal Zone, so your chap will have to leave Alexandria."

Just a few weeks before, Morgan might have hesitated, but he didn't now. The salary was more than double what Mohammed got on the tram.

"I am very grateful to you, Robin."

"Does that mean he'll take the job?"

"Yes, of course he'll take the job."

Mohammed was pleased and excited, as Morgan knew he would be, but he had one minor reservation. "Am I to be a spy?"

"I don't know. Perhaps. Is that beastly?"

"Yes, of course." He considered it for a while, then smiled archly. "But not very."

There were several weeks still before he had to leave, in which his papers were finalised and his security pass prepared. By now a quiet resignation, very near to peacefulness, had come down over both of them. It was understood that their closeness had always been an interlude, and that separation inevitably lurked in the future somewhere.

This newfound serenity took concrete form one night, not long before they had to say goodbye. Mohammed's brother had gone away somewhere and they had the Home of Misery to themselves. Yet there seemed nothing to do that was out of the ordinary. Now, like castaways washed up on a beach, they lay gently twined together on the bed, staring upward at the ceiling, idly caressing each other. Morgan's hand wandered, as it sometimes did, but instead of the usual refusal, Mohammed went perceptibly slack. There was a tiny moment of deliberation, before he leaned back, untying his linen drawers.

"Do what you want," he said.

It didn't seem possible that he meant it. Morgan looked at him in consternation. But his confusion felt ungrateful and, instead of speaking, it was more natural to act. He pulled the material aside and there it was, the shocking object one had imagined so often.

He thought, of course, of Montazah, but this event was more languid, without the terror of possible discovery. Both of them looked down without speaking, observing like solemn spectators, as Morgan went to work on his friend. The rhythmic tugging, when it wasn't applied to oneself, was surprisingly hard work. At the moment of climax Mohammed pushed his hand aside and gave a small grunt, almost like a word.

After which he became very brisk. He seemed cross as he cleaned himself with a piece of cloth, sighing once or twice. And his voice sounded irritable as he asked, "Are you happy now?"

"Yes," Morgan said truthfully. "I am."

But the real happiness was in the hours that followed. It was too late for him to go home and when they lay down to sleep together Mohammed suddenly wrapped an arm around him from behind and lay snugly against his back, holding him. It was the first time in his life that Morgan had ever shared a bed. He had shared rooms, of course, many times, but never had there been this compact assembly of limbs and skin in the dark, the touch of warm breath on the back of his neck. Something in his life had been made whole and complete, he thought, but the momentousness was inseparable from silence and drowsiness. This was not a clamorous triumph.

There were just a few days before Mohammed had to leave and it seemed that they were at the station almost immediately, saying goodbye. Between them they had wrestled his heavy bag, which seemed to be made of tinfoil and brown paper, all the way from the Home of Misery, and after all this sweaty labour the moment of farewell seemed somehow empty. Nor was any touch beyond a handshake possible, not under the eyes of strangers. *Good luck. Goodbye. Thank you.* The politeness was nearly intolerable. But as the train began to pull out of the station, some of the buried emotion reached the surface, and Mohammed's voice called suddenly out of the clamour: "Don't forget me, don't—"

It was like a curtain coming down at the end of an act.

* * *

Back in England, Maimie Aylward finally died. But Morgan knew by now that he wasn't ready yet for home. Mohammed would have leave at some point; they would see each other again.

Then a cable came from London. He was to be Head Searcher for the Red Cross in Egypt, which meant he was to supervise those for whom he'd been working till now. Although he didn't much care for promotion, he was tentatively pleased at first, because he hoped it might mean more leisure time. But very soon he found himself enveloped in a row: Miss Grant Duff was unhappy.

She had always been a complicated sort, quivering on the verge of unnamed affront, but her outrage now had found a focus. There had been several moments when it had seemed worryingly to Morgan that she might be in love with him, but what she displayed now was very far from love. Whenever he came near her, her lips drew tightly inward and her eyes rolled like those of a skittish horse.

"It is a want of confidence," she said. "The leadership does not believe in me."

"Oh, come," he said, very eager to placate her. "It's not as if I'm in charge."

"That is exactly what it is," she said. "They have put *you* in charge."

She used the word "you" like a pair of tweezers, picking Morgan up by the neck to examine him and finding him insufficient.

He didn't care enough for a fight. He saw that it mattered greatly to her—indeed, it was her whole life—how she was seen by other people. She regarded him as a usurper, a sly intruder who had levered her from her seat. He wrote wearily to London, asking them to undo the appointment, but was overruled.

This made everything much worse. She ceased to speak to him at all and turned away when she saw him, her face pinched and pale. She opened letters that were addressed to him. It very soon became insufferable, and he went away for a while to escape, to the Nile temples and the pyramids. Nothing had changed on his return and he had to find more inventive consolations. Music was one, and he banged out his Franck and Chopin on Irene's old upright. He started a few new friendships and allowed them to dictate some of his social arrangements. He thought of taking up his Indian novel again, but felt too far from it, and settled for some journalism instead.

More solidly, he found himself taking interest in the idea of a larger subject. Since Mohammed's departure, the city had felt somehow deserted, and he thought now that he might fill it up with the past. He had long been aware of an invisible history, underfoot and all around him, but perhaps, he thought now, it might be possible to recreate it in words. Since space was controlled by the military, he would travel through time instead. He had recently been reading Gibbon again, with almost sensual enjoyment, and he hoped he could summon lost centuries as vividly and enthrallingly.

He thought of the book as a sort of reconstruction, the building of a vast ghost city. Aside from a few stray ruins, a hunger for practicality and commerce had razed the ancient world, leaving grit and grimness in its place. The footsteps of kings, emperors and patriarchs had been covered over by pavement; no trace of them was left. No less an absence were the great spiritual philosophies that had taken form here and been eclipsed by others. Alexandria was made of debris and displacement, and its air of grubby nostalgia demanded some appeasement.

Of the people with whom he discussed his project, none were as enthusiastic as Cavafy.

"Oh, excellent, Forster," he declared, snipping a cigarette in half, his usual miserly habit. "I myself have always been poised between history and poetry. I could have written either, and perhaps I have made the wrong choice."

Morgan felt encouraged enough to confide, "Greece will be at the heart of the book, just as she is at the heart of Alexandria."

"No longer. Alas, my dear Forster, no longer. The Hellenic Empire has long since disappeared. She is merely an influence and an echo."

"But the echoes are not negligible. I have thought of your country as my stronghold for sentiment, ever since my student days."

Immediately Cavafy became sorrowful, and turned his face away. "Oh, the Greeks," he cried. "Never forget about the Greeks that we are bankrupt. That is the difference between us and the ancient Greeks and between us and yourselves. Pray, my dear Forster, that you English never lose your capital, otherwise you will resemble us—restless, shifty, liars."

He had tried to flatter Cavafy, but had never been allowed to draw near. Nevertheless, his project almost put their friendship on a new footing. The advice came in a torrent, nearly all of it useful and encouraging. Had Morgan read Plotinus? Did he know about Philo and the Logos? Was he up on his Athanasius? He, Cavafy, had some books that Morgan simply had to read.

As he researched in preparation, Morgan realised that he and the poet were embarked on a similar labour. He thought of this book as a resurrection, restoring a graveyard to life. And in his own work, in his own way, Cavafy was doing the same thing. Dipping into myth and ancient history, veering off into the modern streets, too, his poems stitched between an old, lost Alexandria and the immediate, sensual, modern one he lived in. In his words, the past quite literally drew breath.

But Cavafy lived here, after all. What pulled Morgan so powerfully? He hadn't responded warmly to Egypt when he'd first arrived. When he considered it, he decided that it was precisely because Alexandria felt like a place—almost a country, alone—separate from what surrounded it. And what stirred him most deeply was that it was a mixture: an interbred miscegenation, a bastardy of influences and traditions and races. He had learned to mistrust purity—or the idea of purity, rather, because the real thing didn't exist. Everybody by now was a blend; history was a confusion; people were hybrids.

* * *

His own hybrid self missed Mohammed terribly. All his newfound activity was only a means to divert himself from loneliness. Those few months of companionship now seemed irretrievable. Why had he worked so hard to bring them to an end?

His sufferings were private and complicated. Their separation had become a condition, as chronic and persistent as illness. Mohammed wrote every few days, but the letters were polite and said little. He wasn't working as a spy, of course; more as a clerk, and it sounded tedious. He was far away and the prospect of leave was remote.

Just before he'd left Alexandria, Morgan had arranged for Mohammed to be photographed. Now he kept the picture close to him and frequently took it out to study it. Wearing Western dress—a dinner jacket, white shirt and bow-tie—with his red tarboosh, his Egyptian friend sat looking serious, one leg crossed over the other, an ivory-handled fly-whisk in his hand. He stared out of the image, out of the past, into a restless place in Morgan that wouldn't lie still.

Months went by and still they could not meet. It was only in May—half a year since they'd last seen each other—that Mohammed managed to return to Alexandria for a couple of days. He stayed with a friend in Bacos and Morgan visited him there. Still fearful of being spotted by somebody he knew, they spent a day at Mex, beyond the western edge of the city, where they swam among the rocks and sat on a hilltop in the sun. He was reminded of the scene he had written, where Maurice and Clive played truant from Cambridge: this had something of the same illegitimate leisure.

He had often thought about *Maurice* recently and wished he were writing it now. How differently he would handle the relationship at the heart of it! His imagination had squared up so timidly to the reality. And by contrast, how like a bad novel his life would have been, how mean and small, if this had never happened to him.

"Give up your job," he told his friend now. "Come back to Alexandria to stay."

"And what work will I do?"

"It doesn't matter. I will support you."

Mohammed shook his head, smiling faintly. When they said goodbye again properly, in the Nouzha Gardens, he told Morgan, "Two days have passed like two minutes, yet I think perhaps it is best like that."

"But why?"

"If I walk with the same friend every day I have sometimes wanted another. Now we shall again be anxious for one another for six months and then have the time of happiness."

Morgan didn't think he could bear another six months. Damn the military zone! Mohammed couldn't leave it, nor could Morgan get in.

* * *

When Mohammed did abandon his army work soon afterwards, it wasn't to return to Alexandria and to Morgan. Instead he went back to Mansourah to stay. His life had thrown up a double calamity in the form of two deaths: first, very suddenly, his father, and then, just two days later, his brother—who had drowned while swimming in a canal.

Mohammed had loved his brother. And yet, although the drowning was a mystery, he hadn't enquired too closely. "What is the use?" was all he said, when pressed. "If only it was the rest of my family instead."

This disaster brought Morgan, finally, to Mansourah for a visit. Mohammed had inherited the house—or rather, as Morgan now realised, three tiny houses joined together. Two of them had been let out and his friend was living in the third, although it consisted mostly of one dirty room, crowded with bits of furniture, in a muddy lane close to the station, in which poultry wandered between puddles.

Lying in bed together on the second night, Mohammed said, "I am thinking of marrying my brother's wife."

"Is that possible?"

"Many people do. No dowry has to be given, so it's cheaper. There is also a child, who needs a father." After a pause, and in a different, quieter voice, he added, "I want to be a happy man in my own paternal home."

"I understand," Morgan told him. He knew that what sounded like a statement was, in fact, a question, and that his answer was a form of permission.

Earlier that evening, Mohammed had told him about how, in Kantara in the Canal Zone, he'd been seduced by an English soldier. The man had cadged a cigarette off him, then taken him back to his tent. The exercise had been repeated the next day. But the story didn't make Morgan jealous, any more than the prospect of Mohammed's marriage did. Bodies could collide, in their confusion of appetites; what mattered was something different, which he struggled to put a name to.

During his visit, the two men had wandered the esplanade along the edge of the Nile; they had visited some of Mohammed's friends, and taken a boat trip on the river. They had had themselves measured by a tailor for a suit that they would own together, a little too big for Mohammed, a little too small for Morgan. In the evening they had washed in the passageway under the stairs, pouring tins of water over each other. And when they had got into bed they had wrestled and tickled one another like children, Mohammed screaming playfully all the while that he was going to kill his friend.

This kind of companionship had far more value to Morgan than their few, fumbling physical encounters. Sex could be forgotten, or made into something that it wasn't, but feelings were much harder to erase. There had been moments, from their time in Alexandria, when they had simply sat together talking quietly, or smoking cigarettes in brotherly contentment, when he'd felt that they were removed from other people. Paired off. And it had come to him then that there might be many men like them, in the past as well as the present, who had been together in a similar uncelebrated way, encircled by invisible emotion.

Invisible but powerful. Affection was like a colour, or a scent on the air; you couldn't seize it in your hand, but it lingered, it lasted. When he and Mohammed were gone, he thought, some trace of their joining together would still be here: a ghost haunting an empty room.

Nor was their parting an inconceivable idea any longer. There were signs that the War might be drawing to a close. The end wasn't yet discernible, not even a topic for conversation, but Morgan could sense a time when he would have to leave. He and Mohammed back in their proper compartments, lives entirely separate from each other. When that happened, he wanted to know that his friend was all right.

* * *

In the end, Mohammed did marry, but not his brother's wife. Instead he married her sister. The perfunctory change in plans reflected something deeper: he'd told Morgan that he'd read about love, but didn't know what it meant. The arrangement was practical, nothing more, yet no less effective for that. *I feel I was not in the world the time before, everyday I am so happy.*

With Hom and then with Masood, Morgan had learned to accept the inevitable. The men he loved all married. It didn't cancel out what had gone before—or what was, in this case, ongoing. So he had made his peace with the idea, even before something else occurred, next to which all other worries seemed thin.

When Mohammed had come to Alexandria again recently, Morgan had noticed that his back looked hollow. But when he was asked about it, he'd become irritable.

"It's nothing," he said. "I am having stress about money. Nothing more."

But Morgan remembered that there had been complaints for a while now, about being weak and listless. He felt a faint chill deep inside, like an underground stream, and it didn't come as a complete surprise when—shortly before he got married—Mohammed wrote to say that he'd been coughing up blood.

The word that went through Morgan's mind was the name of the disease that had carried his father off. Lily had spoken about it with respectful dread, and something of the same tone infiltrated when he wrote a difficult letter. But the reply that came was close to laconic. *I think my illness is what you say, consumption but the doctor did not tell me thinking that I may be very unhappy. I do not trouble much about my illness I believe that only the death is my relief from this troublesome world.*

In real distress, Morgan became very calm. He continued with his usual life, mild and diligent, but under his perpetual half-smile the centre of his attention was elsewhere.

A different doctor, whom Mohammed went to see at Morgan's expense, gave some reassuring news: he thought the condition had been caught in time. With care and a healthy regimen, the young man ought to pull through. Morgan very much wanted to believe this. And when he returned to Mansourah in December, not long after the Armistice was declared, it did seem that Mohammed had put on some weight again. Nor was his mood despondent. Taking advantage of the wartime economy, as well as a loan from Morgan, he had recently begun trading in cotton, buying it in the countryside and bringing it to the city to sell to dealers, and the work had cheered him up.

His marriage had also rooted him somehow. The change was indefinable but obvious. Morgan glimpsed Gamila, his wife, mostly in passing: a shy, pretty figure, very young, almost a girl still, who left the room as soon as he entered it. She put him in mind of some kind of country creature, who bolted at the least sign of disturbance. But she had made Mohammed happy, and he heard the two of them laughing together when he wasn't with them, a sound that stirred him in a complicated way.

How could it be otherwise? He wanted things to be well with his friend, but there was no doubt that he'd been displaced. Since his last visit, the tenant had moved downstairs, and the more spacious top floor—two rooms, a paved hall, a kitchen and bathroom—had been taken over by the young couple. There would be no more lying snugly together in the warm dark; Morgan had his own room now.

Nevertheless, the emotion between them was unfeigned, not to mention deepened or, at the very least, renewed. Life was more or less in balance and, though it was hard that some distance had intervened, it wasn't unfitting that it should have happened now. It was one's duty to be optimistic, and it helped in this endeavour that his relations with Mohammed, though surrounded by complexity, were in themselves simple. In a certain way, things between them didn't change. It was the greatest event to touch his life so far, and it made him proud. In some indefinable way, he felt he had grown up, he had become a man. Something had finally *happened* to him.

This knowledge consoled him in his last two months, which were otherwise difficult. He had to prepare himself for the future. Great events had blown him here in a strange, anomalous gust, and now they would carry him back again. He dreaded his return. He was glad that the War had ended, of course, but he suspected that the world had changed irrevocably and he doubted it was for the better. Everything he had heard about England in his absence had deepened his idea of it as a dirty place: its manners, its morals, its thinking, all contaminated by the fighting, infused with a dark, new, compromised spirit.

And although he had resisted and strained inwardly against it, Egypt had touched him more than he knew. It was hard to think he might never come back. He had started writing his book on Alexandria, and consequently the city had taken on a different solidity. It had become freighted with history and legend, not a small part of which had to do with Mohammed.

The work was far from finished and this aspect of the country, at least, he would be taking back home to England with him, to complete. Everything else he would be leaving behind. Now that it was inevitable he almost wished he could slip away without any final moments: board a ship at midnight, fade into the dark.

But Mohammed would be all right, he thought. The consumption, if that's what it was, seemed to have been beaten down in time. When Morgan returned to Mansourah for a last visit, his friend had a physical fullness he hadn't seen for a while. It was heartening that his health did seem so much better. He had fattened out a bit and hadn't coughed up blood, he said, in many weeks. He no longer felt perpetually exhausted.

All this was good, and the sound of Mohammed giggling with his wife, privately, in their room, didn't bother him as much as before. He was leaving his friend better off, he thought, than when he'd first met him as a tram conductor in Alexandria, living in one rented room with not much money, perhaps not lonely but certainly alone.

Though when the two of them went for a walk early on the second morning, into the fields outside the town, Mohammed became plaintive. They had a good life in Egypt, could Morgan not stay? Why did he want to go home? He had asked these questions in letters recently too; he knew how to work on Morgan's weakest places.

"Do you think I haven't thought about it? I don't want to go, but I'm afraid I must. I have obligations. I have my mother."

"Fetch Mother back here with you to Egypt. She will be my mother too."

"That isn't possible." He smiled into his moustache at the idea, but at the same time it gave him a pang to think of how little Mohammed had understood of what his English life was like. How he wanted to mix the two! To bring Mohammed to his home, to show him to his friends and relations, let them think what they liked. It would be such a relief not to care.

But in fact it had only been two or three weeks before that he had mentioned his Egyptian friend to Lily for the first time, and he'd been careful to slip in a reference to his marriage.

"Can you not find me a job in England? I will come imme-diately."

"I'll try," Morgan told him insincerely. "But I think you wouldn't be happy."

"Anywhere you can find work for me, I am gratitude to you. Even India. I should like to travel there with you next time you go."

"Perhaps one day you will," Morgan said—but that idea was impossible too. India was another life, another love; he couldn't think of bringing Mohammed there.

The flat landscape they were strolling through reminded him very much of Cambridge, stretching away mistily to knots of trees and farm buildings. They climbed down into the bottom of a ditch, where Mohammed undid his trousers to allow Morgan to fondle him for a few minutes. He was only half-hard and Morgan only half-enthused. Neither of them commented on what they were doing, and it didn't seem important to bring matters to a climax.

Two weeks later he stood at the rail of the ship that carried him away. Water in every direction, no land visible. Nothing solid to fix on. The farewell that preceded this journey was as difficult as he'd feared, in part because it contained no meaning; everything that mattered had come before. To dwell on it was pointless and, perhaps for this reason, his mind wasn't with Mohammed, but with the poet.

Morgan had gone to see him a few days before in the Rue Lepsius to say goodbye, and they had stood on the balcony, drinking raki, looking out towards the eastern harbour. In the dusk, all the faults and failures of the city were annulled; a soft breeze carried in from the sea.

The two men had chatted in their usual desultory way on historical topics, before a silence crept in between them. Then Cavafy had said, "So. You are going home."

"Yes."

"How I wish to be going with you. I have always thought of myself as an English subject, even though I am a Hellene." He sighed happily. "But I am used to Alexandria. Even if I had money now, I'm not sure that I would move, though the place disturbs me. A small city can be a great burden, don't you think? For a man like me, an unusual sort of man, a large city is essential."

"I don't know. I have never lived in a large city myself."

"I should leave this flat, certainly. Though on the other hand, I have everything I need here. There is the brothel downstairs, which caters for the flesh. There is St Saba nearby, where my sins may be forgiven. And there is the hospital opposite, where I may die."

Morgan had heard this joke before and soon afterwards, when Cavafy fell to wondering aloud whether to move or to install electric lighting instead, he knew that it was time to go.

From the street below, he turned to look up. The pale face was still visible on the balcony, and even from a distance it seemed inscrutable and strange, an oddity in what surrounded it. His mind went back to the visit three years before when he'd heard the first poem. "The God Abandons Antony". *Bid farewell to her, to Alexandria whom you are losing.* He waved a hand and perhaps the poet waved back, it was hard to be sure.

* * *

From almost the first instant he stepped ashore in Gravesend, the country that revealed itself to him was one he knew, and also did not recognise. He tried to break the surface, to sink into what he knew. He rushed about, visiting friends and family. He stopped with Aunt Laura and the Bargers and Edward Carpenter; he saw the Merediths in Belfast and took a two-week holiday with Goldie in Lyme Regis. But it rained without stopping at Aunt Laura's and Florence was a wonderful confidante when one was writing to her but, alas, a little dull as company, and Carpenter more interested in lecturing than in listening, and Hom's family life was depressing, along with Goldie's gloom and misery over the state of the world, although the cottage they stayed in was nice.

If he kept dashing about nevertheless, it was because sitting still was painful. And at home of course there was his mother, from whom he felt even more removed, owing to the Great Events he had to keep from her.

Though what mattered most had to stay concealed, confession lurked always just below the skin. Past and present almost came together one morning at the breakfast table when he opened a letter from Mohammed, telling him that Gamila was pregnant. If the child was a boy, his friend added, he would be called after Morgan. This was more than Masood or India had ever done for him, and he found himself knocking over the milk jug and becoming disproportionately upset. He was appalled at himself for making a scene.

But Lily was unexpectedly sweet to him, stroking his hand while he struggled to explain.

"It's my nerves," he said. "I haven't yet accepted that I'm home. It was a great strain, being away for so long. I meant to be gone for three months, and it turned into three years."

His voice sounded brittle to himself, but his mother was unusually in tune with him. She had been making an effort since his return, and he'd been pleased to be welcomed—for the first time since his childhood—by family prayers read in his honour. The emotion between them was best contained in ritual.

"I too thought it would go on forever," she murmured. "Or the end of my life, at least."

Which was nearer now than before. She had noticeably aged while he'd been gone. In shape and thickness, she was more than ever a pillar; time had smoothed away some of the sharper edges. Nevertheless, he resolved afterwards not to put himself into her power in that way again. It wasn't safe to break in front of her; the truth had a way of seeping through the cracks.

His one moment of weakness aside, Egypt could usually be held at a distance. The closest he could come was in writing about it. He was still busy with his Alexandrian book, which carried him back in imagination at least, but now he also began writing journalistic articles and reviews, many of which were about the country he'd left behind.

For the rest, it was a topic best reserved for the breakfast table, where the newspapers provided fodder for outrage. The end of the War had stirred up hopes in many subject peoples, and some of these hopes had been dashed. So Egypt bubbled and stewed, while loud voices shouted from mosques and Coptic pulpits alike. Blood had been shed, and at first it was English blood.

"Forty dead," Lily announced in shock one morning, the headlines vibrating in her hand.

"Really, it is one thousand and forty. But the thousand are Egyptians, and they don't count."

"Don't be unreasonable, Morgan. You can't expect me to care about people I don't know, ahead of my countrymen." After a moment she conceded: "You, I suppose, do know an Egyptian or two."

Of course it was true: his main, abiding fear was for Mohammed. He saw everything now through his eyes. His loyalties had crossed the front lines and there were whole days when he felt quite limp with anxiety and outrage. When he read about Egyptians being arrested, Egyptians being shot or jailed, he saw only Mohammed's face. Though the outlets for anger were small, limited to rhetorical flourishes in certain newspapers.

Then, in the middle of the upheavals, a letter came, written in French, from a village near Mansourah. Mohammed had been arrested, it told him; he would be in jail for six months.

Nothing more was explained, but it sent Morgan into panic. He wrote back immediately, but the reply that followed didn't make the situation any clearer. All that he understood was that a fine of ten pounds needed to be paid, or Mohammed's sentence would be extended by three months. He paid the fine.

At the same time, the news coming in from India was equally disturbing. First reports were short on detail, but there had been some kind of massacre in Amritsar. A British general, confronted by a seditious crowd, had decided to let loose on them with rifle-fire.

Morgan's own memory of Amritsar was sketchy: he had visited the Golden Temple hastily, between trains, under a threatening storm, and retained only a vague impression of water and marble, and of holy books being fanned to keep them clean of impurities. He didn't know anybody there. So it was hard to visualise the shooting, the panic, the death, in the way that he could in Egypt. Perhaps because it was far from the recent theatre of war, India had fallen somewhat off the mental map of late.

Out of these events, a longing to see Masood came over him. He had avoided thinking of his Indian friend for some time, but now he allowed himself to dwell on him again and on some of what had passed between them. That tall, powerful frame, that long, handsome face with its despondent eyes and droopy moustache! Oh, he had missed him, though he couldn't allow himself to know it; he had felt the physical distance between them intensely, and the more painful distance that had opened between their lives, which was impossible to measure.

Masood was at present in Paris, attached in some vague, informal way to the Peace Conference. He would be drifting over the Channel shortly, and would continue to drift afterwards, among his English friends—at least one of whom was filled with anxiety at the prospect. Morgan wanted the coming reunion so badly that he pretended he didn't want it at all.

But when the moment finally arrived, it was as if Morgan was twenty-seven again and Masood was coming for his first Latin lesson. He was late, as always, and with the same distracted assurance he'd shown on their first meeting. Though age was wearing on him—he was noticeably stouter, his face a little looser—he remained tall and comely, his eyes were still sad, and his talent for rhetoric was undimmed. "Ah, my first and only English friend," he cried, picking Morgan up in his arms and planting kisses on the top of his head. "I have thought of nothing but this doorstep since setting foot in Europe!"

It wasn't true—he had bought a whole new wardrobe in Paris and had seen many mutual friends already in London—but Morgan forgave him everything.

"I am happy to see you, Masood."

"Happy? *Happy?* What a pale, pathetic English word. You must not be 'happy' to see me. No, you must be enraptured, transported! You must be *overjoyed*. I have no use for 'happy'. Let me come inside, please, I am desperate for tea."

He greeted Lily and the maids with the same mournful ebullience; he had brought gifts for everybody, and his large spirit infected them all. He overflowed a sofa languidly, and his voice twined through the house. He had become very loud and orotund, and his inertia was wearying, but by the time he moved on a couple of days later the mood that hung over England like a pall seemed to have lifted a little.

Morgan saw him again a few times over the coming weeks. The vague dread of anticipation had given way to a renewal of intimacy. They didn't talk about what had happened in India; that was on the other side of the world. Instead they spoke about the last six years and how their lives had changed.

It took Morgan a while to mention Mohammed. Against all logic, he felt that this transfer of affections somehow constituted a betrayal. But eventually, blushing and stammering, he came out with it. "I had what you might call a romance. Or no, more accurately, it was love. While in Egypt."

"Yes, yes, it was obvious. You were dissembling with me."

"I was angry with you."

"I know, I am guilty of everything, I deserve the most extreme punishment, but let's not talk about that now. I want to hear about your great love affair. I demand to know everything."

They were circling the pond in Regent's Park at the time, a long autumn afternoon waning slowly around them, and the happy commotion of children and dogs and ducks only underscored for Morgan the strangeness of what he was describing. Had he really done those things? None of it sounded real. Yet once he started speaking, he couldn't hold back.

When Morgan mentioned Mohammed's child, he saw Masood flinch.

"He has named his son after you?"

"Yes, there is a little baby Egyptian named Morgan. Well, it is only his second name, but still. I am very pleased. Born last month."

He couldn't help himself; he wanted to punish Masood a little. His Indian friend by now had two sons, Anwar and Akbar. He had asked Morgan in an airy way whether he would be a guardian to his boys, but it was a gesture, nothing more, and both of them knew it.

Now Masood sighed and waved a hand and said, "I will name all my future children in your honour."

"No, you won't. You will promise and promise, and do nothing."

"I have already conceded, I am a failure as a friend. Forgive your wretched servant, please, who cares only for your welfare." Masood took his hand and slapped him lightly on the wrist.

"What was that for?"

"It is punishment, for your recklessness."

"Do you think I have been reckless?"

"You have been courting danger, yes. You know it very well."

"But you don't resent my happiness?"

"How could I, when it is what I want most in the world? I am glad for you, my dear fellow. But you must promise me that you will be more sensible and careful in the future. What is going on now with this tram conductor of yours?"

Mohammed's experience had wrecked the whole year for Morgan, the more so because he couldn't speak openly about it. Now he did, and the relief was palpable. Mohammed had eventually been released from prison, after four months inside. Only then had he related what had happened. In his version, two Australian soldiers had tried to sell him a firearm, which was tempting, because of the lawless state of the country. But he had refused their price, insulting them in the process, and in revenge they had had him arrested for trying to buy a weapon. It was a serious charge. He had been sentenced to six months' hard labour and a ten pound fine. In prison, he had been beaten and badly fed and treated with contempt.

Morgan couldn't entirely believe Mohammed's account of buying the gun, but he didn't say so, out of loyalty. And there were other elements of the story that he couldn't mention either—such as, for example, that Mohammed had performed sexual favours on the guards in order to obtain leniency, nor that he spoke openly now of his hatred for the English, calling them cruel, and of his desire for revenge. These things might not reflect well on his friend.

Masood listened calmly, nodding from time to time. In the end he merely said, "It is the same in India."

"Not so bad, surely?"

"Oh, yes, it is bad. It is all up with you English and your Empire. A matter of time now, you will see. You will be pushed back onto your little island."

"Where you have always been a most welcome guest, I might add." He upset himself and almost cried. "It is not *my* Empire, Masood, why will you never admit it?"

"Friendship is your Empire, Morgan, I know that very well. I am only teasing you. Please remember that you were a welcome guest in India too. Though you are too afraid to come back."

"I'm not afraid of it."

"When will you come?"

"I don't know, this isn't the time to decide. Perhaps it won't be soon. I have my mother to think of. I abandoned her during the War, I can't do it so quickly again."

But he continued to think about it, and the subject returned a few weeks later, just before Masood's departure. Morgan had gone down to London to see him and they were sitting in the garden of a mutual friend, chatting inconsequentially, when a bereft sensation came over him. "Perhaps," he mused aloud, "I must come out to India again, if I am ever to finish my novel."

"Your novel! Your Indian novel!" It was as if the idea were striking Masood for the very first time. "How is it going? Are you close to completing it?"

Morgan laughed with unfeigned merriment. "It's hopeless, really. I should throw it away."

"Oh, nonsense, you are only being modest. I know you too well. It is a work of genius and it is almost done."

But it wasn't a work of genius and it was nowhere near done. Over the last six years—since starting *Maurice*—he had barely touched it. Not long after getting back to England, he had made a serious attempt to pick it up again, but that had ended quickly after a few days. He was usually a calm and methodical worker, but the words wouldn't join in any sensible way. There had been a terrible afternoon when he had come close to screaming dementedly over it, alone in the attic. He had put it away after that and not looked at it again.

Instead he had occupied himself with his articles and his Alexandrian book. He was always busy, always working, but none of it was creative and at certain moments, when this came clear to him, he fell into despondency. He saw his middle years as a continuation of the same. He had a small paunch and the beginnings of baldness, and the reddish tinge of his nose seemed permanent. He felt he was a spent force, his finest time somewhere behind him. He didn't think he would ever complete his novel.

* * *

And yet, after Masood had finally sailed, the Indian story remained behind, bothering him. As before, in India, Masood's absence enlarged the presence of his book. By now he had a curious relationship with all that unfinished material. He could see it from a little way off, with its promise and its shortcomings. There was something in it, something unformed as yet, which pulled at him. But in order to proceed, he would have to become involved in it again, with the almost sensual imagining that its private world required. He wasn't sure how to do that.

"Simply by taking up your pen," Leonard Woolf told him.

There weren't many people before whom he could throw out his writerly woes, but with the Woolfs he could. They paid such attention! Though without always fully understanding.

"It's not that simple," he protested. "I do take up my pen. I am fingering the keys, as it were, but I seem to produce only discords so far."

"Well, persist. Your problems are not unusual."

"Do you think so?" Morgan was genuinely surprised; his lameness felt unique to him. "I was reading it over recently and I lost all hope."

"No, don't thwart yourself. Really, you are worse than Virginia. You have to finish. If I could order you, I would."

This conversation was only possible because for once they were alone. A great busyness usually surrounded the Woolfs, but today the entourage had withdrawn. He knew everybody in the group that had accreted around them; as individuals he mostly liked them, but collectively they made him shrink a little. They were all so interwoven and intimate, changing relationships and sexual tastes the way other people changed hats. To say nothing of their cleverness, which was sometimes cruel, and used against friend and enemy indiscriminately. He couldn't air his failures too completely in front of them, and it was mostly to Leonard and Virginia that he turned.

"I told Masood that perhaps I need to go back to India," he said now. "The place is vague in my mind, so much has come between. Egypt, the War, other writing. I have almost forgotten it."

"Go back then," Leonard told him brusquely. "If that is what you need to do."

The advice was so hard-edged that it seemed like an object. Leonard did not speak whimsically. And of course, he had spent years of his own life out there, in the East; he knew very well what was involved.

Morgan said faintly, "Perhaps I will."

Virginia was sitting nearby, smoking one of her shag cigarettes. Her presence had an intensity that made his spirit lean backward. Yet he had also grown to like her, with her long, lantern-shaped face, inhabited by sharp intelligence. She studied Morgan intently with the two bright nails of her eyes, then told him, "You know, I can't imagine you there."

"But I have been there already. For six months."

"Yes, I know. You corresponded with me. I am simply say-ing I cannot picture you in that place. The failure is mine."

Though somehow, with Virginia, the failure seemed always to be his.

* * *

His Alexandrian book was done and in the aftermath there was little to keep him occupied. His old talent for idleness took over, with its attendant self-reproach. Months passed, leaving no mark.

He kept in touch with Mohammed, of course, but the news that came wasn't good. Little baby Morgan had sickened and died, and that was sad enough. But Morgan had never seen the child and his very existence seemed like a fable. Far more real and distressing was that Mohammed's health was also under strain. Since his time in prison, the old sickness, consumption or whatever it was, had returned. And he still struggled for work, and was noticeably more bitter that his English friend couldn't help him.

There was nothing to be done. Mohammed's life had been touched, but not changed, by Morgan's, and his fate had been shaped by his station. Race and class were a kind of destiny; very little could dent them. Morgan himself had been decanted back into the vessel that had made him. It was better to stay there, at least for now; and if he flowed elsewhere in the future, it would probably not be to Egypt.

India, then. Even though he couldn't go yet, it continued to call to him in various voices. One of these was Masood's. Since his visit to England, a great tenderness had been restored, and it was in this tone that he wrote to say that he had set some money aside to pay for Morgan's journey: a touching, if not practical, suggestion.

At almost the same time another message came through

Malcolm Darling, who was back in England on furlough. Between rabid diatribes on the Amritsar massacre, which seemed to preoccupy Malcolm to the point of obsession, he brought a fresh invitation from His Highness, the Maharajah. Would Morgan be prepared to drop everything forthwith and come to India as his Private Secretary?

"He asked me that once before," Morgan said. "I don't even know what it means."

"Oh, the Indians like titles," Malcolm told him. "It's merely an administrative position, a bit like being a guardian to the constitution, although there isn't one. An Englishman is in the post at the moment, but he has to go on sick leave for a few months. He had a small accident. Fell out of a train."

"I can't do it, Malcolm. I long to go, but I can't."

It was quite true: inwardly he strained in that direction, till he made himself quite East-sick. And after a few months, feeling that he was committing an infidelity, he wrote quietly to Dewas, asking whether the position of Private Secretary had been filled yet.

He didn't expect a reply. But just in case one came, he raised the matter with his mother. They were sitting together after dinner, reading companionably, when he lowered his book and said, "How would Mummy feel if Poppy left her again?"

She sighed and marked her place with a finger. "It would depend on where he wants to go."

He told her about Dewas and the possible invitation. He was watching her expression carefully, but she seemed unperturbed.

"Can this princely state not do without your assistance?" she asked.

"I daresay it can. I have a different motive. I mean my novel—my Indian novel, of course."

"Oh, yes," she said vaguely.

"Perhaps you don't remember it. It has been stuck for some time, but only because all the details of India have become blurred in my mind. I need to go back, to refresh my impressions."

"Well, go if you must, dear," she said, opening her book again. "But do take care out there."

It seemed too much to hope for that she would accept the blow so calmly. Though it probably wouldn't matter, because he doubted the invitation would ever come.

And then, of course, it did.

He was again on holiday in Lyme Regis with Goldie when the cable arrived. The message was wordy but vague, and he stood in the hallway reading it over several times, before going through into the drawing room, where Goldie was working. His bemusement must have been obvious, because the older man looked up and murmured, "Everything all right?"

"Yes, I think so. That is, I have been asked back to India."

"Oh, how dreadful." Goldie set down his pen. "Are you very pleased?"

"I don't know." It was almost a shock that the impossible had suddenly happened, and what was distant had come into reach. "He wants me to leave immediately."

"Not for anything would I return there. If there is celestial punishment, and if my sins were very great, the Almighty would send me. But no Maharajah has the power."

Goldie had spent the War in a morbid pacifist funk, closeted away in Cambridge, wanting, he said, to absorb the full horror of the time. At the very start of hostilities, he had drafted his scheme for a League of Nations and had been pushing the idea along ever since. The Covenant of the League, adopted at the Peace Conference, had made him feel powerful again, and his mood had improved considerably. Though he had been very exercised again of late by the parlous state of the world—everything, from the famine in China to the lynching of negroes in America, upset him greatly—since coming away with Morgan he had undergone a transformation. He had passed his days in comparative contentment, wrapped up in his dressing gown, scribbling away on his translation of Faust. And he spoke now with a grave tone, but his sensitive mouth betrayed amusement, and the little tassel on his mandarin cap jiggled merrily.

Morgan had already started out the door. "I am going to cable my reply."

"No pause for reflection? Is that wise?"

"What?" Morgan was confused. The question seemed meaningless for a second. "There is nothing to reflect on," he said. "I am going. Certainly I am going."

* * *

Now that the news was definite, Lily lost some of her good humour. In his last few days she became toneless and inconsiderate, but he knew it was out of love for him, and bore it. And on the night before his departure, she wrote a little note, with some of her gentlest words. *I feel I got up days ago, and that you have been gone a very long time. The house seems sorrowing for you—such a desolate feeling as if it knew you had really gone and were not in London for the day or away on a visit. I felt in a dream when I was out, rather as I felt when war was declared.*

It was not the house that was in mourning; it was his mother. But not even her sadness could stop him. Twelve days after sailing from Tilbury, he was in Port Said.

He had arranged to meet Mohammed onshore, but to his astonishment, just as he was struggling to disembark, a familiar face welled up beaming in the crowd. They clasped hands and stared. It had been two years since they'd seen each other, and for a long moment he didn't understand anything.

"Are you not glad to see me, Forster?"

"I am, of course. But how did you get onto the ship?"

"I had to bribe. Everything is baksheesh, as you know. Here are expensive cigarettes, my gift to you. The box is not full, because I had to give to many people in order to find you. But I think you do not like me any more."

The ship was full of people; there was nowhere to demonstrate his liking. While they toured the second-class decks, the most that was possible was to bump flanks occasionally through their clothes. It was a cold night, with low, scudding clouds, and Mohammed was thickly wrapped up. Suddenly he stopped and with his blue knitted gloves took hold of Morgan's hands and said, "How are you, friend, how are you?"

"I am well, very well. And how are you?"

Instantly, his face fell. "I am sick. I have lost four pounds. And Gamila's father has become bankrupt. Life is not good."

Morgan stopped him. "I have only a few hours," he said. "I don't want to be sad. Please, let's talk only of happy things."

Mohammed brightened again. "Yes, I agree. Let us pretend." They were standing at the rail, watching the coaling barges move immensely through the gloom, and he suggested now, "Let's go ashore and drink some coffee."

It was only a five-minute ride to solid land. On the motor boat, Morgan tried to see how thin Mohammed really was, but he was wearing a heavy greatcoat—one of his own cast-offs—and his body was hidden from view. Perhaps it was better that way; it didn't help to know too much.

It was good to be standing on Egyptian soil again, next to his friend. He hadn't been able to visualise such a moment until now. They drank a Turkish coffee together and collaborated on a postcard to his mother, before walking out along the canal. A sea-mist was coming in and the water dissolved at the edges. Even the figures of people near the docks seemed substanceless, unreal. "It is like a dream," Morgan said.

"Yes," Mohammed said, though perhaps they were speaking of different things. For the first time a silence dropped over them, and they walked half-pressed against each other, shoulders touching, down the mole to the statue of de Lesseps. Only the feet were visible; the body disappeared upwards into night. They stood looking at it in silence for a few minutes and then went on along the deserted beach, where, a little way back from the sea, they found a hollow in the sand to sit in.

"So," Mohammed said at last. "India."

"India, yes. For a year, perhaps."

"Let me come with you."

"Next time," Morgan said, avoiding his friend's gaze. He quickly added, "I shall stop with you on the journey home."

"But how long will you stay? You are here now for only four hours. What is so important in your India that you must arrive there so fast?"

"On my way back I will stop with you for longer."

His voice had become hoarse with suppressed emotion. Both of them knew why they had walked out here, into the dark, and it was no surprise when he leaned over and reached his hand through the folds of Mohammed's coat.

His friend sighed, but leaned back accommodatingly. "Foolish," he said, shaking his head.

"All have their foolishness, and this is mine."

T he dullness of the evening sky hung heavily, reflecting Morgan's mood. It had been a long and tiring journey, the train nowhere near as clean or comfortable as on his previous visit. And the road from Indore was rough, running straight between small, dispirited trees, doing nothing to uplift him. His thoughts were all of indecency and failure, so that when the car passed a dead cow at the roadside, a ring of vultures hunching and bobbing around it, the image seemed like an omen. *That's how it will end.*

Ever since leaving Bombay, he had been musing on what lay ahead. He had accepted a position at the royal court, where his duties felt unclear and his abilities insufficient. He was sure he could be of no use to His Highness. Much more worrying, however, was the prospect of being a liability. His sexual imaginings had been rampant ever since stepping ashore and he felt almost capable, after his time in Egypt, of putting them into practice. But that way lay disaster; he could not—he *must* not—be weak. He told himself: *the least I can do is to cause no trouble.* But he had no faith in his own character, so that the rotting cow carcass spoke louder than his resolve.

His despondency lasted all the way to Dewas. But when they arrived at the New Palace, the Maharajah was capering joyfully outside the front door.

"Morgan! Morgan! So fine to see you. I have been waiting some time. Let us send cables immediately to announce your arrival. One to Malcolm. And one to your mother! Then we must find some Indian clothes for you, we are going to a party tonight. Where is my secretary?"

He wore no head-dress and his face—although eight years older now—had the impish delight of a child. Morgan cheered up.

He was cheerier still once he had been taken upstairs to his rooms and dressed in jodhpurs and silken waistcoat and a scarlet turban, and then driven off by carriage to the Cavalry barracks to watch a play performed by a visiting troupe of actors. He squatted on the floor for as long as his hips could bear it, before retreating to a chair at the back of the hall. The noise and colour and strangeness confirmed indisputably that he had, finally, arrived.

It was unsettling and comforting to know that he was the only white man in a radius of twenty miles.

* * *

Nothing so far had gone according to plan. He had written twice to Masood from England and wired from Aden en route, but still his friend wasn't in Bombay to meet him. He had taken himself from the quay to the Thomas Cook offices, but there was no letter. Even more problematic, Masood had promised him some money which he needed to live on, and there was no sign of that either.

And there was nothing from Dewas. He had apparently been stranded. He fell back on the hospitality of friends living nearby and it was only on his second day, while he was at the Post Office sending off yet another wire to Masood, that two frantic courtiers had come rushing up to him. They had been looking for him in the wrong place, or at the wrong time, or under the wrong name—anyhow, it had all been wrong.

After that things had gone better for a while. On the journey up to Dewas he had been looked after very well. But for the first few days after his arrival, all his worst fears again seemed true.

The place was incomprehensible. The first time he'd come here, he had been an honoured visitor, staying in the guest house, and the doings of the palace were remote and fabulous. But now he was in the thick of it and what had appeared dazzling from a distance was merely baffling from up close.

He had a long interview with the Maharajah on the first morning, where his official duties were explained to him. "You are in charge of the gardens, the tennis courts, the motor cars." His Highness counted off his responsibilities on his fingers. "And we must not forget the guest house and the Electric House."

"The Electric House?" Morgan's despair knew no bounds. "I can't fix anything electrical. And I understand nothing about motor engines. Your Highness, I had expected to be dealing with matters of reading and writing, those are my fields of expertise."

"Call me Bapu Sahib, please. Don't worry, your expertise will not go to waste. I would like it very much if you would read to me every day, some enlightening piece which we can discuss. This was part of my education with Malcolm and it is necessary to continue. And all the palace post will go through your hands too."

"But, Bapu Sahib, the tennis courts . . . "

"All will come clear in time. Do not distress yourself. What is most important is to understand the rankings of office. Let me write them for you, then you may study afterwards and remember."

Though Morgan studied, he struggled to remember. It was so unbelievably complicated. "There are four categories," the Maharajah told him, while he wrote. "There is first the Royal Family. Then there are the great Maratha nobles, followed by the secondary nobles. Then there are the rest, the lesser nobles, whom we call Mankari." He looked sadly at Morgan. "In this last lot, you will be the first."

He went back to the subject of the Ruling Family. There were his brother and his son, his wife, his brother's wife and his aunt. Each had their own names and titles and had to be salaamed with two hands, using the whole hand in each case. A similar courtesy was to be extended to the Dewan, meaning the Prime Minister, the Agent to the Governor General and the Political Agent.

"The last two, as you know, are British representatives, but when dealing with them you are to consider yourself an Indian. Now let us discuss the Council of State."

"I'm a little lost."

"Wait a minute!" He went on ruthlessly, enumerating countless officials of descending importance.

"I shall never get this right."

"Yes, you will. Besides, it doesn't matter in the least, except in the case of Brother and those others whom I have specially mentioned."

Among the Ruling Family, Morgan's task was made slightly easier by the absence of the Maharajah's son, who was in the hills, and his wife, who had left him, or been banished—the question was disputed—five years before. Nevertheless, other royal personages swarmed, trailing their glory and their titles. It was all very frightening.

And made worse, he was soon to discover, by the appalling disrepair that surrounded him. Everything was confusion and mess. When he'd last been here, eight years before, the New Palace was under construction—but it was still under construction now, and what had previously been built seemed to be falling down. Under his window six almost-naked men did work that one man could do, handing a tiny basket of earth between them to no apparent purpose. The same futility was evident across a much wider area, where half-dug holes pitted the ground between sheets of abandoned marble.

And further afield, a similar chaos held sway. Roads had been started that petered out into grass; beautiful fruit trees were dying in the heat. A thousand pounds' worth of electric batteries stood decaying, with no use for them until the Electric House could be enlarged. Numberless servants underpinned this enterprise, all of them seemingly idle and incompetent.

It was just as bad indoors. Everything had warped and buckled in the heat. An assortment of new musical instruments—a harmonium, a dulciphone and two pianos, one of them a grand—could not be played, because their frames were cracked and peeling. Taps dripped continually and could not be turned off. An unused suite of dining-room chairs was vomiting forth its innards. When he opened a cupboard in the bathroom, he found it stacked, inexplicably, with teapots. He asked for a bookcase and it collapsed instantly under his hands. A large rodent of some kind was gnawing a hole in the canvas ceiling on his veranda. Nor did it help that the two Indian officials Morgan relied on to assist him in his duties could speak very little English.

When he told all this, as diplomatically as he could, to Bapu Sahib, the response was delight. The Maharajah clapped his hands and giggled like a girl.

"Do not fear, Morgan!" he cried. "All will be well!"

The same kind of gaiety ran through the court. Nothing appeared to matter very much. When Morgan had first arrived in Bombay the festival of Holi was still in progress; the two courtiers who had escorted him were streaked with bright paint. The same colours stained everybody in Dewas, and there had been the raucous party at the Cavalry barracks on his first night. Then April Fool's Day came, and he was offered trick cigarettes and whisky laced with salt, and an attempt was made to send him on a pointless errand to a remote shed in the garden. It was all games and foolery, a sort of childish bawdiness that made even the driest officials fall about in laughter. Indeed, Morgan joined in, and his first ominous mood soon faded away.

* * *

Not long after his arrival, he was taken on an outing to visit a local village. Walking along the banks of a river, where nature was still unspoiled, the train of villagers that followed their party became most excited at what they emphatically said was a rearing snake. To Morgan's eyes, the snake appeared to be a small, dead tree, but common opinion declared him wrong: it was certainly a snake, they told him, of a vicious and poisonous kind. It was on the other side of the water, too far away to harm them, but it was necessary anyway to throw stones at it. One of these stones, hitting it full-on, revealed that it *was* a small, dead tree. Much hilarity ensued, which turned to consternation when it was decided that the Sahib was disappointed, and very much wanted to see a real snake, which was nowhere close to hand.

Morgan thought of this moment as typically Indian, and somehow revealing, because of the lack of certainty that enclosed it. One ended by being unsure whether the branch might not have been a snake after all. This doubt would not have lasted back home in England, but here, under the strong, enormous sky, no answer was ever quite enough. There was a mystery at the heart of things, he felt, which might derive from the gap in language and religion—but which might, just as plausibly, derive from the landscape or the weather.

The same sense of mystery—a tiny blurred place at the edge of perception—carried into all his dealings here. There was hardly a conversation or a custom that didn't leave him perplexed in some way. It wasn't that things weren't explained: Masood had always tried, and so had Bapu Sahib, and there were whole tomes written on the subject of India. But even the plainest explanation seemed to throw up more questions; an opacity remained, impervious to language.

This applied also to his work. Not his smallest confusion related to the doings of the court, which he was supposed in part to oversee. But never could he fully understand the logic of even the simplest arrangement. Why were scores of rupees spent on festivals and pageantry, for example, when the palace itself was falling down?

The Maharajah's intimate life was another area of mystery. His wife, the Maharani, had come from Kolhapur, and thence had she fled again. Kolhapur was a powerful state, far more powerful than Dewas, and Bapu Sahib appeared to have created a frightening enemy through this personal rupture. Strangers would appear in the court from time to time, who were said to be Kolhapur spies. But whether his wife would return, whether or not they were divorced, and what the reasons were for the split: none of this was ever made clear to Morgan.

He remembered the Maharani from his first visit, and knew that the glimpse had been a privileged one. But Bapu Sahib had since taken another companion, Bai Saheba, who didn't feel the need to keep invisible. She lived in a ramshackle house near the entrance to the city, where she lolled about on carpets in a courtyard, surrounded by attendants. She would frequently visit the palace, or Bapu Sahib would go to her, and on each occasion the journey would involve a loud spectacle of horses and soldiers and finery, drawing great attention to itself. But although His Highness referred to her as his Maharani, and she had borne him three daughters already and was again pregnant at this moment, it didn't seem that they were properly married, which was confusing. Why was there a great need for modesty and circumspection in one case, but not in the other?

Morgan knew that there were concubines of different ranks in Hindu society, and thought perhaps she was one of these. But when he very delicately tried to bring up the topic with Bapu Sahib, talking of golden concubines and silver ones, His Highness laughed uproariously. "She is my *diamond* concubine," he said, which only muddied the matter further.

* * *

Masood's absence at the docks had been worrisome, but it turned out that he'd been visiting educational establishments in the jungle and had received none of the messages. Now that he knew Morgan was here, he hastened up from Hyderabad for a visit.

Both of them were edgy, because of the royal surroundings. "Well, it isn't much of a palace," Masood observed. "More like a big, ugly house. Mine is much better."

"For God's sake, don't say that when you meet him. Decorum must be maintained."

"Your salary, you mean. And your good standing. You're as rotten as the rest of them."

But they were smiling as they embraced. Time had made everything easier.

Masood had brought three attendants with him—a Parsi clerk and two servants—who followed behind, carrying luggage and files. Much of this was for show, Morgan realised, because he couldn't stand to be overshadowed by a mere Maratha king. And once inside, he immediately began to bully the Mayor of the palace, Malarao Sahib.

"The Nizam of Hyderabad, for whom I work, is entitled to a twenty-one gun salute," he told him. "I forget what Dewas Senior merits . . . ?"

"Fifteen," Morgan said quickly, noticing Malarao's unhappiness.

"Hmm. How wonderful. But we have twenty-one." And he ran a fingertip distastefully across a dusty surface.

By now Morgan feared the worst. But when the time came for him to meet the Maharajah, Masood was the soul of politeness. He was more pompous than usual, but in a deferential, self-demeaning way. Even when he questioned His Highness about the constitution—which was being drawn up eight years ago and was still being drawn up now—he did it with enormous, elaborate respect. It was as though the ritualised humility that he'd parodied in his early letters had suddenly come true.

And Bapu Sahib matched it. Was Masood quite comfortable, were the furnishings and the food to his liking? He was an Indian brother, his name had been mentioned so often, and nothing would be too much to ask, he had only to request it. There was a great deal of solemn nodding, and it seemed for a while as if two kings were in the room, discussing matters of state.

But when they were alone together, Masood became himself again. He swaggered and twirled the ends of his moustache, in which a strand or two of silver was showing. At night it was too hot to sleep indoors, so they retreated to the roof. Morgan had been making his bed up there since he'd arrived, but—Masood told him now—it was on the wrong side.

"No, no, no, only an Englishman and a fool would sleep over there. You simply have no idea . . . you must face the town. Yes, here, much better. Can you not feel the breeze? Call the servants and have the beds moved."

The beds were moved from one end of the roof to the other. And when the lamps were doused he felt intensely happy to be lying near his old friend, talking softly back and forth in the warm dark.

Over the next few days, the Maharajah treated them to fine food and entertainment and outings. He even sent them to the top of the mountain of Devi on an elephant. But despite all the finery and expensive fare, Masood never lost his disapproval of Dewas. He didn't show it to their host, but when he was alone with Morgan he muttered in a haughty way about all the incompetence surrounding them. The heaps of rubble and masonry were a visible reminder of everything, in his opinion, that was wrong with the princely states.

"True independence will correct all this," he said, as he sipped tea from a china cup on the veranda. "It isn't really India, it's a grotesque caricature that has been bred by the intermarriage of your Empire and our silliness."

"We didn't invent the Princes," Morgan said mildly. "They were here already."

"Not in this form. Look at the waste, the excess. Do you know there is a squirrel nesting in one of the pianos?"

"Yes, I saw it." Morgan couldn't suppress a giggle.

"Oh, and look at this. It's too much. While we are drinking tea!"

He was referring to a line of servants who trooped past just then, each carrying a commode. As they marched away, trailing a faint, unpleasant odour behind them, he sighed and raised his eyebrows.

Morgan giggled again; it was funny and sad. If the English left, as they no doubt would one day, what would the Indians set up in their stead? Would it be less ridiculous than the Raj?

The same question touched them both a day or two later when he and Masood drove over to Ujjain. It was a holy city and Morgan thought his friend might enjoy the spectacle of the ghats along the river, with their hectic displays of worship. It was never less than entertaining. In Benares, on his first visit, Morgan felt he had come closest to something essentially Indian. With the bodies being burned on the riverbank, and the ribald pandemonium of boats and temples and shrines, a vision was evoked of how this country might have functioned if no white man had ever come here.

But although Ujjain's river was a paler imitation of that scene, it stirred up horror in Masood. There were hundreds of sadhus going about their business, washing themselves or chatting or praying, some almost naked, many painted brightly or smeared with ash, a few even sitting on beds of spikes. Masood stared at a group who were drinking tea, his face seeming to broaden with the emotion that filled it, and then rounded on Morgan, as if he were responsible. "My dear chap," he cried in indignation, "I *ask* you!"

What he asked wasn't said. But there was no answer in any case.

* * *

It was too hot to work in the middle hours of the day. He attended to his duties in the early part of the morning and sometimes read to His Highness in the late afternoon. From noon to four he was mostly in his rooms. Though they were spacious—a bedroom, sitting room, anteroom and bathroom, all attractively done in the European style—they could not contain him. Indolence and heat were a bad combination, and his thoughts tended towards carnality, despite his best efforts to stop them.

He remembered the dead cow at the roadside, and the resolution he'd made. But he'd been struggling with himself ever since. It was the first time he fully understood Searight's meaning. The midday light was white and blinding, impaling the dry earth vertically with its rays. Indoors, one perspired and imagined—there was little else to do. And it was hard to keep one's thoughts from finding an object.

Two gradually swam into focus. The first was the

Mohammedan sais who clung to the back of his Victoria when he rode around. He was an unattractive lad of fifteen or sixteen, dirty and thin, who had nevertheless noticed Morgan. There had been an alarming moment when he'd bunched up the front of his dhoti to simulate an erection, and then smiled meaningfully with bad teeth.

Far more promising was the Hindu coolie, who worked with the Sikhs who were installing electric light in the Durbar hall. It was part of Morgan's duties to inspect their progress, and on one of these visits he'd seen the boy running across a courtyard, laughing. A look had passed between them and thereafter the coolie had made a point of salaaming Morgan with great respect, using both hands. He was about eighteen, thin but well-shaped, with a pleasantly gentle expression.

On another occasion, he had brought a chair for Morgan to sit on, making a small show of it, and from then on, the two had been aware of one another differently. A secretive game of smiles and glances went on between them, which quickly became more elaborate. When Morgan next visited the Durbar hall, he was startled by a loud noise behind him; turning to look, he saw the coolie boy lashing the ground, as if to dust it, with a leather strap. He lashed once more, forcefully, then a third time more softly, and all the time he smiled while he lashed. Not long afterwards, when he was sent by one of the Sikhs to fetch some wires and brackets for the lights, he stared at Morgan as he trotted off down the passage. He went around a corner, and then stopped, his shadow visible on the floor, waiting out of sight for the Englishman to follow.

Morgan didn't follow, even when the boy repeated the exercise the next day. It would have been too obvious, too dangerous, to take this sort of action. But he felt his inertia, then and afterwards. His lust was both humiliating and boring, but it couldn't easily be quenched—not even by masturbation, rigorously applied.

The heat was conducive to such barren activities. On one afternoon he resorted to self-abuse three times, and still felt frustrated, as well as ashamed. There were days when the whole earth, pinioned under the white-hot sun, was as empty and aimless as Morgan's mind. He felt a little ill with it, the inside of his mouth and nose dried out, his appetite shrunken. For hours at a time he seemed stupid to himself, even senile, unable to concentrate or remember. At night the sheets on his bed threw off sparks when he moved, and once even gave him a shock. This electricity, coming from nowhere, serving no purpose, was like the sexual charge that crackled around his idleness.

It became worse in May, when Bai Saheba's child, another girl, was born. For fifteen days after the birth, His Highness had to sleep, with most of his court, in the compound where she lived. Morgan would go there in the evenings and stay the night and, on these journeys to and fro, the sais would cling to the back of the carriage and sing what sounded like love songs under his breath. He was singing to Morgan alone and, when he turned his head to look, the boy would part his lips suggestively and smile. It was intolerable! These images, these sounds, lingered in Morgan's head through the hot nights that followed.

It was part of the ritual that mother and child were serenaded by an unholy din of fireworks and music, most of it clamorous and sore on the ears. The discord was like an echo of what was roiling inside him, but there was one particular night when he woke at three in the morning to a different sound entirely. Indian singers were accompanied by a lovely and simple harmony, and he fitted on his turban and rejoined the company. Under the brilliant white frieze of stars, he found himself remembering Mr. Godbole, who had sung unexpectedly to him on his previous visit. That moment, as well as this, were both small but exquisite, reminding him of the order that could lift unexpectedly from its opposite.

* * *

His room was flanked by an inner and outer veranda, and on the doorway from the latter a grass mat known as a tattie had been hung, which had to be sprinkled with water, so that the air which passed through it could be kept cool. A month after Morgan's arrival, his servant Baldeo had come to look after him. As wizened and blackened as ever, still of indeterminate age, Baldeo seemed indifferent to the prospect of being reunited with his old master. Morgan had gone to trouble to arrange his appointment, but none of this effort had softened Baldeo's feelings; he complained and muttered about every duty, and high on his lists of resentments was keeping the tattie damp.

Now it occurred to Morgan that it might be ideal for everybody if the coolie boy could be given this particular job. He spoke to the overseer downstairs, who managed to send the wrong boy. But after another conversation and a hint to the coolie himself, the next afternoon he appeared at the door, throwing his water.

Morgan waited for a moment when they were alone. Then he went out onto the veranda and pretended to inspect the activity. "No, no," he said. "That isn't how you do it."

"No?"

"Let me show you."

He drew close and took the cup from him. Then, inexpertly, he demonstrated how the water should be thrown. In the process, he let his wrist rub against the coolie boy's wrist. It was a tiny contact, but it felt intense enough to strike a spark.

The young man smiled gleamingly.

His voice choked with fear and excitement, Morgan said, "Meet me tonight."

"Tonight?"

"At seven-thirty. On the road near the guest house." He

couldn't arrange an assignation at the palace itself. His Highness had told him he was building the palace in memory of his late father, and it would be too large a transgression. "Do you understand?"

"Seven-thirty," the youth repeated, nodding. There was nothing more to say and after a few more desultory swipes with the water, Morgan went inside, where he was immediately convulsed with guilt. It was one thing to dream and imagine; it was quite another to act, and now he had acted. Or he had made his intentions clear, which was almost as bad. At the same time, inseparable from the sense of sin, he was jangled with anticipation.

Almost immediately, the punishment came. Scarcely ten minutes had passed when he heard a hissing, whispered conversation from the inside corridor:

"The Burra Sahib has given orders to come at night—"

"At night?" A second voice, incredulous.

"Yes, and he will give money—"

Morgan rushed to the door to listen. But the voices, jabbering in excitement, had already drifted away, merging with those of a larger group of workmen who were moving furniture in the State Drawing Room. That bigger conversation took on a note of outrage and he felt sure—he *knew*—that they were talking about him. The first two voices had been those of the coolie boy and Baldeo, he thought now; he had been undone by his servant, from whom no secrets could be kept.

It was terrible, terrible; everything he most feared was about to happen; he had drawn it down on himself. He had always known this moment would come. Soon afterwards there was a commotion downstairs and, feeling sick with terror, he staggered onto the outside veranda to look. He was in time to see Mr. Chavan, one of the senior clerks, jumping into a bullock cart and moving purposefully off in the direction of

Bai Saheba's house, with one backward accusing glance. He could only be going to report the matter.

The shame was, literally, indescribable; there were no words for a sensation one had never fully experienced until now. He wanted to die, to vanish; he wanted the fastenings to be unpicked so that he could be dismantled. He had been invited here on faith and trust, he had been given this appointment because he was Malcolm's friend. And now he had brought disgrace not only on himself but on Malcolm too. Everybody would know; whisper would blend into whisper; it would carry, quite possibly, all the way to the heart of his life, in Weybridge. His mother would hear of it! The horror made him lame. How he wished he could spool time backward; how he wished he had never spoken.

There was nothing to do but wait. Despite the intense heat, he felt cold. In his mind he went back to his first visit to Dewas. He'd recently stayed with the Maharajah of Chhatarpur—that eccentric and likeable man who kept his own theatrical troupe of boys to perform his Krishna plays—and on that first evening, Bapu Sahib had shocked Morgan by making mention of this other Maharajah's tendencies. The remark was something about him being less than a man, and it had been delivered with a smirk and a sneer. It was the facial expression, the tone, that had lingered more than the words, and at the time Morgan had felt disappointed in his new princely acquaintance. He'd thought then that their friendship would be a short one. Things had turned out differently, but the remark came back now with a venomous sting. If His Highness could speak that way—so contemptuously, so dismissively—of another Maharajah, how much more virulent would his disdain be for an inferior, such as Morgan was?

And now here he was, Bapu Sahib, Morgan could hear his carriage arriving downstairs. Perhaps an hour had passed since Mr. Chavan had hurried off on his mission. It was important to behave as he normally did, and he went downstairs to the porch to meet His Highness.

It was immediately plain that the worst had happened. Bapu Sahib's manner was friendly but remote; there was an underlying cynicism to his friendliness. "Where have *you* sprung from?" he said in greeting—words that he had never used before.

Morgan muttered in reply.

His Highness strode briskly to a room on the ground floor, not one he usually frequented. This in itself seemed to betoken a shift in relations; perhaps something was about to be said. On the way they passed a boy painting the wainscot, an effete child who drew the Maharajah's attention. Pausing briefly, he murmured to himself, "Everywhere . . . I cannot get away from them . . . ", before marching angrily on.

What could this mean except damnation? Things were just as bad as Morgan had thought. Or perhaps worse: the Maharajah seemed determined to draw out the agony to its fullest extent. Another comment came a little later about intrigues in a neighbouring court:

"What is the use?" His Highness observed bitterly. "You cannot hide like that bird that pushes its head into the sand. You know which bird I mean—what is its name?"

"The ostrich," Morgan said wretchedly. He knew he was being addressed directly.

"Exactly," Bapu Sahib agreed. He let the moment linger. "The ostrich."

But the most hurtful remark came much later, in the evening, before various assembled courtiers. The conversation was brought around by subtle degrees to a discussion of catamites. "I intend to drive all of them out of Dewas," the Maharajah announced, with a cruel sweep of his hand. "Really, what is the good of such people?"

The other nobles nodded in agreement. Morgan stared at

the tips of his feet. At this moment he could only agree with His Highness: there was no good in people like him.

That night he went down to Bai Saheba's house as usual, to join the gathered throng. He sat at the right hand of his master, who ignored him, and in the faces of the people around him he saw awareness and disrespect.

Then the coolie boy came. Suddenly, among the watchers opposite, he was there, glowering sadly at Morgan. His gaze was filled with mute incomprehension: why had the Sahib not met him as arranged? He had gone, he must have gone, to the road near the guest house at seven-thirty, and waited in vain. Now he was here, staring his reproach across the crowded courtyard.

Morgan ignored him. On previous evenings the boy had sat here in the same courtyard, smiling, pulling down his dhoti to cover his legs, in order to make the Englishman aware of him. But tonight he did not exist—or he existed only as an absence, a blank space unoccupied by desire.

It was the same in the days that followed. As assiduously as Morgan had pursued him, he now un-pursued the boy, deliberately avoiding the rooms where he knew he was working, taking himself elsewhere when the time came for the tattie to be cooled. When he did see his tormentor, the boy always had a half-bemused, half-hopeful expression, still expecting a liaison to be arranged, or perhaps payment of some kind. He had the power to make a scene, so that even his silent waiting figure, loitering in the passage, or outside the garden after sundown, a whitish, accusing outline in the dusk, could strike dread into a soft English heart.

He lasted for four days. Then he went down to Bai Saheba's compound just after noon. It was unspeakably hot—a good time for this discussion, because fewer people were around. Bapu Sahib was drowsing in a tin-roofed shed with a few unconscious courtiers nearby.

"May I speak to you, Your Highness?" It was the first time since he'd arrived that he'd fallen back on this formal mode of address.

"Yes, of course, speak."

"I would prefer it to be private, if you don't mind."

The Maharajah stirred himself; he pretended to be puzzled. They crossed the courtyard to the shade of a tree and settled themselves at its foot.

Morgan hesitated only a moment. He had rehearsed what he wanted to say in advance and there was no point in delaying. Disgrace gave him a peculiar authority.

"My mind is clear at last," he announced. "I feel I can now speak. I wasn't able to before." He drew a deep breath. "As I think you know, I am in great trouble."

"Tell me, Morgan. I have noticed you were worried."

He looked down at the ground, and his attention fastened on a line of ants, disappearing into a hole. This tiny, frantic activity, in the midst of such inertia, consoled him. He said, "I have tried to have carnal intercourse with one of the coolies, and it has become known."

"With a coolie girl?"

"No, with a man." His voice cracked, but he brought it under control. "You know about it, and if you agree I think I ought to resign."

The Maharajah, frowning, straightened a little against the bole of the tree, then collapsed again. "But, Morgan," he said. "I know nothing about it."

The white centre of the day ballooned and spread.

"But I beg your pardon, that isn't possible," Morgan said.

"Oh, yes, yes, I promise you, this is the first I've heard of it."

Morgan still didn't believe him. It had been so clear and so certain. He began to ask His Highness about what he'd meant by his various remarks and moods over the previous days. But there were innocent answers to everything. The ostrich, it seemed, was merely a metaphor; the small boy painting the wainscot had irritated simply by being underfoot, nothing more. Gradually, despite his suspicion, Morgan began to realise that he'd made a huge mistake.

How absurd, how foolish he had been! All the signs and portents that he'd read, that he'd felt so sure about, suddenly took on a different, innocuous cast: everything could be explained. There had been no cynical knowledge. There had been no judgement. He had imagined all of it.

And in the same moment he knew that everything he'd feared was now about to come true. Not because it had been discovered, but because he had revealed it. No external agency had brought him low; instead, he had dealt the mortal blow himself. Even in his extremity, the irony wasn't lost on him.

But Bapu Sahib didn't seem outraged. In the same kindly, worried tone, he asked, "Why a man and not a woman? Is not a woman more natural?"

"Not in my case. I have no feeling for them."

"Oh, but then that alters everything. You are not to blame."

"I don't know what 'natural' is."

"You are quite right, Morgan. I ought never to have used the word." Seeing tears well in his Private Secretary's eyes, he went on hurriedly: "Now don't worry—don't worry. My only distress is you did not tell me before. I might have saved you so much pain. May I know all about this coolie now?"

Morgan told everything. He didn't hold back. In the rush of confession, he volunteered all the tawdry details, including how he had resorted to his *dirty trick* for relief. And when he'd finished, Bapu Sahib exclaimed, "But you are in a very strong position."

"Am I?"

"Yes, yes. I was afraid you had copulated, which might have caused difficulties. But you haven't even kissed him. Now don't worry." His voice changed, thickening in collusion. "Only you must always come to me when you are facing problems like these. I would have found you somebody reliable among the hereditary servants and you could have had him quietly in your room." Seeing Morgan's expression, he waved a hand. "It's true, I don't encourage such people, but it's entirely different in your case, and you must not masturbate, no, no, that's awful."

"What I haven't said yet," Morgan told him, "is that I'm so very sorry at having deceived you—"

He felt as if he was reconciling with his father—a father nine years younger than himself—and the emotion squeezed his voice into a sob. Bapu Sahib almost cried, too, but caught himself in time.

"Oh, devil! Don't do that, Morgan. The only way with a thing like this is to take it laughing."

Laughter didn't seem possible in this moment. But the Maharajah was deflecting them away from embarrassment by brooding on possible candidates. "Hmmm, I don't think you've seen that servant of mine, Arjuna. He is mostly at the Holy Temple in the Old Palace—very delicately formed, like a girl. Or there is a man in the kitchens . . . but he's too old, twenty-eight. Wait, let me think. There is another boy . . . he is a barber, though he does that sort of thing, I believe. But the first thing now is to see that this business with your coolie is safe. I'm sure he meant to do you no harm."

* * *

The lightness that took hold of him in the days that followed gave him the illusion of weightlessness; the information his senses carried took on new poignancy. The hot, dry air was beautiful to him. He no longer felt parched and burnt-out by the light. Instead he could detect, deep inside, the impending monsoon. At night there were often electrical storms, great violent displays of wind and lightning, but the rain didn't fall.

And when the clouds blew away, the giant constellation of Scorpio hung brilliantly overhead. Never before had he experienced those cold points of light like shrapnel in his flesh; never had the sky cupped him so tenderly in its huge palm.

But like the promised rains, the Maharajah's solution didn't come. Soon after their talk, the servant-boy he'd mentioned drifted in for a visit. But he and Morgan didn't take to each other: the boy seemed both arrogant and crushed at the same time. When His Highness asked how the meeting had gone, Morgan shook his head.

"You didn't like him?"

"I'm afraid not, I very much regret . . . "

Bapu Sahib waved his regret away. He seemed vexed for a moment, but his basic approach to this problem was good-humoured and soon, in a jolly mood, he told Morgan that he'd made enquiries and nobody in the court was aware of what had happened. Better still, the coolie boy was not from Dewas; he came from elsewhere in the Deccan, and would be returning there as soon as building work in the palace was over.

"But now tell me something, Morgan," he went on. "I have been wondering. These habits of yours. Have you indulged them in other places?"

"Do you mean England? No, it wasn't possible at home."

"You have been in Egypt during the War. Did you, perhaps, learn these ways while you were there?"

His manner was innocent, but his eyes had narrowed. Morgan understood his meaning. He wanted to blame this vice on the Mohammedans, whom he held responsible for a great many ills in the world.

"Certainly not," Morgan said. "I never saw anything of the kind in Egypt."

"Ah, I only wondered." And he changed the subject; in a minute they were talking of other things.

It was the only moment in this period of trial when Morgan

felt His Highness had behaved less than well. It wasn't proper, he thought, that his behaviour outside of Dewas should be questioned. But for now the matter was put away, out of sight. No more candidates were sent for inspection and the topic wasn't raised again. The whole problem seemed to have been forgotten and very soon the silence hardened into disappointment; the days became long and empty once more.

Into this vacancy, desire swelled again, and he experienced its full futility one evening in the back seat of his carriage.

It had become part of his daily routine to take a drive, once the heat of the day had gone, to a quiet garden about two miles away, where he could sit for a while under enormous trees at the edge of a cistern to think. It was a little island of repose and contemplation in the midst of pandemonium, and he was usually accompanied on these expeditions by the Mohammedan sais, who clung to the back of the Victoria, somewhere behind Morgan, out of sight. On this particular afternoon his thoughts had all been physical in nature, a performance in his mind of what he couldn't accomplish with his body, and by the time he climbed back into the carriage for the drive home he had worked himself up into a feverish state. The bleached, bare landscape was like a thin sail, stretched to its limit by an unseen wind. Morgan's arm lay extended across the top of the seat, and the idea came to him that the sais was about to touch his hand. They were close to each other; they both contained the same idea; only an inch divided them. The notion of the tiny gap closing, of the touch that was about to happen, was too much, and the stretched sail tore and broke. With a little cry, quickly stifled, Morgan ejaculated in his trousers, a visible embarrassment he had to conceal when he climbed down. It had happened without the touch ever taking place—and only as he scuttled away, half-twisted around his shame, he realised that it wasn't even the right sais.

* * *

There might have been some outlet if he'd been able to write. He'd brought the damned manuscript of his novel with him, thinking that being in India might wake the story up again. But the effect, strangely, was the opposite: the continent pressed in on him so hugely that he could barely see it. When he looked at the pages he'd written, they seemed to be about an imaginary place, somewhere he'd never been. None of it was convincing, all of it was unreal. Feeling nauseous, he locked the book away again in his trunk.

He simply couldn't write at the moment. His senses were open to their fullest; the world was moving in one direction only. Better to watch, to take note, to take in. There were always details you could use, conversations that you needed to remember for later, sometimes in unexpected places.

One such occurred now, in the palace dining room. The head engineer of the electric company had been sent up from Bombay with his wife, to install the unused batteries at the Electric House. Morgan was supposed to oversee him, but he knew nothing about electricity and it was a relief when the work was over and the social niceties resumed again. At dinner His Highness took over the burden of conversation and Morgan became quieter.

Then the engineer's wife told a story. On their last visit to Dewas, she said, they had been motoring back to Indore to catch their train when a strange incident occurred.

"We had just crossed the Sipra," she said, "and some kind of animal, we couldn't see what it was, came running out of the ravine and charged our car. We had to swerve aside and almost hit the parapet."

The Maharajah had been drowsy, but he suddenly woke up. "It came from the left?"

"Yes, it did."

"A large animal. Larger than a pig, but not as big as a buffalo?"

"Yes, exactly." She was staring at him. "But how did you know that?"

"You really couldn't be sure what kind of animal it was? You didn't see?"

"No."

He slumped a little in his chair again, becoming morose. "It is most unfortunate," he said.

"But how did you know?"

He didn't want to talk about it; he was staring at the table-top. "Years ago I ran over a man there. I wasn't at all to blame—he was drunk and he ran out into the road. I was cleared at the inquiry and I gave money to his family. But ever since then he has been trying to kill me in the form that you describe."

All three of them were stupefied. Such an extraordinary event, described in such an ordinary voice: it was a challenge to the rational mind. And though Bapu Sahib soon changed the subject and spoke of other things, the story continued to bother his Private Secretary. Magic—a world of omens and portents: this was part of India, too, and inseparable from its mystery. It was a kind of thinking that had been worn away in England, lingering mostly in its literature. So that what struck Morgan most forcefully when he encountered it here was how casually it took place, almost underfoot, an accepted part of everyday life.

He didn't believe—not really—in the supernatural. But he didn't entirely disbelieve either. India scraped up to the surface a kind of buried animism in him, a propensity towards the mystical. Although he'd shed his religion early on, it was only the Church of England that he'd dropped, with its safe morning prayers and Sunday services. He had never ceased to yearn for something rawer and rougher, something closer to the earth, or perhaps the sky, of which the brain could not partake. He remembered Pan rippling through the forest in Italy; he remembered the shepherd boy above Salisbury. Those moments were elusive and few in the life that he'd known, but they were far more frequent in the East. You could hardly walk a few steps without coming across a temple or a shrine, daubed with ghee and reeking of incense, and you had only to look into the faces of those worshipping to recognise blind, atavistic devotion.

In theory, he didn't believe in God, certainly not in the avuncular versions that his own upbringing had formed. But the myriad godlets that Hinduism threw up were a more interesting proposition altogether. The sadhus at the riverside who had so horrified Masood: they stirred something else in Morgan, something not unrelated to envy. And he felt these stirrings at other moments, too, whenever Indians spoke about religion. Though he couldn't let go of himself enough to worship, he had never lost a sense of an ultimate cause, a Thing at the back of things, which propelled events without actually shaping them. Whatever the ruptures and ructions of human life, he felt, the universe operated according to some vast, unfolding principle, and to abandon oneself to its rhythms wasn't a senseless undertaking.

It came to him now that his book might express something of this unity through its structure. It was always a useful moment when a story revealed its deeper nature to him—told him, as it were, why he was writing it—and he experienced such a realisation now. He had a sense of a gathering shape, of an underlying architecture to his narrative. Part of the reason that he'd faltered was because he couldn't see further than politics; to write merely of Indians and Englishmen wasn't enough. But the story had broadened, suddenly, into a much larger channel, in which politics was only one stream. Religion, the lifeblood of India, flowed more strongly, and he saw now that the temple would offset the mosque and the caves; it would replace the one god and the no-god with a multiplicity of gods. If it wasn't order exactly, it was something better, because it more closely resembled the world. Things were not rounded off and resolved; rather, they expanded outwards, perhaps for ever, and his book could suggest that possibility.

Mosque, caves and temple. Three kinds of spirituality; three sections to his novel. A trinity, for its own spiritual reasons, was always symmetrical and pleasing. And it could be made to resonate further, by being linked to the seasons of India: the cold weather, the hot weather, and the rains. Though Morgan himself hadn't yet experienced the latter, the skies had been pregnant and moody for some time and the monsoon would soon be here.

* * *

One evening the Maharajah sighed and said, "That barber I told you about. He has been hanging about the palace. I don't like it. It's no good for the servants."

They hadn't discussed him in weeks, but the interval might not have happened. Morgan said immediately, "I do wish you could get somebody for me."

"I was waiting for you to mention it. There's not the least difficulty."

Kanaya arrived at noon, a time Morgan had chosen because Baldeo was eating his dinner. He was a good-looking young man, perhaps a little effeminate, wearing a coat that was too yellow and a turban that was too blue, with a wispy moustache and thick black eyebrows that formed a single bar over his eyes.

This first meeting was an innocent one. The idea was that Morgan would decide if he liked the barber, and only then would he be asked to return. Kanaya shaved him, his fingers thin and delicate on the Englishman's pink face, and when he was done they smiled at each other.

"Come back tomorrow. At the same time."

He went tripping away under a canvas umbrella, trailing the smell of cheap scent.

The next day he arrived a little late. The shaving ritual was repeated and in the middle of it Morgan stretched out a hand to touch the buttons on his coat. The razor stopped moving, Kanaya stood still. They looked at each other and then Morgan took hold of his sleeve and drew him closer. The little barber smiled and wobbled his head. It was a moment before Morgan remembered that in India this movement indicated assent.

To be sure, he asked, "Are you willing?"

"Yes."

"Yes?"

The reply had seemed too quick. Perhaps they were misunderstanding one another. To add to the confusion, Kanaya resumed his work, moving the razor smoothly over his skin. But when he was finished, and he had packed away his equipment, he came back to Morgan expectantly. "Yes," he said again.

Morgan bent his head clumsily—he was taller than the young man—and kissed him. It was a pleasant if passionless contact, and the Englishman was still nervous, because the other was so calm. But no upset occurred, and he hurried to the door to bolt it.

Almost immediately there was a small explosion. Baldeo had returned early from his meal and was hurling water at the tattie on the outside veranda. Haste and panic! Morgan hurried his visitor to the other door, on the inner veranda, to escape. As they parted, fumblingly, he hissed at Kanaya to arrive on time the next day.

That afternoon, when they met to play cards together, Bapu

Sahib enquired how things were going, and Morgan told him everything.

"That is good," His Highness said encouragingly. "But it is important that, the next time you see him, you make sure of it. Once you have taken action, he won't talk about it to anybody. And something else—you must be sure not to be the weaker partner. You understand me, I hope? You are not to be the lady. That sort of rumour would be bad."

Shifting around uncomfortably, Morgan tried to change the subject. "We are to meet tomorrow at the same hour, that is to say—"

Instantly, His Highness blocked his ears. "No, no," he said. "Don't tell me, because when the time comes I shall think of you, and that I don't want."

The next day Kanaya arrived early, and was gone before Baldeo returned from lunch.

* * *

A week later, the rains came at last. The situation had been dire for some time. The cisterns were so low that Morgan's bath couldn't be filled, and buckets had to be carried in from the fish-ponds outside. The two wells had run completely dry and the gardens, lovingly designed by his predecessor, were a charred plain of dust. Pipes had been laid to water the gardens, but they led from an empty tank, which led in turn to one of the empty wells.

The first shower was mild, releasing odd odours from the ground. But the air had changed, turning misty and pastel-coloured, and there was the promise of more. It came two days afterwards, while Morgan was in the garden, planting seeds. At first there had been only rumbling dark clouds and a few stray drops, but suddenly the sky turned liquid. Violent wind made the rain horizontal, switching direction constantly, and took away the palm roof of the one available shelter. When the storm had eased a little, he staggered back towards the palace, his feet encased in mud.

Just as the dryness had been the defining feature of life, so the monsoon now took over. The rains had come in time to save the crops, and there were celebrations from the local townsfolk, with naked wrestlers and brightly clad women, and the faces of elephants garishly painted. The rush of water was a daily event and, though the heat persisted between showers, Morgan's mind revived. The feeling of stupidity that had slowed him down was washed away. The colours of the world returned, and his perception of those colours too.

It had only been a few days, but his meetings with Kanaya were a regular part of his life now, though they continued to be furtive and fraught. His rooms were on the first floor, at the end of a wing, and visible to the public eye. Both the inside veranda and the staircase that descended from the outside one were on full display, and his bathroom was overlooked by stairs that went up to the second floor. All comings and goings could be observed, and even the interior wasn't safe. There was no such thing as privacy in the palace; the warped and swollen doors meant that few of them could be properly closed, and it wasn't unusual, when one was sleeping, to be woken by the sound of servants creeping about the room.

A possible solution was to try to meet outside the palace. Beyond the guest house was the Naya Bagh, a garden that might provide some cover. One afternoon, they arranged to go there. Morgan went in first, and ensconced himself among leaves. But when Kanaya tried to follow, there was a commotion of shouting and blows: he had fallen into the grip of a gardener, who thought he was a thief. Morgan extracted him and they tried to proceed further, into the countryside beyond, but you could hardly walk five steps without coming across spectators, sitting or lying about, filled with curiosity.

By the time he retraced his steps towards the palace it was fully dark.

Crossing the almost-empty tank in front of the guest house, Morgan became lost. The farce was complete as he ended up wailing Kanaya's name. The barber appeared in a moment.

"Sahib?"

"I don't know my way."

"I help."

He held out his hand. The Sahib took it. As they stumbled together across the pitted mud of the tank floor, they seemed joined in a childlike friendship. It came to Morgan that this, the tenderest moment that had passed between them, was what he was really after: the linked companionship in the dark, a guide who was keeping him from harm. The sex didn't matter so much.

But of course it did matter. He couldn't talk or laugh with Kanaya in the way he had with Mohammed. The barber couldn't speak much English and was, in any case, not very interested in Morgan. He was there to provide a service; he didn't understand anything else. So they were left with the same situation: namely, their bodies, and how to unite them unobserved.

The next day, he talked over the problem with Bapu Sahib.

"You know," the Maharajah said at last, "there is a suite of rooms downstairs where you could meet. Nobody uses them, I think they could be ideal." He explained which rooms he meant. "But it is important, Morgan, that you impress on Kanaya not to loiter in the palace. And he must not talk in the bazaars, that would be fatal. Tell him he will lose his job in consequence."

"I have told him, Bapu Sahib, but I will tell him again."

He had talked sternly to the barber, more than once, who had nodded earnestly in response. Kanaya was frightened of the Maharajah, who had a reputation for treating servants harshly. But in this case His Highness had been kind, going so far as to bestow on the barber a largesse of twenty-five rupees. Perhaps because of this generosity, Kanaya's discretion had slackened, and Bapu Sahib was right to be concerned.

People had begun to talk. Or perhaps they were only teasing; it was sometimes hard to tell the difference. Mocking people for supposed minorite tendencies was common among the courtiers; the Maharajah himself sometimes joined in. But it was one thing to joke and another to ridicule, and Morgan didn't want to cross the line.

When Malarao started to chaff, it was bothersome. Kanaya had a reputation, and his frequent visits to the Private Secretary had been noticed.

"You must be good-humoured in return," His Highness told Morgan. "Do not ever become angry. And I will tease you myself, just a little, so that everybody knows it isn't serious."

It was a good line of defence. The next time Malarao brought it up, Morgan asked him with a smile whether he was jealous. This made the other courtiers laugh, and the moment was softened. Not long after that, the Maharajah made a point of mentioning Morgan's age. This was a less obvious argument, which had to be explained.

"At forty-two," Bapu Sahib told him, "no Indian can keep an erection. That part of life is over. Now nobody will believe that you can be having sexual relations with anybody."

He chortled at his own devious wit.

*   *   *

The new rooms had been a success. Hardly anybody went there, and they had an outside entrance which Morgan could unbolt from within. Despite lavish furnishings, there was no bed, only a big divan in the middle of the main room. The place had a hushed, hot feeling to it, thin strips of light coming in through the shutters. Morgan wanted to roll naked with

Kanaya among the cushions, whispering endearments, but wasn't brave enough to take off his clothes. And the little barber was without imagination or passion.

Morgan did try. He always kissed Kanaya, and often stroked and caressed him. Although he found him too willowy to be really attractive, he spoke fondly to him and made a point of smiling frequently, sometimes to cover his embarrassment. But all of it was wasted. The young man only looked puzzled, and waited for the next order. He seemed to have the soul of a slave.

Morgan became depressed. On a couple of occasions he felt quite close to anger, but that wouldn't have helped either. Any solidarity across race and class, like that which he'd achieved with Mohammed, simply had no purchase here. Affection wasn't part of the arrangement. It was useless to want what couldn't even be spoken, and all that was left was the physical. Afterwards, thinking back on what he'd done, he felt wretched.

He told himself: *give it up*. Send Kanaya away; tell him not to come any more. There would be no more shame, though the afternoons would be long and empty again.

But the shame, he slowly realised, was part of the point. Degradation had its own sensual power, and no sooner was he hurrying away from one encounter than his mind was leaping ahead to the next one. In the morning when he woke up he was already breathless with anticipation and the hours passed with grinding slowness till the appointed time. But the idea was far more thrilling than the act, which was over almost as soon as it started. The two of them lay in a stunned heap afterwards, stickily joined. On more than one occasion at these moments, the image of Searight passed across his inward eye. Scenes like this one were what the other man aspired to, but they provided no upliftment to Morgan. Buggery in the colonies: it wasn't noble.

His dependency on this daily event was starting to dirty his mind. His spirits were low and he was finding it hard to enjoy any aspect of court life. The palace was an inward-facing building and not much light came in from outside. Everything seemed to strain towards religion and away from art. There was a deadness of the mind and it took on, for him, a physical dimension: lately he had struggled to hear even the echoes of his own footfalls as he walked about.

He decided that he needed to get away for a while, to escape. In July he took ten days' leave and went down to Hyderabad to visit Masood: an enjoyable interlude, with no rocky outcrops of pain or pleasure. But when he returned, it was to upset and drama.

"That barber of yours has been foolish," Bapu Sahib told him primly. "No harm's been done, but he was boasting in Deolekr's room that he was under your protection, and he said, 'Sahib's fond of boys.' Wrong of him, that."

The Maharajah spoke lightly, but the offence was serious. When Kanaya appeared brightly at the downstairs suite the next day, Morgan folded his arms angrily.

"You have been talking about me. You promised you wouldn't, and you have broken your promise."

Instantly, the young man collapsed. His repentance was histrionic, but perhaps sincere. Morgan was even a little sorry for him.

"All right, all right," he said severely. "But I can't see you for a few days. Go away now and don't do it again."

But the incident couldn't be damped down so easily. Deolekr Sahib was the Maharajah's Indian Secretary, and not well disposed towards Morgan. He repeated the story, and it spread. Nobody confronted the Englishman directly, but he could see a kind of insolence in certain faces around him. He wasn't respected as he had been before.

Bapu Sahib confirmed his fears. "You mustn't mind," he

told his Private Secretary consolingly. "They don't understand the facts of your case and who is to explain it to them?"

Morgan knew that he was stretching the ruler's indulgence quite far. Miserably, he said, "I wish I could control my desires as you do."

It wasn't meant as idle flattery, but His Highness became impatient.

"Oh, one can't teach those things," he said brusquely. "When you are dissatisfied with your present state of existence you will enter another—that's all."

His present state of existence continued, unbroken. After a few days' lull, he summoned Kanaya again and they resumed their relations.

* * *

A few weeks later, the attention of the court was distracted by the Gokul Ashtami festival, which celebrated the birth of Krishna. Much of the month of August was to be devoted to this event, which Morgan embraced eagerly: his disgrace might be completely forgotten. But, more than that, he sensed a religious happening which could provide him with some material he still needed.

His rational mind was prepared. He had read the Bhagavad Purana and he knew a little about the Krishna birth story. It wasn't entirely unlike the tale of Christ's birth, with the wicked king Kamsa standing in for Herod and the village of Gokul for Bethlehem. But there the similarities ended: in his playful, irreverent earthiness, Krishna left humourless Jesus behind. Morgan had always liked him for this reason, without precisely following the significance of his various incarnations, though he hoped now that something would be explained.

The festival itself was set to last eight days, but weeks before, when the preparations began, confusion had already set in. Why did the Lord of the Universe take the form of a six-inch doll with a mean little face, and why did he require eight different suits, worth thirty pounds, each embroidered with pearls? And what was the point of giving him a mosquito net? More worrying, though more prosaic, was a different question: why were such prodigious amounts of money being spent on flowers and food and decoration and music when the state coffers were so badly squeezed?

It was best, perhaps, simply to be carried by the current of events, and let understanding follow in their wake. The entire court decamped to the Old Palace for the duration, leaving shoes and meat-eating outside. Nothing was supposed to die as long as the festival lasted; not even an egg. A room was made available to Morgan upstairs, which did offer some sanctuary, though the mayhem leaked in at all hours, and there was a holy feather-bed in it which required votive candles burning on the bolster and the prayers of the Maharajah once daily. Sleep was in any case disturbed and intermittent, because of the three bands playing simultaneously in the courtyard and the terrible thudding of the steam engine which drove the temporary electricity supply.

In the daytime it was much worse. In addition to the bands, groups of singers, accompanied by cymbals and a harmonium, offered unending prayers at the altar. Sometimes an enormous horn was blown; sometimes elephants would trumpet. Between all this came the sound of shouting, or the patter of children's feet as they ran and played through the palace. But the racket was merely an accompaniment to a corresponding visual cacophony: people swarmed and rampaged everywhere, the altar was buried in petals, incense burned smokily.

In such disorder, what sense? There seemed to be no form or beauty to any of it. Morgan wore Hindu clothing, but he wasn't Hindu inside, and he struggled to find the logic that bound one thing to another. Yet there *was* logic of a kind, for those who believed. He couldn't find any of it stranger than the more demure rituals of Christmas at home. Seen from a distance, all ecstasy is odd, and this bodily abandonment wasn't worse than any other. Indeed, it was the ecstasy that intrigued him most, when sense and rational thought departed. At certain times of the day His Highness danced before the altar to make his oblations. In contrast to the singers, who were mostly quite rooted, these were vigorous outbursts, with Bapu Sahib leaping happily about, plucking at a stringed instrument around his neck, reciting poems in moments of inspiration, and once memorably flinging himself prostrate on the carpet before the god. His face showed what it meant to lose oneself: all personality had been wiped away. How Morgan envied it, this loss, which was also somehow a sort of gain, but he couldn't emulate it. From inside himself he observed, and made notes for the future, and suffered the minor injuries of envy. He would have given a lot to cavort and caper on a threadbare carpet, or hurl himself headlong before a dressed-up doll in a shrine. But his upbringing, or his Occidental scepticism, held him in. He would always be Morgan, never Krishna, not even in part.

Yet even His Highness, when his rapture ebbed, came back quickly to himself. Not ten minutes after he had jumped around like David in front of the Ark of the Covenant, he was in a side passage, complaining to Morgan about his indigestion. And he was perfectly capable of giving out mundane orders about the palace, or repairs to the motor cars, in the midst of all the other frenzy.

The most startling intrusion of normal life, however, came in another form. Upstairs in Morgan's room one evening, after he had made his daily prayer to the sacred feather-bed, the Maharajah came to sit next to Morgan where he was leaning against the wall. He looked weary and rubbed his eyes.

"Are you tired, Bapu Sahib? Would you like to lie down?"

"No, no, it isn't that. The problem is different. It is that little barber of yours again."

"What has he done now?"

"Well, he is quite shameless, that boy. I was resting in a room here last night and I saw he was sitting in the corner. I paid him no mind. As you know, they are everywhere, these people. After some time he came over and he was massaging my feet. So I knew he wanted a favour."

"Yes," Morgan said, closing his eyes. He knew already what was coming.

"He asked me for employment at the palace. At first I was confused. I told him, 'But you have employment, you are Sahib's barber.' It was the wrong reply. He said, 'Sirkar, I want more employment. I want employment with *you*.' Then he said . . . "

Here Bapu Sahib became bashful; he looked around, even though they were alone, then leaned over to whisper in Morgan's ear.

"Oh, no."

"Yes, yes. That is what he said." He chuckled ruefully.

It was sickening, but all too believable: the foolish young man, misunderstanding his position, wanting promotion, thinking he could be catamite to the king.

"What happened then?"

"Oh, I became very angry, I shouted at him. He ran away in fear and he hasn't come back. But he *will* come back, his sort always returns."

"I shall beat him. I shall send him away."

"You should beat him, certainly. He doesn't fear you enough. But let us not be too hasty about sending him away. It may cause suspicion and talk. We should—"

Here the door opened and two courtiers came in search of His Highness. Their talk abruptly ended, suspended in mid-air, though it continued to unspool in Morgan's mind. It took a great deal to wring rage from him; of all the emotions, it lay deepest. But he was incensed and, if Kanaya had been before him at this moment, he might have lost all restraint.

Morgan would deal with him later, but meanwhile there was the rest of Gokul Ashtami to get through. Krishna's birth was only announced on the sixth day of the festival, which involved the Maharajah thrusting his face into the mound of rose petals that concealed the little idol, and everybody throwing red powder, so that the air turned crimson. The noise reached an excruciating pitch in the same moment, with the elephants joining in the shouting, while a band played "Nights of Gladness" in the courtyard outside.

The next day was the conclusion of festivities. A massive procession was formed to walk slowly, over the space of a few hours, to the tank in front of the guest house. At its heart was a huge palanquin, bearing the image of the god, along with other holy items; before it went an elephant, followed by a military contingent with musical instruments, and then the twelve bands of singers who had been assailing their ears for days. Their energy was ferocious, because release was near, and Bapu Sahib led the last band, walking in front of the palanquin, while another elephant brought up the rear.

They set out at six. The sky was pink with sunset, and their creeping pace meant that full darkness had fallen before the palace was out of sight. Morgan walked barefoot, holding hands with two Hindu holy men, their foreheads ceremonially smeared with red and black powder, and their way lined with boys holding back the crowds. Progress was slow, with interruptions, and it was already ten o'clock by the time they reached the tank. Here the concluding ceremony was performed, in which a clay model of the village of Gokul was dissolved in the water, though what the reason was he couldn't understand. The Maharajah told him that the village represented Krishna, who couldn't be drowned—though it *was*

drowned, by a half-naked man whose hereditary office consisted in this function: he steered the little village, on its sup-
porting tray, with all its tiny clay figures of people, away from
the shore, into the dark. The water lapped and ate; the people, the buildings, melted away. Other offerings followed—
images of Ganesh, sacrifices of corn—before the tray was
brought back and half-heartedly worshipped. Cannons were
fired and elephants induced to bellow, but Morgan had had
enough. His feet were sore, his back was hurting, and he was
hungry and deaf. He'd had the foresight to arrange his
Victoria in advance, and he hobbled over to it to be carried on
the road around the edge of the tank to the guest house,
where he could sleep.

* * *

"You fool. You awful little fool. How dare you?"
As he had the last time, the barber instantly collapsed. His
face had been filled with anxiety, overlaid with hope, but now
the hope had gone. He fell to his knees on the carpet and
clutched at Morgan's feet. He began to wail theatrically, knowing that Morgan would beat him. Morgan beat him. The blows
and slaps were real, but they didn't hurt him. Nor were they
unexpected, for Kanaya had folded his turban into a protective
pad in advance.
When he had boxed the boy's ears for a while, Morgan
went to a chair and sat down. He felt coldly satisfied, though
the surge of power had been exciting. He was breathing heavily, not only from exertion, as Kanaya crawled over the floor to
him and began kissing his feet.
"Now shave me," he said.
The loud sobbing ceased. The barber picked himself up
and began to prepare the razor, drying his cheeks on his sleeve.
Morgan watched him, as if from a great distance, though he

was also watching himself. He had become, for a moment, somebody he didn't recognise. He had never struck anybody in his life before, and the sensation wasn't displeasing, despite the throbbing in his hand.

It was a few days after the end of the festival. He had been waiting for Kanaya to appear, and had observed him loitering at the edges of the palace, waiting to be beckoned. He had made no sign, knowing that he would come anyway. He had developed an instinct for these things. And so sure had he been that the reckoning would take place today that he had dressed in English clothes for the occasion.

His fury hadn't diminished since the Maharajah had told him, though it had become more intellectual while he'd brooded. The arrangement had been perfect; he had given clear instructions; all would have been well if Kanaya had simply complied. But the young man was devious and greedy, and it was futile to expect obedience from him. It was in the nature of a slave to disobey and to be beaten.

The shaving took place in silence, except for the rasping of blade on skin. There was no sensual pleasure in the ritual today. Morgan had no emotion; the little spasm of violence had purged him. The anger was gone.

But so was any fear he might have had. Kanaya couldn't even betray him properly. He had done his worst, and nothing had happened. Even now, when his white throat was nakedly exposed, Morgan knew that he was safe. The barber didn't have enough initiative to murder him; the most he could do was stretch out a hand, once the razor was stowed, to scratch enquiringly at his fly-buttons.

"No."

The hand retreated. Soon the barber did too, carrying his little bag of tools. He'd be back, but in the meanwhile Morgan felt amplified, imperious. He went over to the mirror, ostensibly to check on the shave, but really to examine his own features. His face was pale and fanatical, and somehow rather beautiful.

They resumed their meetings in a couple of days, but everything had changed. The coldness continued from Morgan's side, and the subservience from the barber's. The wistful desire—only felt by the Englishman—for something more human and tender had gone. Instead, the imbalance of power that had always been present had now waxed to the full, pushing softer possibilities aside.

In their sex now, he was rough with Kanaya. He could see that he was hurting him sometimes, and that knowledge excited him. The moment of retribution—when he'd beaten the pleading barber in his room—had awoken something. He'd felt strong, his authority beyond question. All the force of the Empire had filled him for a second. Gentleness and kindness weren't possible in their relationship any more, not even as a longing. The young man was in his power, and he treated him accordingly.

It wasn't good for him. Seventeen years before, writing his first novel, he had created a scene of cruelty which had excited him sexually. A broken arm being twisted in its socket, the idea of force deliberately causing pain: his mind shrank from it, while his body responded. Never in his real life had he felt an impulse to match it; it had remained fictional, a literary vice—until now.

Although no serious damage was inflicted, the desire was a dark one and it made Morgan unhappy. It was as if a hand had roiled the bottom of his character, releasing clouds of mud into the water, so that he couldn't see clearly. It would be easy, he thought, to continue like this: to allow one weakness to unlock the next, so that he toppled slowly headlong into his basest elements. Moral decay, if it increased your power, had its own logic, its own rewards. Once begun, the fall might be hard to arrest.

Feeling sad and guilty, he told all of it to Mohammed in a

letter. He hoped the confession might relieve him, or that his friend might absolve him, but received only a reprimand by post. *I got nothing to say except that you are so silly. I am very sad for that game. I am looking forward to see you and to blame you about your foolish deeds, foolish deeds.*

* * *

At this time, fate handed him another respite. For some weeks now there had been plans for a royal trip to Simla, to see the Viceroy, Lord Reading, whom Bapu Sahib hoped to persuade to come to Dewas to inaugurate his new constitution. This journey had been put off more than once, but it was decided that now would be a good moment to make it.

Morgan immediately applied for leave which was due to him, so that he could extend his absence. Three weeks away from Dewas and Kanaya: a chance to restore his better nature. He returned, however, to another crisis, which threatened to grow larger.

His predecessor in the court was a Colonel Leslie, with whom he'd had some amicable correspondence over the last months, but the letter that was awaiting Morgan now wasn't friendly in the least. *I know that some people feel when they get east of Suez that not only the Ten Commandments are obsolete but also the obligations and etiquette of English society.* His crime, apparently, was to have opened some of the colonel's correspondence, thinking that it related to official business, before forwarding it to England.

His face grew hot as he read and re-read the haughty words. It always took him some time, when he'd been insulted, to arrive at the correct emotion in response. But he knew that this couldn't remain a private matter. He hurried off to find Bapu Sahib, only to discover that he was at prayers and couldn't be disturbed.

While he waited, he considered the situation. He knew that Colonel Leslie had gone back to England to recuperate through the Hot Weather, but it had always been his plan to return to his job. Perhaps, Morgan thought now, the colonel had become threatened. Perhaps he believed that his position had been usurped.

And when the Maharajah turned up, his suspicions were quickly confirmed. Before Morgan could speak, Bapu Sahib said, "I've had a letter from Colonel Leslie. He says he shall undertake no more administrative work since it is not appreciated. It is an unpleasant letter."

"So is this."

"Oh, dear. Oh, dear." Bapu Sahib seemed to contract with dismay as he read. "This is very bad. I am so sorry on your account, Morgan."

"I was rather concerned that I might have caused you trouble."

"No, no. He has been jealous of you for some time. He has been writing to me to say that I prefer you to him. Which of course is true. I am very sorry."

So bound up was he in the coils of diplomacy that it took Morgan a couple of days to comprehend that he'd been offered an escape. Colonel Leslie was expected to arrive in a few weeks, at the end of October: a perfect time to say goodbye to Dewas. He would book his passage home for January. The remaining two months he could spend with Masood in Hyderabad.

When he told this to Bapu Sahib, the response was regretful. The Prince of Wales was due to make a royal visit to India in November, and he would have liked Morgan to remain at least that long, to see him through. But the Private Secretary had made up his mind.

"I shall be very sad to be without you, Morgan," the diminutive monarch told him. "But I do understand."

His position had always been temporary. Even without Colonel Leslie, Morgan had been thinking of going soon. But now that it had become official, he too felt sad. He knew that these months would haunt him later in England, like a strange and spectral dream, a vision seen in a fever.

But it was, in every way, time to go. His relations with Kanaya had resumed, and he was too weak to break them off. The memory of these indulgences, he suspected, wouldn't make him proud. Nor would his achievements at the court. All the works that had been in progress when he arrived had since been stopped, for lack of funds. Bapu Sahib's predecessor had already sunk the state into debt, and every royal extravagance since then had gone unchecked, sucking the coffers dry. The palace itself stood up in the middle of the landscape like something anomalous and misconceived. It was unfinished when he'd first seen it, and it remained unfinished now. Perhaps it would always be like this.

* * *

His remaining two months in Hyderabad—with his first and most important Indian friend—were happy. The royal palace, with all its weight of responsibility, had lifted from him. Everything felt new and fresh; even foods he had been eating for months seemed to have a different taste. The weather was fine, the company congenial, and it was a relief to be among Muslims again, whose problems were at least comprehensible to him. He had loved Bapu Sahib, but Masood he also understood.

From this contented vantage point, he could reflect back on his last few days in Dewas. The farewells had taken on a moist and maudlin quality. He had been profusely thanked, and presented with the second-highest honour the state could confer: the Tukojirao III Gold Medal. Except that—money being in short supply—it was only a temporary medal: the sun's face had been scratched out inexpertly onto it with a pin, and the ribbon was a makeshift scrap of red cotton.

"Soon," Bapu Sahib had told him, "a proper medal will be struck, and then you shall exchange."

But Morgan didn't want to exchange it: the improvised imitation was far more apt.

He had been forgiven much, he knew. Damn the little barber! If he hadn't entered the scene, Morgan wouldn't have acted so vilely, or felt so wretched and insignificant in consequence. Only glancingly did he wonder how things might have looked from the other side. Perhaps Kanaya, too, was cursing Morgan's arrival and the moral downfall that followed. But that was hard to believe. Kanaya could only have been in it to bolster his standing in the court, or perhaps for financial reward.

He hadn't received much of the latter. Though the Maharajah had raised his salary, of course; and when Morgan had finally left, he had given him some money. Kanaya had responded by counting it despondently and telling him that it wasn't a lot.

"How ungrateful," Bapu Sahib had said crossly when he heard. "Did he ask for a chit?"

"No. Should I have given one?"

"You did well not to. It might have made talk when he showed it about, and now all will soon be forgotten. But it shows how utterly he has failed to appreciate the high position he had with you—and your goodness to him."

Morgan shifted uncomfortably. "Will you send him away?"

"No, I think not. I shan't scratch him off the budget, despite the way he's treated us both, because I can't forget that he was useful to you earlier in the year."

But Bapu Sahib's generosity couldn't erase the guilt. He knew that he had failed to be kind, and had, moreover, caused anxiety for His Highness. After a few days in Hyderabad, Morgan felt relaxed enough to confess the whole story to

Masood. He told him everything, not holding back even the most unpleasant details.

If he'd expected to be chastised, he was pleasantly surprised by his friend's reaction. Masood shook his head despairingly and laughed. "Oh, Morgan, Morgan. Are you never going to change?"

"I doubt it, at this late stage."

"I think the time has come at last for me to take you to a woman. I know a few who might oblige. Come, think about it. A voluptuous Indian lady, with breasts like mangoes. It might save the day, just when there is no hope left."

"I'm afraid it's too late for that."

It was good to be able to talk with his friend in this way; sex, which had always divided them, now united them a little. In part, this was because they had reached a certain age. Masood had thickened in girth and his life had thickened around him too: he was happy in his job and full of enthusiasm and plans. Property and family and future had filled him out. Morgan, although he was poorer in all these things, had accepted that his friend would never be his lover—not in the way he'd once wanted. But the loss was also a sort of gain, because a new gentleness had sprung up between them.

Zorah, Masood's wife, wasn't there this time when he first arrived. Morgan had met her on his last visit and they had tentatively warmed to one another. Each of them had tried hard and in the end a mutual admiration had resulted. But she and the boys were away for a few days, so that for a while it was like bygone times, when he and Masood were young. They lived in the zenana, the part of the house usually reserved for women, sleeping next to each other on a back veranda, with vines hanging overhead.

Other friends were present too. Some were new acquaintances, whom Morgan had never met. Some, like Sherwani and the Mirza brothers, he had encountered before. All of them were warm to this English visitor, whose name they often heard. As on his first trip to India, he was treated as one of the company—an honorary Indian. This involved frank airings of their political views in front of him, with no protection of his feelings. There was no malice in it, for they had nothing to lose. The Khilafat issue—the cutting up of the Turkish Empire after the War—had outraged Mohammedan sentiments and pushed Indian Muslims, who had long supported the British, towards the National Congress. Now all were united behind Gandhi in his push for civil disobedience.

It was into this swelling tide of nationalism that the Prince of Wales was stepping. Almost everybody in Masood's circle was opposed to the royal visit. For the past six months Morgan had been among Indians who were attached, sentimentally and politically, to the British Crown, and it was startling to suddenly hear the opposite. How hated they were, the English! How unwanted, how mistrusted! And how very far from understanding what they'd done.

He himself, as usual, was subtly conflicted. Sitting with Masood, surrounded by his friends, he was keenly attuned to their feelings. If he had been born here, with a different shade of skin, he too would be roused. But at the same time, part of him always wanted to protest, though in a very small voice. He had heard the noble justifications for Empire, not only from British politicians, but from high-minded friends like Goldie, and it was hard to give them up entirely. It could all have happened so differently, if it had simply been carried out with civility and politeness. It was a smallness of soul, a narrowness of the heart, which had done for Goldie's high ideals. Ill-breeding had undermined the whole edifice. He couldn't help believing that on a certain level this great dream was dying because of petty rudeness in railway carriages.

But it *was* dying; there could be no doubt of that. The change of tone among the English living here betokened that.

Some were even admitting aloud that they would have to leave—not now, perhaps not even in the next few years. But one day there would be an end to the Raj, which meant the end of the Empire.

He would get a little taste of it a month later, when he accompanied Masood on an official tour to the south-west corner of the state. There had used to be a British cantonment in Lingsugur, but it had been abandoned in 1860, and only the relics of colonial occupation were left behind. It was oddly moving to wander through the ruins of old bungalows, catching the sound of ghostly conversations, or to touch the stucco walls of what was once a bandstand. The cemetery, too, carried the inscriptions of past lives, not all of them under the ground, but gone anyway—gone. No mourners came to remember the dead. No English left now; neither the language nor the people. It was curious how touching the vacancy was, when he didn't especially care for what had filled it. Wind and weeds were the only things alive.

* * *

He had booked his passage home for the middle of January. His plan was to disembark in Port Said and spend a few weeks with Mohammed along the way, if the military situation permitted. Unrest and upheaval there had continued to simmer, breaking into outbursts of violence from both sides. The big concern, from Morgan's point of view, was that the boat might not be allowed to dock.

It had been arranged that Mohammed would come to meet him on board. He was working now in Port Said, but they might be able to spend some time travelling together. He was a father again—a daughter had recently been born—so that his family obligations were powerful, too, but there would be the chance of a few days without anybody else in attendance.

As the boat entered the Suez Canal, Morgan was in an excellent mood. The voyage had been good, with few people on board and most of them pleasant company. A kindly purser had moved him from his first, shared cabin on the inside of the vessel to a charming outside one that he had to himself. From the porthole, as well as from the deck, he could see the delicate colours of Suez flowing slowly past, and take in its temperate air. More than anything, though, he was charged with the anticipation of seeing his friend in a day or two.

The boat arrived early in Port Said. This was a new worry, because it was possible Mohammed didn't know of the change in schedule and might not find him in time. But not long after they'd docked, there was a knock on his cabin door and he opened it, smiling.

It wasn't Mohammed; it was the purser, with a letter that had been delivered to the boat. When Morgan unfolded the single page, the familiar handwriting made his heart leap. But only for a moment. Mohammed wasn't able to meet him, because he had fallen ill again. Morgan should come to Mansourah.

* * *

"I am very sorry, Forster."

"No, my dear fellow, it's I who am sorry. What has happened to you?"

"I don't know. About two weeks ago, no, three, I received a great pain. Then I became weak and I was vomiting blood. I think it is the old sickness again."

"And how do you feel now?"

"Because you are in front of me, already I feel much better."

But Morgan could see that Mohammed was very ill. He had lost so much weight that his ribs stood out starkly in his chest and his breath came with an audible wheeze. A little later, when he needed the bathroom, he could barely hold himself upright and had to lean on the wall for support.

It didn't make him proud later that Morgan's first thought was a selfish one. Through the weeks of debauchery in Dewas, his imagination had frequently travelled over the sea to Egypt. What he'd done to Kanaya he wanted done to him by Mohammed, and in his mind he had dwelt often on this moment. But he could see in an instant that no more carnality was possible. His friend was hollowed out, a husk of his former self, so that it seemed a strong wind might blow him away.

Then Morgan became very calm. He knew now with a clear certainty that Mohammed was dying. He also knew that he himself could survive it.

Where had it come from, this new steadiness of spirit? When Mohammed's illness had first showed itself, three years before, his reaction had been panic. His fear then was not so much that his friend might lose his life, but that he might lose his friend. Now, when that prospect seemed sure, it didn't break him into pieces.

He didn't dwell on the future too much. It seemed more sensible, not to say helpful, to approach the matter practically. Money would make things easier, and that he could provide— although not in an unlimited way. Mohammed's circumstances were dire: no job any longer, no income and no savings. His wife and some of her relatives were dependent on him, and his baby daughter was herself quite ill, in the hospital at the moment. Morgan had enough in the bank at home to look after him for six months, or perhaps a year. But he didn't want to send a large sum, which he thought would soon be lost. It would be a better idea to find somebody reliable, living nearby in Egypt, who might be depended on to pay over a monthly allowance.

What he also needed to do, quite urgently, was to take Mohammed to see a specialist in Cairo. So far he had been treated only by a local doctor who was, as far as Morgan could tell, a quack and a thief. But he didn't know the name of any suitable person, and to get one he would have to speak to some of his expatriate friends.

He went to Alexandria. He was away for a week and by the time he returned to Mansourah he had found somebody who would help with payments. Gerard Ludolf, who had been assisting him with research on Alexandrian history, was happy to be of use in this way. He also had the name of a doctor in Cairo who specialised in consumption, and had made an appointment to see him.

This man was English and plump and round, the embodiment of appetite and good health. Morgan introduced Mohammed by name, and nothing further was asked. But when the examination was over, it was to Morgan that the doctor turned, not to his patient. Even before he spoke, the news was visible in his face.

"I'm afraid it's what you feared," he said.

"Is there anything that can be done?"

He shook his head. "Not very much. The disease is far advanced. A matter of months, perhaps even weeks. I'm sorry."

It didn't seem possible that they could be sitting in a normal room, on a normal day, discussing such things. Not even Mohammed appeared concerned, while he studiously did up his buttons. So that it didn't feel unnatural for Morgan to ask, delicately, "Will he . . . that is, will there be much suffering?"

"Not necessarily."

The reply was really no reply at all, and through the hot vacancy in its wake the two men walked silently back to their hotel. Each was plunged in thought, and separate from the other. Until the Englishman lifted a hand and touched his friend on the shoulder.

"It doesn't matter," Mohammed said. "I think he doesn't know."

"I'm sure you're right."

"He says it is consumption, but he doesn't know. My doctor in Mansourah . . . " And he began a complicated account of what that charlatan had told him, a story involving money and false hope.

"Of course," Morgan said, when he was done. "You are young, you have power. You will get better."

"Yes. And if I do not, that also doesn't matter."

* * *

Three weeks later, it was time to go. Mohammed accompanied him as far as the train station in Cairo, and as they pulled up outside in a carriage Morgan was murmuring distractedly about a parcel that he would send soon, with medicine and clothes and tins of food. It was easier—it always was—to speak about plans rather than feelings, but Mohammed cut him short.

"Don't let us talk of anything, except that you will see Mother soon. My respects to her. And then you will see Mrs. Barger, my respects to her. And you will see Bennett . . . " He began to name various other friends and family, who made up Morgan's life, although he had never met any of them.

Inside the station, all was confusion, until they found the right train. In the compartment, a small space of quiet presented itself, at the centre of which the two men sat thoughtfully next to each other. The fact of parting felt curiously distant.

Mohammed jogged him gently with his elbow. When Morgan looked at him, he said, "My love to you. There is nothing else to say."

"Yes."

"I will get out now, and wave from outside."

"No, I'll come and say goodbye on the platform."

It was crowded and noisy outside and Mohammed was half in conversation with an acquaintance he'd bumped into, so that he didn't hear the request the first time.

"What?"

Morgan wanted to remember his friend's face cleanly and, with faint desperation, he repeated, "Take off your spectacles."

"Why?"

"You are more beautiful without them."

"No." He shook his head irritably.

Almost immediately, it seemed, the train began to move and Morgan had to run to get back on. He leaned through the open door for a last look back. Now, too late, the moment did pierce him. He knew he would never see this face again, except in memory and photographs, but Mohammed had already turned away.

CHAPTER SEVEN
A PASSAGE TO INDIA

On his first trip up to London, he bumped into Virginia. He was despondent and aimless, and when she suggested he come back with her to Hogarth House, he was happy to accept.

It did help to sit for a few hours in Richmond with the Woolfs, talking over his time away. He had barely been home for two weeks, but already he was at odds with his familiar life, ruing a loss he couldn't name. It wasn't only Mohammed's impending death, which already seemed like a fact; it was Dewas and the Maharajah, as well as Masood. He had been given a glimpse of other Morgans that he might have been, and then they were whisked away again.

It was impossible to express all this. His funk had immobilised him, so that he couldn't find the words. Instead he mumbled half-sentences about his mother and Bapu Sahib and, when asked about living in a palace, all he could talk about was the sparrows that had flown around the rooms. "I used to shout at them sometimes. One got caught in the electric wire. There it hung, until it wrenched its claw off and flew away . . . "

A silence followed, while they stared at him, perturbed. Despite himself, the image had conveyed something personal. He felt like a small, soft creature, hanging by one foot.

It had been the hardest homecoming of his life—worse, even, than the return from Egypt after the War. England felt passive and indifferent to him. He was withdrawn and remote with his friends. People had got used to his absence. Even Lily had only been briefly stirred, before sinking again into private abstraction and lamentations about her rheumatism.

And his own mind, of course, was elsewhere—behind him, or in some theoretical future. He was waiting for something, though he wasn't sure of what. Mohammed would certainly die, but that wouldn't change Morgan's English existence. Perhaps he was thinking about his book. Though in fact he hadn't looked at it in months.

Just the previous week, however, he had taken a momentous step. On an impulse—which had, he realised, been brewing in him for months—he had burned all his erotic short stories in the fireplace at Harnham. They had been piling up in the attic for years, written at feverish moments of compulsion, though less to express than to excite himself. That kind of agitation seemed like a hindrance to him now rather than a liberation; he had discovered in Dewas how lust could block the channels.

But if he'd imagined that his little act of destruction would free him up to work, he was mistaken. In the aftermath, he felt more stuck and inert than before. It wasn't that India was far from his mind any more; if anything, it was too much with him. But writing was removed from life, and he didn't have that distance, that clearness.

He discussed the matter with Leonard. Not on that first visit, but during lunch a few weeks later, when he felt less leaden. He thought he should abandon the book, he said. It wasn't anything solid as yet—a fragment, rather, which should probably stay that way.

"You ought to read it again," Leonard told him.

"I don't see the point."

"You might, if you read it. You need to try to finish it, even if it's not a success, or how will you really know that it's a failure? The first step, in any case, is to look at what you have."

The advice wasn't startling; he had thought of it himself. But somehow it was comforting to be steered by somebody else, who had implicit faith in him.

So he returned to his fragment. Which was, in fact, more substantial than he'd thought. And Leonard was right: reading what he had gave him a sense of how he might forge ahead. More out of curiosity than passion, he found himself taking up his pen.

* * *

Although he'd dipped into his manuscript from time to time, it had been years, really, since he'd worked properly on it. Not since 1913, before *Maurice* had thrown him off track. And then life, and the War, had taken over. Trying to find his way back into it now, after so much had intervened, was both harder and easier than he'd imagined. His story felt remote from him, and whatever feelings it had once aroused had long since cooled.

Fiction was too artificial and self-conscious, he thought, ever to convey anything real. More than that, his way of seeing things had altered, so that his original conception seemed faintly absurd. His literary idealism had drained away. He no longer imagined explaining the East to suburban England through his words; people everywhere, whether Indian or British, felt like shits to him.

So his characters, he felt, weren't likeable. No, they had been forged in angry gloom, scored and scratched by their maker. It worried him sometimes that he'd succumbed to pessimism; he'd always thought of despair as not only a moral but also an aesthetic failure. On a crude level, he feared that nastiness was boring, and that none of his creations would hold attention for long. Or perhaps he simply struggled to be in their company himself.

Years before, in writing the early books, he had thought of characters as a form of vegetation, and what he had here, he thought, was a shrubbery. Low, tangled forms, vibrating in the wind. He lacked a lone tree or two, standing in heroic isolation against the sky, but his newfound cynicism worked against it. To compensate, he found himself building up the atmosphere instead, tilting the narrative out of true. The weather, the stones, became portentous, but they hadn't yet delivered up their meaning.

Still, he went on. And as he returned to it, day after day, the words gradually became his again. Fire did spark occasionally between the bits of dead coal. He had bought an ornamental toy in India, a little wooden bird, green with patches of red on its wings and sticklike yellow legs, which he set up on the edge of his writing desk, and it looked impartially on as he struggled with himself. His trysts with the pages in the attic became the unacknowledged centre of his existence. Though there was a persistent sense of unreality to the hours he spent there. The truth, he suspected, would always be in actual events, which continued to pile up around him.

Deep inside himself, he was braced for news of Mohammed's death. In some way, he wanted to hear it had come: only then, he thought, would he be free of dread. Pity and worry obscured the image of his friend, while he awaited what couldn't be escaped.

Meanwhile, they wrote to each other. *I think we shall meet each other if not in the world it will be in the heaven.* Not even lines like these wrung Morgan's heart too much. He had been dwelling in his mind, as honestly as he could, on his memories of Mohammed. It seemed to him now, in his most lucid moments, that perhaps he had exaggerated their passion. From his friend's side, there had been little harshnesses, little instances between them when Mohammed had been hard or hurtful, which he'd chosen to sweep aside. He remembered now, more than he would like, that final goodbye in the train station in Cairo: the irritable way that Mohammed had refused to take off his spectacles and how, as the train had pulled out and Morgan had kept his gaze fastened desperately on his friend, Mohammed had turned away to speak to somebody else.

Such moments made him think that the picture he'd built up—of a glorious, immortal union—had been untrue. He'd needed it, to persuade himself and others that his life had served up at least one big success. He had loved Mohammed, certainly, but what could Mohammed realistically have felt in return? He'd been excited and flattered, of course, to be courted by an Englishman. And he'd been eager for the financial help too. He might have felt gratitude or politeness or pity. But love, in the way that Morgan had experienced it . . . ? No, he didn't think so.

These candid reflections were difficult, but they also helped to insulate him. The prospect of Mohammed's death hurt less. He and his situation were very far away; in a sense none of it was entirely real. When the end came, it might be a sort of fiction too.

So he told himself—but his heart lurched into a different register when Mohammed's health abruptly faltered again and the tone of his letters became very dark. An especially bare one upset him deeply:

> dear Morgan
> I am sending you the photograph
> I am very bad
> I got nothing more to say
> the family are good. My compliments to mother.
> My love to you
> My love to you

My love to you
do not forget your ever friend
Moh el-Adl

Morgan understood quite viscerally what was behind these words. It must be awful to feel so weak and sick and to know that the last light was flickering. But it would be over soon for Mohammed, and Morgan would be the one left behind. For the first time he had a sense that what lay ahead of him would be much bigger than he'd imagined.

Another letter followed, just a few days later:

dear Morgan
I have got the money today from you and thank you very much for it
I am absolutely bad I don't go out I can't stand
I am very weak
How are you no more today
My love to you
My love to you

No signature, no name. And that was perhaps appropriate. Because as he stood reading the letter on the grass behind the house, hiding his face and his feelings from his mother, Mohammed was already dead.

* * *

It took a few days for the news to reach him. Morgan had accompanied Lily to the Isle of Wight so that she could visit her friends, the Misses Preston, and two letters followed him there on the same morning. One came from Gamila and one from Mohammed's brother-in-law. Neither of them spoke English and the messages had been written on their behalf by somebody else, in formal, stilted language, though the meaning was plain.

After everything—all the mental preparation, the fore-knowledge—it was still a shock to see the fact written down. A small sound escaped Morgan; not quite a word, not quite a cry either. Then he had to prepare a public face, to cover any unruly emotion.

He read and re-read the letters in the coming days, as if they might yield up something different. They did contain other, extraneous information, not relevant to the main fact, but skewing it off centre. Mohammed had owned sixty pounds and three houses. He had left Morgan a ring, which would be sent in due course. Gamila and other family members were in need of money.

The news left vacancy in its wake. He didn't care about the ring. It was hard to feel anything, except bewilderment, not least about Mohammed's financial circumstances. Perhaps after all there'd been deception about money? The doubt was added to his general uncertainty, taking form in a dream that same night, in which Mohammed came out from behind a curtain, taller than he'd been in life. No words passed between them, but it was understood that his friend was asking for forgiveness, which Morgan didn't know how to give him.

A few numb days passed before the horrible moment when Mohammed's death finally became real. Still sequestered with the old women, he had gone for a walk by himself on the Downs. He was sunk in recollection of the last few weeks he'd spent with his friend in Helouan, a resort south of Cairo. Mohammed's health had briefly rallied and they had been blessed with mild weather, so that the interlude had been strangely peaceful. One afternoon, on an outing in the desert, the two of them had become separated, and he had heard his name being called. *Margan, Margan*. The slight mispronunciation made the memory vivid. Now, absurdly, he called out in reply. He was completely on his own and the three lonely syllables sank into the sky, the grass; no answer would ever come.

Over the months that followed, he dreamed of Mohammed on most nights. Perhaps he occupied all the sleeping hours because he'd been banished during the day. There was nobody Morgan could talk to about him, except for those—like Florence Barger or Goldie—who had only known him from a distance. There was something humiliating, too, in a display of grief when the relationship had been unwitnessed. No, this was to be a private suffering, like lust or literature, lived out mostly in his dreams.

In these nightly visitations, Morgan always knew that his friend was dead. But that didn't stop him from appearing, sometimes with a face or a body that wasn't quite his own. There was no romance in these encounters, although it always felt that one or both of them wanted something. The most unsettling dream came many months after Mohammed was gone, when he took the shape of a young man dressed in black, with a small but distinct moustache. He didn't resemble Mohammed physically, but the feeling that he evoked made his identity obvious. Morgan knew that he ought to follow him, but his dream-character was like his actual one and he delayed. He knew somehow that the young man was going to get on a train and there was urgency, but when he tried to catch up with him his legs were suddenly heavy. They ended in a bathroom, filled with other figures who departed, leaving them alone. Then they spoke, but seemingly about nothing, both of them standing naked, Mohammed smiling all the while.

Even this dream wasn't troubling sexually. The most disturbing aspect was waking up, and knowing that Mohammed never would. That was what was terrible: his friend couldn't even know that he was dead, precisely because he was dead. All that was left of him was a handful of rotten remains in the Mansourah burial ground.

In the beginning, he had seen himself as a speck looking for another speck—that was how death felt. But as the months passed, deeper emotions came to the surface. Morgan wasn't obsessed with Mohammed so much as oppressed by him: there was a pulse of pain, a deep ache inside him constantly.

* * *

There was refuge in writing. On a surface level, he was quite sociable, seeing a great many people and acquitting himself well in company, but an essential part of him had become deeply withdrawn, hardly noticing the outside world. This part, when it wasn't contemplating death, was happy now to retreat to the attic and to work. Alone for hours at a stretch, not even really in the attic any more, sunk into some crevice in his head.

Anguish obscures, but grief is limpid. It was in this state of curious clarity that Morgan returned at last to the moment in the caves on which he'd foundered almost nine years ago.

Nine years, stuck in the dark! Poor Miss Quested had twisted in every direction, trying to escape. At least she had finally acquired a name that became her, Adela, though the driest, most sticklike part of her remained Morgan. There had been times when he felt he couldn't abide her another second, while she struggled and writhed to get away from her attacker.

But whose hands were grabbing at her? At one moment they belonged to Aziz, at another to the Indian guide—but mostly, he suspected, they were his own, ineffectually shaking his creation. In any case, none of it convinced. The seizing of breasts, the choking and hitting, the strap of the field-glasses twisted around the throat—all of it was forced, willed rather than felt, the rhythms out of alignment. He had never been good at writing physical calamities, though the emotional ones came naturally.

It was better to start cleanly, he decided. He made a fair copy of what he'd roughed out before, throwing the old pages away. And tried again.

And was quite suddenly back there, in the Barabar caves, on that morning. Alone, enclosed in the rock. The darkness was complete and of a piece with the stony smoothness beneath his fingers. The echo seemed present, under the silence, and it took a physical form: somebody else was there, moving when he did, stopping when he did, mirroring him. A presence, an outline—no more substantial than that. But who was it? No way to know. The other remained a mystery.

Almost immediately, he was in despair again. More than anything, he would like to throw the scene to one side, but of course he couldn't do that. He was the author, after all; he had created the question and so it was his job to provide the answer. He couldn't leave the central event of the plot unexplained.

And then the thought came to him, so strongly that he spoke it aloud: "Why not?"

Why not let everything turn on a mystery?

Immediately, in a quiet way, he became excited. The moment he thought it he knew that the lack of an answer was, in fact, the answer. He had circled around the question for nine years, while all along the solution was almost underfoot. He'd been casting around, in search of the cornerstone of the scene, but he'd been looking in the wrong place.

Dry, earnest, ignorant Adela. All this time, she'd been in love, longing to be touched, and her longing had transmuted into violence. Imaginary or real or ghostly: let it remain mysterious. He wouldn't explain what had happened, because he didn't *know* what had happened. As a writer, he'd felt he had to provide answers, but India had reminded him that no answer would suffice. There had been so much he'd seen and heard in that country which had baffled him and which rational thinking couldn't penetrate. Mystery was at the heart of things there and it would be at the heart of his novel too. It was right that there should be an obscurity at the core of events, echoing the physical shape of the cave, around which the characters and events would dance. One could move outwards from that absence, suggesting infinite expansion.

He especially liked this idea, because it seemed to work like certain pieces of music did (Beethoven's Fifth Symphony, for example) which left him with the sensation that something was heard once the orchestra had stopped, something that hadn't actually been played. Now, in an extended clarity, he saw the way forward. He had wanted the story to open out, and suddenly it had, in the most Indian of ways, into wider questions about the universe. And when he took up his pen again to write, for the first time in years his hand trailed behind his head, trying to keep up.

Wearing Adela's skin now, which fitted him better than he liked, he burst out of the tunnel, into the blinding light. At the end of his recent visit he had gone travelling with Masood and one afternoon he'd tried, against all sensible advice, to climb up to a hilltop fort and had got himself into bad trouble with cactuses. It was horrible to fall headlong through them again now, lacerated and torn on their spines, his own frenzy entrapping him. He flailed and cried—but did break free in the end, into the open plain, the horizon remote. There was nothing to hold him back now and he ran, he ran.

Nor did his velocity slow in the coming days. Even when he had left the Barabar Hills behind and was back again behind the Civil Lines in Chandrapore, the words continued to braid and flow. He was writing quickly and decisively, sure of his footing, and more sure of where he was going.

"I have come unstuck with my novel," he told Leonard, when they next saw each other, then immediately corrected himself. "That is, no, rather the opposite. I mean to say, I have *found* my path again. And I have you to thank, for urging me to persist."

"It is moving again?"

"Yes, it is moving quickly."

"I'm very glad." Leonard eyed him shrewdly, sucking on his pipe. "Now perhaps you will let us publish it for you."

Instantly, Morgan folded into himself. His writing, along with his grief, was in a private area of his life; he hardly spoke about it to anyone. He needed to keep the work secret, exactly like a certain kind of relationship. Talk of publication belonged to a future, theoretical world.

"I wish you well with the Hogarth Press," he said.

"We pay generously, let me remind you. Ten pounds for every thousand words."

But money bored Morgan.

"In any case, I am bound to Edward Arnold. I have been promising him my Indian novel for a decade now."

"Well, not your Indian novel then," Leonard said irritably. "Don't you have something else? What about this history of Alexandria you have been talking about for years?"

It still hadn't appeared. Morgan had signed an agreement with Whitehead Morris in Alexandria, and entered upon the most hopeless publishing process he'd yet experienced. The representative of the company in Egypt, the nervous, colourless Mr. Mann, seemed to have no idea what was involved in putting a book like this together. There had been endless back-and-forth discussion about maps and illustrations and, though he had finished the bulk of the text not long after his return, it had taken another three years before the proofs were ready. He had read from them aloud to Mohammed in Helouan, and they had sent his friend to sleep—perhaps their only purpose in the world so far.

"It will appear at the end of the year," he said uncertainly. "That, anyway, is what they tell me."

"Nothing else lying around?"

"Well, there is one possibility."

"What might that be?"

"I have been wondering about collecting together all my Egyptian writings. You know, all the bits and pieces that I have done for the papers . . . "

Leonard liked the idea. Among the occasional pieces that Morgan had cooked up for the *Egyptian Mail*—entertaining impressionistic vignettes about English life in Alexandria—there were twelve that immediately suggested themselves, which would need only to be slightly rearranged. The Hogarth Press would bring it out the following year; they would call it *Pharos and Pharillon*.

Very quickly, Morgan decided that he would dedicate the book to Mohammed. The gesture felt important to him. But he didn't have the courage to address him by name, which would have drawn questions and curiosity. So he chose a cryptic camouflage instead. The dedication was in Greek, to the god Hermes Psychopompos—the conductor of souls. Others might not understand, but he did. He liked the allusion to conducting, it was amusing, but there was a more serious meaning too. One soul could help another: Mohammed had done that for him, probably without meaning to, although the afterglow continued to radiate.

His long leave-taking of Mohammed had gone on inside him, out of sight. He didn't forget his *ever friend*. It had started to matter, though it hadn't in the beginning, that he get hold of the ring that had been promised him. Almost five months of letters and requests and money passed back and forth before he finally held it in his hand. Then he didn't know what to do with it. A plain, brass circle, glinting dully in his palm. There were so many associations with a ring like this, but all of them belonged to a Western world, a world of men and women, which neither he nor Mohammed were part of. What did the ring *signify*?

Nothing, perhaps. It was merely an object. He owned only two other items that had belonged to Mohammed, both given as gifts when he'd first left Egypt—his conductor's whistle and a pencil. He sometimes wore the whistle around his neck, where it hung uselessly. Nor could he do much with the pencil. But he took comfort in these little keepsakes, if only because they had once touched the living skin of his friend.

He took to wearing the ring himself now, putting it on at least once a day, hoping to summon the past. But walking on the Chertsey Mead one morning with the ring on his finger, he understood that it would, in fact, be better to forget. His efforts of memory didn't bring back what was gone. Everybody he loved would vanish into these incoherent misperceptions when they died, and then he himself would die too. There was only the present moment, and Mohammed could never be in it again.

* * *

Among the decisions Morgan faced was what to include in *Pharos and Pharillon*. As he reflected on it, he thought that he would add another four pieces to the book, and one of them would be his essay on Cavafy. It had caused a ripple when it had first appeared in the *Athenaeum*, but perhaps it would have more effect between covers.

He had stayed in contact with the poet, though their friendship had never grown strong. Despite his own fulsome tone, to say nothing of his efforts on the other man's behalf, the replies he received were always polite and distant. On his recent visit to Alexandria he had dropped in on Cavafy at the usual hour when he was at home to callers, the Palamas whisky set on a table in readiness. Morgan had hoped to create a stir, but he'd only been greeted with dry surprise, overlaid with irony, as though he hadn't ever left.

Nevertheless, his faithfulness didn't waver. He was loyal to the poems, if not entirely to their creator. He had managed to get some of them published, but though he continued to lobby for fresh translations, these were hardly ever forthcoming. Into his Alexandrian book he had inserted "The God Abandons Antony" between the two parts, the history and the guide, and now he put the same poem, the first one he'd heard, into *Pharos and Pharillon*. In addition, he ended the book with his piece on Cavafy, in the hope that it would linger in the memory.

To his surprise, Mr. Mann didn't let him down. Whitehead Morris brought out *Alexandria* at the end of the year, and it received appreciative and thoughtful reviews. And more of the same was to follow when *Pharos and Pharillon* appeared just a few months later, and sold unexpectedly well. There was, it seemed, an eager anticipation of something new from his pen, and these books would fill the gap until a novel arrived.

He had apparently become a writer again, despite his best efforts to slip away. He wasn't exactly sure how this had happened, but it wasn't only other people who saw him like this: even in his own eyes, the vocation had somehow assumed him. He was spending long hours alone now, with his book. It had been years since anything had claimed him quite as fully. But despite the flow that he achieved, there were still times when he was hauling his own props around an empty stage. He could become so depressed by it that he wanted to spit or scream, but mostly stared blankly instead.

He had lived for so long with an unfinished book that the idea of finishing seemed unreal. But there were questions, contingent on completion, which had to be attended to, and he turned his mind to them now. One of these was the matter of the dedication. From early on, it had felt that the book belonged to Masood. At different moments, as their closeness had waxed and waned, he had nurtured the idea and let go of it again, but now, as things narrowed to a close, it seemed obvious that the writing had been, all along, connected to his friend. Even the initial idea, however lightly thrown out, had been his. But more than that, the very presence of India in Morgan's life had only happened through Masood. Everything in it, and everything behind it, had flowed from him, and led back to him again.

Nevertheless, there were the formalities. He wrote to Masood, asking for permission. *Suppose it is finished, will you accept it?* He knew the answer in advance, but immediately had qualms. It seemed like a very flawed gift. But insufficient as it was, his writing was really all he had to offer.

Other worries took over. How to express it? At first he thought it should be by initials only—*to S. R. M.* But over time he relented and inclined towards spelling the name out. *To Syed Ross Masood.* No more was really necessary, but it didn't seem enough. He didn't want to put their intimacy on display, of course, but people might not understand how solid their friendship was, and he wanted it conveyed. Perhaps he could add something? *In Memory and in Expectation?* No, that was too formal. *In remembrance of the past sixteen years and in certainty of the years to come?* No, no, no. Too cumbersome and overwrought. More even than in the narrative which followed, the right words counted, though perhaps only to Morgan.

Of course and as usual, Masood didn't seem to care too much. He was volubly grateful, but the wording of the dedication didn't concern him. And there were other irritations between them. Morgan was deep into the second half of the book by now and the courtroom scenes presented their own special problems. He wasn't even sure of the most basic details, such as whether a case as serious as the one he was describing would take place in a small, provincial court. The law, as it was practised in India, was an abstruse subject; he needed Masood's help. It was important to him that he represent the reality correctly, at least in its technical aspects. But when he sent the relevant material over to India, to be inspected and pronounced upon, he got only a few perfunctory corrections and the injunction that he shouldn't change a word of it.

All this might have been cause for conflict, but by now he and Masood understood each other too well. After the last Indian visit, their letters had been full of a comfortable closeness. *You can have no idea my dearest how very much your love for me helps me to bear all my troubles. I love you so much that whenever anything new happens to me I cannot help thinking of you at once. I long to make you share it but become desperate when I realise that you are far away.*

In the past, lines like these might have excited Morgan with their promise, but he knew better by now. They were true, but also untrue. They meant something, and they didn't mean anything. Somehow, between them, it had always been this way.

* * *

Another problem was the title. Nothing obvious had thrown itself up, and he couldn't put off a decision much longer.

In the end, the solution came from an unexpected quarter. He was paying a visit to Edward Carpenter, who had moved to a Guildford villa not far from West Hackhurst. The old man had lost much of his allure in recent years; he was pleasant company, but repeated himself a great deal. He exerted no new fascination and, after a couple of hours, Morgan was almost relieved to be leaving.

As he headed for the gate, Carpenter asked him, "When do you go next to India?"

He kept trotting down the path in the twilight. "I have only just returned. Or no, it's been a couple of years already, but it feels like only last week. I don't know that I'll ever see it again."

"In your dreams, you will." And, smiling, he began to intone, in a special, sonorous voice: "Passage to India! Lo, soul! Seest thou not God's purpose from the first? The earth to be spanned, connected by . . . connected by . . . what was it again?"

Morgan stopped at the gate. There seemed to be a quick, strange smell on the air, which almost instantly disappeared.

"Where is that from?"

"It is *Leaves of Grass*. Have I told you that Walt Whitman was my very dear friend long ago?"

"Yes, you have told me." It was one of the stories that Carpenter too frequently repeated, but Morgan had first heard it from Goldie. The rumour was that Whitman and Carpenter had once been lovers. If it was ever true, the gloss had gone from it, and he didn't want to listen to old memories again. He waved a hand and said goodbye.

But the words kept on unrolling in his head, with their pleasing rhythm and shape. *A passage to India*. Yes, that was it—simple and unadorned. The phrase said nothing in itself, but it seemed to point the way ahead. And, not disagreeably, it reminded him of sitting aboard ship, talking to Searight, all those years ago.

* * *

The momentum of coming unstuck hadn't lasted. Despite his ignorance, the courtroom scenes had been easy to write, but what followed was much harder. The third part of the book exerted him once again to the utmost. Dewas and Chhatarpur provided the physical details, but the religious content came mostly from the Gokul Ashtami festival, which protruded like a knob on a smooth surface, drawing undue attention to itself. He was trying to explain what couldn't be said in words, or not in words that he knew.

More than anything, he felt, writing showed his own failings to him. The struggle that was involved was a demeaning and dutiful one, a matter of grinding craft rather than lofty art. Not that he was a fake; his interest had always been *real*. But he saw in others a hunger, a voracious need to comprehend or capture life by transforming it into language, which he didn't share. There had always been something a little self-conscious and studied about his writing life; it involved an effort of will, which wasn't true of the genuine practitioners. If he never picked up his pen again, he wouldn't feel greatly diminished.

On a weekend visit to Monks House, the country retreat in Rodmell that Leonard had recently acquired, he found himself announcing his futility. While playing bowls on the lawn, his attention went to the big round ball in his hand. It occurred to him that writing, in his case, had never taken on this smooth, spherical quality; the perfect circle eluded him.

"You know," he said suddenly, "I don't think I am a novel-ist."

He had offered this observation without any secret motive; in that moment, it seemed like the truth. He felt Leonard and Virginia stirring. His remark had caught them both.

Unexpectedly, Virginia said, "No, I don't think you are." She spoke sincerely, without malice; she was recognising something. They were discussing a fact, like his hair or his eyes.

"Ah," he said eagerly, turning to her. Virginia was a witch, or at least a High Priestess; she might absolve him. He wanted very much to hear what she would say next.

But Leonard had become most uncomfortable. His hands, which habitually shook, took on extra agitation.

"Oh, what rot," he snapped huffily. "You write novels, therefore you are a novelist—what else to call you? You have always tried to be someone apart, but your struggles are like everybody else's. I wish you could accept that. Now please, Morgan, do bowl."

Morgan wanted to protest: he *was* someone apart, he always had been—even if he had to play bowls like the others, because no guest at Monks House was spared. The ball trundled dispiritedly, stopping well short of its target, and Leonard clicked disapprovingly with his tongue.

"You know," Morgan told them, as they went in for lunch soon afterwards, "I'm not at all downcast about my literary career."

Nor was he. If his novel failed, well then, it failed. It was merely a matter of literature, not real life, which was far more important. He had other things he could fall back on.

He knew it now: this would be his last novel. He had threatened it before, but this time, he thought, it was true. Beyond the imaginings in India, no feature broke the horizon. He could feel that something had been used up. If he'd stuck to what was familiar and safe, a comfortable tapestry of tea parties and English scenery, he might have kept a quiet industry going, writing numerous books of a similar nature. But the world that interested him was disappearing, or already gone, buried under motor cars and machinery and the smoke of war. Writers should see ahead, not constantly be looking behind them, and his powers couldn't keep pace with history. There would be no more books like this one.

Still, if it came off, it might be a fitting conclusion to his novelistic career. At least it was different from most English books, and different too from other books about India. In his best moments, he suspected that he had created something new. But his best moments came seldom, and their power didn't last for long. Mostly, as things narrowed down on the end, he just thought it very bad. Getting it finished was often a slog, and he put in the hours with his teeth lightly clenched, a distant turbulence troubling his bowels.

Long before he reached the closing pages, he'd prepared them in his mind—though not gladly. In the early stages of writing, he'd thought of his book as a little bridge of sympathy between East and West, but as he'd progressed he'd realised that it couldn't be. Between him and Masood, between England and India, there had seemed to be an understanding, a joining, which was always just ahead, in the future some-where—until you realised it was impossible and that the story had really been one of a slow drifting apart, a widening gap. But the sundering had never been as final as it was in these last pages, when he spoke it aloud.

After he had fiddled with the words a bit, getting them right—the concluding rhythms were important—he decided it was over and put down his pen. Then he opened his diary and recorded the fact, using Mohammed's pencil, which he had kept near him for the purpose. The twenty-first of January, nineteen twenty-four.

Eleven years. He had expected it to feel momentous, but in fact it felt like nothing. As if he'd finished one small task and could move on in a minute to another. Everything that had happened in the last eleven years should have been present in the room, but somehow it wasn't. There was no trace of India or Egypt, of a World War, of an unpublished novel or two complicated loves. There was only the unruly heap of pages covered with his writing.

He felt he ought to do something more. It was still early and the rest of the day stretched vacantly ahead. He wrote a quick letter to the Woolfs, announcing that he was finished, but after that—aside from the prospect of posting the letter—there was nothing else to keep him busy. So he stacked the pages neatly and sat at his desk for a little longer, humming vaguely to him-self, before growing hungry and wandering downstairs in search of tea.

* * *

It was five months before the book appeared, in which life lost its central impetus. There was a great deal of typing to be done, and the proofs to be attended to. But the time for changing one's mind was almost behind him; the deed was nearly irrevocable.

In this abeyance, Aunt Laura died. He had never been close to her, but he was sorry she'd gone. She had been his only surviving link with his father—or perhaps that was her house, West Hackhurst, the sole commission his father had completed in his short career as an architect. Aunt Laura had lived there for forty-six years, and now she left the lease to Morgan in her will.

This bequest caused great turmoil in their household. Lily and Morgan had only recently purchased Harnham, the Weybridge house, which till then they'd been renting. Now they had to wrestle with the prospect of selling it again and making a big upsetting move.

Lily was very resistant. Although she was disturbed at Harnham by the noise of children and dogs, she was more disturbed by the idea of West Hackhurst.

"She was always unfriendly to me," she told Morgan. "I was always beneath her. I don't need her charity now."

"She was very sweet to you in the last months."

"Only because she'd lost her mind. It hardly compensates."

It was true: Aunt Laura had always regarded his mother as an unfit addition to their family, because of lowly and suspect origins. So there had been relentless sneering and sniping from the upper ramparts of class, and it was only when she'd become addled towards the end that Aunt Laura had eventually softened. But Morgan also knew that this wasn't the real reason for Lily's reluctance.

The move signified something conclusive in her life. A last

phase, a coming home to rest. His mother was seventy years old now. There wasn't much energy for fresh starts, new beginnings. He had his doubts about whether West Hackhurst would be as final as she feared—there were only thirteen years of the lease still to run—but he understood the symbolism involved. He steeled himself for a long period of dithering ahead, in which Lily wavered between one option and another, and talked about keeping up two houses.

For himself, he recognised that a different period in his life was opening up. Although his mother would always be in charge, he was a householder at last. This position of authority corresponded with a solid status in his professional career that had recently taken shape around him. He wasn't sure exactly how, but there was a renewed air of respect about his name, which came at the same time as his book.

A Passage to India appeared in June. It was always a peculiar moment when he held a published product in his hand. What had been, till then, a mental state or a bodily condition had somehow been transformed into an object. There had been several moments recently when other people had spoken about it, using its title, which still sounded odd to his ear, and he had had to remind himself that he, Edward Morgan Forster, had created it. Now it had actually entered the world, multiplied and disseminated far beyond its source, and had taken on a separate life of its own.

Until now, he had been more ashamed of it than anything else. The struggle to get it written, to say nothing of the nine-year hiatus while he'd been stuck, had marked him with the feeling of failure. Nothing worthwhile could have emerged so tortuously. But almost immediately after it appeared, his feelings changed. Maybe it was only defensiveness, but every word of it belonged indisputably to him. The writhings and convolutions of spirit that had attended its birth now only added to its value. Nothing less would have done!

His pride was boosted by reviews. The critical tone was laudatory—and not only from the newspapers. Among his friends, almost everyone seemed to be reading it, and the response was wonderful. There was none of the backstage whispering that had hurt him before, and which had seemed directed more at the *idea* of his writing than at the books themselves. People had got used to the notion that E. M. Forster was a novelist—or perhaps it had taken this long for him to accept it himself.

Very rapidly, it became clear that he had done something marvellous. There would be dissenters—there always were—but the general agreement was that he had quietly triumphed. Everybody had finally given up on expecting anything new, and then he had slipped it out. He had written a great book, apparently, a masterpiece: the best of his career. And the timing, with questions of Indian independence so much in the air, couldn't have been better.

What pleased him most about the book, however, was something he couldn't publicly declare. He had eventually decided on the wording of the dedication, after wrestling with it for weeks. *To Syed Ross Masood and to the seventeen years of our friendship.* In the end, the simple formulation made him happy, but he was happier still at the thought of their two names, joined together in this way, proceeding forth from Weybridge into the wider world. People he had never met would know that he had an Indian friend who had been part of his life for a long time.

Seventeen years! He'd had to do the calculation, and been a little unnerved by it. On one hand, Masood was so much an element of his emotional being that he seemed always to have been present. On the other, it felt like just last week that he had come up the front steps, dark and strange and handsome, for his first Latin lesson. Masood had been a very young man then, and now he was entering his middle years, a husband

and a father, becoming stout and soft. Their friendship had once promised a great deal, but it had let Morgan down and made him sad. He couldn't ignore that, but there were also times when the longevity of this affection cast a glow over the rest of his life. Not much had happened between them, it was true, but they had certainly loved one another, and that wasn't nothing. No, it was very far from nothing, even though there was no way to hold it or measure it and—when you looked straight at the place—there did seem, after all, to be nothing there.

Of course, it was typical of Masood that he managed to be both effusive and laconic about the book. He told Morgan that it was magnificent, and then barely referred to it again. No doubt he was happy to have been honoured in that way, but at the same time it was an *English* honour, happening far away from real life, which was in India. Or so Morgan surmised. As usual, there wasn't much to go on, except the sparse communications that made their desultory way from Hyderabad.

And it was also typical of Masood that, on the legal points where Morgan had relied on him for guidance, he had been wrong. The case, it turned out, would *not* have been held in such a small, provincial court. Masood had told him otherwise. On this and other aspects of Indian life, not all to do with the law, his friend might have helped him, but did not. It was most frustrating.

Now that the book was in print, everybody was free to have their say, and naturally the admonishments and corrections began to fly. Most were of a minor nature, though even these pricked sharply. Morgan had been wrong about the six-spot beetle, which, instead of being deadly, was utterly harmless. References to the 'Burra Sahib' among the English community were quite wrongly used. Dog carts and Lieutenant-Governors were outdated. These sorts of mistakes were humiliating, even though they were small and forgivable. Much harder to deal with, because more significant, was the suggestion that he had misrepresented the English in India.

Naturally, it didn't come as a surprise. He'd been braced for accusations of this kind. But the outrage was still unsettling. Certain shrill denunciations were easy to dismiss and when Rupert Smith wrote to him in a fury, breaking off their friendship, he knew he wouldn't feel the loss too keenly. Far more worrisome were the letters from retired Civil Service officials who explained in reasoned tones that he didn't know his subject. He was merely a visitor who had never actually *lived* in India; he had spent time with Indians, it was obvious, but hadn't extended the same courtesy to the British out there.

He was perturbed at first by these charges, because they might contain some truth. He'd been among the English in India, but he'd disliked most of them so intensely that he might not have seen them accurately. But as he cast his mind back to some of the conversations he'd had, some of the things he'd witnessed, his own outrage stiffened inside him. He had written what he'd perceived, as honestly as he could, and if that made his judgements seem unfair, the perceptions still remained. To be honest and to be fair were not always the same thing.

* * *

But denunciation was by far the smallest part of what came his way, and in any case he'd always dealt well with it. What he had never coped with was approbation, and it was pouring down on him abundantly. Without especially wanting to be either, he found himself suddenly both famous and wealthy.

It was pleasant, and also not. He didn't want the letters, the excitement, the attention; yet it was hard not to feel amplified by them, into something more than one was. It gave enjoyment, but left discomfort in its wake.

Quite astonishingly, he was recognised by people he'd never met. One such incident, which occurred around now, unsettled him deeply. He was visiting London and had been taking afternoon tea in the Lyons Corner House in the Strand, when he sensed the awareness of an older woman on the other side of the room. She was with a slightly younger companion, who seemed oblivious, but across the crowded aisle her glances kept returning to him. It wasn't displeasing, and so it didn't happen entirely by accident that he steered a course past their table as he exited, then paused behind a convenient pillar while he searched his pockets for his spectacles.

"I do believe," he heard the older woman declare, "that that was Mr. E. M. Forster."

"Who?" her companion enquired.

"The author, my dear. *A Passage to India*. You must have heard."

"Oh, *yes*. But where is he?"

"He has gone now. You were not observing."

"No," the younger lady admitted sadly. He could sense her disappointment. "I would have liked to see him."

"He was not well dressed. His trousers are a few inches too short. But his book is remarkable. So everyone tells me. I intend to read it very soon."

"I shall certainly read it too. Now that . . . now that I've seen him."

"But you didn't," the other reminded her. "*I* did. You were too much absorbed in your sandwich. Is this butter quite fresh, do you think . . . ?"

Their voices disappeared for a moment into the general haze of conversation and Morgan was about to depart, when a new observation arrested him. One of the women—he couldn't tell which—said distinctly, "I have heard that his life is unhappy."

"Really?"

"Well, lonely. He lives with his mother, you know. There has never been a wife. And he is not a young man any longer."

"How sad. He isn't an adventurous sort?"

"That is it, my dear. He is a timid soul. They say he hasn't really lived at all, except in his mind."

"Still. That is something. He has imagination, at least. He has written a wonderful novel."

"Yes. I really must read it." And their voices sank again into the background noise, which may only have been roaring in his head.

The subject of this discussion caught sight of himself now, as they might have seen him, in a gilt-edged mirror on the opposite wall: a curious, contorted figure, one leg wrapped around the other, right hand clasped in the left, tousled head tilted to the side. The angle of the light wiped out the surrounding room, so that he seemed to be standing alone in the middle of an immense whiteness. A snowy, frozen landscape, on which the sun was nevertheless pouring down. Arctic summer: nothing moving, nothing alive, and yet the sky was open.

That isn't me, he thought, but in fact it was. Everything about this man was wrong. But the reflection would never show the truth, which he wanted to shout aloud. *Do you know what I have made*, he would ask them, *out of almost nothing? I have performed miracles! I have turned water into wine, I have seen angels dancing on the head of a pin!*

But standing before the two ladies—whose powdered, astonished faces resembled those of the women who had tended him all his life—he was suddenly at a loss. He was on the verge of some significant action, but what it should be eluded him. He'd felt that he might shout, but the voice that emerged was very small.

"I have loved," he told them. "That is, I mean to say, *lived*. In my own way."

There seemed nothing more to add. A few crumbs had appended themselves to the mouth of the older lady, trembling in the silence that followed. Or perhaps it was Morgan who trembled. In any event, things shook while they stood still.

Until he turned and did truly exit this time, spoiling the effect by stumbling on the raised edge of a carpet.

So terrible or trivial was the memory of this incident that he mentioned it to nobody. Not even to the pages of his diary, which had heard worse confessions. Though his life had become very full, and it was possible he simply didn't have the time.

* * *

He would return to India one more time, in 1945, at the age of sixty-six. His life had entirely changed and this visit in no way resembled the previous two. On the earlier occasions he had been relatively unknown, especially in these parts, a private figure stopping with friends who often belonged to what in those days was called Second Society. But he was a famous author now, sought out by the loftier echelons of British India. He dined with the Viceroy and other high officials. He was in the country for three months, at the invitation of PEN, the international writers' organisation, and he took part in conferences, delivered speeches and radio addresses, signed autographs for admirers. His opinion was sought on matters not always related to writing.

The larger world itself was profoundly different. It had just been through another immense convulsion, with revelations about human nature that stunned the imagination, although India, as far as he could see, wasn't interested—everybody he met there spoke only about themselves. Europe and America, it seemed, did not exist; they had been cancelled. India itself was on the verge of major transformation: in just two years it would at last be independent, and the signs of violent pregnancy were becoming visible on the air.

Even the manner of journeying was different. No more the slow two-week arrival by ship. Instead he was there in three days, travelling by flying boat at a speed and height that had once felt like the symptoms of a declining world. But rather than the future, it was the past which seemed to infuse the flight with melancholy, as he floated over, and touched down upon, many of the places that had been part of his early life. First France, then Italy, then Egypt, all passed beneath the wings, full of memories, haunted by ghosts.

The same could be said about both his home and his destination. In England, he had suffered a great displacement recently on the death of his mother. She had been ill for some time and in March of that year, at the age of ninety, she had grown very weak. It became clear that the end was near. Morgan had slept in the passage outside her room on that last night, and in the morning they had said goodbye to each other.

"I shan't be long with you," she'd told him.

"No," he replied. "But I shall have your love."

He was very glad, afterwards, for that moment. It was a bond of great complexity that was being annulled and it would leave its guilts and regrets. His mourning wasn't small. He had been preparing for it imaginatively over the past ten years, but there was no way to conceive of how deep the event would go. It struck a bass note in him, close to the centre, which vibrated outwards through the rest of his life. In the beginning he had sometimes wanted to die too. He broke down at peculiar moments, often out in public, feeling how alone he was, remembering some arbitrary conversation or image. But it was also true that part of what wrung him was the awful knowledge that her vanishing had lifted off a great weight, so that he felt he could breathe more easily. It was terrible to feel that; he did not want her gone. On the contrary, he conjured her continually. He had put honeysuckle on her pillow when he'd left; he would take back a leaf from an Indian tree to lay on her grave.

Her death had made it possible for him to be there—a sort of gift. The journey served also as a great distraction, because she had never been to that country, it had no association with her. In that sense, India was clean.

But India, too, had its departed dead. For by now the two Indians who had meant most to him—who were, in fact, the reason for his previous visits—had both gone.

Masood had died first. His life had reached a high point in 1929, when he had been made Vice-Chancellor of Aligarh Muslim University, as the Anglo-Oriental College was now known, like his father and grandfather before him, and it had seemed as if a circle was being closed. But it was a brief triumph. Politics at the university and tensions with the British authorities, partly his own doing, had ousted him five years later. In compensation, the Begum of Bhopal had made him Minister of Education in her state, but his spirit had already been broken and three years later he suddenly died.

The news came through the most impersonal of channels, a report in *The Times*. The moment that he read it had been one of cold, white shock for Morgan, the world briefly encased in ice. It didn't seem possible, but the fact was there for everyone to see, in print. The story was still unclear, with a suggestion of something sinister, but over the coming weeks it would emerge that he had died merely of kidney failure. An ordinary, unexceptional death, then, at forty-seven. They had always spoken, only partly jokingly, of becoming old men and sitting together under a tree in India. Now Morgan found himself under the tree alone.

Recently Masood's old habits of not communicating for long periods had returned, and when he did write he expressed himself with such circular pomposity that he might not have bothered. Morgan had felt far from him for some years already, and yet the past was suddenly very near. There had been a time when everything that mattered had seemed possible between them. Something of that feeling, of hope and excitement, had continued to flicker somewhere, and flared up again now in a brief blaze of anguish.

He did travel to Aligarh, but couldn't bring himself to pass near the house where they had lived together for only a week, a quarter of a century ago. He'd heard that it had been left abandoned, to fall slowly into ruin. Masood's two sons had gone into trade, and he blamed that for a great deal—though they couldn't know, of course, what they were treating with such indifference. But he didn't think he could bear to see it, or carry what it might stir up.

Nor did he visit Dewas. The Maharajah had died six months after Masood, at the end of the same year. But the condition of his demise had been far more ignominious, and far more public. The downfall of His Highness had already been gathering shape when Morgan knew him. Profligacy with state expenses, rumours of maladministration: they had already begun to define his reputation in the eyes of his British masters. Things had got worse when his son and heir, the Crown Prince, had become convinced that his father was trying to poison him and had fled. When the finances of the state became truly untenable, the Maharajah had got into negotiations with the Indian government, who could have helped him. But it all turned sour, and each side began laying down conditions that the other would not fulfil. The tipping point was reached when, on a pilgrimage to the south of India, Bapu Sahib and his entourage had abruptly turned left and gone instead to Pondicherry, still a French enclave, and taken up station there, refusing to leave. A disastrous move. His Highness had thought, perhaps, that it would strengthen his hand, but in fact he had unwittingly resigned the game. A provisional government was set up in Dewas under his son, and he was never to return. He died in Pondicherry four years later, possibly of a broken heart.

Malcolm had been to see him in his exile, and Bapu Sahib, he reported, had laid his head down in his lap and wept like a child. That was awful to hear, and Morgan had been very exercised on his behalf. The British authorities—as they had been with Masood—were both correct in their dealings and utterly wrong at the same time. Their wrongness derived from the inability to see the human being under the strictures of protocol. Nobody who hadn't met them could know how lovely each of these men was in his excellent moments.

All of it now was in the past, and probably best left there. It was self-defeating to be looking backward continually, when you had only one existence and it was always slipping through your fingers. Grief could undo every solid structure if you let it. Nevertheless, he was unable to get away from Aligarh without one last abrasion of the heart.

He had come there at the invitation of the university, in order to receive honorary life membership of the Student Union, so there was no way to escape that particular patch of the past. Even to walk about there transported him back to his first visit with Masood, and the unfavourable impression the place had left on him. Nor had it improved meanwhile, as far as he could see. There was an atmosphere of dust and corruption and religion which made it hard to breathe. And the sly Vice-Chancellor, with whom he had to socialise, had always been an enemy of Masood's.

His duties done, it was to this man he had to turn for help. "Before I go, I very much want to see . . . "

"Yes, yes. It is already arranged. One of the students will take you there."

The university mosque was neat and clean, but the cemetery attached to it had an overgrown and abandoned air. Masood's tomb—and that of his grandfather close by—was shockingly neglected. The grass on top had been allowed to overflow the sides and the marble hadn't been cleaned in many months. It didn't look as though anybody had come to visit in a long time. Dead only eight years and, it seemed, already forgotten.

The student appointed to be his guide was one of the gaunter, more fanatical-looking types, and he was keen to point out the inscription by Iqbal on the maqbara. But Morgan cut him short.

"If you don't mind," he said, "I would like to be left alone with my friend."

The boy looked taken aback. How could the dead be your friend? But there was no other word for the man under the ground, who would be—for the one left behind—never quite gone.

He fussed for a few minutes around the grave, pulling out weeds and clumps of dead grass, but very soon there seemed to be no point. Then he wept a little bit, but without much heat, for everything that was past. The next day he would be on a train to Calcutta and he would never come back here again. But that scarcely mattered: there was no real communion with a mausoleum and what counted was in any case invisible. The only defence against time was what he had learned in Egypt: that true affection left something behind it, something that lingered, with its own mysterious life.

So he gave himself over instead to the present, finding a seat nearby in the sun where he could think for half an hour. He dwelt on Masood for a while, but couldn't help himself from dozing off. He wasn't a young man any more and his body frequently let him down. Though in many ways it always had.

And was that truly so terrible? The day was warm, there was the comforting sound of bees in a bush close by, the shadows of birds swooped across the graves. These things mattered too: they were part of Life, and beautiful, and therefore important.

Eventually he felt able to leave. Though he wasn't quite sure of the procedure. He stood at the foot of the grave, waiting for an appropriate goodbye to strike him, but none did. In the end, you could only nod and rub your eyes without clearing them and then wander back along the way you'd come, down the path to the gate.

Where the gaunt student, it turned out, was crossly waiting.

"You are ready?" he wanted to know.

It wasn't clear what he meant: the official visit was over, and Morgan had only to depart. But he nodded anyway and smiled at the young man.

"Yes," he told him. "I am ready."

Acknowledgements

In my research, I have relied first and foremost on E. M. Forster's own writings, both fiction and non-fiction, including his diaries (Pickering and Chatto, 2011) and letters (edited by Mary Lago and P. N. Furbank; the Belknap Press of Harvard University Press, Volume One 1983 and Volume Two 1985). For permission to quote from his published work, I am grateful to The Society of Authors as the Literary Representative of the Forster Estate. For permission to quote his unpublished writing, I am grateful to The Provost and Scholars of King's College, Cambridge, and The Society of Authors.

I wish to state that I have seeded quotes from *A Passage to India* at certain unrelated points in my novel, in order to suggest the wide range of sources from which Forster may have drawn his material. I should also point out that where I have used actual dialogue recorded by Forster (and others) in letters or diaries, I have sometimes altered the words a little, on the assumption that nobody recalls conversations, even their own, with complete certainty. On the other hand, I have tried to be as accurate as possible in evoking the India of Forster's time, down to modes of address and the use of place names. For the same reason I haven't modernised spellings, with the exception of a couple of words.

I am also indebted to four biographies of Forster. It

would be hard to surpass P. N. Furbank's superb two-volume *E. M. Forster: A Life* (Harcourt Brace Jovanovich, 1977, 1978). Mr. Furbank was also kind enough to meet with me to share some of his personal impressions and reminiscences of Forster. I have used information, too, from *Morgan* by Nicola Beauman (Hodder & Stoughton, 1993), *A Great Unrecorded History* by Wendy Moffat (Farrar, Straus and Giroux, 2010) and *E. M. Forster* by Francis King (Thames & Hudson, 1978). Helpful, too, was the *Paris Review* interview with Forster conducted by P. N. Furbank and F. J. H. Haskell in 1952, which appears in the First Series of *Writers at Work* (Viking Press, 1958).

In addition, I have been helped by Miriam Allott's introduction to the Abinger edition of Forster's *Alexandria* and *Pharos and Pharillon* (edited by Miriam Allott; André Deutsch, 2004); Elizabeth Heine's introduction to the Abinger edition of *The Hill of Devi and other Indian Writings* (edited by Elizabeth Heine; Edward Arnold, 1983); and Philip Gardiner's notes to *The Journals and Diaries of E. M. Forster* (edited by Philip Gardiner; Pickering and Chatto, 2011).

Biographies of other figures connected to Forster that I have drawn on are, in no particular order: *Cavafy* by Robert Liddell (Duckworth, 1974); *Edward Carpenter* by Sheila Rowbotham (Verso, 2008); *Lytton Strachey* by Michael Holroyd (Chatto & Windus, 1994); *The Priest of Love* by Harry T. Moore (William Heinemann, 1974); *Leonard Woolf* by Victoria Glendinning (Simon and Schuster, 2006); and *Virginia Woolf* by Hermione Lee (Chatto & Windus, 1996). I have adapted excerpts from *The Diary of Virginia Woolf: Volume II 1920-1924* (edited by Ann Olivier Bell; diary copyright 1978 by Quentin Bell and Angelica Garnett; the Hogarth Press, 1978; reprinted by permission of the Random House Group Limited in the United Kingdom and Houghton Mifflin Harcourt in the USA). For permission to quote Virginia Woolf

I am grateful again to The Society of Authors as the Literary Representative of her Estate.

For historical background on India at that time I have used *Raj: The Making and Unmaking of British India* by Lawrence James (Little, Brown, 1997); *Women of the Raj* by Margaret MacMillan (Thames and Hudson, 1996); and *Raj, A Scrapbook of British India* by Charles Allen (Book Club Associates, 1977). Invaluable for my Egyptian section was Michael Haag's wonderful *Alexandria, City of Memory* (Yale University Press, 2004).

Other books that helped me were *The Forster–Cavafy Letters* edited by Peter Jeffreys (The American University in Cairo Press, 2009); *Aspects of E. M. Forster* edited by Oliver Stallybrass (Edward Arnold, 1969); *Concerning E. M. Forster* by Frank Kermode (Weidenfeld & Nicolson, 2009); *E. M. Forster, Interviews and Recollections* edited by J. H. Stape (St Martin's Press, 1993); *E. M. Forster's India* by G. K. Das (Macmillan Press, 1977); and *Islam* by Alfred Guillaume (Penguin, 1954). Ronald Hyam's *Empire and Sexuality: The British Experience* (Manchester University Press, 1990) provided the quote from Kenneth Searight's poem which appears on page 7. The line from Cavafy's "The God Abandons Antony" on page 238 is from the first English translation by G. A. Valassopoulo, which appeared in *Pharos and Pharillon* in 1923.

I am very grateful to the School of English at the University of St Andrews and the Wilhelmina Barns-Graham Trust for a generous residency in 2012.

My thanks for their insights to Tony Peake, Alison Lowry and Margaret Stead. In addition, I am grateful to Fourie Botha, Ellen Seligman, Nigel Maister, Peter Cartwright, Neel Mukherjee, Tamsin Shelton, David Davidar and Aienla Ozukum for their critical perceptions; to Anat Yakuel, for a space to work in; and for his help on my visit to the Barabar Caves, to Manish Shavoren.